TORN

A Forensic Romance

ANGELA APPLEWHITE

Virtually Published Media

For
Mark, Emily & Nora

Contents

Part I

"Fear and pain should be treated as signals not to close our
eyes but to open them wider."

~ *Nathaniel Branden*

Prologue

THE OTTAWA GAZETTE

Army Training Turns Deadly

Derek Johnson, Staff Reporter

CHATHAM, Ont. – February 14, 2012

A weapons commanding officer killed two recruits during a
live-fire drill yesterday.
The incident took place at Cedar Springs Range and
Training Area. The 134-acre property is situated southwest
of Blenheim near Chatham, Ontario.
The deceased soldiers' names have been withheld. Details on
the events that led up to the shooting remain sketchy. Army
headquarters in Ottawa released statements saying that the
training commander opened fire on the two privates and
then turned the gun on himself. All three men were
pronounced dead at the scene.

The instructor would have been an expert with assault weapons, including the C8A3 magazine-fed rifle he used to execute his fellow soldiers. The firearm is a general-purpose, light-weight rifle and is considered a personal weapon in a war zone.
Further reports from 4th Canadian Division Support Base Petawawa suggest drug involvement. However, army officials refused to comment on the tragedy.

Our prayers go out to the young soldiers' families while the public awaits an investigation from the Canadian Army.

Chapter 1

$\mathcal{I}$N THE QUIET CEMETERY, the last rays of sunlight glinted off the black granite headstone and blinded Nicholas Wade. He shifted his position and met the gusting wind full on. It shoved against his sturdy stance, pressing the desert tan fatigues close to his body. He dug his heels into the ground and turned away from the sudden bluster.

A man stood staring down at a grave. His stance—a sorrowful chin pressed into his chest—echoed Nicholas's regret. He turned away from the man when a distant sob tugged his head to the left. The woman kneeling a few paces away clutched her shoulders. She swayed, pouring inconsolable grief onto the burial plot in front of her.

A few weeks ago, a powerless gloom hung over Nicholas as he watched the coffin being lowered into the grave at his feet. Torment wrapped around his gut then and seemed to strangle him from inside. Letting go with abandonment wasn't an option. He turned away from the woman. How would he reconcile this injustice?

Rather than a military monument, a black stone marker headed the grave in front of him. Six inches thick with the name already sandblasted into the granite. The army was wrong.

Someone should have listened. Nicholas should have listened. When Kevin came to see him at about 1500 hours that afternoon back in December, Nicholas stopped working on his report long enough to pay attention to another outlandish conspiracy.

"The generals know about it," McBride had said. "Someone is operating a profitable business distributing drugs throughout the entire military. They are doing it from the inside and no one gives a damn."

"That's not what you put in your report, McBride."

"I tried. They fucked me over instead. Told me to do it again, or they'd write me up for psych and throw me in the tank without even waiting for the results. I wrote what I wrote."

"You have proof of this?"

"Proof?" He pointed at his arm motioning a syringe.

"I can't take this anywhere without something concrete," Nicholas said.

"You want me to get you that something? Look—" McBride waved a hand in the air like he was calling on an invisible muse. "I've been known to dabble a bit, but only when it's necessary. I take the occasional go-pill too." He raised a hand to stop Nicholas's protest, even though Nicholas hadn't responded.

"Others are using enough to lose their minds and shit." He gestured in midair again. "I can tell you things."

Nicholas had heard a similar story for almost six months. If it wasn't weapons smuggling, it was human trafficking and prostitution. "Look, McBride I've got to finish this report," he said. "Let's meet up tomorrow." Nicholas had pushed from his chair. "I'm interested in what you've got to say, but I wish you could get me someone to corroborate this story."

"What? You don't believe me now? What the fuck am I saying? You never believed me. All these months I've been coming here, pouring my guts out to you and you do what? Not one fucking thing." McBride turned his back to Nicholas and flicked a dismissive hand.

The woeful sobs a few yards away reached Nicholas again. They pulled his attention back to the grave at his feet. He stepped forward. His vision cleared and the name on the tombstone sharpened. Second Lieutenant Kevin Elliott McBride.

Nicholas's fists tightened at his side. If he had only listened. If he hadn't ignored the cries for help from a man he called his friend, McBride would be alive today. In the army's eyes, the three deaths at Cedar Springs Range that tragic day dishonoured McBride's military career. His was the only name struck from the Canadian War Memorial. His death, not in service to his country, meant nothing. The army abandoned his legacy.

Nicholas stared at the letters blasted into the stone. The deep carvings burned into his brain. The last time he saw McBride, his face was twisted in misery, maybe even fear. Haggard was the only word that described the creature that stood in Nicholas's office. He'd become a shadow of the man Nicholas knew and admired for half of his eighteen-year career. Nicholas had recommended the military hospital for rehab treatment. He should have driven McBride there himself.

His friend's death was on him. He would fix this wrong. The truth, unknown and buried, couldn't end here. Second Lieutenant Kevin McBride's legacy deserved recognition.

Chapter 2

MAY 7, 2012 · WESTBURY, ONTARIO

TWENTY MINUTES BEFORE MIDNIGHT, Savanna Jones stood under a dark satin sky. A few stars glimmered from the inky blackness despite some moving cloud patches.

She shivered when a swift breeze tickled the loose hairs beneath her ponytail. The dark blue forensic jacket she slipped on before leaving the lab hardly kept her warm.

She pulled the zipper to her throat and double checked that she had locked the door to her Volkswagen. Her messenger bag slung easily over one shoulder. A quick glance to either side confirmed that she was alone on the street. BlackBerry in hand, she crossed the quiet boulevard.

Cuddling at home in a warm bed, exhausted from long and delicious lovemaking would be her choice. But not tonight. With Richard, her husband out of town for the next six months, her only action were a weekly kickboxing class and her forensics job.

She mentally shook her head. *Focus,* she scolded and pushed the unsettling thoughts away. The house she headed toward seemed to stand alone in the corner. In fact, it was the last in the row of dormer-style bungalows, built a quarter century ago in a community of mostly law-abiding citizens.

She lifted the cellphone and tapped redial then placed the phone to her ear.

After two rings her partner, Mathew Quinn answered. "Yeah." Sleep still muzzled the normal timbre in his voice.

"How far away are you with those keys?" She asked.

"Huh?"

They had been covering each other for eight years. He the police officer, she the civilian forensic scientist. The midnight summons had always been a part of their routine. Half an hour ago when she called, he was already asleep, but promised to bring the keys she'd forgotten. Though she loathed dragging him from bed, she needed him out here.

A third look, this time into the unfamiliar corners of the house could turn up the necklace that would make all the difference. The investigating team had searched the place last April when the police arrested the owner, Colton Moore, on charges of kidnap, false imprisonment and rape. Forensics had even gone over the place again in July just before the trial started. The house had been vacant since then. It was possible the necklace was still here.

"So where are you now?" she asked Quinn.

Before he could respond, a scream cracked the dark silence with the energy of a newborn.

Savanna froze on the spot. "What was that?" she said into the phone.

"Something going on out there?" her partner asked.

"I heard a scream." Savanna grabbed the flashlight sticking out from her messenger bag and ran toward the house with the phone still to her ear. She flicked the beam around the tiny square bunga-low, focusing on the two small front windows. Nothing. She hurried to the side. Her torch light trailed along the scaling grey siding.

"See anything?" Quinn's voice sounded more awake now.

"Nothing yet." She continued to the left side and around to the front again. Her heavy breathing and a dog barking in the distance were the only sounds vibrating through the cool night air.

"Savanna?"

"I'm here," she said. "I think the sound came from inside."

"Okay. I'll be there soon."

She kept moving the light, her ears pricked. Maybe the noise was more distant than she first thought.

A cry whimpered from below her.

Savanna jerked to a stop. She peered closer at the two-brick wall surrounding the basement window. Three small shoe soles imprinted in mud. She stooped, keeping out of sight from anyone inside. The windowpane was broken.

"Someone's here," she said to Quinn. "Looks like a 10-84."

"Wait for me." He hissed as though he too needed to conceal his voice.

"I'll take a quick look."

"Not without a key, Savanna. Wait."

She leaned closer to the broken window. A loud bang followed by whimpers echoed from inside.

"It sounds like someone is hurt," she whispered into the phone. Hopefully it wasn't another woman. Considering what went on out here last year, this house was bad news for unsuspecting females. "I'm going in." She clicked off the call.

Savanna carefully mounted the three broken steps. The hinges on the screen panel squeaked when she pulled the metal frame. She held it open with one foot and grasped the front door knob.

On the off chance that it was unlocked, she twisted. The cool nickel chilled her already sweaty palm, but the door wouldn't budge. Determined to get inside, she shoved her shoulder against the wooden panel. It bounced her onto the lower step again.

There must be another way in.

She shifted the torch light to the crumbling cement at her feet. It had disintegrated into sand and pebbles. To the right, her torch illuminated a pile of small stones forming weeping tiles against the window wall. They provided the only solution left to her. The rock she grasped fitted perfectly into her palm. With a single smack, it shattered the plate glass window next to the door.

Savanna used the rock to clear the sharp edges, then reached in and twisted the lock on the door. She poked her head inside and shifted the torchlight around. Nothing moved.

She crept into the small living room. The narrow light above her shoulder reflected from a large wall mirror hanging over a worn sofa. The matching chair faced a dark laminated stand that supported an oversize flat-screen TV. Its remote control lay askew on top of a coffee table covered with dog-eared pornographic magazines.

No question someone was squatting in the house. Savanna tiptoed further into the room, but halted when a small voice whimpered.

"Shh," someone else warned. The tense conversation rose from the basement. Definitely children.

"Hello," Savanna said. "I'm with the police. I need to see you out here." Her forensics crime scene jacket came with a badge. Hopefully, it was enough to hold any potential suspects until Quinn arrived.

She followed the whispers but froze when she thought a shadow moved in the open doorway leading to the kitchen. She whipped the light in that direction, but it was her own reflection in another large mirror. She'd forgotten about the mirrors. They hung throughout the house. Still, she entered the kitchen and flicked the switch. The room flooded with a yellow glow. It smelled of stale takeout food. The countertop had seen better days. A banged-up wooden block with two knives and a pair of shears stood next to a white-ish plastic drain tray.

Savanna left the room and crossed the hallway to the half-opened door leading to the basement. A damp, mouldy scent floated up from below. She peered into the darkness, recalling that the light switch dangled from a bulb in the ceiling halfway down the steps.

Thirteen months ago, when they investigated the house, the stairs creaked and shook under the trampling weight of the investigating team. As she descended now, each step seemed even weaker.

Scrambling feet scurried around before she reached the bottom. Soft cries whined and hissed from the right of the stairs.

Her pulse quickened as she listened.

"Shh," a voice said. "They'll hear us."

"Hello," Savanna spoke into the silence. "Is someone hurt?"

No response.

She poked her head around the corner. The stair light didn't cover the entire space, but a standing mirror reflected the other side of the room. She made out the edge of a laundry tub and a white washer-dryer set next to it. Nothing moved back there.

"You shouldn't be in here right now," she said. "I'm sure you know that. This place is private property and unsafe."

"It hurts," one of the voices cried again.

"I told you to shut your mouth," said another.

"I want to go home."

Two boys, Savanna guessed. And the younger was injured.

She guided her hand up the wall and found the switch she knew was there. A dull light illuminated the small basement. When she pulled the door closing off the area under the stairs, two pairs of eyes stared up at her. Their pupils enlarged under the glare of her searchlight like frightened refugees.

The taller boy raised a hand to shade his eyes. The other one dropped his chin and cradled a bleeding hand to his chest. The wound looked bad.

"Come on out." Savanna forced a bit of steel into her voice. Without a police uniform, she needed instant obedience. She stepped back and waited.

The older one leapt to his feet first. Just as Savanna thought, he tried to dash past her.

"Not just yet, sir." She caught him by his jacket.

He struggled and pulled to escape.

"Do you really mean to run and leave him here when this was your idea?" She had no way of knowing who cooked up the scheme that landed them in an abandoned house in the middle of the night, but her accusation settled the boy.

He frowned and turned his face away from her.

"I'm Savanna. What's your name?" she asked.

He turned to look at her again, his little mouth pouting. "Elvis."

"And you?" She turned to the younger boy.

He hiccupped, then said, "Eric."

Something sharp had sliced opened the meaty part of Eric's

palm, just under his thumb. A steady stream of blood leaked from the wound.

"Let's go upstairs," she said. "Elvis, I'll need your help while I call an ambulance. Okay?"

He nodded.

Once upstairs and secured on the worn couch, she gingerly took the injured hand and glanced at Eric's tear-stained face. He had stopped whimpering, but fresh tears leaked from his wide brown eyes.

"That must really hurt," she said, "but I can see you're brave. Can you tell me what brought you guys out here so late?"

Elvis turned his head away, but Eric spoke up. "We wanted to see it," he managed through his tears.

"See what?"

"Don't tell her," Elvis said and shoved an elbow into the younger boy's ribs. "She'll tell the police that we did it."

"Did what?" Savanna kept her eyes on Eric's wound as she inspected it for a foreign object.

"Nothing." Elvis was adamant about keeping their secret.

"If you did nothing wrong, no one will blame you," Savanna said.

Elvis assumed his signature pout and sharpened his gaze on her. "You wouldn't believe us anyways."

Right. He saw an adult stranger. Not the most trustworthy person in an eleven-year-old's view.

"Okay," she said. "There's too much blood to see what's going on inside. We need to clean it up. Can you help me with that?"

Elvis nodded again.

"Good. Help Eric to the sink, and we can start washing the blood away." To keep Elvis from bolting again, Savanna kept him talking. "If you tell me what happened," she said, "I'll let my partner know how helpful you were."

The boys looked at each other and then at her. "We came to see…" Eric spoke first, then they both blurted out, "the dead body."

Savanna stared speechless for a moment. "A dead body? Here?" she finally asked. "Are you sure?"

"See, I told you she wouldn't believe us," Elvis said. "We heard his brother talking about it." He pointed to Eric.

"Okay. Have you seen it?"

They both shook their heads.

"Did you come out here on your own?"

Elvis glanced away from her. "Yes." He sounded offended, but she still wasn't sure about the veracity of his claim.

"Did your brother say where—"

A noise clattered from the front of the house and startled them. They all turned to look at the same time. Though they saw nothing, Savanna motioned with an index finger on her lips for the boys to stay quiet.

She hurried to the living room and caught someone disappearing out the door. The broad back looked like a man's.

"Hey. Stop," she yelled. "Who are you? Wait."

She followed, but the figure disappeared behind the house. Savanna pursued him. Just as she cleared the side of the small building, she tripped over something and went down. *What was that?* She scrambled to her feet again and fumbled her cellphone from her pocket. She found the searchlight app and zipped the phone around on the grass.

What looked like human fingers stuck out from a blanket. Savanna gasped and hopped back. The darkness surrounding her had swallowed up the person who ran from the house. Not a sound emanated from the shadows. For all she knew, someone stood only a few feet away, watching her.

Chapter 3

MAY 14, 2012 - OTTAWA, ONTARIO

Major-General Emmanuel Corbett was the one person least likely to sway a vote in Nicholas's direction, even in the best circumstances. At least not since his sanction. So why Nicholas had been ordered here two hours before he left for his new post baffled him. Frankly, he got the feeling Corbett knew the ill-timed summons would cause him to miss his flight to Kingston.

He straddled a silver maple leaf centring the navy carpet in the middle of the office. In desert tan camouflage, the general circled him. A slow glide that resembled a coyote stalking a wounded prey. His injured eye batted feverishly and seemed to look in an opposite direction than the healthy one.

"Do you think you're the only man in this army to bury a friend?" Corbett asked.

Nicholas's eighteen-year military career rested on Corbett's opinion, but MacBride's coffin still haunted him. He tightened his jaw and fought the urge to tell Corbett what he really thought.

"With all due respect, sir," he said. "This isn't about a single soldier. The epidemic pervades all ranks, and now three men are dead."

"Their deaths have nothing to do with the army."

If Corbett believed that a soldier killing two fellow soldiers and then turning the gun on himself wasn't an army problem, then there was something weird going on here that Nicholas couldn't understand.

"I respectfully disagree, sir," he said. "An incident of this magnitude is abnormal among Canadian soldiers and even more bizarre for Second Lieutenant McBride. I believe that this incident was the result of the abuse of neuro-stimulating drugs unofficially endorsed by certain divisions."

"You are wrong about this, Lieutenant-Colonel Wade."

"I don't believe I am. It's devastating when—"

"May I remind you that this is not why you are here in Ottawa? You are on my team to investigate why our soldiers are dying on the battlefield. You are here to use your specialized medical skills to analyze our current battle-ready gear, to address the weaknesses and to develop solutions to combat those weaknesses. You are not a neuroscientist, and you're certainly not a spokesperson for the army."

Nicholas and Corbett never agreed on much, so no one was more surprised than Nicholas when the Major-General chose him for the team of scientists and specialists he handpicked for his task force eight months ago.

"I am aware of my assignment, sir. But when soldiers are forced to run for cover from their own troop members because of mental impairment, it deals an unconscionable blow to trust and morale."

"Regardless, you are not responsible for the press releases issued from these headquarters."

"Turning a blind eye to soldiers operating while staving off mental health issues and sleep deprivation with amphetamines and other drugs isn't an issue that we can hide behind. The issue needs to be addressed, sir."

"Lieutenant-Colonel, are you overlooking the fact that Second Lieutenant McBride violated the Canadian military's drug-free protocols? That killing two men from his squadron while hopped-up on drugs is his fault and his fault alone?"

"The fault is… was McBride's, but certainly not all the blame. As such, his contribution and service to this country should not be forgotten, sir."

Corbett halted and squared himself to his full height just under Nicholas's chin. "First of all, no one in this army is forgotten," he said. "Dead or alive. It would do you good to remember that when you're shooting your mouth off in the media."

Three weeks ago, Nicholas gave an interview to Global Research, a magazine unpopular with the army. The controversial story highlighted an increase of substance abuse in the Canadian Army. The magazine asked the army's upper brass to comment on the claims. In response, the army cited the editor-in-chief for slander and forced an injunction against the article.

Nicholas had been the first person Corbett ordered to his office. With no reason to deny his involvement, he admitted to the interview.

"What about the families?" Nicholas asked. "They, along with the Canadian public deserve to know the truth, nothing less."

"That truth does not come from you. The Canadian Army's report is official, whether you agree with it or not. If we confirmed that McBride was a rogue officer, then that's what it is. When the media comes calling, you need to keep your mouth shut."

"It was the silence that killed MacBride three weeks ago, sir," Nicholas bit down. He too had dismissed McBride as an addict. By the time he took a second look, it was too late.

"The army's silence is the public's protection," Corbett said.

"When impairment causes lives, silence is hard to abide."

"Then I suggest you find a way. We are in the business of training soldiers, not sissies or snivelling schoolboys."

Why was Corbett revisiting this issue? He had already kicked Nicholas off his team and forcibly stalled his career for an entire year. So now what? Something nefarious festered under his blustering. Nicholas wished he would get on with it.

"I didn't call you here for your opinion. You've been reassigned. The city of Westbury needs a forensic pathologist. That's you for the next year."

Westbury? Blood pounded at Nicholas's temples. *How the hell did Westbury fit into Corbett's plan?*

"You have two days to present yourself to Coroner Scott Miller," Corbett said. "Pick up the details from Captain Renée when you leave this office."

If Nicholas wasn't struggling to curb his anger, he might find this funny. "Sir, I'm scheduled for the RMCC in Kingston. I'm needed there."

"Get over yourself, soldier. You're replaceable."

Following his interview, a committee of generals stripped Nicholas of his access to army intelligence. They assigned him to a teaching post at the Royal Military College in Kingston, Ontario. He raised his objections then, but soon reined in his rage when Corbett ordered him handcuffed and escorted to barracks for insubordination. What could he do while locked up? But this new move from Corbett was outrageous. It reeked with the stench of revenge.

"Your future with the army is uncertain," Corbett said. "I suggest you take the next year to do whatever you need to clean up this mess. I don't care whose ass you have to kiss. Just don't create any more damage. And remember, soldier, if this goes sideways, I would personally see to it that you're rendered permanently expendable."

This was classic Corbett. The moment the man believed a soldier of lower rank threatened his authority, he retaliated with sabotage.

"Perhaps after this year," Corbett said, "you'll finally learn to play by the rules. Westbury is hardly notable. The military should use the city to house a prison, not to station an airbase."

Corbett was wrong about Westbury. The city carried a single astronomical risk just as menacing as a sniper's rifle. But Corbett didn't need to know that. "I'm a forensic pathologist, sir," Nicholas said. "Westbury is as good a place to practice as any other."

"You're lucky your sanction still permits you to practice medicine. For the next year, I don't want to see you, or footage of you, in any media. If you so much as help an old lady across the street make sure there are no cameras or bystanders with cellphones around to capture your heroics. Do I make myself clear, Lieutenant-Colonel?"

"Yes, sir."

"Now get out of my sight." Corbett released him with a contemptuous flick of his arm. "You're dismissed."

Nicholas raised his right arm to touch his forehead in a swift salute. Corbett was missing the point. Nicholas intended to investigate who was really responsible for the three soldiers' deaths. Posting him to Westbury worked more in his favour than Corbett realized. But regardless of where on earth the man sent him, there was no way in hell he intended to stand by and let an honourable soldier go down in history as a murderer.

*N*icholas shot from Corbett's office fuming and stopped in front of Captain Renée's desk.

The tall wiry man with frameless glasses looked up. "Here you go, Lieutenant-Colonel Wade." He handed over the file before Nicholas said anything.

"Thank you, Captain," Nicholas took his reassignment orders, then returned Renée's salute. He exited the outer office and rather than wait for the elevator, he sped down the sixteen flights of stairs. Each breath kept the explosion seething inside him at bay.

Corbett had no right. Before this year was over, Nicholas would see that the Major-General swallowed every single threat to his career.

On the ground floor, the exit door opened before he reached it. His fury spiked another degree. He wasn't in the mood to deal with Gerald Brock, a sociopathic soldier with captain's bars. He saluted Nicholas a dismissive flick that barely rose above his cheekbone. Then spread his massive chest blocking the doorway.

"Permission to speak freely, sir," Brock snapped.

The captain was a big man, about an inch taller. As an Armour Officer, a senior gunman with the Royal Canadian Dragoons, his size was an asset in the dangerous job where he and his team engaged with the enemy from a Leopard II tank. He was used to manoeuvring a fleet of high-tech, battle-tested vehicles in hostile territory. Since his first mission, Brock acted as if he always faced the enemy. His team branded him as an intense soldier.

Two years ago, at a local bar in Trenton, Nicholas had witnessed Brock trying to pick up a young woman who flirted with him. When her date showed up, she changed her mind.

Brock claimed the man was disrespectful. He grabbed the girl. Her partner stepped between them and Brock reached for a pool cue and swung it. The man ducked just in time to avoid the blow that would have definitely broken his jaw.

Nicholas intervened and escorted Brock outside. The captain raged and eventually shoved Nicholas. When he followed up with a right hook aimed at Nicholas's face, Nicholas blocked the punch and kicked Brock in the knee and brought him down, twisting his arm behind him. A few soldiers witnessed the skirmish. Once Brock's temper cooled, Nicholas released him and he scrambled to his feet again. But the captain suffered the humiliation.

Since that night, the story among the officers was that Nicholas was Brock's sworn enemy. Yet, Brock merely whispered his comments while his salutes bordered on contempt.

Now, the same wild, steel-grey eyes that regarded Nicholas that night, scrutinized him. Still struggling to hold his temper, Nicholas guessed what was coming. "Permission granted," he said.

"You had no right broadcasting the army's business to those trouble makers, Brock started. "You have a big mouth."

This from a man who had been grounded multiple times for bullying other soldiers.

Nicholas flexed his fists. "Is that all, Captain?"

Brock's top lip tightened and curled to one side. "Upper brass will finally see you for what you are," he snarled. "Nothing but a coward hiding behind a brain."

Speaking of cowards, Brock was one of the few low-level officers who voiced his disapproval after Nicholas had already left the room. Nicholas levelled his stare with Brock's. "In that case, I'm sure the generals noticed you from day one," he said.

The muscles in Brock's jaw flared. A growl rumbled from his

throat. "I'll be more than happy to see you kicked out of the army in disgrace," he glared.

"Noted. Now, Captain. . ." Nicholas leaned in close enough to smell the steroids secreting from Brock's sweating armpits. "If you ever salute me like that again, I will see that you spend a few weeks at a training camp until you learn how to formally address a superior officer. Do I make myself clear?"

Brock snapped to attention and raised his right hand in an official salute, his eyes straight ahead. "Sir, yes sir."

"Now soldier, don't force me to say it twice. Get the fuck out of my way."

Chapter 4

THE CONSTANT DAMPNESS FROM two days of rain crept into the forensic lab and along the hallways of the Coroner's Office. The continued cool temperature offered no promises for the weekend.

Savanna raised a hand to knock on Coroner Scott Miller's door but paused when she noticed the door was slightly open. She tapped.

"Come in, Savanna," he called out to her.

She pushed the door open and stepped inside. "Good evening, Coroner."

He greeted her with his usual anticipatory thin-lip grimace.

She'd been expecting this summons since she broke in and entered the Lamon Street crime scene last week. But Miller had been out of town until this morning. His text lit up her BlackBerry only half an hour ago. *Meet me in my office before you leave tonight.*

Whatever he wanted must be rather important to summon her this late on a Friday night.

"Sorry about the time," he said when she closed the door.

Her glance flicked to the clock above his desk. It was already 6:30 p.m. How did he know she was still at the lab, anyway?

Miller pushed away from his antique oak desk. At sixty-one, the coroner and the desk exhibited the same heirloom qualities. His elbow-patched grey blazer hung open on his straight, sturdy frame. Curly white hair framed his oblong head. And in the yellowing ceiling lights, his fair skin appeared soft and pallid.

"Let's sit over here." He pointed to the comfortable chairs and coffee table to the left of the entrance

"First," he said, "I won't be attending Doreen Bellamy's discovery meeting on Monday."

Savanna had requested the meeting on behalf of the investigating team. She and Quinn, along with the two detectives on the case, pushed more than the assistant Crown attorney for a murder charge against Colton Moore. "Why?" she asked.

"I'll get to that in a minute."

The mystery surrounding this meeting increased by the second.

Miller smoothed a hand over his curly hair. The wiry loops bounced up again, defying his efforts. "I want to update you on the new chief of forensics status," he said.

"Another postponement?" She didn't bother to hide her cynicism.

"Not really. Keria Koff is engaged elsewhere and can't relinquish her responsibility right now."

"She cancelled? I thought her appointment was a done deal."

Miller raised a hand. "Not to worry, we already have a replacement."

Savanna relaxed into the chair again. Waiting for a new chief of staff to show up had already delayed her scheduled vacation. "Who is it? she asked, "Anyone we know?"

"His name is Dr. Nicholas Wade."

"Wade?"

"Do you know him?" Miller looked hopeful.

"I don't think so. Should I?"

"Well, it's actually Lieutenant-Colonel Wade, but under the circumstances, his military rank doesn't matter. He'll get the job done in spades. Personally, I would accept a few hours of his time just to have his name on our roster."

"Really? What's so special about him?"

"He's been a military man since he was eighteen. Interned with the RCMP during college. Graduated from medical school at twenty-three. Also worked for the UN for some years."

"The UN?"

"Yes, like Koff, he was part of the five-year mission for the UN International Criminal Tribunal for the former Yugoslavia, including Kosovo in 2000."

Savanna pursed her lips. The Westbury Forensic Department needed a highly skilled chief forensic pathologist. But a boy genius from the army and the UN? How long would their operation hold the new chief's attention? Maybe for a full ten minutes.

"What brings him here?" she asked.

"The position."

She snorted. "A doctor with the entire alphabet after his name is interested in Westbury?"

"He's on special leave from the Canadian Army. Under some kind of a cloud."

"Special leave, under a cloud? I didn't think those terms went together. Has he been exiled to Westbury?"

"Something like that, I suppose."

"Well, he should make an interesting boss," she said and stretched to push from the chair. "I look forward to working with him."

"Glad to hear it. You're his assistant for the next year."

She couldn't have stopped the cringe if she tried. "His assistant? I belong in the field, not feeding a doctor's ego." She caught her snarky tone and reined it in. "I just meant that—"

"I get it. You have reservations," Miller said. "I was hesitant at first too, but I've come to recognize how good he can be for us."

"Why me?" Normally, an opportunity to learn from a seasoned doctor would intrigue her, but fetching for a disgraced army officer, who likely had a chip on his shoulder, seemed less appealing. "If Dr. Wade is as talented as you claim, wouldn't he prefer to work with another doctor?" she asked.

"Maybe, but I don't have another doctor. You're the perfect match for him."

"As his adjutant?"

"If need be, but that wouldn't be necessary. I've already assigned Josie Hale from records to that position."

"What's involved in this assignment?"

"All of it, really. Whatever he needs—morgue duties, fieldwork, lab assignments, training, court prep. The usual. Most of all, bring him up to speed on the Moore case. The accomplice and the possible psychotropic drug connection are still our priorities."

"Coroner, you forget that I'm on leave for two months at the end of May. That's in two weeks."

Savanna scheduled the time off to travel with her husband, well-known Canadian classical pianist Richard Reeves. He'd flown to New York for rehearsals the day after Valentine's Day. His six-month tour began last weekend in Toronto. In those three months, he'd returned home only once. The lonely nights without him had already started to affect her work.

She met Miller's gaze. The torch that burned so brightly in his eyes for the incoming chief a moment ago extinguished under a grimace. He sat back and ran his palm down his purple tie. "I have to postpone your leave," he said. "Indefinitely."

Her head jerked back. "Did you say postpone?"

"Actually, I meant cancel."

"What?" Savanna shot from the chair as though struck with a jolt of electricity. "That's ludicrous. I scheduled the leave months ago."

"In light of what we're dealing with, it just isn't possible right now. Your absence would leave us too shorthanded."

"Why do I get the feeling that this is less about our recent case-load and more about Dr. Wade?"

"Look, with Wade coming in we have an opportunity to put an end to this Colton Moore case. Both the mayor and the police chief are breathing down my neck to clean this up. I need you here."

Six months ago, a judge had sentenced Colton Moore to four years in prison for kidnapping, false imprisonment and sexual assault. Yet, Savanna could trace his intrusion into her life as far back as thirteen months when she met his victim, Sally Starr.

It was another wet evening in April, Savanna had detoured to the Westbury Police station to see the criminal division commander, Detective Superintendent Rupert Hannigan. She was ready to leave when a young woman ran into the station. Realizing that she had reached safety, she stared at Savanna and DS Hannigan through puffy, black and blue eyes.

Her thin legs shook under her slight frame. The simple pink cotton dress she wore did nothing to protect her shivering body against the cold night air. A rip clear down the front of the garment threatened to expose her nakedness, but shivering fingers clamped it in place. Crusted blood clumped her ash-blonde hair hanging limply on either side of her face. And deep sorrowful sobs interrupted her attempt to explain that four nights ago, on her way home from the university's student pub, someone grabbed her.

Because of Sally's brave interviews with the police, Moore was picked up in a few weeks. He was tried and convicted. But three weeks ago, and only six months into Moore's sentence, the police uncovered further evidence against him in another crime. Theresa Filito, a twenty-three-year-old woman, found murdered and stuffed into a ten-gallon drum, carried Moore's semen inside her.

Without further evidence, the Crown Attorney's Office delayed charging Moore with murder. To build the case, the police needed to find the person who transported the drum to the dockyard. Neither the detectives on the case, Dave Thomas and Ronald Fontaine, nor the Westbury Forensics team were any closer to identifying an accomplice.

Miller cleared his throat, but Savanna spoke first.

"Quinn and I trained Wessel to take over my CSI duties," she said. "I'm sure she or another scientist can assist Dr. Wade."

"Wessel can't do it."

"Not only is she capable of taking over, she's been looking forward to the assignment."

He sighed. "Not anymore. She's pregnant."

That announcement curbed Savanna's growing irritation. "Oh." She sat down again. "Oh, that's wonderful news."

"Though that shouldn't change things for a few months, Wessel requested a change in assignment." Miller said. "In either case your absence wouldn't have worked. I need you here on this case and assisting Wade."

"I can't help that."

"Recent budget cuts have tied my hands," Miller said as though she hadn't spoken. "I have limited funds for hiring. I got Wade. Now I need you to help him."

Savanna sank deeper into the chair. What would she tell Richard? Her promise of support meant travelling with him for two months. Plus, living without her husband for close to a year wasn't an experience she wanted to endure.

She'd started packing already. She'd also cancelled the newspaper and their raw milk delivery. She'd even written a list of interests to pursue while Richard rehearsed. She looked forward to the break from examining bruised, battered and violated corpses. A few weeks free of speculation, and testing and peering through a comparison scope. She deserved this time to recharge with Richard.

Miller moved to the edge of his chair and pushed his elbows into the armrests. "If you leave now, I'll end up with a mess on my hands," he said. "I need you here."

She shifted in the chair. He was right. How could she leave now when Moore's accomplice still roamed Westbury's streets, picking off women? The two months leave would be nothing but angst. Yet, abandoning Richard wasn't the answer either.

"What kind of time off can I expect?" she asked.

"The best I can do is the vacation you have left."

"Two weeks? I need more time." Without Richard, she became lost in the taxing and often gruesome details of her work. "What about weekends?" she asked. "Maybe someone else can fill in."

Miller offered her a sympathetic gaze. "You can discuss that with Wade. It will be his department as of Monday."

Monday. She'd have to explain all this to a new boss and hope he would understand.

"He'll attend the discovery meeting in the Crown's office," Miller said. "Once the case is closed, things will look a lot different. Is there anything we could do to speed up the process?"

Still bewildered with her cancelled leave, Savanna shook her head. "The wait times for forensic results are longer than they were a year ago," she said. "The lack of testing equipment increases lag times every day."

"What about the missing necklace? Anything?"

"No. Quinn and I searched Lamons Street a week ago. No traces of it anywhere. I'm hopeful about the psychotropic drug found in both women's DNA though."

"Really? I wouldn't have thought that was much of a lead. It's probably just a street drug."

"Maybe, but someone from the local Canadian Air Force base came to see me yesterday morning."

"Who was that?"

"Said he is based out of Petawawa but is using the local air base as his centre while he investigates rumours of a psychotropic drug that's been *wreaking havoc* on Canadian army bases. His words."

"The same drug?"

"He said the information he received led him to this part of the country."

"Is he an officer?"

"He introduced himself as Second-Lieutenant Scott Allen. He also said he has no way of procuring a sample and wondered if we might share what we know with the army."

"What's your take on him?"

"Seems genuine enough, but he did ask that I speak to no one else except him because of the sensitive nature of the situation."

"Well, this isn't the first time the Canadian Army asked for our support. And if this is going to help our case, then I see no reason why we can't share our info. How do you get in touch with him?"

"I have his personal cell number."

Miller looked thoughtful for a moment then sighed. "What we need is a break. A godsend. Somebody walking in and confessing. But all we get are more problems."

Savanna sat up. Maybe they already had a break. Two days ago, one of Quinn's informants gave him a tip. Jimmy said something about a cheese barn on Lucan Street in Exeter. She flicked a glance at Miller and decided against mentioning the tip. Quinn thought Jimmy was *spinning a yarn*. But, rather than chase their tails, she saw no harm in following the only lead they'd had in weeks.

Chapter 5

Ethanol and hydrogen peroxide fumes met Savanna when she walked into the serology lab. Two weeks away from her trip and Miller cancelled her extended vacation. Explaining the situation to Richard would take some doing. This time when he asked her to quit her job, she'd have to come up with more than *someday*.

"Damn. Damn and double damn." Catching herself, she looked around. No one was here to witness her mini melt down. *And why should they?* It was after 7:00 p.m.

She tugged her task chair from under the table and noticed that the triple frame hanging above her work station had tilted to one side. She reached up to straighten it. Her gaze lingered on the three photos of her best friend's family vacationing at Disney in Florida last March. Rebecca, always the diva, sported a Maleficent headpiece, complete with horns. Ben and the kids wore Mickey hats and Disney smiles.

In the photo of her father at her wedding, he was kissing her forehead with a sad faraway expression. Savanna knew the reason for his doleful mood, but she shifted her gaze to the thirty-year-old "mommy and me" shot. She was three years old. She held hands with her mother. Sometimes she thought she could recall the warmth of Ana's fingers on hers. Her father had said that this particular photo was the only time he captured the striking resemblance between them.

Savanna agreed, but she saw the differences too. Dark-honey and bronze undertones highlighted her latte skin tone while her mother's tanned complexion radiated with a pinkish hue. Straight rich chestnut brown hair framed Ana's beautiful face. At three, Savanna's hair was a mass of mahogany curls.

She straightened the frame and dropped onto the chair. When she felt lonely, her thoughts strayed to her childhood. With Richard gone for the next few months, and her leave cancelled, reminiscing was going to be a regular pastime. How depressing.

Well, she didn't do depress. She needed to do something to change Miller's position on her leave. Without a husband or a gaggle of kids to head home to, she might as well follow up on Quinn's informant's tip. Finding a lead to Moore's accomplice would get her out of here and on the road with Richard.

Prior information Quinn obtained from James Keizer had turned fruitful. But her partner described Keizer as a strung-out clerk. Jimmy worked the night shift at Walmart. He didn't seem to know much, but he heard about an illegal drug cook shop operating out of a cheese barn in Exeter. When Quinn had asked who would use a cheese barn to make drugs, Jimmy said that the stinky cheese snuffed out the chemical scents.

"The drugs took over the boy's brain sometime ago," Quinn had said.

"He can't be that far gone if he's able to hold down a job," Savanna had insisted. "Maybe what he says has some merit."

Quinn wasn't convinced. "The boy is like Duff Man. He says a lot of things." Duff Man was another one of Quinn's references from "The Simpsons" cartoon TV show.

Savanna wasn't so keen to dismiss Jimmy's ramblings. With nothing to do tonight, she might as well look into the address. If this place was a regular business, there was still enough time to make it to Exeter before closing. What she would find out there was anybody's guess. But looking into the claim certainly beat doing nothing.

She grabbed her trench coat and the scarf she slung around her neck that morning. Maybe going as a student would get her further than if she went as an investigator. A pair of fake glasses and an extra scarf she used before lay at the bottom of the drawer where she kept her purse. She headed for the door. Almost out of the lab, her blaring BlackBerry halted her stride. She should ignore it. Instead, she plucked it from her purse and read the screen.

"Dr. Wagsmith?" *Why would her doctor call her cellphone this late?*

"Good evening, Savanna," he said.

"Is something wrong?"

"No. Not at all. I'm following up on your physical. I thought you might want to know as soon as possible."

Her throat clogged. It couldn't be cancer or leukaemia or anything as damning. No fatal disease killed her mother. She'd died in the line of duty, as they say. Except, Ana Jones was no longer a soldier when someone shot her. She was a journalist.

"Know what?" Savanna asked.

"You're pregnant,"

The words echoed in her head, but somehow their meaning lagged. She stood frozen to the spot, trying to decipher the definition of, *you're pregnant*. When the answer worked itself to the fore-front of her brain, she returned to her desk and lowered herself onto the task chair.

"Are you sure?" she asked.

"Of course I'm sure. According to my calculations, you're just over three weeks."

"Three weeks?" It had been three months and three days since Richard left. They met only once during that time two months ago. "Sorry, Doctor, that can't be right. In fact, it's impossible. Can you please recheck?"

She listened into the quiet hum on the line. The silence wasn't eerie at all. In fact, it carried none of the awkwardness of a long pause in a short conversation.

"All right, Savanna. Here we are. You are right about the timing, I'm mistaken. You are now entering your fifth week of pregnancy."

A tremor gripped her and she melted against the chair. She'd met Richard in New York back in March. It must have happened then. "But," she said. "I'm still menstruating and… and I'm on birth control. The patch. . . It's supposed to work."

"And in most cases, it does, but sometimes other medications can interfere with the contraception. You were on antibiotics a couple months ago for a bladder infection. Remember?"

Oh God, she couldn't be pregnant now. "Doctor," she swallowed, then tried to breathe away the obstruction in her chest. "Can you please check again?"

"I can, if you like, but the results will be the same."

Her hand lifted to still her spinning head. *Pregnant.* Four years ago, after she and Richard returned from their honeymoon in Barbados, she lost the child she had been carrying. Back then she had thought the miscarriage was the universe's way of punishing her. She'd even entertained the possibility that she would make it to menopause without having a child. The other part of that possibility would have her facing this news, where scenarios and options would trip her and raise memories she buried too deep to untangle.

Wagsmith dragged her back to the present. "Given your history," he continued, "this news can be a bit overwhelming."

Was that it? She *was* overwhelmed. Richard was going to be away for half the year. How could she do this without him? She shook the fog from her head. "What… What happens now?" she asked.

"I need to see you every two weeks for the first three months and then we can take it from there."

"That often?"

"I know that seems excessive, but it's necessary. The clinic is open from 9:00 to 1:30 in the afternoon on Saturdays until the start of summer. Call my office in the morning and set something up with Monica. We can talk about your options then."

She winced. *Options?* She had only one option. Richard needed to know, and he needed to know this weekend.

Chapter 6

IT WAS EVIDENT THE CLEANING staff had already rolled through the serology floor when Savanna entered the bathroom. Toilet bowls greeted her with seats lifted, and industrial strength Mr. Clean overpowered the ethanol floating in the corridors.

She entered the first stall and locked the door squeezing her ringing BlackBerry to her ear with one shoulder. Her fingers tugged the button of her pants open, then she levered down the zipper and shoved her pants to her hips.

The line connected. "I wondered where you got to after work," her best friend said.

"I'm still at the lab." Savanna stretched the waistband of her underwear, exposing the birth control patch stuck to her hip.

"Of course," Rebecca Dubai said. After a moment of silence she asked, "What's wrong?"

Savanna froze. *Another win for best friends.* Seventeen years of multiplying the good and sharing unforeseen crazy between them, Rebecca could detect the slightest chink in Savanna's armour, even over hundreds of feet of fibre optics.

Savanna scratched the thin beige patch with her thumbnail

until the edge loosened. She should have waited until she saw Rebecca to give her the news. Her best friend's reassurance in person would have soothed the hot anxiety piping through her veins now.

With a quick jerk, she yanked the patch from her skin. "I'm pregnant," Savanna blurted out through gritted teeth while pressing her hand against the stinging spot.

While her words resonated and reached into the pass, Savanna rustled her pants into place and left the stall.

"Oh my god," Rebecca finally said. "You're serious." Her voice started bouncing.

"What are you doing?" Savanna asked.

"What do you think? The mummy dance."

"There's a mummy dance?" She imagined Rebecca's curly strawberry hair flopping around her smiling face.

In front of the bathroom mirror, Savanna covered her forehead with the scarf and wrapped it around her hair. She draped the second scarf over her shoulders and pulled on her trench coat. She pushed on the fake glasses. The square black frames covered half her face. A scratch marked the corner of the left lens, but they still worked.

She left the bathroom and pressed the button for the elevator. That's when she noticed the silence. "Rebecca?" she asked. "Are you still there?"

"We're happy about this, right?"

Savanna leaned against the cold marble wall. "Richard is gone for months. What will I do?"

"You'll be fine. You've got me, and this is such good news."

"A baby. It's frightening." The elevator arrived. She stepped in and pressed P1. The phone connection held on, though a bit spotty. Once she reached the car, she climbed behind the wheel and switched to the Bluetooth speaker.

"You're worried," Rebecca said.

"A bit."

"Then stop worrying. How did it happen? You've been on the patch forever."

After two failures with the pill, Savanna switched to the patch. "It didn't work," she said. "Or stopped working."

"I thought those things were bulletproof. Anyway, this is a good thing, just what you need in your life right now."

"Uh hmm."

"You're going to be a mummy."

"What if I'm no good at it? Soccer moms and minivans terrify me."

"Nichole and Peter don't scare you."

Savanna started the car and guided it to the exit. No, Rebecca's kids didn't scare her because she loved them, and would give her life for them if she had to. "That's just it," she said. "My only experience with babies is Nichole and Peter. I wouldn't know what to do to stop the baby from crying in the middle of the night."

"None of us do. You'll figure it out as you go."

"I'm a forensic scientist. What do I know about parenting?"

"You're the last person who should worry about having kids. I will never forget that the week before high school graduation, when everyone was trying to get laid, you turned down a date with Connor Watson, heartthrob and panty-peeler rolled into one, to scavenger hunt with a group of six-year-olds."

Savanna grinned and pulled onto the street.

"Not convinced?" Rebecca asked. "I've got more. What was the first thing you did when you moved to Westbury?"

"I—"

"That's right." Rebecca was in full command of her evidence, and nothing Savanna said was going to stop her. "You volunteered at the youth centre and showed up late at your job interview, almost losing your internship."

"That's not exactly how it happened."

"You are the same woman who scheduled your wedding day and honeymoon around your days off from said youth centre."

"You're missing the point here."

"What point?"

"Those kids aren't mine. What if it's not meant for me?"

There was a moment of quiet on the line. "You didn't always

feel that way," Rebecca's voice softened. "I know you didn't. When Nichole was born, you cuddled with her for hours. And when Peter came along—"

Tears stung Savanna's eyes. "Stop it," she said.

"You practically moved in." Rebecca ignored her protest. "Don't get me wrong, I loved it, but Ben worried our little guy would think you were his mother."

"Okay fine, but—"

"You're nervous, maybe even scared. I get that. You have your regrets. I know that too. Just don't let that frighten you into thinking you can't do this."

Savanna blinked fast to clear her vision. The memories took her too far back. She'd never heard of anyone actually turning back time, so why she held onto a secret wish to relive her past, she would never know. They promised never to talk about her mistake, not even to Richard. That promise had worked, until now.

"Come on over and we can celebrate," Rebecca said.

"I can't. Not now. I'm heading to Exeter."

Chapter 7

NICHOLAS STRADDLED HIS NEWLY rented BMW G3 motorcycle and pulled away from the spot directly in front his house. Despite the angst needling him since he drove into town again last night, an adrenalin rush shot up his spine as he revved the bike into the highway traffic.

The machine's power reminded him of his rebellious pre-teen years that started the day after his grandfather's death. That was twenty-seven years ago. He was just eleven-years-old. It had taken his enrolment in the army seven years later to redirect his defiance.

He sped through the light traffic, following a westerly dipping third quarter moon. In a clear sky like that, he betted on success. Forty minutes later, he slowed and turned onto Lucan Street in Exeter. The GPS coordinates brought him to a bright yellow wooden barn in the centre of a gravel lot of about 22 by 150 meters. He pulled onto the driveway.

Several tall trees in spring bloom and a four-foot rock wall separated the barn from the plant nursery next door. To the opposite side and around the perimeter, detached trailers with the name, "Steel Plant Nursery" bordered the rest of the property. It was likely that both businesses shared the lot.

Letting the engine idle under him, Nicholas snapped the kick-stand to the ground and pushed from the seat. The property looked deserted, not unexpected for a Friday night. He came prepared to answer questions and ask some of his own. He knew one thing. He wasn't leaving until he got inside.

Nicholas blew air from his lungs and looked around. The place didn't look like a drug manufacturing and distribution plant. He spotted no high-tech cameras, no heavy-duty floodlights and no security guards carrying partially concealed, illegal weapons. Instead, the rustic barn looked as though they sold second hand furniture, yet the air was scented with a pungent odour he couldn't quite identify. A few lamps hung from the building casting a dull light into the yard and large shadow patches provided enough coverage for him to move around unnoticed.

He dug into his jacket pocket and extracted the paper and double-checked the location. It had taken him an entire three weeks after McBride's death to find this address. He certainly hoped it led somewhere. As unsophisticated as this place seemed, he crept forward. The appearance could be a mere deterrent. To verify its purpose, he wanted to take a look around before he found a way in.

He snapped the kickstand back into place and guided the bike to the rear of the property. Though the barn was painted on the front, rough, aged wood formed the backend. A dark sloping roof, one loading door and an office entrance completed the structure.

Nicholas shut off the engine, dismounted and searched for cameras again. He spotted none, yet the short hairs on the back of his neck spiked. Seeing no one, he pulled out his phone and started snapping photos of the building, the perimeter, and the trailers on the edge of the property. Then he tried the doors, but they were all locked.

He stuck close to the building and repositioned to the side. Long wooden stairs led to a second-floor entrance. He mounted the steps with break-and-enter on his mind. The loose floorboards creaked under his weight as he scaled them two at a time.

An unlit bulb centred the doorframe, probably burnt out. He loosened the bulb as a precaution and tried the lock. He hadn't expected it to turn and release, but when it didn't budge, he went with plan B and pulled a small tool from his pocket. He crouched to eyeball the lock then set to work. Within seconds, an audible click released the metal tongue.

As soon as he stepped through the small doorway, an overpowering mixture of sour milk and athlete's foot rushed up his nostrils. He stumbled back and pulled the door closed behind him. *Cheese? It was a cheese barn?* Either this was the wrong address, or a really clever way of concealing an illegal drug operation. The place was its own deterrent. No need for a security alarm.

Almost twenty years as a soldier with ten tours of duty under his belt, he didn't intend to let a warehouse full of cheese intimidate him. He pulled a bandana from the knee pocket in his cargo pants and tied it around his nose, then opened the door again. After one long inhale to fill his lungs with fresh air, he slipped into the room and pulled the door shut. The moment his foot hit the cement floor, Nicholas knew he wasn't alone.

Chapter 8

WHEN THE LOCK TURNED OVER, Savanna ducked behind one of the fully-stacked racks. The door opened. Mounds of cheese concealed her location. The smell was especially dank from her corner and she pulled the scarf over her nose. She shivered from the ten-degree temperature in the barn, wishing she wore a winter coat instead.

Two minutes earlier, guided by the light from her BlackBerry, she picked the lock. Eight years with a police partner had taught her something about how to slip past locked doors. She had never had to use it on anything this unorthodox. Inside, she locked herself in and crept down the wobbly steps. Before she got a chance to look around, someone followed her. Panic crawled down her back now.

Savanna released the scarf over her nose and carefully reached a hand out to get her bearings in the dark. The racks were stacked close and her hand connected with a hunk of cheese.

The door closed again.

She exhaled the tense breath and pushed to her feet. She counted the seconds, allowing the person enough time to clear the area before she made her way up the stairs and out of the noxious, smelly barn. When the door opened again, she bristled and returned to her hiding spot.

On arrival, she'd noticed a switch at the top of the stairs and expected overhead lights to expose her, but whoever entered started a cautious descent in the dark. The weak stairs shook and rocked as they had under her weight only minutes earlier. One thing for sure, this wasn't the owner.

She lifted the scarf to her face again and exhaled a cautious breath. Where was the direct path to the door? She would make a run for it.

A scratching noise halted her attempt to move forward. *What was that?* Footsteps ran from the opposite side of the barn, across from where she hid. Savanna's blood ran cold. Someone else was already inside and she hadn't known.

A loud crash rumbled and shook the wooden barn as though a bulldozer had ripped it from the ground.

"What the…"

Scuffling.

"Shit. Argh." The swearing and agonizing growl came from a man. Lighter footsteps pounded up the stairs.

Savanna's scalp prickled. She froze.

The man's voice trailed into grunts and curses. The door opened and slammed closed.

"Shit," the man said again.

Was he injured?

What should she do now? When she arrived, entering the building seemed like a bad idea, and then it didn't. She'd come all this way. Why leave again without a glimpse of what Jimmy thought went on at this address? Their entire case depended on getting answers to Moore's accomplice and the drugs they used. But she'd found nothing and was in danger of being identified. Then again, with all the activity here tonight, this place was ripe with more than the cheese.

She should have informed Quinn about her plans, but as a police officer, he needed a search warrant to enter locked doors.

Rather than allow such limitations to hamper her entry, she leaned heavily on the technicality that she wasn't really a police officer.

Now on high alert, she sidled in the darkness and tiptoed toward the stairs.

"Is someone here?" The voice she'd heard earlier.

She froze. Nape hair raised, mouth parched, she wondered what to do next. "This is private property." The words somehow left her mouth. "Who are you?" She asked. Better to sound authoritative rather than scared, like she felt.

"You're the security guard, then?" he asked.

Though she expected some level of aggression, the commanding tone caught her off guard.

"Look, we need some light in here," he said. "Thanks to your friend, I'm caught under something. You must know where to find the light switch."

He was trapped? Well, that could work to her advantage, especially if he broke in. She pulled out her BlackBerry and spotted the light around the barn. The room was filled with racks from floor to half a foot from the ceiling that stretched twelve feet high, and cheeses of all types: Swiss, Cheddar, Gruyère, Brie, and some others she couldn't name— filled the shelves. The giant round thick slabs sat in rows and columns with a few inches of space between them. Some of the metal racks, like the one toppled over, were on wheels.

She shifted the light in the stranger's direction. His feet in large camouflage sneakers stretched toward her. He leaned against one of the fallen metal racks. He wore green cargo pants and a brown leather bomber jacket covering an army camouflage t-shirt. She couldn't see his left leg clearly. Like he said, it was caught, though with his size, it looked rather easy to move.

She shifted the light to his face and her breath hitched. *Now who wears a bandana around their face?*

"Having light wouldn't matter to you," she said. "You can wait here for the police."

"What's my crime? Stealing cheese?" Her threat didn't even faze him.

"Breaking and entering at least," she said. "You were obviously up to something since you arrived wearing a disguise."

He laughed, though it sounded more like frustration than humour.

"I'm glad to see that I amuse you," she said.

"I've been called many things, but a cheese bandit? That's fresh, unlike the cheese in here. What gave me away?" he asked. "The leather jacket?"

"I'm more concerned with that bandana."

He yanked it down. "Don't tell me, you're a cheese lover," he said. "This place takes some getting used to."

A healthy tan enhanced his clean-shaven jawline, broad forehead and square chin that seemed chiselled from stone.

Her clever comeback stuck in her throat while she stood there gawking at his military haircut and trying to follow his green, no, amber, maybe they were honey brown eyes that glinted under the cellphone light.

"I'm not here to steal your ripe cheese," he said. "I'm looking for some information and I was given this address."

That sounded similar to her reason for being there. She slid the light over his body again. He was six feet tall or more and built like that, he was probably military, or maybe the reserves. The typical psychotropic drug user, like the one she was trying to trace.

"Did I scare off your contact?" she asked.

"What are you talking about, lady?" He shifted a bit then gritted his teeth. "Look, if you think I'm here for some illegal reason, go ahead and call the police."

He called her on another threat. "Like you," she said, "I was given this address. You must be the contact."

"I don't suppose you feel like lending your contact a hand here?"

She took one step toward him and stopped. "How do I know what you say is true? You did pick the lock to get in here."

"And how did you get in? You have a key?"

Sarcasm aside, he had a point. "Okay" she said. "I'll try to push that away." She pointed to the constraint and stepped around him. She positioned the phone on the ground with the light shining up then gripped the wooden rack with her gloved hand and started pushing it away. It strained her muscles but weighed less than she thought. So why did he need help? He heaved and together they shoved the heavy rack from his arms.

As soon as he was free, she grabbed her phone and cleared his reach. He sat up but remained on the cement floor.

"So?" she asked. "Are you going to tell me who you are?"

"I believe this will go better if we remain anonymous."

"Really?"

"Yes… Really."

She spotted the light on him again.

He was looking down at his left leg with an annoyed grimace. "But if we're going to get anywhere," he said, "we need at least a modicum of trust."

"You're the one who wants to remain anonymous."

"You didn't come here to learn my name and I sure as hell don't think who you are will help me at this point."

"Fine. Let's forget names for now and just tell me what you got."

"What I've got? May I remind you that you're here to provide me with information?"

"Be like that then." She turned and started up the rickety steps again.

"Wait," he called out. "I'm going to need your help."

"Why should I help you when all you want is to pump me for information."

"Because as far as I can tell, you don't have any?"

"Are you always this tetchy, or is it the smell?" She sighed. This trip was a waste of time. "If you have nothing to say," she said, "why did you come out here?"

"Perhaps you have nothing to do with why I'm here. Maybe what I'm looking for isn't even in this bloody barn."

Without the light from her phone she couldn't see him very well. And whatever it was he was doing sounded as though he was trying to lift the building off its foundation. "Well good luck with it then." She had reached the door at the top of the steps.

"Are you going to walk away?"

She hit the light switch on the wall. A yellowish glow illuminated the man. He was twisted away from her.

"That's good of you," he said, his words thick with sarcasm. "Thanks." He turned his head in her direction. With the light spotting directly in his face, she was no more than a figure on the stairs.

That's when she noticed a rip in one of his pant leg and a dark patch spreading outward. She gasped.

"What now?" He flashed that cranky expression again.

Maybe he needed the light to assess the extent of his injury and decide whether or not to extract the object that stuck out from his left leg.

If she left him here, he would probably lose too much blood before someone else showed up. He could probably manage to free himself, but then climbing the weak stairs would be tricky. She made her way down the steps again.

"Here, let me take a look at that," she said watching him gingerly inspect the wound. She stooped next to him and his scent, heavy with attractive male and damp with fresh blood, started working on her. She froze as the smell poked at a lost memory.

"Do you faint at the sight of blood?" he asked.

She shook her head, more to clear it than to answer his question. "I'm fine. Are you hurt anywhere else?"

"Isn't this enough?"

"Calm down there fella, just figuring things out." *Big boys don't cry, but they certainly do yelp lots when hurt.* Most of the thin blade had pierced his leg.

From the cylindrical handle and the two inches that stuck out from his thigh, she guessed the object was a palette knife, about an inch and a half wide. "I need to see what's going on under there," she said pointing to his pant leg.

He grabbed the blood-soaked spot with both fists and tore a hole in the fabric, then grasped the handle and pulled it from his leg. Blood gushed from the wound.

"Why the hell did you do that?" she yelled.

He grunted.

She reached for his bandana and untied the knot. She used it to cover the wound, pressing down as hard as she could. What did she know about dealing with a live, wounded man? All her cases came to her with death preserving the mystery that killed them.

She watched his eyes while applying pressure. The anger had left him and he studied what he could see of her face in silence.

She eased her hand away from the wound and tenderly inspected the area surrounding the bleeding gash.

The muscle beneath flexed.

The contraction shot an electric surge up her arm. She snatched her hand away and bit her lower lip to stop the warmth burning her cheek. With her latte complexion wrapped under a disguise, he would hardly notice that though blood didn't bother her, feeling the pulsating muscular leg of a well-built man who wasn't her husband, made her a bit jumpy.

"I don't think there's anything inside," she said.

"Me either."

"I don't know what's on that thing." She pointed to the palette knife he extracted from his leg. "Given what's stored in this barn, you could be riddled with bacteria by now. I have something in my car that can clean this until you can get some medical help." She met his gaze. Hazel.

His eyes were hazel and they scanned her face as though he was trying to imprint an image for later review.

She swallowed. "I'll be right back," she said.

"Are you sure you're coming back?"

"If I don't, get yourself to a hospital."

She left him and ran across the yard to grab a few items from her kit.

When Savanna returned, there was something frantic and twitchy about the way her lame, tight-lipped informant shuffled on his butt. She watched him for a moment. He had inched closer to the stairs where he sat back, propped up on his elbows with his wounded leg raised on the steps.

"To help the bleeding," he said when she looked questioningly at him.

"Good thinking," she agreed, a little unsettled. "Okay, I have some saline solution here. I'll bathe the wound and cover it with this stuff." She held up the gauze. She didn't have as much of a first aid kit as she thought.

"It will hurt," she said. "If you're squeamish, look away." She didn't really think he was, but she'd seen police officers drop in the morgue like chloroformed flies. She could never tell who would faint and who wouldn't.

When she checked his face, he wasn't following her handiwork, but staring at the braid that had fallen from her scarf and lay on her shoulder. She pushed it behind her with a thumb and focused her attention on the cut. "Ready?" Without waiting for an answer, she squeezed the solution onto the wound.

He didn't even blink. Instead, his focus remained on her scarf, as if trying to see beneath it. Since she had readjusted her disguise when she went to retrieve the bandages from the car, he couldn't see much.

"Put your finger here, will ya?" she said, holding thick gauze against the open gash that wouldn't stop bleeding. "I don't have anything to wrap it for pressure." His bandana was already soaked through. "I'll use this," she said and removed the scarf draped around her shoulders. It had been a gift from Rebecca. She brushed aside any thought of an explanation and wrapped it as tight as she could around the man's leg.

"Are you a doctor or something?" he asked.

"Or something." She tucked in the end. "How's that?"

"It will do," he said.

"Glad to hear it."

"Thank you."

She pushed to her feet. "I'll help you out of here, but I suggest you hitch a ride back to wherever you came from. Operating a vehicle could aggravate your blood loss."

"I'll need your shoulder to get up."

She stooped down again, and he draped an arm around her shoulder. His heat penetrated her trench coat and light sweater. The sensation caught her off guard. She pushed up too fast.

He grunted.

"Sorry," she said and grabbed for his midsection to steady herself. The feel of well developed, rippled abs pushed back against her palm. She snatched her hand away, but was totally unprepared for his weight. They toppled to one side. This time, his quick shift in the opposite direction saved them from falling over.

"Sorry," she said again. "Are you okay? Do you need a minute before we try the steps?"

He held on to the shaky railing and some seconds passed before he answered. "I'm good to go."

By the time they made it onto the gravel outside, the weather had cooled. Still holding onto each other, they both paused to inhale the night air.

After a moment, Mr. Tall, Tan and Anonymous looked down at her.

"I see you didn't find the cheese appetizing either," he said.

"I didn't."

He smirked and directed her to his bike hidden behind a dumpster.

"Is there some sort of medical facility near here?" he asked.

So, he's not from this area. "South Huron is about fifteen minutes east of here," she said.

"How did you get here? I didn't see a car when I pulled in."

"I'm parked next door."

"Don't suppose you can give me a ride to the emergency room?"

Not certain she wanted to spend more time with him, she met his eyes. He didn't seem hung up on his athletic body and handsome face. How refreshing. That in itself was attractive.

God, what was she thinking? She dropped her gaze. Most women might find him attractive, but she was married. Admittedly something other than his good looks paralyzed her for a moment when she first laid eyes on him, but attractive? And this wasn't working out like she'd hoped. She came here for information and ended up playing nursemaid to an uncooperative informant.

Savanna started for her Passat, not yet decided if she would drive him. Behind the wheel, she observed his tall figure leaning against his bike, which was clearly visible from the adjacent parking lot where she'd stashed her car. As she watched him, she adjusted the scarf around her head again, pulling it down over her forehead and wrapping the ends more securely around her neck.

How did he know she wouldn't just drive away and leave him stranded? He seemed honest enough, even if he wasn't cooperating. And one way or the other, she needed to find out who he was and what he knew about the operations in that foul-smelling cheese barn.

Chapter 9

$\mathcal{T}$HEY WERE ON THE ROAD driving away from a third quarter moon when Savanna turned to look at her passenger. His head leaned against the headrest, his eyes closed. His Adam's apple stuck out from a long, thick neck.

"Are you in pain? she asked.

"Nothing I can't handle. Thank you." He sat up and looked over at her.

She startled and swung her eyes back to the road. "You can repay me by telling me what I want to know," she said and shoved the fake glasses up on her nose.

"And what exactly is that?" he asked

She was over her head now and thought it best to wing it. "Someone gave us both this address because they thought . . . Well maybe they thought you had information to share."

"Who left you the address?"

She snuck him a glance. "Is it that important that you have a name? A source."

"A source? And did this source give you a date saying when I would be out here? A time? A name?"

Who was he? The Riddler? Pointing out her folly. "Nothing like that," she said.

"What exactly did your source say?"

"What did yours say?"

"Nothing about cheese. And how do you suppose the person knew when I would show up?"

"What?"

"How are we supposed to exchange information if we don't even have a code word, or something?"

"What are you trying to say? That this was a set up?"

He was silent for a moment, then asked, "Who was your partner in the barn?"

"What partner? You mentioned that before."

"The person who stabbed me in the leg and took off."

Savanna shivered. Entering the barn had been riskier than she realized. The person could have been Moore's accomplice.

"You don't have a clue, do you?" he asked.

She shook her head. "No."

"Then why were you there?"

"I told you—"

"Were you looking for a hit?"

"A hit?" The car swerved when she turned sharply to look at him. "You think I'm… That I'm a…?"

"Isn't that why you showed up there?"

"No. It's not."

"Then you are just in over your head?"

"There it is," she snapped, happy to see the hospital sign. She pulled to the side and took one of the vacant spots directly in front of the building. She was familiar with the hospital and knew that this door served both the emergency and the main entrances.

By the time she helped him from the car, the blood had saturated his entire pant leg. The doors slid open as they approached. A few people exited. Her patient paused to take a breath. He leaned against the wall with his arm still around her shoulder.

"You've lost a lot of blood," she said. "No wonder you were talking so crazy."

He eyeballed her, but said nothing.

"If you're going to pass out, now is a good time," she said. "You're in capable hands."

His hazel eyes roamed over her face.

"Not me." She pointed to the two nurses and a doctor attending patients. "Them." Savanna led her charge to a free chair against the wall.

"Sit here for a moment and I'll see about getting someone to help you."

"Look, I'm—" He started to say, but she cut him off.

"I won't be long. In fact—"

"Savanna, is that you?"

She recognized the voice right away and turned to face the woman behind her. Janet Whateley's short dark hair curled neatly around her ears. The lucky white patch covered part of her forehead and remained obediently in place over her left eye.

"Janet," Savanna said and hugged her. "You're working tonight? Good."

Janet was the most sympathetic emergency nurse this side of the moon. She was Florence Nightingale and Wanda Sykes rolled into one wonderful human.

When they released each other, Janet pulled back and gaped, wide-eyed. "What's this?" she asked pointing at Savanna's headdress. "You coming from a costume party or something? Why the heck didn't you call me? I could have at least gotten you something to show off your—."

"Ah, no. I'll tell you about it later. I brought you a patient. He's hurt pretty bad."

"The only type of men I seem to meet these days."

Savanna hid a grin and avoided the stranger's eyes.

When Janet laid eyes on him, she did a double take.

Savanna quickly transmitted the *nothing like that* signal.

"I tried to stop the bleeding," she said. "But there wasn't a lot in my kit to help."

"He's lost a lot of blood. He's not a haemophiliac, is he?"

They talked about him as though he wasn't sitting right there and when Savanna looked over at him, he watched them with an amused expression.

She adjusted the glasses on her face again. "Well, are you?" she asked him.

"No. I'm not."

"All righty," Janet said. "That's good news. Let's get into an exam room and see what we've got."

"I'll get that wheelchair." Savanna dodged Janet's wink and scuttled toward the counter. When she returned, their patient shrugged from his leather jacket and handed it to her. Then he slid into the wheelchair.

They made it as far as the check-in desk when the entrance door slid open again. A rush of fresh air ushered in two paramedics pushing a gurney. They scurried to clear a path.

"What do you have there, Dan?" Janet asked one of them as they zipped past her.

"A stabbing. Caucasian male, about nineteen. Intoxicated. Vitals are stable but—"

"Sherry," Janet yelled to her colleague behind the counter.

Their stranger wheeled his chair to the gurney. He touched the victim's neck. "He's going into shock," he yelled.

Savanna followed him. "What are you doing?" Savanna hissed.

He ignored her. "This man needs medical attention now," he said.

Sherry hurried over and pointed down the corridor. "Room four," she said and hastened ahead of the ambulance attendants pushing the gurney.

"Page Dr. Riser, stat," Janet said to the young man coming toward her.

He nodded and hurried to the phone on the wall.

Janet wheeled their patient to room two and hoisted his muscle-bound frame onto the raised bed.

Savanna never took her eyes off him. "Suddenly you're a medic?" she asked.

He looked her over without a word. Janet grabbed scissors and cut into the scarf wrapped around the wound. Savanna bit her lip.

How would she explain that to Rebecca? She looked up to see their patient watching her. She dropped her eyes to his leg again.

The cotton swabs hardly contained the gaping wound. Underneath, the cut was red, swollen and raw with a bit of tissue pushing through. If he was in pain he certainly didn't show it.

"I've to get some equipment to clean and suture this up," Janet said. "Are you up-to-date on your tetanus shots?"

"Got the last one only six months ago."

Savanna grimaced. *Why couldn't he be that cooperative with her?*

"Okay," Janet said. "I'll be right back." Her friend eyed them and ducked behind the curtain.

Savanna hung his jacket on a nearby chair and pulled it closer to the bed. She sat down.

He followed her every move without saying a word.

"Maybe we got off on the wrong foot," she said. "You said you came out here for some information, maybe I can help. Just tell me who you are and what you're looking for."

"Haven't we already established that you know nothing?"

She clenched a fist, to stop herself from poking his wound like she'd seen in the movies. "I was in the barn for a reason," she said. "I must know something."

"And if I hadn't come along when I did, you would be lying here rather than me. Maybe even—"

She leapt from the chair. *Okay.* So, she had acted on a whim and it didn't turn out as she had hoped. In fact, she *could* have been killed, but did he think she wanted to keep hearing it? "You don't want to tell me what you know," she said. "Fine, I don't scare that easily. Good luck with your search and best of luck with this." She waved a hand over the wound.

"I'm not trying to scare you," he said. "Just pointing out the obvious dangers."

What, so now he cared? She scanned the length of him lying on the small bed. The rip in his pants exposed his jockey underwear, navy and hugging a thick muscular thigh. She swallowed. His flat stomach under the sweater rose and fell with a calm, quiet breath. His hand under his head lifted his chest and pressed firm pectorals against the thin t-shirt. With a body like that and a high pain toler-ance, her suspicion that he was military was probably right. When she reached his handsome face, an amusing smirk lifted his lips.

She turned away to cover her embarrassment. "You're in good hands with Janet," she said.

"You're leaving, Savanna?"

Her name sounded chillingly familiar coming from him. Goose bumps pimpled her skin under the trench coat. She half turned. "What happened to remaining anonymous?"

He shrugged. "What about my bike?"

"Don't look at me. I can barely drive stick. Don't you have someone you can call to pick it up? If I were you, I would do it soon, while it's still dark."

"I would much prefer if you drove me back to get it."

"Not going to happen, Mr. Tight Lip."

Janet returned then, pushing a cart with gauze, tools and vials.

Savanna looked one last time at the man on the bed and turned to her friend. "Jan, can we talk for a moment?" she asked.

Janet worked part-time at Westbury General for six years before she found a permanent position on the nightshift in Exeter for the last year. She was still commuting. Since the move Savanna hardly saw her. They made a point to have dinner at least twice in the last year.

They stepped outside.

"This man," Savanna said. "Well, to be honest, I don't know him."

"Kinda gathered that."

"I can't explain now, but can you not give him any more infor-mation about me? He didn't know my name until you mentioned it in the waiting room."

"My bad. Sorry about that."

"Don't worry about it."

"How did this happen anyway, or can't you say?" Janet raised her eyebrows and gave Savanna a saucy glare. "I won't say a word, promise." She made the zipped motion with her fingers across her mouth.

"Nothing like that," Savanna said, feeling a bit heated. "A rusty palette knife impaled his thigh. We were in a cheese barn."

"Okay. Not the freakiest accident I've come across in the emergency room. And not the most romantic place for a rendezvous either." Janet grinned.

"Would you stop." Savanna said, faking annoyance.

"I'll keep your information under wraps, but I'll have to ask him for some ID. Do you want to know who he is?"

"That would be helpful." The guilt that pricked her neck lasted for a split second. Finding out this man's identity could take her investigation in the right direction. "Whatever you find would go a long way. I'll call you tomorrow." Savanna leaned in and wrapped her arms around Janet. Her friend worked too hard, driving back and forth on a daily basis. Her once lean, but muscular figure now felt thin and boney under her nurse's uniform.

"Got it," Janet said.

Savanna glanced back at the curtain and checked her watch. She had barely enough time to catch a red-eye to Montreal.

Chapter 10

ESPITE THE DULL THROBBING in his upper left leg, a sense
of calm surrounded Nicholas. He leaned against the
island in the kitchen in his new home, then reached for the television remote and lowered the volume of the newscast.

He grasped his cellphone and dialled Lieutenant-Colonel Brent
Warner, then single-handedly popped the cap off the oxycodone
prescription he picked up from the pharmacy last night.

"Brent," he said when the line connected. "I need to call in
another favour."

"What happened? You fell and can't get up?"

Nicholas smiled into the phone and supported his weight on his
right foot. "Smart ass," he said.

His best friend for twenty years was second in command at the
Royal Canadian Air Force base in Westbury. Their friendship began
the day Nicholas lost the officer cadet unofficial beat-down on his
first day at Shilo, the Canadian Forces training base in Manitoba.
He was eighteen and bound for the army. Brent, two years older,
had signed up to follow his dream of becoming an air force pilot.

"Would you be able to provide me with login access to the air
force base's network?" Nicholas asked.

"I don't see why not. You got any equipment there?"

"I have an Apple Airport router."

"I was thinking more like a Synology router."

"I can get one. I plan to head out soon anyway. I can meet you back here this afternoon." *Here* was the townhouse Brent had scored for him. A heritage bungalow in the old north district of Westbury.

"Don't worry," Brent said. "I'm headed to your place to see if you survived the night."

Last night, Brent picked him up from South Huron and brought along Officer Cadet Saunders to ride Nicholas's bike home. Nurse Whateley sutured the cut on his upper thigh with eight dissolving stitches, injected him with antibiotics and prescribed oxycodone for the pain. He took the drugs to numb the throbbing in his leg and the ineptitude that left him feeling a little humiliated.

"Didn't know you cared," he said to Brent.

"Somebody's gotta cover your sorry ass."

One of these days, he'd remind Brent how miserable he'd been just before Nicholas introduced him to Marie, the woman he called his soulmate and married ten months later. Still, the man was on the money. It had been some time since Nicholas had someone in his life who really cared about him. Fraser McDaniel, his old friend and mentor, had said it best a few weeks ago. 'See how life looks when you're staring into the eyes of an irresistible woman'.

"One complication at a time, man," he said to Brent.

"Right. I have a spare router Marie is no longer using. I'll bring it."

"Thanks. Appreciate it."

Nicholas rested the phone on the counter and tossed one of the pills in his mouth, then chased it with a bottle of water. He looked around the house. Still littered with unpacked boxes filled with whatever he would have needed for a year in Kingston. *Why the hell did Corbett send him here instead?*

Friday night when Brent drove him to see the house, they'd entered and immediately Nicholas started listing its cons: dull lighting, trendy interior decor with exposed brick and ceiling trusses. But the pros: the investment property was rented fully furnished and belonged to Marie's boss, an interior designer. The gourmet kitchen was overkill. He would have preferred a gym.

Nicholas attempted to vault onto the quartz countertop, but the injury curtailed his movement. He grabbed a chair and used it to climb up. Closer to the light fixture, he scrutinized the bulbs in the track and popped out one. It fell into his hand with ease. Nothing was that easy, and last night was proof.

His entire operation fell apart the minute he'd entered the cheese barn. Then Savanna, the woman who thought he was her contact, rendered him incapable of asking questions. She'd taken the lead almost immediately. Though he refused to provide answers, their cat and mouse game told him nothing about what she knew. Yet if she hadn't helped him, his leg could have been worse.

He popped out another bulb from its socket. He'd left his full name and address with the nurse when he completed the forms she handed him. They seemed like friends and Nicholas was sure Savanna would contact Janet to get his info. He expected to hear from her soon.

He'd just popped the second bulb into place on the light track when the front door opened. Brent appeared from behind the wall separating the entrance. His short wavy blond hair looked damp. The man couldn't grow a buzz cut if he wanted to.

"Remind me to get that key off you before you leave," Nicholas said.

Brent threw him a lopsided grin. "I expected to see you on your ass and out of your mind with those pain killers," he said.

"Sorry to disappoint."

"You look like you're in good enough shape to make it to Officer Cadet Saunders thirtieth birthday bash tonight. You owe him for saving your bike."

Nicholas grimaced, but nodded. "I might be good for an hour or two."

Brent heaved a picnic cooler onto the counter.

"What's that?" Nicholas asked.

"Marie thought you looked a bit emaciated when she saw you."

"And she plans to fatten me up?"

"Get you ready for the dating scene out here."

"You're kidding me, right?"

Tall and fit, though not as much as he was before his eight-year-old twin boys. Brent was still broad in his upper body, and a bit fleshier than Nicholas.

His clear blue eyes widened. "Don't look at me," his friend said. "I'm just here to set up your computer and password on the air force's VPN."

"Good. The sooner I get on the better."

"I can't get you the high-level access you want though, but once you're logged in, your movements will be undetectable."

"With authorized access, I can do the rest."

"If you say so. I'll get to it."

Nicholas lowered himself onto the counter and scooted off the edge. He landed with his left foot first. Pain shot up his quad muscles. "Argh." He groaned through gritted teeth and grasped the counter. *Were the bloody pills ever going to kick in?*

"So," Brent said. "You gonna tell me how you ended up in an emergency room in Exeter?"

Nicholas threw him a sidelong glance and hobbled to the fridge. The bizarre events scrolled around in his memory as he decided which version made him look less foolish. "Want a beer?" he asked.

"Too early for me."

Nicholas didn't care about the hour. He wanted a distraction from the pain in his leg. He twisted the cap off the bottle and put it to his head, then hobbled back to one of the stools at the island. He avoided Brent's glare.

"Is it Corbett or the injury that's got you drinking your breakfast?" Brent asked.

Nicholas massaged the area around the stitched-up wound. "I was following up on a lead last night when I ran into some unexpected trouble." He wasn't about to mention that his trouble was an unarmed, slightly disguised woman who thought he was her contact.

"A lead? To what?" Brent asked.

"Two days before McBride died he tracked me down and handed me a piece of paper with three words—*Exeter* and *Major Mac*. I figured out Exeter. I have no clue who or what Major Mac means."

"You're not thinking Corbett's involved, are you?"

"I don't know who's involved. I'm just following the leads."

"Do you think you should be dicking around with the army's reputation like that?"

"You think that rampant drug use, the murder of two soldiers and suicide give us a stellar reputation? Something fishy is going on here."

"Fishy? Are you serious?"

"Tell me this. How is it that McBride was able to shoot two armed privates without one of them taking him out? Three soldiers are dead and their families still don't know the truth."

"I think it's time to leave well alone and let the families grieve in peace."

Nicholas placed the beer on the counter. "The first time McBride came to me, I dismissed his ravings as drug-induced and sent him away. He returned three months later. That's when he gave me the note. The next thing I heard he was dead. Killed two soldiers and took the gun to his head. I was wrong not to help him when he needed it. The least I can do now is try to figure out what happened. I owe him and the other men that much."

Brent raised a hand. "Wait a goddamn minute, this is not on you. Don't start thinking—"

Nicholas bristled. "He and the others before him were mentally fatigued and sleep deprived before the drugs," he said. "They needed help, but someone hopped them up on non-army regulated psychotropics and sent them back to the war zones. There's no resting in peace, Brent. Their deaths aren't irrelevant, and neither are the last two years MacBride spent in agony trying to get someone to listen."

"But you did listen. You did something about it."

"Not enough and then it was too late to get to him, to save him.

I waited too long. Somebody knows what's going on and I'll find out who."

"Damn it, man. You really need to watch your back. This could get dangerous."

Nicholas reached for his beer. "It's already dangerous," he said. "What about you?"

"What about me?"

"Do you use anything to deal with the mental fog when the flight hours pile up?"

"I've popped the occasional go-pill, but I try not to make a habit of it. Sometimes I want to get home to my wife and my boys rather than sleep in another city for the night."

"And if you don't have something on you, what do you do then?"

"I don't take the chance. I stay put."

"It's a real problem. I see the end results and I'll tell you, the drugs aren't worth it either."

Brent's glance dropped to the beer bottle Nicholas held. He turned away and entered the office without another word. After a few minutes he returned to the kitchen. "You're connected," he said. "I hope to God you're wrong about this, but this should get you what you want." He handed Nicholas a piece of paper. "You're now Captain Ishmael."

Ishmael. He hadn't used that name in a while and for good reason. "Don't you have something that I haven't used before?" he asked.

"Why? Is Ishmael burnt?"

"It's just—" Nicholas didn't want to explain how he got the name in the first place. Now that he was in Westbury, he preferred to leave the decade-old memories in the past where they belonged.

"Just what?" Brent prompted.

Nicholas shook his head. "Never mind," he said.

"I swear, Corbett's really got you going."

Nicholas shrugged and took the paper. "I appreciate this and the house, too. I owe you one."

"You owe me nothing. This doesn't bring us close to even. Just don't let McBride's ghost lead you into more trouble with Corbett."

Nicholas frowned. That's exactly what he intended to do, follow the ghost until he found some answers.

Chapter 11

———————

AVANNA NESTLED BETWEEN THE silky white sheets on the plush king bed at the Ritz-Carlton. Her husband spent his time away from home in pampered luxury. She lifted her head to find him. Richard, wrapped in the hotel bathrobe, perched on the edge of the antique desk scanning the menu. Apparently, their pre-breakfast lovemaking had increased his appetite.

She dropped her head onto the pillow, realizing that she would have to wait until they ate before she could lure him between the sheets again. That's when she intended to tell him the news. *Honey, we're having a baby. Hmmm. Not quite right.*

Last night on her flight from Westbury, the words came together more poetically in her head. She needed more flare. Maybe she should tell him about the cancelled leave first.

"Why didn't you tell me you're pregnant?" Richard's voice asked from across the room.

"Aah," Savanna yelp. Her head jerked back. *He knew?* She threw frantic glances around the swanky hotel suite. Nothing indicated her new maternal state. Unless her BlackBerry flashed the word pregnant in neon colours, there's no way Richard could have guessed.

"How…" She sputtered. "How do you know?"

"Monica from your doctor's office called your mobile line."

Savanna stifled a groan. *The woman could have waited until she was back in town. Thanks, Monica. Very professional.* She slipped from between the sheets and heaved from the bed.

Richard opened his arms and pulled her into his lean body.

She cuddled against the rough fabric of the bathrobe. "I know we said we would try again someday," she said and leaned in to kiss his cheek. "That someday came sooner than planned."

"Ah," he said. It wasn't really a response, just a noise.

"What do you think?"

"I think it's an awkward time."

"I know, but it seems babies are unpredictable that way."

"We haven't had the best experience with pregnancy. Are you sure this is a good time?"

"I had nothing to do with the timing. It just happened."

"Will this change our plans?"

"I'm sure our lives will change, but not right away."

His arms dropped and he stepped away from her. "I wished we'd discussed it first."

Savanna shivered from a sudden chill and reached for the second robe draped over the back of the chair. She swaddled her disappointment in the scratchy cotton and turned to Richard again. "Discuss it?" she said. "I was as surprised as you when Dr. Wagsmith called me. I kept asking him to check again."

"I suppose you want me to come home now?"

A tiny spasm squeezed her stomach, but she kept her focus on him. "No. I never thought that."

He shook his head. "It didn't go so well last time, Savanna."

"I know."

"And now…" He pinched his nose bridge. "I'm on tour. I'll be away for months." Frustration edged Richard's tone and she couldn't tell if it was concern or dread.

"The baby doesn't change our lives right now," she said, unsure that was true. This new revelation ushered in loads of apprehension. Not to speak of the guilt that resurfaced the minute the doctor told her she was pregnant.

"It's still very early," she said. "I'm in my fifth week."

"You weren't much further along last time. How will I know what's going on with you when I can't be there?"

She took Richard's hand and caressed his knuckles.

Those same fingers tenderly touched her naked belly the first time she told him she was carrying his child.

They had been dating for nine months. Before Richard, she took the pill. On her busy schedule, she sometimes forgot the occasional dose. At the time, she never worried since the birth control was meant merely to regulate her cycle. She hadn't dated anyone in more than a year, not counting the rather attractive chef who turned on more than her taste buds her last day at a forensics conference in Montreal. He had filled in for the resident chef and was in town for one more night.

Then along came Richard who was a hopeless romantic and courted her with old-fashioned charm. She stepped up her vigilance on the birth control and thought she never missed a day.

A couple weeks after the start of spring, she visited her doctor for a routine pap test. The next day he called to say she was pregnant.

The first time she had become pregnant six years earlier, she'd made the decision not to keep the baby, and later regretted going through with the procedure. Though she never told Richard about that mistake, regardless of his response, she knew she would never go there again.

Their courtship was still in its honeymoon phase. She loved her job and enjoyed the combined freedom and intimacy of dating Richard. They saw each other as often as they could. The evening she decided to tell him, they had just made love and she lay on her stomach in his king-size bed. Richard stroked her naked back. She relaxed, silently going over how best to tell him. Children hadn't yet come up in their conversations. In the end she just blurted it out. His fingers stopped moving and she held her breath.

He touched her shoulder and she flipped over onto her back. Her palms covered her lower belly as if the child threatened to show its face through her skin.

Richard gently lifted her fingers, then started tapping her belly. She squirmed, a little ticklish. He continued to tap and then started humming a lullaby.

A week later he left Westbury for Boston where he was scheduled to perform for two nights. When he returned, he asked her to marry him. She said yes. He insisted on an away wedding, saying it would be faster. All she needed to do was to buy a dress and get her father to clear his calendar. Rebecca, Ben and Nichole, their then four-year-old daughter made up the wedding party. They spent a week in Barbados, with a promise for a second trip when Savanna had more time in her schedule.

Two months into the pregnancy, she stood up from the toilet and gasped. Blood had tinted the water in the bowl. Her first thought was to get to the doctor, but before she could cross the room to the sink, a burning pain tore through her lower belly and she doubled over.

Blood splashed onto the floor at her feet. "No," her plea was no more than a whimper. When the blood trailed down her legs, the shaking started. "No. No. No. No." By then she had been cupping a palm over her vagina to save her two-month foetus.

The pain blinded her, but she felt Richard's arm around her and his palm against her belly. "I'm here," he said. "I'm here."

Her bloody fingers lay on top his hand and in that moment, she thought they could save the baby if they just held on. Four years later, they were stronger together.

She laced her fingers through Richard's and met his eyes. This time it would be different. "I'll call you every night," she said. The telephone wasn't the same as having him there, but knowing he was coming home to her was enough.

"It's more than that," he said, looking down at their entwined fingers. "I'm no longer a young man. I wouldn't be able to keep up with a child." His hand gripped hers.

Her mouth gaped ready to deny his claim, but his words scrambled her thoughts. The assertion seemed very unlike him. She wondered if there wasn't more to what he was telling her. She touched his chin. "You're only fifty-four and stronger than you think," she said. "I have faith in you."

Richard pulled away and started pacing. "This is too stressful," he said.

That was an interesting response. Savanna met his gaze. "It wouldn't be any less so in Westbury while you're out here."

Richard jerked to a stop in the middle of the room. His chin dropped to his chest. "I really wish you had waited and given me time to settle in again before you started this."

"You don't have to do anything." She wasn't sure she meant it. His absence scared her too.

"It's after the birth that concerns me," Richard said. "The prospect of raising a child at my age scares me more than a little."

"Men have children in their fifties all the time."

He snickered. "I'm sure they do." He stared into the carpet again as though unlocking the mystery of its design would be easier than dealing with their conversation. "Maybe in a couple of weeks," he said with less hesitation. "When you join me, we'll have more time to sort this out."

Damn. Double, triple damn. She turned away from Richard, rubbing her neck. The news of the baby was meant to soften the news about the cancelled leave.

"What is it?" Richard asked.

"There's something else."

"What?"

"Miller cancelled my leave. I can't spend months with you as we planned. At least not yet."

"When were you going to tell me about this?"

"It's the other reason I came out this weekend, to tell you."

"Jesus Christ, Savanna. This is a disaster." Richard raised his voice.

"The choice was either postpone the leave or lose my job altogether."

"Then why didn't you just quit and let Miller clean up this mess himself?"

"That's not something I want to consider now. There are other solutions to this."

"Did he give you any time at all?"

"I'll have two weeks in a few months. I'll join you then."

"When is that?"

"Later in the summer."

"When in the summer?"

"Mid-August, maybe."

"That's three months away."

"I know this is not what we planned, but it's a solution that could work."

"Dammit, Savanna."

She waited for him to calm down, but he just stared across the room as though seeing the world for the first time in unmistakable high definition.

"Have you told Kenneth?" he asked.

"I haven't said anything to my dad yet. I figured we'd invite him to one of your concerts and tell him together."

"Kenneth in my audience?"

"It would mean a lot to him to hear the news from both of us."

"We should hold off the announcement."

Savanna's breath hitched. "What? My father is the first person we should tell."

"I will be gone until the fall and you can't join me for any of it. Kenneth isn't going to like that."

"What does it have to do with him?"

"He blames me, Savanna."

"What for?"

"Your miscarriage four years ago. He thinks it was my fault."

"Richard, that's silly. My father wouldn't blame you for that. And that's no reason why we shouldn't tell him."

"Let's wait."

"I don't understand your reasoning."

Richard reached for her. She'd grown flustered from their conversation and welcomed his touch.

"I want to make this work," he said. "Without the leave, you would be alone for most of the pregnancy."

"I think I might be able to get the time off. Perhaps later than we planned, but I can still join you."

"Well, until that can happen, or we're sure that you're coming out here, let's hold onto the news for a little while."

"I don't know. That could cause some issues on the job."

"It wouldn't be for long. I want the tour to gain some momentum before my name is in the media about the baby rather than the success of the tour."

"What about my father?"

"I don't want him to think that I left you all alone with this."

"Richard… I"

"I'm still trying to make up for the last time we lost a baby."

"That wasn't your fault."

"His opinion is important. You know that."

"I know, but keeping the pregnancy from him… That just seems—"

"It wouldn't be for long." Richard interrupted the image of her father's face darting before her.

When her husband inserted a hand under her robe and caressed the small of her back, the tension that lodged there for the last few weeks softened. He kissed her lightly on her lips then let his tongue tease the corners of her mouth.

"How long?" she asked.

He moved behind her and loosened the belt on her robe. His palm smoothed over her hips and around to her pelvis.

The sensations distracted her.

"Get Miller to change his mind about the leave," Richard said. "Then we can tell your father and everyone else about the baby when you're traveling with me."

"That could be weeks away." Plus, it wasn't Miller she needed to convince. Dr. Wade was her new boss as of Monday.

Richard slipped two fingers between her legs.

She gasped as a single notion circled her thoughts. A growing pregnancy was the worst kept secret.

Chapter 12

———————

SAVANNA SCRAMBLED UPRIGHT IN BED. Her hand found the ringing cellphone with automatic precision.

"Savanna, it's me," Quinn said before she spoke.

The tension in his voice forced her drowsy eyes open. "What time is it?" she asked.

"Just after 2:30. Dispatch said you're back in town. I'm coming to get you."

After one night with Richard, she returned to Westbury on Saturday afternoon and headed straight to the lab. She intended to spend a few hours searching through the files in the Moore case, but thought better of it and brought the files home with her.

She pushed hair away from her damp face. Her head still swam from the headache and queasy stomach that had chased her under the covers. *Sleep deprivation maybe.*

"What's going on?" she asked Quinn.

"We've got a body at Ford Drive and Mackenzie."

"The McGuire Landfill?"

"Yep. An anonymous tip called her in."

"Did you say her?"

"Dispatch said it was a young woman."

"Who found the body?"

"Don't know. Two uniforms checked it out and confirmed. It appears she's been dumped."

"Do we know who she is?"

"No identification yet, but, get this."

"What?"

"She's missing her right hand."

Quinn's words sent a message down Savanna's spine. She swung her legs off the bed. Her stomach lurched when she stood up. She reached for the wall. *Could this be morning sickness?*

"Okay," she said to Quinn. "I'll be ready in ten."

"Make it five." He disconnected before she could reply.

She lowered the phone from her ear and stared at it, then hurried to her closet.

Moments later, fully dressed, she left the bedroom to search for nausea relief while the landfill victim filled her thoughts. Up to now the investigating team wasn't certain if the owner of the hand discovered at the Lamons Street address was dead or alive. But if this body belonged to that hand, then they were looking at multiple victims in the Moore case.

A few flavoured Tums in a bottle presented themselves when she opened the cabinet next to the fridge. She popped one on her tongue and dropped a couple into her pocket. Eyeing the soup bowl and tea mug on the counter, she thought she should put them into the dishwasher, but left the kitchen. Why hurry to clean up? Richard was away for another few months. He wasn't the neatest person she knew, but dirty dishes on the counter was his one pet peeve.

While the Tums dissolved on her tongue, Savanna wondered if Dr. Milano would attend the crime scene. They could get the ball rolling with a few non-invasive samples from their Jane Doe and start a comparison test against the stray evidence in the Moore file. Well, she could try anyway.

True to his word, Quinn arrived at her door before she pulled her hair into a ponytail.

Her partner's glance rolled over her face. His boyish features squinting into concern. "You look awful," he said. His bottle brown eyes never missed anything. "Come on. I have some black coffee in the van. It'll wake you right up."

Quinn bolted around to the driver's side. He moved like lightning for a stocky built man. He often reminded her of the first policeman to visit her grade one class. In eight years, he had never given her reason to doubt his loyalty. She trusted Quinn with her life.

She tightened the elastic on her hair and followed him. He climbed in before she reached the passenger door. When she heaved herself onto the seat beside him, he shoved a silver thermos at her.

She waved it away. "I'll be fine."

"Suit yourself." He dropped the flask in the cup holder and started the van. "You should stick to notes and I'll video the scene," he said as they pulled onto the street.

"You got me out of bed to hold your pencil, officer?"

He chuckled, and in the dim light, his pale face flushed and blended with his reddish hair. "You forgot to remove your rock," he said motioning to her hand.

"Right." Savanna unfastened the gold chain around her neck and threaded it through the ring, then refastened the tiny lobster clasp. She never wore the ring on duty.

Ten minutes later, the rotting scent that invaded the van from the McGuire Landfill was enough to put Savanna off boiled eggs for some time. Quinn parked just inside the entrance and they suited up and grabbed the forensic kits from the back.

Savanna tried to breathe normally, but the stench trapped her against the forensic identification van while she pulled on a crime scene jumpsuit. *If a bit of decay freaked her out this early, what was she to do for the rest of the night?*

"Come on, Jones," Quinn said. "I want to leave this place before sunrise."

He hurried toward the floodlights illuminating the northwest corner of the landfill. Every few seconds, he covered his nose with the crook of his elbow, then pulled it away again. "It's best not to see everything out here in broad daylight," he said.

Savanna agreed. The odour threatened to dislodge the small

dinner she'd eaten earlier that night. She wrapped her fingers around the tube of menthol she pocketed on the way out the door. She shouldn't. Masking unwanted scents covered up evidence. Professor McLachlan drummed that fact into her head in his first biology lab fifteen years ago when she whipped out the small jar to combat the sickly smell of death.

She released the tube and pulled her hand from her pocket, then coughed and covered her mouth before she inhaled another whiff of the putrid rank floating around the landfill. Surely, McLachlan hadn't meant for her to endure such torture when her stomach hovered on queasy. Somehow, she needed to adapt and fast. With the wind whipping the stench around, that was easier said than done.

"Was I wrong to drag you from bed?"

She gasped and jerked to a stop when she collided with Quinn. They were the same height, making it easy for him to peer into her face.

"You're looking a bit ashy," he said. "Coming down with something?"

She shifted away from him and headed toward the police flood lights. Trust came with the job and after eight years together, honesty was a given. She never lied to Quinn, not really. Omitting parts of her personal life wasn't lying. Yet, telling him about the baby meant breaking her promise to Richard. Her stomach flip-flopped. "I just need to get used to the smell," she said.

"That's taking you longer than usual."

"It's worse than a sewer out here."

"I agree, but you've always been much better at this than me. Tonight, I'm not so sure."

Her jaw muscles quivered. She bit back the truth. Right now, she needed to trust Richard. "Whatever's going on with me will clear up the minute I get out of here." She hurried past Quinn, her stomach sinking along with her courage.

Chapter 13

$\mathscr{T}$HE CLANGING COMMOTION THAT thundered into Nicholas's sleep startled him from the chair. He stood straight. That was a mistake. Pain sliced through his leg. He doubled over. When the clanging rang out again, he straightened and shot his glance around the unfamiliar space. Not a war zone, but a white kitchen, in an extremely modern house with boxes stacked at the entrance. *Right. He lived in Westbury now.*

Overhead track lighting glowed from the wooden beams arching across the ceiling. He surveyed the open doorways—the office, the bedroom, and the small bathroom off the front foyer. Nothing moved.

The sound shrieked again, this time less piercing. *The telephone?* The thing was so artsy, he hadn't realized it was functional. Maybe someone was looking for the house's owner. Nicholas crossed the room and read the display.

He sighed and lifted the receiver. "Brent, did you forget the keys to the Cormorant here?" he asked.

"Yes. Have you seen them?"

"What? Are you sure?" Nicholas started for the office where

76

Brent spent most of his time while he was at the house. "Do you remember—?"

Deep laughter through the line cut him off.

"You're an idiot," he said.

"You're losing it man," Brent howled. "Not yet a city doctor and you're off your game."

"Count your lucky stars that you're heading out of town, or I'd kick your—"

"You'll get your chance in a few weeks, old man."

Nicholas grinned. Two years older than him, Brent was coming up on his fortieth birthday in a few months. "Right," Nicholas said, rubbing his neck. "Hey can you keep your ears open for any talk of Major Mac when you're out there?"

Brent was silent for a while, then said. "Not sure I want to get involved in this."

"Shields down, man. I'm just looking for a trail."

"All right. I'll let you know if I hear anything. Since you're in town with nothing much to do, keep an eye on the family for me, will ya?"

Nicholas bristled at the sarcasm and the request. "You sure you want to trust me with that task?" he asked.

"I'm not saying get all bodyguard on them. Just run the boys out to the park once in a while. Marie would appreciate the break."

"Right."

"Over and out."

"Safe flight." Nicholas settled the receiver back into the cradle. *Kids, what would he do with them?* He turned to the reading chair where he had fallen asleep earlier. He left Saunders' birthday party and headed home about 2330 hours. Rather than going straight to bed, he sat up reading. He couldn't decide if curiosity or self-pity lurked behind his thoughts.

A half bottle of beer sat on the floor next to the documents he'd been reading. He picked them up and arranged them into a neat pile. The reports outlined an ongoing operation to track manufacturers of active pharmaceutical ingredients, APIs, which were then smuggled into Canada to produce psychotropic substances.

Fatigue pressed down on him. A few beers at the bar weren't enough to bring on sleep at the speed he required. The reports and another beer should have done the trick. And before Brent's call, his method was working.

Nicholas emptied the contents of the bottle into the sink and reached for the cabinet where he kept the oxycodone. Beside the prescription was extra strength Advil. He chose the over-the-counter version and tossed two in his mouth, using a glass next to the sink to chase them with water.

A few hours of sleep should ease the throbbing pain. He headed for the bathroom in the dark but jerked to a stop when his cellphone blared through the house. He considered letting it ring off. Instead, he reached for it and slapped it to his ear without reading the screen.

"Don't tell me," he said, "you lost your flight manifest?"

"Pardon me?"

Heck, not Brent. His eyes found the clock on the wall next to the refrigerator. 0230 hours. Did anyone around here ever sleep?

"I'm trying to reach Dr. Nicholas Wade. Do I have the right number?"

At this hour? "This is Nicholas Wade," he said.

"Coroner Miller here."

"Sorry, Coroner. What can I do for you?"

"The police dispatch desk just reported a dead body at the McGuire Landfill. Detectives Thomas and Fontaine are attending the crime scene. They need a doctor on site. Eric Burke is on tonight. I tried calling him, but there was no answer. He tends to ignore the phone after hours. Have you had a chance to look through your personnel files?"

Nicholas closed his eyes briefly. "Not yet," he said.

"Michael Milano is a good pathologist. He's from the hospital environment and is a bit green in the field. However, Savanna Jones is back in town and on duty tonight with Officer Quinn."

Savanna? Could this be the same woman from the cheese barn?

"She often assists Milano," Miller was saying.

"I'll take the call," Nicholas said. The stiffness in his leg tightened. He should have gone to bed.

"Good time to get your feet wet and observe the team in action." Miller sounded relieved at his decision.

"Agreed. What's the address of the landfill?" He committed the address to memory.

"Good luck, Dr. Wade."

"Thank you. Good night, Coroner."

Eyeing the untouched pile of personnel files on his desk, he walked over and shuffled through them with Savanna Jones's name echoing in his head. The name was too unusual. The woman in the cheese barn wore a disguise and tried her best to keep her face away from him. But he couldn't take his eyes off her latte skin. The photograph in her file might help.

He met most of his forensic staff on Thursday afternoon when he arrived in town and stopped by in an unscheduled visit. Savanna Jones had been out on a crime scene call.

The next day when he checked in at Westbury Police Services, he met her partner, Forensic Ident Officer Matthew Quinn. Nicholas took the opportunity to introduce himself to the head of the criminal investigation division, Detective Superintendent Rupert Hannigan, who was meeting with Dave Thomas, one of his detectives.

According to Miller, Jones had discovered the connection between Colton Moore and the recently murdered victim, Theresa Filito. For the next year, he would rely on her dedication, starting with background on the ongoing Moore case. He plucked the file bearing her name from among the stack and flipped it open.

He squinted. *Was he hallucinating? Probably an effect of the beers and the Advil.* He blinked a couple of times, then threw his head back and laughed, howling loud enough to disturb the neighbours. He looked again. What the heck? This couldn't be.

That woman who walked into his life and walked out again ten years ago now wore her hair straight. He recalled the dark, rich brown with tawny streaks that blended with her skin tone. He wanted to be wrong about this woman. Of all the professions in the world, she had to choose his.

He exhaled and stared at the photo. Her chocolate eyes pulled him in and for a moment, he relived their single night of passion. Those same lips that seduced him ten years ago, appealed to him last night. Their fullness was so alluring, he almost missed what she said.

He dropped the file on the kitchen counter and slammed his hand down on it. *Savanna Jones*. It took him only a decade to learn her name.

The afternoon in Vancouver when their eyes met, her mesmerizing gaze had penetrated every cell of his being. Her slow and deliberate admiration blazed a fire in his belly. In the next second, her glance focused behind him. By the time he deciphered danger in her expression, she had already sprinted out of his reach.

He jerked his head in the direction she ran and watched her race into the busy street to save a child who stood frozen in the middle of the oncoming traffic. Nicholas's heart slowed, perhaps even skipped a beat. He slung his leg over the seat of his motorcycle and revved the bike into the traffic, hoping to allow her enough time to reach the kid. Only, he didn't notice the heavy-duty Ryder box truck until the last minute.

A cacophony of screams from onlookers drowned the screeching tires on the hot pavement. But his mystery woman was as brave as she was beautiful. In a move worthy of combat training, she dove for the boy. Her arms wrapped around his tiny body. They rolled toward the fence.

Hours later, as though none of it mattered, she strolled into Scully's student bar and curtsied to the loud cheers that acknowledged her courage. That night, Nicholas wanted more than anything to know her name.

When she and her friends invited him to celebrate their last night on campus, he accepted just to be near her. Learning her name, though, wasn't part of the invitation. They encouraged him to join their game. The rules insisted that he choose a character from a novel or movie, and not once during the evening was he allowed to use his real identity.

"Call me Ishmael," he had said.

She rewarded him with a smile. As the drinks kept coming, the conversation turned nostalgic, and the close-knit group surprised him. Not once did any of them slip up.

After the party, when she agreed to walk with him, he longed to be himself again and stuck out his hand for a true introduction. She slid her fingers into his palm and placed the other hand on his lips.

"Tonight," she said, "our real names don't matter."

It was the last night before he left the country for a mission to Afghanistan. Rather than spend the hours with his fellow soldiers, Nicholas was content to call himself Ishmael.

He snatched his hand from the file folder as though touching it generated the memories. *Savanna Jones*. He finally found her, but she had forgotten him.

Nicholas grabbed his cellphone and found Miller's number topping the recent calls list. He couldn't take this call. She was the last person he wanted to see tonight, or any other night.

He limped around the island in his kitchen. Somehow, the decade hadn't erased her from his memory like it had done for her. He would never forget the instant attraction and heat between them. The flirting that grew into passion by the time he kissed her, and the tenderness in every stroke of pleasure her fingertips blazed under his skin. It took him months before he accepted that she got away. Now here she was.

"Pull it together, Wade," he said out loud. When had he become such a coward? Determined not to let memories divert him from his mission, he hobbled through the living room and headed to the front door, grabbing his jacket on the way.

With that one night between them, the year would drag like a bug stuck in molasses. He grabbed the car keys and headed for the door. Time to clear the air.

Chapter 14

DETECTIVE DAVE THOMAS AND his partner, Ronald Fontaine, were two of the few detectives in the Westbury Police Services who knew how to treat a crime scene.

"Evening guys," Savanna said.

"Don't suppose you brought the doc with you, Jonesy?" Fontaine asked in reply.

"Sorry." She shook her head while scanning his outfit. He was over-dressed in a grey silk suit that accentuated his olive skin and jet-black hair.

He was the taller and the more stylish of the duo. Tonight, his formal attire contrasted with the trash heaps towering twelve feet high. Fontaine stood on a clear spot looking around and rubbing the back of his neck.

Quinn stopped next to him. "I have a pair of overalls in the van that might fit," he said.

"I'll take 'em." Fontaine stepped gingerly over the debris and followed Quinn to the van.

Dave Thomas stood with two uniform officers pointing around the landfill. Savanna started for the body, but the rotting smell in the immediate area seemed worse than what she already encountered.

Her stomach lurched. She wrapped an arm around her face and turned in the other direction.

"Going somewhere, Jones? The body is that way."

She stood toe-to-toe with Thomas and tilted her chin up to him. White, even teeth shone back at her from a rich dark complexion and then disappeared behind a slight grimace.

He scratched the fresh stubble, barely noticeable on his dark skin, and peered at her.

"I'm here," she said.

"I don't suppose you know which one of your doctors is on call tonight? Whoever it is, he's running late."

"I'm just hoping it's Milano. Burke is allergic to night-time crime scenes."

Thomas lowered his chin and peered around the yard. His expression registered disinterest, but she knew what that look meant. While he engaged her in conversation, he processed as much of the scene as he could see. When he finally looked at her, he zeroed in on the hand touching her stomach. "You doing okay? You look a bit green."

"I'm fine." She flinched at another denial, but her personal problems didn't belong in a crime scene.

"Someone dumped her here," Thomas said.

"Anyone witnessed the act?"

"No one is admitting to it. I sent the constables to search for fresh tire tracks."

Savanna nodded and walked with him toward the body. They stopped a few feet away from a large trash heap lit with police flood-lights.

After more than ten years investigating dead people, Savanna still fought the urge to avert her eyes. This time, she kept her focus on the dead woman. Whoever left her had positioned her corpse face up, about twenty yards from the main entrance, with her remaining arm extended as if she had fallen.

"How old would you say she is?" Dave asked.

Savanna stepped forward for a closer look. The face had taken on the stiff, lifeless appearance evident in death, but a subtle innocence still lingered in the soft freckles dotting her nose bridge. Round and supple cheeks, plump with subcutaneous fat, most common in younger people, revealed her youthfulness. She was likely in her early twenties. Probably still holding onto her dreams and wondering if she'd turn out okay. What could have happened in her life at such a tender age to bring her here, murdered and mutilated? Did she even live long enough to know what a broken heart feels like?

"About twenty," Savanna said. "Perhaps twenty-two."

"Jesus Christ. Where do they come from?" He exploded in a fit of rage whenever they investigated a homicide victim younger than thirty.

Savanna raised the digital Nikon she took from Quinn and zoomed in on the deceased's appearance. A few random shots of her long brunette hair, framed around her face tested the focus. "It looks as though someone arranged her after placing her here," Savanna motioned to the twenty-foot mound.

"Not unheard of," Dave said.

The wind picked up again as Savanna continued to photograph the area, capturing the body in long-range images. When she thought she saw something move, she bent closer. The quick gust whipped a mixture of rotten egg and sulphide in her face. She covered her nose with the back of her hand and inhaled deep breaths from the rubbery latex glove.

"How long has she been out here?" she asked.

"Dispatch got the call around 2:00 a.m. The first officers on the scene reported nothing unusual."

"Really?"

"Well, nothing unusual for this place."

Savanna palmed the camera again and stepped back to increase the distance but stumbled on the debris under her feet. Catching her balance, she straightened.

"You sure you should be out here, Jones?" Dave asked.

Her skin tightened down her back. She turned and eyed the tight-lip grimace he wore all night. "What about you, detective? Holding it together?"

Palms up, he stepped back. "Just checking."

Determined to get through the night, she turned away from his inspection.

"Is there anything in the rubble?" Dave recorded every question he asked and her responses.

"No more than you already observed," she said. "Just an approximate description."

"We didn't want to get too close before you and Quinn got here."

"Well, her clothes seem intact for a woman missing an arm. They're soiled with something, could be blood. I can't tell you too much now. I don't want to move her until the doctor gets here."

"And where is he already?" Dave's impatience rose to a tipping point.

"I'll like to get her bagged before the rain starts," Savanna said. Noticing moisture on the corpse's cheek, she leaned in closer. "Did it already rain out here?"

"No," Fontaine responded this time. "Why?"

Savanna pulled a pen from her saddlebag and used it to push back the scarf. "Her clothes are wet," she said. "Soaked through, actually."

"No rain within the last twenty-four hours," Dave said.

Savanna hovered a latex palm over the dead woman, then touched her index finger to the left cheek. The flesh wrinkled on the surface like thawing meat, without yielding like regular tissue.

Savanna leapt to her feet. "Quinn, call the coroner's dispatch desk and find out Dr. Milano's location. We need to get this body out of here fast. She's frozen."

"Did you say frozen, Jonesy?" Fontaine asked.

"Yes."

Thomas moved closer and bent over the body. "How can you be certain?"

Savanna stooped beside him and brought the dead face under the Nikon's powerful zoom again. A glimmer on the girl's flesh was unmistakable. Through the camera's eye small beads of a clear liquid trickled down her cheek.

"Well," Savanna said. "She's as stiff as a board and I don't believe it's rigor. Yet there's little decay. She's secreting some type of fluid, and as far as I know, dead people don't sweat."

"She might have been killed during the winter."

Savanna raised her head skywards and down again. Windy conditions persisted as the clouds drew closer. A raw scent, like uncooked animal flesh assaulted Savanna's nose. Her stomach lurched with a little more vigour than before. She snapped her head away from the body. "What's that smell?"

"What smell?" Thomas sniffed in the direction of the body.

"It's familiar and disgusting at the same time," Savanna said.

"Can you identify it?"

She leaned in again. The foul scent attacked her again and a wave of nausea surged up her stomach. She jumped to her feet and clamped a hand over her mouth. "Raw pork," she choked out, then leapt away from the immediate crime scene.

Quinn stood a few paces away, talking into his cellphone.

She shoved the camera at him and broke into a run. When she could no longer hold onto the churning pushing its way to her throat, she halted mid-step and a forceful gush spurted from her mouth.

Bent at the waist, her stomach heaved and contracted, spewing its contents into the landfill. After a moment, the spasms subsided. She straightened and rubbed her ab muscles. It felt like she'd just completed a hundred sit-ups. She felt a presence and heard something in the distance. She swung around peering in the other direction. She saw nothing. Could be an animal. Enlarged shadows from moths buzzing around the faint lamp lights flickered in the darkness.

She turned again and Quinn walked toward her, carrying a bottle of water.

"You okay?" he asked.

Short breaths caught in her chest, undermining her efforts to conceal her tension. She took the water. "Thanks." After a rinse, she turned to him. "I'm fine. Is Milano on his way?"

"No. Dr. Wade is coming instead. You sure you're okay?"

Self-consciousness washed over her. "We need more photos before the doctor arrives," she said.

"On it." He hurried away, leaving her alone.

Savanna filled her mouth with water, rinsed, then repeated. Quinn had said Wade was on his way. *Damn. Why did their new chief take the call?* Didn't matter. She'd need to make him see that collecting samples tonight for a comparison test was a giant leap forward in the case.

She plucked a fresh tissue from her pocket and pressed it to her mouth, then turned toward the floodlights. She lifted the bottle to fill her mouth again and a movement to her right pricked the back of her neck. She scanned the darkness and spotted a man emerging from the shadows and heading in her direction.

Dull light hid him in darkness. Her stomach clenched. Within seconds, a faint glow revealed a square jaw and the angle of his chin in a face that seemed familiar. Then she noticed his limp. Her breath caught. *What was he doing here?*

Chapter 15

THE TIGHT-LIPPED INFORMANT Savanna met in the cheese barn stopped in front of her. He watched her as if she would explain why they were meeting again.

"You are Dr. Wade?" She threw the first accusation.

In response, he lifted an arm, holding something that danced in the breeze.

She looked down and reached for the white fabric. A handkerchief? She held it to her nose. The clean scent dulled the landfill odour enough for her to recall his rippling masculinity under her care.

"I owe you a scarf, but I think a peace offering is more appropriate."

A handkerchief and a peace offering. *What should she expect next?* She raised her eyes to meet his. "Thank you," she said.

"I thought you would have gotten my full dossier by now."

"Janet?" Savanna hadn't heard from her friend since they'd run into each other in the ER. She'd tried calling her and left a message when she got her voice mail.

"How is the leg?" she asked. "Should you be on it right now?"

"I'll live. What about you? I see the landfill is not as forgiving as the cheese barn."

"We all have our limits."

"Are you feeling better now?"

"Much, thank you." She swiped hair from her face and looked toward the floodlights. "I'm glad you're here, though we didn't expect you."

"We worked so well together before. I thought—"

"Are you mocking me, Doctor?"

He studied her for a moment. An unreadable expression flickered across his face before he spoke. "The opportunity for a second chance is rare. Like you said last night." He stepped closer and stuck out his hand. "Let's start again."

Gripping his handkerchief in one hand, she peeled the latex glove from the other and slid her palm into his. Her fingers seemed delicate in his masculine size grip. Long fingers and a thick heel with a callous left by a scar clasped her hand.

"Welcome aboard, Doctor."

"Thank you for the second chance."

"Does that mean you're willing to tell me what you know about the cheese barn drug operation?"

The corners of his mouth flickered. "I should have seen that coming, but this is not the time or place. We can pick that up at a less pressing hour."

"I can live with that. I'd also be interested in knowing how you found out who I am."

"Coroner Miller called. Told me Savanna Jones, my new assistant, would work the crime scene tonight. With such an unusual name and the bedside manner of a morgue assistant, it couldn't be a coincidence."

"If you're complaining about my bedside manner now, Doctor, wait until I assist you in a morgue without the aid of well-aged cheese."

His grip tightened and her fingers tingled from the slight pressure. Still she didn't reclaim her hand from his and he showed no signs of releasing her fingers.

"Can you tell me something about what we have here?" he asked.

"Yes. The state of the victim's body is unusual."

"How so?"

"I believe she was frozen at some point and is now thawing fast. With the clouds moving in and the wind picking up, removing her is our top priority."

"In that case——"

"Jones." Quinn came running up behind her new boss. "Are you still feeling sick?"

She withdrew her hand from Dr. Wade's and shoved it in her pocket. *What had she been doing, standing there enjoying his…* She stopped before another word entered her head. Instead, she tried to concentrate on Quinn, but she felt her boss's scrutiny tracking her every move.

Quinn peered into her face. "I've never seen you throw up before," he said. "Now I'm sure you're coming down with something."

"I'm fine now," she said though her stomach quivered as she spoke.

He turned toward the doctor. "Dr. Wade, we didn't expect you tonight."

They knew each other? She raised her eyes to her boss again and found him still inspecting her.

"As Ms. Jones pointed out," he said. "Moving the deceased takes precedence."

Her partner nodded. "Savanna can assist with the body, and I'll see what else the detectives need."

She dragged her eyes from the doctor's face and willed her mind to do the same. A slight frown was forming around his mouth and she guessed that he read more into her throwing up and wasn't willing to let it go that easily. Turning toward the crime scene, she grimaced as the queasiness churned again.

"Ms. Jones." Dr. Wade's crisp tone pulled her around to face him one more time. He studied the hand on her stomach.

She snatched it away.

"I'm concerned that you may not be well enough to continue here," he said.

"I'm feeling much better now."

"Your partner can finish up without you."

"Maybe you should call it a night." Quinn said. "I thought you looked a bit pale earlier and then—"

What is this? Converging testosterone? "I've got this," she said and snapped on a new pair of latex gloves. "I'm well enough to assist with the body."

"A morgue assistant will be here shortly. You're free to leave."

Who said anything about leaving? She had a job to do. "If you don't require assistance, Doctor," she said, "I'll work the site with my partner."

His intense gaze surveyed her face. Not a single expression creased his steady brow.

"Is there another body over here I don't know about?" Dave's voice sounded irate.

She turned.

He hurried toward them, his thick lips tight. "If you folks don't mind, I'd like to get on with this."

"Detective Thomas," Dr. Wade said.

"Dr. Wade." Thomas's tone rang with familiarity. "You're here for the body, I take it?"

Savanna looked from one to the other. *Did everyone know this man?*

"That's right," Dr. Wade said, then turned to Savanna. "Ms. Jones, I'm sure you would agree that zero contamination is our main responsibility here."

She pushed back the annoyance needling her and pulled two more gloves from her pocket, then walked toward him. "I agree, Doctor," she said and offered them to him. "I'll take every precaution, but you'll need these."

Again, the steady unreadable stare examined her before he took the gloves from her outstretched hand.

Savanna turned and stalked toward the crime scene. *Pick up my pencil. Dab my brow. Pull my microphone closer.* Was that the other side of the responsible and steadfast soldier she should expect for the next year?

"Let's go," she said to Quinn, feeling the doctor eyes still on her.

She might have won the duel between them, but a war brewed just below his watchful surface. She needed to make sure she won that one too.

Chapter 16

Forty-five minutes after driving away from the crime scene, Nicholas stood over the frozen body in an autopsy suite at Westbury Forensic Services. The young woman lying dead in the McGuire Landfill reminded him too much of his work in Kosovo in 2000. He'd been twenty-six then. The bleak and harsh reality of young bones in mass graves left a lasting impression.

Like his new assistant, he wanted to get the victim into the morgue before the rain. Completing her external exam tonight would save evidence that might be harder to separate after thawing.

Nicholas tugged on latex gloves and flexed his fingers before removing the paper bag from the victim's remaining hand. Without a forensic photographer, he relied on Savanna's apparent skill with the camera.

She started with the body, while Officer Quinn took notes and sketched onto his pad. If he hadn't been aware of the close relationship between partners, he would swear they were a couple. They worked together like a seasoned team, consulting each other and syncing notes.

After he and Morris bagged the victim for transport, he'd turned to ask Savanna for close-up images of the spot, but she was already photographing the area.

"And, Doctor," she said as though they were already in the middle of the conversation. "I can make sure we have physical copies, in various sizes, by Monday morning."

"Thank you, Ms. Jones." They agreed to start over, then out of nowhere, once her partner joined them, friction sparked again. *Was it something he said, or did?*

The McGuire Landfill was far beyond an adequate working environment during the wee hours of the morning. Perhaps here, in this morgue, under better conditions, they would become an awesome team too. Given time, she may even recall that they met before. *What made her forget him?*

The door opened and interrupted his musing. He turned as Morris entered the room. The morgue assistant had changed into green scrubs. "A storage unit is ready for this victim, Doctor," he said.

"Thank you. Morris, have you worked with Savanna Jones before?"

"Yes, sir."

"Is she usually incapacitated in the field?" He hadn't meant to ask, not like that, and as soon as the question was out, Nicholas felt like a schmuck. *Too late.*

Morris's pale face flushed. He dropped his eyes. "I don't know if I'm the right person to ask. We've never worked a crime scene before tonight."

"How is she in the morgue?"

The technician looked up then, his blue eyes measuring whether his new boss really wanted his opinion. "I prepped and cleaned up for Dr. Milano and Dr. Burke while Savanna assisted," he said. "She always seems to be ahead of Dr. Milano, but not so he would know it. And on more than one occasion, she corrected Dr. Burke." Morris shoved his hands in his pocket and shuffled from one foot to the next. "But like I said, I really don't know her that well."

Nicholas watched the young man for a moment, thinking he

knew Savanna well enough to have a crush on her. He let silence linger between them.

"I'll prep and join you," Morris said.

"No need. Prepare an implements tray. I'll take care of the external exam tonight."

If it wasn't just the crush talking, Savanna was a competent forensic scientist, crime scene investigator and morgue assistant. She'd taken the time to integrate her skill sets and was a valuable asset to her lab. *Admirable.*

Nicholas turned when Morris came in with the tray. "Doctor," he said. "I noticed you limping. I don't mind staying to speed things along."

"Much appreciated, but no sense in us both losing our Sunday morning. I need you alert next week."

"Got it."

"Good night."

Nicholas was about to turn away when he noticed Morris lingering. "Something else?"

He looked hesitant.

Nicholas waited, letting the silence pressure Morris into speaking up.

He flicked Nicholas a sidelong glance and bit his lip, then said, "Savanna said I should tell you that she knows where to find the victim's right arm."

"She did?"

Morris nodded.

"Thank you."

"Good night, Doctor."

"Good night."

Nicholas stared after Morris as he shuffled from the room, then turned back to the implements tray. *So, it's going to be like that.* Not only did she intend to thrust up the shields without warning, she planned to take the lead at every turn, too.

This could either be the beginning of an interesting relationship or a challenging one. His mission was too important to run into roadblocks this early. He'd just needed to get close enough to convince her that they had a common enemy. "Hmm." That might mean he'd have to tell her what he found in the cheese barn.

Chapter 17

$\mathcal{A}$FTER SHE AND QUINN bagged the last pieces of evidence collected from the landfill, Savanna released a deep, throat-rumbling groan, trying not to let the growing frustration leak into her muscles. When she asked Quinn to drop her at the lab, he looked at her like she had grown another head.

"Two hours ago, I couldn't pry you out of bed," he said. "Now you're going to work?"

"I need to get some samples."

"Couldn't you do that tomorrow?"

"Not without authorization. There's a new chief in town and he does things a little differently."

"How are you going to change that tonight?"

Dryness scraped Savanna's throat as Quinn's words hit her. She had no intention of permitting defeat before she even got started.

She swallowed. "Since our Jane Doe is still frozen, he's probably conducting the external exam as we speak. I can get my samples before he puts her away."

"Maybe trying to think this much in the wee hours of the morning numbs my brain, but I don't see those dots connecting as clearly as you do."

"You will. Give it time."

"Does this have anything to do with Miller's request that you stay in town?"

The skin on her arm pricked and she whipped her head away from him to look out at the thousands of sparkles lighting the city. "Closing this case benefits all of us," she said. "We'll sleep better at night when it's over."

"I get that. Can't say I agree with working through the night, though. You should head home."

Not willing to agree, Savanna bid Quinn a good night and entered the morgue on the basement level of the forensic labs. She shivered as the cold hit her. Maybe she should have taken Quinn's advice. *No, she'd follow this one through.*

A hand without a body and a body without a hand presented a scenario that was a given to most—they belonged together. In forensics, nothing was certain, not even when well tested.

Savanna wanted to match the dismembered hand to the victim, and test hair and blood samples for the psychotropic drug found in their previous victim. It may be a hunch, but it was a hunch worth pursuing. There was no turning back now.

She left the change room dressed in green scrubs, her ponytail tucked under a cap and a rubberized apron tightened around her middle. She hurried through the quiet hallway, looking for a light under the closed doors. Dr. Wade probably chose the smaller autopsy suite.

A thin beam lining the dark floor at the end of the hall confirmed her suspicions. She halted and pushed the door quietly, in case he was recording. The strong white light blinded her for a moment, but she blinked a few times to adjust.

He stood at the first module—a steel table attached to a large floating steel cabinet with a sink. Everything was still spick and span. Not much had been done yet. Nicholas Wade worked with his head bent over the corpse, his face hidden from her view. The LED beam from the over-head adjustable light outlined his blue surgical cap and one broad shoulder slanted toward his subject.

Amid the landfill, his stiff posture even on an injured leg

prevailed, sturdy and unaffected by the nauseating odours. Here he seemed intent on his task. An army trait, she guessed—unshakable in any surroundings.

For a moment, she loathed disturbing him, but that was her cowardice talking. If she were to collect the samples before he stored the body for the night, disturb him she must.

Wearing her morgue rubber loafers covered with protective booties, she crossed the floor without a sound. "Dr. Wade," she said before reaching him.

His head snapped up and his thick eyebrows squinted together, as if trying to recall where they met before. "Ms. Jones? I wasn't expecting you here at this hour."

"Are you alone?" The question came out more breathless than she intended.

"I thought I was," he said.

She looked away from his intense gaze to study the defrosting corpse between them. The twenty-year-old amputee melted onto a white sheet. The linen would have collected any debris from the body. The liquids seeping from her corpse drained into the sink below her head. She looked as though she just collapsed after a vigorous exercise routine. "Doctor," Savanna said. "Would you be interested in matching the limb we found two nights ago to this victim?"

His eyes gleamed between the facemask. Her spine fluttered under his attention. That happened in the landfill too. She thought she had been cold then, but now the warmth circling in her stomach caught her off guard.

She swallowed and forced herself to concentrate while she waited for his reply.

"Perhaps on Monday," he said. "I'd like to complete the external examination now."

She nodded. "I'll help with the debris extraction. Then we can drain her and remove the wrapping." She stepped forward. The fetid odour that had emanated from the body in the landfill was now more pronounced and drifted up her nose. She raised an arm and inhaled, then lowered it again.

"Are you sure you're up for it, Ms. Jones?"

She grabbed the small tea strainer from the implements table and swiped it through the water puddling around the dead woman. "I'll make you a promise, Doctor," she said, thinking of her prenatal state. "When I'm not up to it, I'll let you know."

"Fair enough."

"Plus, your leg must be in agony by now, high pain threshold, or not."

"Is my injury the reason for your appearance here now?"

She wondered when he would get around to asking. "Actually, I was hoping to collect serology and DNA samples to cross reference against the Colton Moore case."

"The Colton Moore case?"

Debris clung to the fine mesh when Savanna lifted it to the light. She reached for the second pair of tweezers still on the tray and a sample jar. "Yes," she said. "Are you aware that a severed hand was found on Moore's property?"

"No, I wasn't aware of that."

"When we met last night, you thought I was looking for drugs."

"Yes. Were you?"

His tone stung more than the question. How could he ask her if she was a junkie? Just like that, without knowing her. "Yes, I was," she said. "And I assume you were too. Am I right?"

He stopped working and looked over at her, his hazel eyes sharp, even at this hour in the morning. They measured her with patience.

"A moment ago, we were discussing the victim," he said. "Now you're accusing me of chasing the dragon. If you have a problem you would like to discuss—"

"Just a minute," she interrupted him. "We're heading down the wrong path here."

"We are?"

"Yes. Last night I was on the job." She shifted her gaze away from him. It was unsanctioned fieldwork, but he didn't have to know that, not yet anyway. "Well sort of," she said.

"You were there because of a tip you received?"

"That's right. The point is, someone is manufacturing a

psychotropic drug they are selling as a recreational substance. It's not only more powerful than your run of the mill go-pill, it's deadlier. Moore's last victim died of an overdose of the stuff."

"I see."

She wasn't sure he did, really, but he was listening. "Were you looking for information on a similar drug?" she asked.

Again, his gaze narrowed.

"For a case, I mean," she clarified.

"You could say that."

Savanna frowned. So, she would have to pull the details from him. She exhaled and returned to collecting sediment and transferring it to a vial that she then labeled.

"According to the notes I found on the case," he said, "Colton Moore was sentenced to four years for kidnapping, false imprisonment, and sexual assault. Why is the case still open?"

"That one isn't. But a week ago, the police found evidence pointing to his involvement in another case."

"After his incarceration?"

Savanna didn't miss the surprise in Nicholas Wade's tone. Coroner Miller and DS Hannigan had sounded just as shocked two weeks ago when she presented the evidence.

The cords in her neck tightened again. Colton Moore had played them all for fools. Having another crack at him in the upcoming murder trial forced them to leave nothing to chance this time.

"A witness saw someone dumping Theresa Filito's body at the Carlyle Docks," Savanna said. She carefully slid a fine-toothed comb through Jane Doe's brunette hair. "We believe the person who transported the body is an accomplice."

"The police haven't identified the suspect?"

"Not yet."

"Then how was Moore implicated?"

Savanna reached for an evidence bag and dropped the comb with fibres into it. "The evidence was DNA. A semen sample taken from the victim's well-preserved body matched Moore himself. He had intercourse with her."

Nicholas Wade's gloved hands halted for a moment then continued to clean Jane Doe's fingernails. "That's a rather unusual complication," he said. "You found her frozen in a ten-gallon drum three weeks ago, but your serology evidence connects her to Colton Moore."

"Her time of death supports the connection."

"And what's that?"

"According to the stage of the corpse's mummification, Milano estimated TOD at twenty to twenty-two weeks. She was placed in the drum immediately, or within two hours of her death."

Wade nodded. "And given the weather conditions," he said, "the winter months would have preserved the body from rapid decay."

"That's our theory, supported by the evidence we collected. However, with the oncoming spring weather, conditions inside the drum were bound to change. Somebody knew enough to get rid of the drum before it started to absorb heat."

"Are you thinking, based on this young woman's clothing that she, too, might have been killed in the winter?" Wade asked.

Savanna nodded. "And possibly by the same method—a drug overdose."

"If you find the drug's origins, then you'd have found the accomplice."

"Exactly."

"It's possible that this unfortunate woman's death has nothing to do with the Moore case."

"And it's possible that it does. The analysis would confirm either way."

He reached for the aluminum basin. "Ready?"

She nodded.

He handed her the basin. Together, they drained the water surrounding the corpse and removed Jane Doe from the transport wrapping.

He pulled his face mask under his chin and she was struck again by his handsome features. Her stare lasted past the polite stage and she had to force herself to look away.

"You believe now is the best time to conduct a thorough investigation of this victim?" he asked.

"Given all I've just told you," she said. "I thought you would be eager to collect this victim's DNA for tox. We would have an answer one way or another."

"Are you asking that we ignore the procedures of this lab to satisfy your hunches?"

She stifled an irritated sigh. "These are exigent circumstances, and we're here now. If we wait for identification, this case will be placed at the bottom of a long list, and it will be weeks before I can compare samples. I prefer to know as soon as possible."

"I understand your urgency, but I prefer to schedule this victim into proper procedure."

"It seems rather pointless to put her into storage for another month when we could at least collect samples now. What's the harm in that?"

"The harm, Ms. Jones? It's late and, since you're bent on finding evidence to substantiate your theories, you just might. That's dangerous."

Only minutes ago, she thought she could trust the lingering sincerity in his gaze, but what's this now?

"What is your objection to taking the samples now besides your arbitrary decision, that is?" she asked.

"I'm not objecting."

Was he doing this on purpose? "You're not?"

"I just want to be certain about your motives."

Her motives?

"You've made your case quite clear," he said. "Though coloured heavily with bias."

She squirmed from the sudden prick of his words. "If I seem eager to move this case forward, Doctor," she said, "it's because Westbury has lived with this monster much longer than a few days. If we're no closer to finding Moore's accomplice in a year, a murderer will continue to terrorize us, while you will leave the city to reclaim your former glory."

His eyes found her fast.

She refused to back down or look away. Her cheeks burned. She could almost read the questions in his stern expression. Perhaps with what little she knew, she had no right to speculate on his circumstances. "Are you giving your consent?" she asked.

He softened his posture and hobbled toward her, his limp more pronounced. "I hope, Ms. Jones, that we learn to trust each other much sooner than later. It would make for an easier working relationship. Give me an opportunity to study the cases before I give my consent."

Soldiers, she thought, they must always have it their way. "I hope your decision doesn't take too long, Dr. Wade," she said.

He turned away from her. "It's late and I think we should call it a night." He tugged the body onto the gurney.

Great. Now what? How was she to move this case along if she couldn't even get along with her boss, much less persuade him to perform a simple test? Now all she had to rely on was Sally's necklace. And she didn't even have that.

Chapter 18

____

NICHOLAS COLLECTED HIS BIKE from the hospital's underground parking garage and glided it onto the street. As he rode into the dawn, the will power he needed to push Savanna Jones away from his thoughts wavered.

The sun rising over the buildings in the distance reminded him of the last time he saw her ten years ago. That night she couldn't take her eyes off him.

"I think I like looking at you," she'd said.

His heart had slowed. He'd been so smitten with her, knowing she felt the same was enough to make him lose his cool. "I've wanted to say something like that all night," he said.

"Why haven't you?"

"That's the kind of thing that scares nice girls away. And I didn't want you running away too soon." He waited for a roar of laughter, but a sweet smile twinkled in her dark eyes.

"Anything else you're keeping to yourself?" she asked.

"There is one question."

"Uhm-hmm?"

"Does your heart belong to anyone?"

"Not anymore." Her eyes left his briefly. When she looked at him again, sadness lingered around her smile.

"What happened?"

"He broke my heart."

"And you've hated men ever since?"

"No, but I've hated him." She laughed.

"I pity the fool," he said and laughed too.

He watched her wondering if she would disappear when he kissed her. From the moment she entered Scully's student bar that night, he watched her every smile, every gesture, every playful frown and not a hint of deception dimmed the sincerity in her smile.

Nicholas traced an index finger along her latte cheek and, just as he thought, a silky firmness charged his excitement.

"And no. In case you were wondering," she said. "I don't spend the night with strange men."

"I didn't think we were strangers after this afternoon."

"You're right, we became more than strangers when you tried to sacrifice your beautiful 1947 Indian Chief motorbike to save my life."

He held her gaze and the terrifying moment lingered in the silence between them. "You know about motorcycles?"

"Not really."

"Then how'd you know about mine?"

"I read the stamp when I saw it parked outside Scully's pub earlier tonight."

They laughed, then she spread her fingers over his. Her soft touch drew his attention to their hands, and he studied them in the moonlight. He wanted to feel that touch on the more private parts of his body as much as he wanted to know her name, but he enjoyed the mystery in their anonymity.

"Are you going to try to impress me by saying you read Melville's entire Cetology chapter?" she asked.

"No," he said, closing the distance between them. "I'd need to find another way to impress you. I didn't finish the book, and I only made it through three pages of Cetology. But tell me now, Miss

Dagny Taggart, when was Atlas Shrugged introduced into the UBC's curriculum?"

"It wasn't. I received the book from my father last summer. I did nothing but work and read that book."

"Did you read Galt's entire speech?"

"I did," she said, lifting her chin. "I found it fascinating. What about you? Have you read the book?"

"Now you'll really think I'm trying to impress you."

"Why?"

"I read it too." He paused. "And I read the speech out loud."

She stared at him, then she smiled. "So did I."

They laughed together again. Later, as he escorted her home, he pushed again for her name. When he kissed her for the last time, the sun had already broken the horizon and he was sure something more than a chance encounter connected them.

"Westbury," she said from the opened door at the top of the steps. "That's where you can find me."

And here he was. In Westbury. Nicholas slowed the bike. He pulled into the spot in front of his house and eased the helmet from his head. The night started to recede and a bright orange ball rose from the horizon.

"Hmmm." The year ahead was a long one. Savanna's apparent amnesia was a blessing for both of them. He could do without the distraction.

Chapter 19

MONDAY MORNING, QUINN CAUGHT up with Savanna before she entered City Hall. Not a fan of what he called legally brewed coffee, he grasped two large Starbucks cups.

"Morning," she said.

He took a swig from one cup and handed her the other. "I think that one's yours," he said.

Savanna squinted at him and reached for it. They drank coffee flavoured the same, though until recently, she took hers black. "The usual?" she asked.

"Yep."

She handed it back. "I'm off milk again. Sorry. Doctor's orders." *The truth.* "Cramps are back." *The lie.* She'd have to be extra nice to Quinn for all her lying in the coming weeks.

Quinn took the cup. "I wish your cramps knew when it was my turn to buy."

Savanna winced and held the door open for him. "Sorry," she said.

"That time of the month again?"

She grimaced. She would never get used to Quinn discussing

her monthly like he was her bestie girlfriend. "Hey," she said changing the subject. "I got something."

"What's up?"

Savanna looked around the lobby. The early morning foot traffic and multiple dings from the elevator drummed out their conversation. Still, she pulled Quinn into a corner. City Hall wasn't the best location to discuss her illegal activities.

"I went to Lucan Street on Friday night."

"What?"

"The location Jimmy gave you."

"I know what it is. Why the hell did you do that?"

"I wanted to see if there was anything to it."

"I should have known you would go there. Why didn't you call me?"

"Because—" She avoided his accusing stare.

"Because you broke in."

"Well, how else would I get in?"

"It's called a police warrant."

"And how were you going to get a warrant without a shred of evidence? You didn't even believe Jimmy."

"Was he telling the truth? Did you find anything?"

"Not really."

Quinn rolled his eyes. "What's that supposed to mean?"

"Well. There's more."

"Keeping your partner in the dark isn't the brightest idea right now."

"I was going to tell you."

"When?"

"Now. Plus, since it wasn't exactly sanctioned, the less you know about it the better."

"Did you find anything?"

"I found Dr. Wade."

"This is serious, Savanna. If a break and enter is reported, how the hell are you going to explain?"

"I am being serious. I found Dr. Wade there. Well, he came in after me, but he was there."

Quinn's eyes bulged. "Holy shit. You're not kidding. Did he say what he was doing there?"

"I couldn't get a thing out of him."

"Is that why you went to the morgue after the landfill?"

"Partially, but it didn't make any difference. He wouldn't tell me what he was doing there."

"Holy shit," Quinn said again and sipped from one of the cups.

"Someone else was there," Savanna said. Whoever it was arrived before I did. The place was dark. I couldn't see a thing. None of us could. It was only after Dr. Wade was injured that I switched on the lights and well, that's when we met."

"What the—"

"My point is Jimmy could be right. There might be something going on in that barn."

"What the fuck?"

Savanna's BlackBerry rang and cut off Quinn's disapproval. She plucked the phone from her purse and read the screen. Scott Allen. Actually, his army rank was second lieutenant.

"Who's that?" Quinn asked reading her screen.

Savanna tilted the phone away from him. "A friend," she said. "Look I have to take this. Go on up and secure us good seats. I'll be up in a minute."

She intended to tell Quinn about the soldier contacting her, but she wanted to keep her word for now to see where the relationship was going. Mostly she wanted Scott to divulge more information about the drugs and his investigation. Revealing his identity could spook him.

"You're not stepping out on your old man, are you?" Quinn asked.

The comment vexed her and she screwed up her face at him. "Don't be an ass."

He grinned and she turned away and answered the call.

"Scott," she said loud enough for her partner's benefit.

"Savanna," his gruff voice rasped over the line. "Any movement in the case?"

Her heart dropped. More questions rather than answers. "We

found some information that could point us in the right direction," she said thinking of the dismembered arm at Colton Moore's house. "It'll be some time before we can process the evidence to get any answers."

"Okay. I have something you might like."

She perked up. "Really? What?"

"Sorry. Not over the line. Can we meet?"

"Sure."

"The Starbucks on the corner of Dundas and Wellington around, say noon?"

"How about quarter after?"

"Sure, that works. See you then."

"Yeah—"

The phone clicked off.

These military types. Someone should teach them how to deal with civilians.

Chapter 20

F ONTAINE LOOKED UP FROM his tiny note pad when
Savanna entered the boardroom. "Morning, Jonesy," he
said. His dark hair glinted in the sun streaming in the floor-to-
ceiling windows. In his Harry Rosen suit, he could have been
mistaken for the lead Crown attorney.

"Good morning, Detective." She pulled out the chair beside
Quinn. And where, she wondered, was Dave Thomas? They needed
all the support they could muster to take this case all the way.

Quinn grunted. From the way he shifted in the chair, glancing at
the round gold-face clock on the wall behind Fontaine's head every
two seconds, she realized he'd had too much coffee. Her explanation
about Friday night probably added to his stress.

A tray of freshly-baked sugary snacks infused the room.
Savanna had gotten through the morning with only one incident of
puking. She wasn't about to tempt fate with the chocolate-covered
donuts on the table.

"I can't believe you requested the meeting," Quinn said. "I'd
much rather work on closing my open cases than sit here and
attempt to talk Doreen Bellamy into doing her job." He took
another swig of coffee. "You know what she's like," he said.

Savanna pulled copious notes from her briefcase and flipped through them. "This meeting has nothing to do with Doreen's character or mine."

"I'm surprised you got this far."

"What do you mean?"

"You think Bellamy is going to move this case along any faster based on your say so? That woman couldn't even bother to show up on time."

Quinn's assertions were wrong. They had to be. Their DNA evidence held enough proof to get Moore into court within weeks, rather than waiting months. She checked her watch. "Doreen agreed to the meeting," she said. "And I don't expect her to act on my opinion. The evidence speaks for itself."

Battling Doreen Bellamy was one more hurdle she could do without today.

"Yeah," Quinn said, "but the assistant crown attorney had the evidence for a week now and…" Quinn swallowed his next words when the boardroom door swung open.

Savanna swivelled in the chair.

Dr. Milano entered and held the door for someone behind him. Nicholas Wade limped into view, neck tall and shoulders back. His hobble avoided leaning too much support on the injured leg. His hazel eyes found her as soon as his feet crossed the threshold.

She sat very still as he inspected her and conducted an exploration of her own. Her lower lip twitched when she realized he was even more handsome in daylight. A generous mouth with lips that—

"Are you even listening to me?" Quinn's voice darted past her ear.

Her stomach fluttered. She snatched her eyes from Nicholas Wade's face.

"Good morning, everyone," he said. "Ms. Jones." He offered her an easy nod.

"Good morning, Doctor," she said and ducked her head to caress the tingling at the back of her neck. "Where is Doreen already?" she muttered.

Quinn grunted again and grabbed some pages from her notes. They read in silence for a while.

When Savanna raised her head, Dr. Wade leaned against the wall next to the coffee machine and carried on a conversation with Detective Fontaine. Michael Milano fingered a chocolate dip donut from the tray and returned to his binder. She wondered how much longer they would need to wait.

"How'd you get on with the major on Sunday morning in the morgue anyway?" Quinn asked.

Savanna flipped the page in her notebook. "Lieutenant-Colonel," she said.

"What?"

"He's a Lieutenant-Colonel, not a major."

"Whatever." Quinn squirmed and released her notes and reached for his coffee. "So?"

Before she could answer, Doreen slammed into the boardroom a full twenty minutes late. "Good, you're all here," she said. "Let's get on with it."

Quinn leaned in. "With that attitude," he said, "Bellamy will take over the Crown's office in no time."

Savanna bit her lower lip to stop the snicker bubbling in her throat.

"I hope we don't intend to take up the rest of the morning, Mrs. Bellamy," Fontaine growled when he sat down and threw her a menacing glance.

"Sorry, Detective," she said. "The delay was out of my control."

"Next time," Quinn said, "send word, and we'll all show up late too."

Doreen's arctic blue eyes sliced through him, then she turned her chill in Savanna's direction. "Savanna, I need you in court to explain the Zestril overdose in the Cordova case."

"Sorry, Doreen. That's the wrong case, we're here to discuss the Moore and Filito cases."

Doreen sat back in her chair. "Really? Well let's hear what you have. The eye witness can identify this accomplice then?"

"Victor Mason," Fontaine said. "He saw a man drive a dark

coloured van to the Carlyle Docks and off-loaded the drum, then left again."

"That's it?" Doreen asked. "What about the van? Do we have a definite colour?"

"No. He just knows that it's dark. All vans on site matching his description were searched by the forensics team."

"Whatever you found must have been rather important to warrant this meeting." Doreen's frosty tone bit into Savanna again. "What is it?"

"Something you might even think trial-worthy. First of all, none of the evidence taken from the body or the drum matched what we found in the vans in the dock yard."

"What about prints?" Doreen asked.

"The only prints we lifted were Mason's and the dock employees' who admitted touching the drum. However, the blood we found is not the victim's. She's type A-positive. Another sample on the rim of the drum was type B-negative and from a female."

"And we identified it as female blood how?" Doreen asked.

"We distinguished an identifier—the plasma contained an extra coagulation factor."

"English, if you don't mind." Doreen didn't bother to hide her irritation.

The woman might be self-important, but she was the best prosecutor to take this case to court. "We focused on the hormones directly responsible for gender differences," Savanna said.

"Okay. But, how do we know the blood wasn't placed there by the dock manager after the drum was pried open?" Doreen asked.

"We tested the only females on staff," Savanna said.

"So, are you concluding that a woman placed Theresa Filito in that drum?" Doreen's eyes widened.

Savanna suppressed a sigh and met Doreen's gaze. "The evidence proves that another female was present, one injured enough to leave blood behind."

"You found unidentified blood. What else?" Doreen's pen drummed slower on her notepad.

Savanna watched as the sleek Mont Blanc rhythmically bounced on the pad. "The hair taken from Theresa's clothing during her examination showed the same DNA profile as the female blood found on the drum," she said.

"That woman again," Doreen said. "Do we have any further evidence on who she might be?" She turned her gazed to Detective Fontaine.

"It's a very real possibility that she's another victim," Fontaine said.

Dead silence fell on the room and all eyes measured him as though he recommended a hit on the deputy mayor. The idea that another body waited somewhere out there, not yet discovered, disturbed them all.

"We'll look into that possibility." Fontaine jotted a note on his tiny pad.

"That's not all." Dr. Milano cleared his throat. "We found Adderall in Theresa Filito's system."

"Was she an addict too?" Doreen asked.

"The evidence doesn't support it." Milano sat upright. "The marks on the victim's arms were fresh," he said. "Her veins savagely ripped at the needle sites. Bruises on her wrists and ankles indicate she was tied up for some time. She was gagged with a type of nylon rope. The barbiturates found in her system would have incapacitated her almost the entire time. It's very probable that the drugs were forced on her."

Nicholas Wade's crisp white shirt caught Savanna's attention. She lifted her eyes to meet his. Soft brown amber warmed the hazel glint. A wicked wave of déjà vu needled her. It was as though she looked into those eyes before and drew comfort from the reassurance that lived there. She caught her breath and dropped her gaze.

He loosened his solid blue tie and sat forward. "Any other nootropics present in her blood?" he asked.

"We haven't been able to put a name to all the substances we isolated." Milano flipped through his notes. "Savanna is working with the RCMP on what we've been able to isolate."

No doubt Dr. Wade's question connected to his cheese barn search. Their eyes met and she knew he guessed her thoughts.

When he spoke, it seemed as though he directed his assertions at her.

"Detective Fontaine might be right," he said. "It's probable that the unknown female is a victim as well."

Savanna's surprise registered in her arched eyebrows before she caught herself. Two nights ago, she accused him of killing time until his sanction ended, maybe she was wrong.

"That would mean we might have a serial rapist with two murders under his belt," she said.

"Serial rapist? Really, Savanna." Doreen's objection held enough scorn to render the idea null and void. "Using that type of language is reckless and borders on fear mongering. We need more victims before we can start thinking in those terms."

Savanna's jaw slackened. "You have enough to bring this case to a judge," she said. "You don't need a morgue full of dead women."

"Are you kidding me?" Doreen snickered. "Every bit of this evidence is questionable and guarantees that I'll be laughed out of court. I need something concrete."

"Since when is DNA not concrete?"

"We have no clue when Moore had intercourse with this woman. You gave me no evidence that Moore killed her. He and his lawyer could prove she was still alive when Moore cast her from his bed. Get me something I can work with. Get me the accomplice."

"We're working on that, but you can't allow Moore to skate on murder because—"

"Alleged murder," Doreen interrupted. "It's all speculation until I have—"

"A smoking gun?" Quinn asked.

"You've got enough to file the charges," Savanna snapped.

"May I remind you," Doreen said with definite scorn, "Moore is in prison for rape, kidnap and false imprisonment because I put him there. Stick to your test tubes and leave the legal matters to me."

Six months ago, Doreen won the Crown's case against Colton Moore. Now she acted as though the new evidence somehow undermined her victory. What little proof they held was strong enough to charge him. Theresa died soon after having intercourse with Moore. It wasn't a leap to consider he was the main suspect.

Doreen grabbed her notepad and sleek pen. "Thank you all for coming," she said. "I'll be happy to do this again when we have solid evidence to discuss." She pushed from her chair and left the boardroom.

Savanna sighed. It took the assistant Crown prosecutor less than forty minutes to dismiss everything they'd worked on for the last two weeks. Impossible though it may be to work with her, unless they provided evidence she deemed court-worthy, the case would go nowhere. Sally's necklace was still her only lead to the accomplice.

Chapter 21

When Doreen Bellamy dismissed the forensic evidence with alarming speed, Savanna slumped into her chair and sat there looking whiplashed. Nicholas decided to wait for her. With the exception of Quinn, the others filed from the room.

If the assistant Crown prosecutor continued to poke legal loopholes in their investigating evidence, the case would never get to court. This was his department now, and there was nothing he hated more than inconsistencies.

Savanna's dazed expression lasted only a moment. She packed her notes and pushed from the chair, but Quinn stepped into her path.

"So now what?" her partner asked. "That was everything we had."

Savanna faced him. "We still have the necklace," she said. She didn't look convinced.

It was the only information in the physical file Nicholas found. A single handwritten note referencing the missing necklace.

"Do you have a photograph of it?" Quinn asked.

"No, but I can get one. I'll call Sally."

"Okay. I'll comb the records from the last few months and see what I come up with."

"Sure thing. It's a good place to start. We can go through what you find later." Savanna maneuvered her rolling briefcase around her partner. She stopped when she spotted Nicholas. "Dr. Wade, you're still here, good. Do you have a moment?"

He returned Quinn's departing nod and pushed from the chair. His leg had become stiff during the meeting. He massaged the area. "I was hoping to speak with you too, Ms. Jones," he said.

"You okay, Doctor?"

"Fine, thank you."

They entered the corridor together. "Have you made a decision regarding the samples for testing?" she asked.

He'd expected the question, but she obviously didn't want to wait until they reached his office. "Glad you brought that up," he said. "I ran into a problem and I'm sure you know how to solve it."

"Me?"

He nodded. "The information seems inconsistent as though some material is missing."

"Oh, yes." Her gazed moved to the briefcase she pulled behind her. "There are two reasons for that."

"Can we talk about it in my office?"

The minute he closed the door, Savanna seemed to have lost sight of why she was there. "Since when is DNA evidence not enough to charge a suspect with murder?"

Nicholas glanced at her. In a pale blue pantsuit with her hair in a single braid, she looked far more professional than when he met her in the cheese barn and the landfill.

At one point that morning when their eyes met, he thought she remembered him. Then the moment passed and she returned to her notes. As he listened to her argue with the assistant Crown prosecutor, he couldn't imagine her forgetting anything. He half-expected her to announce her intentions to charge Colton Moore with murder and try the case in court herself. She would probably win too.

"Doreen doesn't take this case seriously," she said with fierce determination still flaming in her chocolate eyes.

He peeled his gaze away from her expression and limped behind his desk. He, too, believed the case seemed straightforward. In his opinion, Bellamy's dismissal of the team's collective efforts smelled of some other grievance rather than the evidence presented. That wasn't why he called Savanna here, though. He wanted a look at those files. Yesterday during his search, he'd noticed the aging computer system and the database software seemed archaic by army standards. Surely Westbury Forensics kept detailed records of every case.

"I hope you understand now why I'm eager to collect DNA samples from our Jane Doe," Savanna said.

A fierce stab shot through his leg. He squinted and raised a hand. He needed total focus for his first day on the job and opted for Advil rather than the prescription medication. He was starting to regret that choice. "Can we put that on hold for a minute?" he asked. "First of all, let's sit." He grasped the chair arms while he eased into the seat.

She took one of the wooden armchairs facing his desk. Her fury seemed diffused as she waited for him. "Can I get you something to help with the pain, Doctor?" she asked.

"I'm okay now. You were saying about the files?"

"Unfortunately, our staff was downsized in the middle of this case and many of the records, though duplicated, are not computerized."

"I see. And the other reason?"

"I have the active copy. The other is in archives."

How on earth was he supposed to work like this? "May I have them?" he asked.

She shoved her jacket sleeves to her elbows and reached for the briefcase. "When I left the lab on Saturday night, I took most of it with me." She heaved a stack of documents onto his desk. "I thought if I spent time carefully assessing our evidence, something new might pop out. I didn't think anyone would need them before today."

"Even after our discussion last night?"

"You can blame me for delaying your decision on the samples."

He stared at the pile of at least fifteen to twenty files. "Did something pop out?"

She crossed her legs and balanced a notepad on her knee.

Nicholas followed the length of her thigh, then looked away before he met her gaze again.

"Just the previously noted holes," she said. "I feel like we have exhausted this lot." She tapped the files. "Or, we're missing something crucial. That's why I believe we can benefit from running a comparison test with our new victim."

The urgency in her request was starting to make sense. "After this morning's meeting," he said, "I'm noticing the similarities to the Filito case. If you have some time now, we can review the forensic evidence together."

Her eyes widened. "Now?"

"Do you have something else more pressing, Ms. Jones?"

"No."

"Good," he said and pushed from the chair. "Let's move over here." He started for the conversation area in the corner of his office. "Perhaps fresh eyes would spot a connection previously overlooked. Something acceptable to Mrs. Bellamy."

Savanna sat forward, her eyes gleaming again. "Let's start with the connection between Moore and Theresa," she said.

Another victim's first name rolled from her tongue as though they discussed a group of friends. In many of his assignments where he dealt with the deceased, he never knew their names. Savanna's insistence that the victims were more than another case reminded him to try harder to reintegrate himself into a civilian society.

It was almost lunchtime when they ended the session. Her ideas and the evidence persuaded him that not only was a comparison test necessary, it was the only course of action left to forensics to move the case along.

"Given the twists and turns in this case," he said, "I think I understand why Mrs. Bellamy is skeptical."

Savanna tensed. "You do?"

He nodded. Each retelling complicated the circumstances even more. "I'll handle the communications with the Crown Attorney's Office," he said.

"Are you saying we should run everything through you?"

"It's just another tactic to satisfy legal."

Concern replaced the gleam that flickered in her eyes. "Tactic?" she asked.

Wasn't that a civilian term? "Is something wrong, Ms. Jones?"

She opened her mouth, then closed it again and looked away.

"You don't agree?" he asked.

"Well, I would hate to think that we had to resort to tactics to get through the next year rather than dealing with the evidence head on."

He sat up in the chair to dodge that direct hit. "Are you questioning my commitment, Ms. Jones?"

"Is your commitment questionable?"

"Well, I'm here."

"Why? Just following orders? Westbury is not as sophisticated as some other Canadian cities. For most, it doesn't even stack up. We can't sway a political vote one way or the other."

Nicholas took a moment before he answered that one. *No rose-coloured glasses here at all. Why was she so jaded?* "Why are you still here?" he asked.

"Still?"

"Yes. Still."

"I have… I have commitments."

He dropped his eyes to her left hand. Not a single piece of jewellery. Not even a watch. "Well, Ms. Jones, I do too."

"Do your commitments have anything to do with your visit to the cheese barn two nights ago?"

He wondered when she would bring that up. He was determined not to discuss the subject with her. "It may," he said, "but this case is important too."

"Glad to hear it."

"So, like I said, I'll communicate with the Crown's office to cut down on misunderstandings and misinterpretations. More than that," he paused making sure he had her full attention, "I agree with you."

"You do?" She perked up.

"I'm all for collecting the samples to conduct a comparison analysis. The autopsy is delayed until we have an identification and are able to notify the family."

"I'm relieved to hear that you're on board, Dr. Wade."

His head tipped up and the smile that played around her mouth ignited his memories again. He recalled the invitation in those curved, full lips, the memory of them that followed him around the globe after their night together. Again, he glanced at her ring-free left hand. The absence of a ring didn't mean the absence of a husband. And why was he checking anyway?

"When do you suppose that would be?" she asked.

"I'll let you know this afternoon."

She nodded.

"Depending on the case load, our days may run late. Will that be a problem?"

Her mouth opened. "I ah. Well…"

Nicholas didn't think his question was that complicated. "I would like to see your evidence trail to the accomplice," he said. "That might mean starting from scratch."

She focused behind him for a moment before she spoke. "Despite what Doreen Bellamy said, we haven't been sitting on our hands, you know."

"Wasn't suggesting it." If he were a betting man, he would say that her defensive attitude was about something else.

"I've never had problems with working late," she said.

"I know."

"How—"

"From my brief research this morning, you're the same Savanna Jones that worked day and night for four months to crack the home invasion cases that left three elderly people dead, aren't you?"

She tipped her chin upward. "That's me," she said.

"Mayor Campbell even gave you the key to the city."

"Why do I get the feeling you're heading toward a point?"

"Is that why you haven't updated the photo on your ID since then?"

"My identification photo?"

"Yes. As a matter of a fact, your entire file hasn't been updated since then. Does that have something to do with the staff shortage?"

"It may." She squinted. "Is my personnel file a matter of urgency, Doctor?"

Ten years ago, she didn't squint. She smiled. Now, her contemplation questioned his motives.

"Not urgent," he said. "Just necessary."

Chapter 22

_S_avanna trailed the empty briefcase behind her as she entered the serology lab.

"Afternoon all," she greeted her colleagues. The two women and the single man were the only scientist left in her department after the recent downsizing.

One of the women waved a blue latex hand at Savanna and returned to her test tubes.

Savanna caught Jenny Wessel's smile, an apology written all over her smooth, dark complexion. Savanna tipped her head to one side and smiled back.

Jenny had no reason to be apologetic. She'd never worked a crime scene before. Adapting to the new position, even with Quinn's help would be stressful, especially since she was pregnant with her first child. Why take the risk?

"Let's have lunch this week," Savanna said.

Jenny nodded.

Savanna longed to share her news too, but she couldn't, at least not for the next few months—if she had that long.

At her station, she exchanged her spring coat for the lab version and dropped her purse into a half-empty file drawer, then she stashed the briefcase under the table. She couldn't believe how horribly the meeting with the assistant Crown prosecutor failed this morning. But all was not lost.

Dr. Wade took his role seriously and intended to deal with the Crown's office. She held out hope for him, but only if he intended to spend his time on more pressing matters than her ID photo. *Why in the world did he bring it up?*

She reached for her chair and paused when the white telephone mounted over her table rang. She lifted the receiver and shouldered it to her ear while she opened a bulging filing cabinet. "Savanna Jones here," she said, fingering through the files.

"It's Mark down at security. There is a Sally Starr asking to see you."

Sally, Really? They hadn't seen each other in months. During their last conversation a few days ago, Savanna had no updates on the necklace. She hadn't expected another call so soon, and certainly not a visit. Maybe Sally found the piece of jewellery at home tucked securely into her mementos.

Savanna rubbed her temples. If the necklace wasn't missing, then she had one less lead to Moore's accomplice. But she was getting ahead of herself.

"Shall I send her up?" Mark asked.

"Ah, no. I'll come down." Having Sally in her lab while she still investigated this case was definitely a mistake.

Sally Starr was a twenty-year-old student at The Westbury Human Resource Institute before Colton Moore kidnapped her. The horrific ordeal overshadowed her existence and forced her into isolation. She even quit school. For the first few months, Sally imprisoned herself in her apartment, fearing another attack. The only time she emerged was to face Colton Moore in court. His conviction changed little. In the last couple months though, she started seeing a therapist.

Savanna found Sally pacing in front of the security desk. "Hi there," she said.

Sally jerked to a stop. Her blue eyes widened in a sad heart-shaped face. A neat bun pulled her natural blonde hair to the nape of her neck. Sally was pretty with a fair complexion, the type that burned easily with prolonged sun exposure. She wore a light grey tracksuit that made her look even paler.

"Hi," she said glancing around her. "Sorry to show up like this."

Savanna smiled and touched her elbow. "I'm happy to see you, she said.

With practiced reflexes, Sally withdrew and tucked her arm closer to her side.

Savanna eased her hand away. "How have you been?" She asked.

"Okay." Sally offered her usual weak smile. "I know you're busy, but I wanted to talk for a bit."

Savanna had promised Scott Allen she would meet with him over her lunch break, but the concern tightening around Sally's mouth urged her to take the time to listen. "Of course," she said. "How can I help?"

The security desk buzzed with the usual activity. Sally's breath quickened as she surveyed the lobby.

"We'll have more privacy over here," Savanna said and led her to the far corner. "Let's sit down." She pointed to the two armchairs and a coffee table, then turned the chairs away from the busy entrance.

Sally perched on the edge of one chair and clutched her purse to her chest. They sat facing the glass wall with a view of the tree-lined lawn and the parking lot beyond.

"I'm hearing rumours about Colton Moore," Sally said.

"What rumours?"

"I'm hearing that the Crown Attorney might charge him with another crime. Do you know anything about it?"

Savanna couldn't talk to Sally about the trial, if in fact there was going to be one. "I'm sorry, but I'm not the right person to ask."

Sally turned ashen white. "So, it's true then," she said and lowered her voice to a whisper. "Does that mean I have to testify, again?"

Savanna wanted to reach out and comfort her, but she feared spooking Sally again. "It's possible," she admitted.

"But this will be all over the news."

Savanna nodded slowly though she failed to understand the woman's resistance.

"I don't think . . ." Sally turned her gaze away from Savanna and toward the view beyond the window. "I don't think it has anything to do with me," she said.

Savanna had hoped Sally might want to help convict Moore for Theresa Filito's murder. It was likely that Theresa was one of the women Sally heard while Moore held her captive. "You're scared," Savanna said.

"I've worked hard to erase his face from my memory. I don't ever want to see him again. I don't want that smirking grin in my dreams anymore. I keep praying that Doreen Bellamy would never call me."

If this morning's meeting was any indication, it was possible that Sally would never see Moore in court again. "You have every right to your fear and doubt," Savanna said. "But remember, nine months ago your testimony put him in prison. In fact, a murder conviction for Colton Moore could help you move on with your life."

Sally nodded. "I thought of that."

"What about your family? What are they saying?"

Sally shook her head.

"Have you spoken to them?"

"How could I? What should I tell them?"

"They would want to help you through this ordeal."

Sally's hand trembled.

Savanna wanted to help, but she couldn't relate to Sally's devastation. The experience shamed and scarred her, maybe for life. Savanna decided to back off and change the subject. "I've been asking around about your necklace," she said. But it would be easier with a photograph. Do you have one? Even digital would be okay."

"I might. I'll have to look for it."

"That would be helpful."

"Okay." Sally vigorously rubbed her right thumb into her left palm as though she was trying to erase a stubborn mark. "The necklace was my grandmother's," she said. "She gave it to me on my sixteenth birthday. I wore it the night…the night I was taken. After I woke up in that place, *he* ripped it from my neck. Now I have a scar to remind me of my grandmother."

"I'm so sorry. I'll try my best to find it. Send me a photo if you have one."

"I would be so grateful to have it back."

"I'll do what I can, but I can't make any promises. In cases like this, some items never show up again."

Sally picked at her fingernails. "You're right, you know," she said. "I am afraid."

"What scares you the most?"

A loud male voice barked an obscenity from the entrance.

Sally startled and shrunk into the chair. "I don't want to testify," she said. "If I go back to court, my face will be all over the news this time. I told my family that it was only a kidnapping. I was too ashamed to tell them everything. Now the whole story will come out in court. Everyone would know that I was raped. They'd know that I lied."

An ache gathered in Savanna's throat. *No wonder she was so scared.* She touched Sally's arm. "All the more reason to speak to them first," she said.

Sally winced, but Savanna kept her hand in place until she made eye contact.

"Perhaps face to face is better," Savanna said.

Sally's eyes widened. "You mean go home?"

"A brief visit may help. This is your life, not Moore's."

"I don't think I can face them. I could never admit it. Especially the…the abortion."

Savanna swallowed, understanding a bit more of Sally's resistance. Some secrets were harder to reveal than others. She moved her hand from Sally's arm. "You're the one who decided to get help for what happened to you," she said. "That decision started you on the road to recovery. Now is the time to let your family help you."

Sally's pale face flushed. She leaned forward and lowered her voice to a tight whisper. "You don't know what he did to me. I could never tell my father that."

Savanna's stomach clenched. "I don't mean everything. Not the details, but —"

"Never." Sally leapt from the chair and zipped through the lobby with surprising speed.

Damn and double damn. She didn't mean to push Sally over the edge. If she refused to testify, all the evidence they'd collected would be nothing but conjecture, and Doreen would continue to derail every inch of progress.

Savanna raced to the exit, but she was too late. Sally was gone before she could rectify the situation. What would she do now? The only clear option left was teaming up with the army. And since Dr. Wade wasn't talking, it would have to be Second-Lieutenant Scott Allen. He was her best chance to get this case back on track.

Chapter 23

THE SPICY, TOASTED AND woody aromas of Starbucks coffee settled on Savanna's palate. She'd been waiting fifteen minutes, and still no word from Scott Allen. She rechecked her watch. Dr. Wade's staff meeting started in half an hour. If she hung around here much longer, she'd be late.

Not even a text message. Scott probably forgot their meeting, and she was sitting there wasting her time. She sighed and reached for her purse.

"Savanna." The gravelly male voice sounded less gruff than it had over the phone that morning.

She swivelled and stretched her neck. In a pair of jeans and a snug fitting white t-shirt, Second Lieutenant Scott Allen seemed taller than the first time they met. A grin sneered across his lips. Without the green fatigues, she wouldn't have been able to pick him out in a crowd.

The dark Blue Jays baseball cap he wore covered a dirty-blonde military crew cut and shaded his sizeable square face. She stared a moment too long at his log-like biceps, bulging like two barrel extensions from his massive chest. "Ah, Scott," she stammered and pushed to her feet, sticking out her hand. "I mean Second Lieu—"

He held a paper bag in one hand and reached to greet her with the other. His rough paw crushed her fingers.

Savanna winced and tried to extract her hand, but Scott threw his other arm around her shoulder and pulled her in for a hug.

The paper bag he held slapped her chest. Ammonia burned her nose. She lurched back.

"No titles, please," Scott whispered. "Not here. Just Scott."

"Of course." She held her breath and managed a weak smile. He was one of those bodybuilders who thought sniffing ammonia before weight training sessions improved his strength.

Savanna freed her hand from his and turned toward a corner table tucked away from the lunch crowd.

Scott followed her and reached for a chair.

"Trouble at the base this morning?" Savanna asked.

"What do you mean?" The chair dwarfed under his bulk when he sat down.

"I thought soldiers were always punctual," she said, "or did I get my timing wrong?"

"Oh, that." He pulled a wrapped Subway sandwich from the bag. "I stopped for lunch," he said. "I figured you wouldn't mind waiting. It was for a good cause."

She stared at him. Was he kidding?

He peeled the wrapping away and bit into the sandwich. Half of it disappeared while sauce dripped onto his chin. "I appreciate you meeting me," he said.

"And I would have appreciated a simple text message."

"Maybe I should have called. Next time, for sure."

He was so engrossed in his lunch; her frosty glare went unnoticed. That was as much of an apology as she would get, she supposed.

"We're willing to help the army with the drug investigation," she said, not really feeling it. "But we're short on leads at the moment."

He nodded. His mouth was too full to answer.

"The OPP outrank the local police when it comes to drug trafficking in Ontario," she continued. "Are you talking to them?"

"Given the gravity of this case, that's a position we can't risk."

She wasn't sure if that was a yes or no but decided to leave it at that. She didn't come here to evaluate the army's investigating methods. As a matter of fact, she had enough of that back at the lab. "So?" she asked. "What information do you have?"

He took his time with the rest of the sandwich. "Word has it that the police found a body dumped in one of your landfills only hours ago." His steel grey eyes measured her reaction while he waited for her reply.

What was this about? The police hadn't yet released that information. Savanna let the comment hang in the air.

Scott held his poker face.

"How do you know about that?" she finally asked.

He nodded and wiped his mouth. "To tell you the truth, I have ears in the department."

Savanna arched back into the chair. She didn't like the sound of this. "Is that right?"

"It's not what you think. He doesn't report on police business. He's a friend of mine. We were just hanging out at the gym this morning when I told him I was thinking about joining the department after my present contract ends. He said I should rethink that if I want to get away from the bad shit. That's when he mentioned the dumped dead woman."

"I'm not really at liberty to discuss the case."

Scott turned his baseball cap backwards exposing a scar high on his oversized forehead.

How come she never noticed that before? It must have been some fight. The wound seemed deep.

His steel grey eyes studied her as she watched him. "My friend didn't give me details," he said. "I thought maybe if the homicide had anything to do with drugs, you might know something about it."

Savanna relaxed. That sounded reasonable. "We know nothing," she said. "The police don't even know who she is."

"That's a shame."

"Yes, it is." Her voice was firmer than she intended. She looked up at him.

He shifted in the chair and crumbled the sandwich wrap. "Intel from Ottawa believes that the drug pervading the army units is one that Health Canada approved for a particular use," he said. "But it's now flooding the streets."

Savanna perked up. "Are you serious?" For a moment there, she was beginning to think that Scott wasted her lunch hour, but this was interesting. "That would mean someone still has access to the outdated active pharmaceutical ingredient," she said.

"We believe the initial form has been altered, a few times."

"You're talking about a flood of poorly designed drugs on the street?"

"Exactly."

"How do you intend to track them down?"

"I'm hoping you guys can help with that."

"Why us? We have nothing to do with drug enforcement. We're forensics."

"I get that, but I thought you assisted the Canadian Army before?"

Savanna recalled Miller saying that they did, but he never said in what capacity. "I'm sure it would have been something within our expertise," she said.

"Look." He leaned forward, and she caught another whiff of the acrid sweat laced with ammonia.

"The army is embarrassed about all this. If the news goes public, things will look bad. This has to be kept quiet until we can get a handle on it. Going with a local forensic angle affords the army better..." He paused.

"Concealment?" Savanna offered.

"I knew you'd understand," he said.

She thought of Miller's assertions that they would benefit from the 'joint' investigation. She also thought of how tight-lipped Nicholas Wade had been with his information. She wondered if she should mention his name to Scott. "Do you have any specific direction you want us to take on your inquiries?" she asked.

"Not really. Test and match anything you come across and give us details on where it came from."

"What about you? Do you have a sample of the limited-edition drug for a comparison test?"

"It's possible I can get my hands on a sample. Let's work together on this. Whatever you tell us would go a long way."

Right. Now it was her turn to come up with something before he made another promise. Wasn't that a screwed-up definition of sharing? Yet it was all she had at the moment.

Chapter 24

———————

$\mathcal{I}$T HAD BEEN TWO weeks since they discovered the twenty-something-year-old amputee in the McGuire Landfill and still the police hadn't identified the victim. To add mystery to an already puzzling problem, whoever she was, Colton Moore had nothing to do with her death. As the forensic results trickled in, none of the DNA evidence in the case matched the Moore ongoing case. Not blood, not saliva, not semen, not hairs nor fibres.

The only similarities Savanna discovered were the abscess-like sores found on the two women's bodies, and the fact that they both used cortisone to treat the bruises. Something else kept nagging at her and though she stared into her comparison microscope until she was cross-eyed, the anomaly disappeared in the fragments.

Her cellphone buzzed. She lifted her head from the microscope to read the screen. A text from Sally with the photo of her necklace.

Hope U R still looking!

They hadn't spoken since their conversation in the lobby. Now Sally was sending her curt messages. Could Savanna really blame her? The one truth that helped Sally reassembled her life after her ordeal, was the belief that she was worth more than her horrific experience. Her involvement in a new trial would shake that confidence.

Savanna opened the photo. The woman wearing the necklace looked familiar. It was the smoky made-up eyes, flirting with the camera that enhanced her provocative confidence. Savanna peered closer. *Oh my. Sally?* She beamed with life. The necklace, a moon face etched in ivory and surrounded by an intricate silver pattern, rested on her chest.

Savanna flipped from the photo to her contacts list to find Dave's number. She touched the phone icon and waited for the line to connect. "Hey, are you at the precinct?" she asked when he picked up.

"I'm here, but I'm heading into interrogation soon. What's up?"

"I've got a lead on the accomplice."

"I like the sound of that. All right. Come on by."

The division was a fifteen-minute walk from the lab. On the last day in May, the temperature was a comfortable nineteen degrees. Everywhere, people took the opportunity to spring their legs from the long winter hiatus. Skin tones from milky white to ebony strolled, ambled and strutted in shorts.

She crossed the traffic lights at Wellington and had to hop onto the sidewalk to avoid a bike courier sprinting toward her against the lights. Someone shouted at him and a street person raised a fist and yelled a few obscenities. Feeling justified, Savanna dropped $5.00 in her box.

The homicide squad room smelled of strong coffee left too long on the burner. Trying not to inhale, she headed straight for Thomas and Fontaine's desk. Only noon and already the phones rang off the hook in the squad room.

"Hey, Savanna," Detective Carter called from behind a Sherlock Holmes mug. "Looking for me?" He stood up from his chair. His blue eyes danced in his pale face. She caught a glimpse of the muffin top bulging over the thin leather belt before he perched on the corner of his desk.

"Not today," she said ignoring his leering. "Have you seen Thomas?"

Before he answered, a loud noise startled her. She turned just as Dave slammed out of DS Hannigan's office. What on earth had happened in there? From the expression on the detective's face, it looked like he lost the battle.

His nostrils flared as he whipped past her. When she turned to follow him, he had already started to retrace his steps.

"You want a piece of me too?" he asked. He'd been butting heads with the captain again.

She needed him in a more receptive mood before she explained her idea. "What are you offering, Detective?" she asked.

He leveled his menacing stare at her.

She matched his gaze and waited, taking care to breathe slow and easy.

Dave's jaw muscles jerked then relaxed. He exhaled then snapped, "Stop that." Before she pretended innocence, he turned away from her, his steps striding rather than marching. "You coming?" He called over his shoulder.

She smiled and hurried to catch up. "What was that all about?" she asked and closed the door to the dull grey interrogation room.

Dave waved a palm, then leaned against one of the two chairs pushed under a small square table. "You don't want to know," he said.

He wasn't exactly the picture of a well-put-together cop at the moment. A rumpled white shirt, loosened necktie, two sharp lines creasing his brow and at least a three-day beard: a look she knew all too well. This disheveled Dave had shown up a few days after she ended their brief relationship five years ago. This time, she left it alone.

He shrugged away from her inspection and stood next to the large mirror built into the wall. "Look at this," he said, jutting his chin toward the mirror.

Savanna joined him.

He flicked a switch and she came face to face with Colton Moore. She crossed her arms under her breasts.

A year and a half ago, when the police finally caught him and guided him handcuffed into the squad car, Savanna watched on the news like everyone else.

Within the first split second, she thought him devoid of humanity. One of the females in the room echoed her thoughts out loud. "What an evil looking bastard," she had said. A scar at the corner of his right eye pulled the lid down.

"No charm in that face," Savanna had muttered.

Shackled at his ankles and handcuffed to the table, his tall, lean body, now gaunt in the orange jump suit, drooped on a small metal chair.

"We brought him in to talk about his partner in crime," Dave said. "He's been waiting for the last twenty minutes, but it seems like his lawyer got caught in traffic."

She wasn't sure if he was serious or if the detectives had played a fast one on the lawyer.

"Fontaine went in to give Moore the news," Dave said.

Moore turned his face to the two-way mirror.

Savanna gasped.

His scar looked even more sinister since his time in prison. He leered, and the longer he stared, the tighter she clutched her arms around her body. He probably guessed he was being watched. His expression swelled with amusement and his sunken, bloodshot eyes widened as he leaned closer to the mirror. The glass between them seemed to melt away under his scorching probe.

Savanna stepped back. Fontaine banged on the table and Moore slowly turned his head. He looked like a demon from "The Exorcist." He tugged at the shackles and muttered something she couldn't quite hear.

"We're hoping he would say something before his lawyer gets here. You're welcome to listen in if you like."

Savanna shivered and smoothed a hand over the small hairs that lifted on the back of her neck. After his trial and conviction, she hadn't expected to see Colton Moore again. She started for the door.

"You okay, Jones?" Dave asked.

"I'll come back when you have more time."

He joined her across the room. "I have a few minutes now. What can I do for you?"

She pulled her cellphone from her purse, searched for the photo Sally sent, then handed him the phone. "This is the missing necklace," she said.

Dave's eyes lingered on the photo. For the entire year they knew her, Sally had never smiled, not even at Moore's conviction.

"This is what you were after when you found the severed hand at Moore's house?" Dave touched the screen to keep the photo in view.

"The very same," she said.

"You really think this is a lead to the accomplice? This thing could have gotten lost in the shuffle."

"If that's the case, we would have found it during our sweep of Moore's locations. Sally said someone ripped it from her neck."

Dave handed back the phone. "What are you hoping for?"

"I would say a miracle, but I know better."

"I don't have to tell you how unlikely recovery is at this point."

Was that the sound of reluctance? "Recovery would be nice," she said. "I'm sure Sally would appreciate it. I think whoever took this necklace still has it and could be Moore's accomplice."

"What? Find the necklace and I'd find my man?"

"Don't mock me, Detective. You know what I'm saying." She searched her contacts for his number. "I just sent you a copy. Maybe you can check to see if anyone tried to pawn it in the last few months."

"Yes, *Detective Superintendent Jones.*" He imitated a salute.

"Oh, calm down. I'm not telling you how to do your job."

He grinned. "Glad to hear. I've had enough of that for the day." Thomas scratched his beard. "If the necklace is out there, it's possible someone's seen it. I'll turn over a few rocks."

"Thank you," she said still a bit jittery. She tucked the phone into her purse. The thought that only a single wall separated her from Colton Moore made her more than a bit uneasy.

"By the way," Dave said, "since we're sharing. I'll send you the official report, but we identified your amputee from the landfill."

Savanna caught her breath. "You did? Who is she?"

"Suzette Anita Morgan, a twenty-three-year-old nurse. Worked the graveyard shift at Westbury General. One of the new nurses, right out of school."

"No one reported her missing?"

"They said she kept to herself and didn't make friends. Remarked that the ones like that usually quit within the first few weeks. They thought she'd quit too."

"And her family?"

"No one knows. One of the nurses said she'd seen Suzette with a man once. When she asked her about him, Suzette said he was her boyfriend."

"Does the nurse remember what he looks like?"

"Vaguely, white guy, wears jumpsuits, sneakers and a baseball cap. Suzette didn't mention a name and the nurse didn't see him close enough to get a better look."

"Someone must know more about her."

"We got her ID from the school, but the personal contact info she supplied was bogus. We're doing what we can to track down next of kin."

"Maybe someone will come forward."

Chapter 25

SAVANNA PILED ONTO THE COUCH, wrapped in her favourite blue silk robe, a Christmas gift from Richard. The chicken salad and a bag of chips she intended for dinner waited on the coffee table until after her call. She leaned into the pillows comfortably surrounding her, and smiled at the sonogram image of the baby she collected from the doctor's office that afternoon. She dialled Richard's mobile number.

"Darling," he said when he picked up.

The distance in his voice magnified her loneliness. Their conversations every night were hardly enough to make up for his absence. She slumped into the sofa to relieve the ache in her shoulders. "How was last night?" she asked.

"It was fantastic. Even better than I hoped."

"I'm glad. I saw the entertainment news this morning. I wanted to call."

"Why didn't you?"

"What, and disturb your sleep?"

"It would have been okay."

Caught up in his excitement, she settled into the soft pillows and smiled into the phone. "Guess what?" she asked. "I have the weekend off. I can fly out to Regina. Isn't Friday your first perfor-mance there?"

"Well, it is, but—"

"Then it's perfect. I can try to arrive on Friday night."

The sound of Richard tapping the music sheet against the side of his thigh crackled over the phone line. "Do you have to come out this weekend?" he asked.

"What's wrong with this weekend?"

"Well, it's the orchestra here. The conductor and I have never really seen eye to eye. Marty is smoothing it all out."

That was more than a little disappointing. Nine weeks pregnant and he'd never seen the baby's ultrasounds.

"I don't think I can handle the distraction if you come out." Richard continued.

Savanna felt tears prickling her eyelids and took a deep breath. "I wish you would think of the distance between us," she said, "rather than how much of a distraction I've been to you lately."

"Darling, I'm sorry. I didn't mean it like that. You know how I get when the conductors are trying to shove their ideas down my throat."

"But I'm not just anyone. I want to come out to see you."

"I don't know. Sawa is the one man who manages to get under my skin with a single word."

"What does the conductor have to do with me coming out?"

"I don't want you caught up in that, not in your condition. It's between me and him."

"You shouldn't worry about me," she said. "I handle much worse here."

"You're right. I'm sorry. Anyway, what did Miller say about the leave?"

Savanna pushed into her forehead with her fingers. She'd rather not talk about Miller. Dr. Wade might not even know about her leave. They had been working together on the occasional Saturday, and for some reason, which she couldn't name, she hadn't wanted to raise the subject with him.

"Savanna? Have you brought up the leave like we discussed?"

"I'm working on it."

"What does that mean?"

"Things are a bit crazy here now. That's why my leave was cancelled in the first place."

"But you will bring it up, right?"

"I will. In the meantime, we've got some weekends."

"I would much prefer if you could get a date for when you're coming out."

She sighed. "Can we talk about the renovations for the nursery?"

"Only if it doesn't include your father coming down to Westbury."

"With things as they are, I think we'll have to tell him sooner than later."

"Just a bit longer. It's all I'm asking."

"If you don't want me to come out this weekend, when will I see you…" Savanna paused and squeezed her eyes shut. The hole in her chest seemed to grow wider as the weeks slipped by. She fought for control. "It's harder than I thought it would be."

"If that's how you feel." The steel in his voice chilled her before he finished his statement. "Why don't I just call off the tour and come home?" he asked.

His manipulation hacked through Savanna like a single blow from a dull axe.

"I've been more than understanding since you left," she said. "I've given you the time you needed and sacrificed my own plans. All I ask in return is that we take some time out for our marriage." She swiped at her wet face with the back of her hand.

He cleared his throat. "You're right," he said, then paused longer than before. "Did you get the flowers I sent? You never said anything about them."

She sighed. Richard apologized with flowers. "Didn't I? I meant to. They were nice."

"Look," he said. "I don't want you getting involved in the drama out here. Regina isn't a good place to visit. We're moving on to Edmonton in two weeks. Meet me there."

"Two weeks?"

"Yes. It's not that long."

"This weekend would work much better."

"But I need you with me in Edmonton. I'd like you in the audience when I play that city."

She held her breath. Edmonton was Richard's hometown, and though they had never visited together, he returned a few times during their marriage on family business. She breathed into the growing heaviness in her stomach. A couple weeks delay was better than not seeing him at all.

"Okay," she said and sank into the couch. "I'll meet you in Edmonton."

Chapter 26

FROM THE MOMENT SAVANNA met Richard, his sensitive nature and adoring attention intrigued her. She admired the way he committed his strength to shield the people in his life from grief and worry.

The Spring of 2008 was especially wet and the rain lasted through the summer. She had accompanied Miller to the home of a deceased older man. The address was in the Old North block—so called because of its proximity to the Thames River. A man in his late fifties had died in his sleep.

The Coroner's Office received the call at 8:00 a.m. that morning. They arrived in the coroner's van at 8:20 a.m. It turned out that Miller had known the deceased.

Savanna was already dressed in her full forensic gear and clutched her hair cap when they drove up to the residence.

They backed into the cobblestone driveway and parked between the ambulance and a black Range Rover aligned on the far side of the driveway in front of a three-car garage. The house was a sprawling Victorian two-storey family residence.

A woman dressed in a pale blue uniform met them at the front door. She held her hands under her breasts as though she supported a baby. Her face released a bit of the tightness when she greeted them.

"Good morning, Daisy," Miller had said. "This is my assistant, Savanna Jones."

"Good morning, Mr. Miller. Miss Jones."

"I'm sorry for your loss," Savanna said.

She peered at Savanna through tear-filled eyes and nodded, then showed them into the house through a large oak door. The home felt warm and smelled of bacon and freshly brewed coffee.

"This way," Daisy had said. "Mrs. Brewster is in the morning room with Mr. Reeves. He came as soon as I called him."

They followed her into the rear of the house. The morning room was an atrium bathed in soft light and offered a view of the well-manicured backyard.

A woman sat in one of the six plush armchairs surrounding an elegant round mahogany table. She held a handful of tissues to her face with one hand. The other hand gripped the man's who sat in front of her, their knees barely touching.

"Mrs. Brewster," the maid announced. "Mr. Miller from the Coroner's Office is here."

The man patted the widow's fingers. "It's time," he whispered. At first, Savanna saw him only from behind. He wore beige linen pants and a matching shirt. The shirt wasn't tucked in. His damp blonde hair grazed his neck.

He turned to them, still clasping the woman's hand. His fingers started to turn white, probably from Mrs. Brewster's pressure. Something about the way he encouraged her to cry and hold on to him seemed endearing to Savanna. "Are you Scott Miller?" he asked.

Miller stepped forward. "Yes. Whatever we can do to make this process easier on the family."

"I'm Reeves, Richard Reeves," he said with no explanation of his connection to the Brewsters.

Mrs. Brewster must have recognized Miller's voice. She pushed from the chair. "Scott, thank you for coming," she practically wailed. "Carlton respected you."

"Marjorie." Miller took her hand. "You have my sincere condolences."

Richard stretched from the chair at that point. His linen shirt crumpled at the tail and Savanna remembered thinking that he probably would have tucked it if he had the time. His face, though flushed, was gentle and handsome. His clear skin creased slightly across the forehead. He looked about fifty.

She blushed when she met his blue eyes. He had been watching her inspect him.

"I'm glad he will be in your hands." Marjorie said to Miller and burst into tears again, then threw her arms around Richard's neck.

Savanna turned away and spoke to the maid. "Can you point me to Mr. Brewster please?"

"Up the stairs and to your right. The ambulance attendants are with him."

"Thank you."

When Savanna completed her routine check, the paramedics descended the stairs with the deceased.

A young man, whom Savanna recognized from the framed photos on the second floor, held Mrs. Brewster.

She guessed he was their son. He looked about Savanna's age and resembled his father. He watched longingly at the stretcher and body bag that housed his father but continued to support his mother.

Outside, as Savanna was about to climb into the coroner's van, Richard approached her. "Is it possible," he began, then paused and squeezed his nose bridge.

He was in pain too. She'd seen it so many times. The supporters holding a stiff posture, too afraid to breakdown. Savanna imagined they, too, wanted to wail like everyone else.

"I'm sorry for your loss," she had said.

"Thank you." Richard met her eyes. "Please forgive me."

"Nothing to forgive. Is there something I can do for you?"

"Is it possible for the family to see Carlton before the autopsy?"

She couldn't answer the way she wanted to and she sensed that he knew. "I'll see what I can do," she said. "If it's all right, I'll take your number and call you if it is at all possible. I will also call if I can't swing it, but I'll do my best."

A few days later, after the viewing, Richard shook her hand and said how much he appreciated her kindness.

"Are you related?" she had asked.

"No. He was my manager for fifteen years."

That's when Savanna noticed his fingers. Long and delicate, though masterful. He shook her hand, and she felt his strength support her as though she was the grieving widow.

His index finger caressed her skin. Each stroke started a new flutter down her spine.

She tried to ease her fingers from his grip. "Goodbye, Mr. Reeves," she said.

He smiled, without releasing his grasp. "Promise that the next time we meet, you'll call me, Richard."

Her face grew hot under his inspection. He seemed so charming and sophisticated. The next day she downloaded his recording of Beethoven's Moonlight Sonata and listened to it at bedtime.

A month later, long after she had put Carlton Brewster out of her mind and moved onto the other victims on her roster, two dozen long-stem red roses arrived. She'd called to thank him, but Richard couldn't talk. He was at the airport about to board a flight.

The following week she bumped into him in the forensic services building lobby as she rushed for the elevator.

"They said you were out on a call," he said and took her hand so gently, she hadn't realized she gave it to him. "I wanted to wait."

But she couldn't talk with him. Not then. Her father had been rushed to the hospital and admitted right away. The doctor said that they needed to operate immediately. His prostate had become inflamed and needed to come out.

She had been so distraught at the time, she told Richard everything. "I need to go to him." She bit her lip to stop the tears.

He squeezed her hand and said, "I'll come with you." On their trip back a week later, she asked him why he dropped everything in his life and flew to Vancouver just to hold her hand.

"I couldn't leave you alone. I wanted to show up for you, the way you show up for everyone else."

Chapter 27

———————

A TEXT MESSAGE CHIMED on Savanna's BlackBerry as she pulled into a parking space under Janet's apartment building.

Use your key. I'm heading into the shower.

Savanna wanted to surprise Janet with her baby news while they were out shopping, but her friend worked the night before and traded running errands for a few more hours of sleep.

It was a beautiful mid-June day and Savanna enjoyed walking around the market, wearing sandals and a simple white dress that flowed around her body. She took her time searching for the perfect gift for Janet.

A few minutes later she arrived at Janet's door, key in hand. *Oh, It's You Again.* The quote printed on the doormat could have been written by its owner. Janet howled with excitement the day they found it at the flea market.

"To let Rick know he's not welcome," she said. Rick was her ex-husband.

Savanna balanced her packages in one hand and inserted the

key. She'd used it once when she threw Janet a surprise birthday party for her thirtieth. Eight friends piled into the apartment. They hid in the reach-in closet, the tub with the shower curtain pulled, and the small space beside Janet's bed.

Savanna turned the key, but the door swung away from her grasp. Janet, still wrapped in towels like she'd just emerged from a Turkish bath smiled at her. "What is all this stuff?" She grabbed a couple of bags.

Still carrying two packages, Savanna entered and bumped the door closed. As usual, Janet's home smelled like oranges and cinnamon. Savanna inhaled and slipped from her shoes. "Hmmm," she said. "Just the remedy to rid my nostrils of hydrogen peroxide." She released her packages on the small dining room table.

Janet reached for a hug. "I thought you skipped town with that handsome G.I. you left in my care a few weeks ago."

Savanna's face burned to her surprise and she planted a kiss on Janet's cheek to hide her flushing. "I picked up some coffee and milk," she said hoping to distract Janet from her line of thought.

"How'd you know I was out?"

"You're—"

"Wait." Janet sniffed the air. "Do I smell Max's bread?"

"You do." Savanna had called in a takeout lunch order at Fran's Diner, their favourite place in the city to eat. Savanna and Rebecca were regulars. More than regulars. Recently, Janet frequented the diner on Saturday afternoons when Max was working.

"You know how to treat a friend in need," Janet said, digging into the lunch bags. She unwrapped the pre-sliced bread first. Still warm, the fresh crusty flavour sent them both into a brief trance.

Janet popped a piece into her mouth and laid her palm over her heart.

Savanna knew not to speak for another few seconds. She washed her hands at the kitchen sink and reached into the cupboard for plates.

"He's working today?" Janet asked after she recovered.

Max, kickboxing instructor extraordinaire, student and bartender, turned bread baker, worked at Fran's for the last six months. His employment at the restaurant had led to an increase in the female clientele.

"He said I should say hello." Savanna laid out the chicken wraps and salad.

"Why is that boy teasing me?" Janet said. Her crush on Max had no logical explanation. She even confessed once to stalking him at the gym a couple times.

"If only he was ten years older," she said dreamily. "The things I could do with him."

"Age has never stopped you before."

"In this case it does. He's too young."

Max was twenty-three and a first-year medical student at Westbury U, specializing in Health and Fitness Science. He'd taken kinesiology as an undergrad. According to him, he kept his life balanced by picking up the odd low-stress talent. His baking was Savanna's latest favourite.

Janet headed down the short hall to her bedroom. "Let me get changed," she said.

It had been a few months since Savanna visited the apartment. She looked around at the soft silver-grey walls they painted three years ago. They held up well and really popped with the bright cobalt blue trims. Rather than art, Janet's life in framed photographs and self-made crafts decorated her 800 by 900-foot home. Savanna appeared in a few of the photos.

The small space suited Janet just fine. Her salary stretched to keep her studies up-to-date with medical technology, maintain her mother's nursing home care, and pay her monthly half of the mortgage. Rick had convinced Janet that she needed to continue the payments if she wanted to split the profits when he finally sold their house.

"I have a great idea," Janet yelled from the bedroom. "Since Miller cancelled your leave, how about we fly out to Victoria and drive up to Tofino. I've been saving for a room at the Wickannish Inn. The beach is one of my favourite places on the planet." She walked out in bright pink jumper shorts, strutting her gangly body, pale legs and swinging arms in need of a tan.

"Well, you could use the sun." Savanna grinned.

"How'd you get so evil?"

"It's baked in, like my tan."

Janet glared.

"The trip out west could work if I coordinate it with Richard's travel plans," Savanna said. "He's playing Vancouver and Victoria."

Janet sat across from her at the round glass table. "We'd have to take some of Patti's chilli and Max's bread for the road trip."

Savanna's mouth watered at the thought. "How do you suppose we'd keep the food fresh during the flight?"

"You are complicating matters. Let me dream for a bit, will ya?"

"I'll definitely come if you promise we can stop for ice cream at that convenience store in Whiskey Creek."

"Would your Lieutenant-Colonel give you the time off?"

"My Lieutenant-Colonel? He's not my Lieutenant-Colonel."

Janet looked at her and grinned. "Thou doth protest too much."

Savanna's temperature rose under her friend's prodding. "I can find out his situation and set you up," she said trying to divert the heat.

Janet's eyes widened. "With him?" she asked.

"If there's no Mrs. Wade ready to bitch slap Westbury's single women away from her man, you can slip right in there. What do you say?"

Janet's shock softened into a dreamy expression. "He is quite dishy. A hero and saviour all rolled into one. Hmm."

"I thought you would like that."

"When he came back to see me—"

"He came back to see you?"

"How else would I check on his wound?"

"He's a doctor, Janet. Whatever he came back for had nothing to do with that wound."

"Yeah, I thought of that. He's so delectable I didn't care. Actually, I'd hoped he was smitten with yours truly. I fawned all over him, asking questions. You know, about a family, to get the low-down."

"So, does he have one?"

"He buttoned down tighter than a strait jacket. Wouldn't say a word until I mentioned your name, then he wanted to know it all."

"What? You told him about me?"

Janet bit into her wrap and made Savanna wait while she chewed. "Let me see," she said wiping her mouth. Her eyes rolled to the ceiling. "I gave him your full name." She started counting off on her fingers. "Your address, your schedule and the little tidbit that your husband is gone for months."

Savanna stared so wide, her head started to hurt. "Janet." Her voice was a mere whisper. "Please tell me you're kidding."

"Of course I'm kidding. What do you take me for?"

"Whew." Savanna smacked her arm. "Why do you have to scare me like that?"

"Wait one goddam minute. How come you haven't figured out if he's part of a set?"

They both reached for the bread. Savanna shoved a piece into her mouth. Buttery soft with the perfect crust. She hoped the baby like freshly baked bread, because she couldn't live without it.

"Well?" Janet asked.

"Sorry. Been too busy butting heads."

"You know, that story of how you guys ended up in the cheese barn together, working on the same investigation, is freaky."

Savanna nodded while she chewed and reached for the basket again.

Nicholas Wade wouldn't agree that they were investigating the same issue. Whenever she asked him about his visit to the cheese barn, he straightened those broad shoulders and insisted that the cases didn't connect. He said that either she or her source was mistaken. Then he clammed up, or changed the subject as though she asked him to sell the secret plans for the new Canadian armoured tank.

She didn't care much for the military way of sharing information.

"You and him not getting on?" Janet asked.

"I think they teach that at the officers' military academy?"

Savanna sat back to put some distance between her and the bread. "Not to worry though. He'll come around." She grinned.

"You've got something up your sleeve," Janet reached for more bread. "Come on. Dish it out."

"Well, I do have some news. I'm pregnant."

Janet froze. "Get out," she said and within the next second her eyes pooled with tears. "Oh God," she said. "You're not kidding. I'm so happy for you." She reached for Savanna's hands. "How far along are you now?" she asked.

"Almost ten weeks."

"Aww. Are you happy?" she asked.

Savanna wrapped her fingers around Janet's. "I'm scared," she said.

"I'm not going to say you shouldn't be, since that wouldn't change a thing. I'll check in often. And call me if there's anything strange."

"Thank you. I will."

"That's the happiest news ever. You've brightened my day."

"It's still a secret. Only you, Rebecca and Richard know. I haven't said anything at work yet."

"Really?"

"Richard wants us to keep the news quiet for now."

"Why so hush-hush?"

"He wants the tour to take centre stage, I guess. For now."

"Your dad will be so happy."

Savanna avoided Janet's gaze. "I know. I have to call him."

"Richard wants you to keep the news of the baby from him too?"

"For now."

"What's his excuse for that?"

The question pricked Savanna. "Come on, Janet. You know how these things work."

She'd lost a baby two years into her marriage and Rick never wanted to try again.

"Do I?" she asked. "Refresh my memory."

"You want to get into that safe zone before you go broadcasting the news. Then if something happens you wouldn't have to bear that 'oh you poor thing' expression from everyone you told."

"And you're lumping your dear old dad in with everyone?"

"Don't be cross with me now, please. I don't think I can stand another tongue lashing."

Janet patted her hand. "I can only imagine how hard it is for you. Richard away and you puking in the morning and hiding it from your boss, the doctor." Janet sat back. "What a load." She screwed up her eyes.

Savanna started to laugh. She laughed so hard, tears ran down her cheeks and she sputtered food across the table. When she felt a cold sprinkle hit her face, her fit stopped. She looked up.

"That was me, you silly goose," Janet said. "You were going to suffocate right in front of my eyes."

"You don't know how relieved I am to finally laugh at all this."

"Good. Now don't let this little secret of yours turn your life upside down when two little words would save you all the trouble."

Savanna flinched.

"Plus, a few weeks might be all you have."

Savanna's hand flew to her stomach. "Can you see anything? Am I showing?"

"Not in your body. Your cheeks are a bit rosy, but I thought that was your Lieutenant-Colonel making you blush like he did the night you brought him in."

That again. "Would you stop? He doesn't make me blush."

"You should watch out. There's definite chemistry between you two."

"If you don't stop teasing me, I'll keep the gift I bought for you."

Janet pinched her thumb and index finger together and touched them to her lips, then turned. Locked or not she couldn't stop grinning.

Savanna handed her the bag from the corner of the table.

Janet opened the gift. "My own baby care package." She was tearing up again.

"Just what every godmother needs," Savanna said.

Chapter 28

IT WAS JUST AFTER 0400 hours, Sunday morning on Canada Day. Nicholas was already leaving Exeter where he'd spent the night casing a few bars. Now he made a U-turn and headed west again. When he turned onto Huron Street, Exeter's water tower came into view against the dark sky.

"I prefer if you came out and take a look, Doctor," Detective Thomas had said. "I didn't call forensic dispatch. I thought you might want to see this one."

With Savanna out of town until tomorrow, Nicholas took the trip alone. Exeter's connection to his investigation had gone as far as the cheese barn and then back to Westbury. This call, he hoped, had nothing to do with it.

The GPS directed him to the same hospital he visited with Savanna two months ago. He knew he had found the right place when he circled the building and yellow tape and police cruisers blocked his entrance to the hospital's rear parking lot. Several reporters had already descended on the crime scene. They stood outside the tape ready with devices.

Police floodlights lit the twenty by thirty-foot parking lot. He drove past the cars lining the street and parked in the next free spot.

Before leaving the car, he slipped forensic booties over his shoes and shoved a cap and latex gloves into his pocket.

Dave Thomas walked toward him wearing a blue latex glove on his left hand. His ever-present rumpled appearance seemed to disguise the well-built body beneath the wrinkled clothes. Nicholas was sure he played a contact team sport, probably basketball.

Right away, Nicholas could tell that something heavy weighed on him.

"Hey, Doc," Thomas stuck out his bare hand to greet Nicholas.

"Good morning, Detective," Nicholas said.

They headed toward the crime scene. "You got here in less time than I expected. I thought the trip would have taken another half hour."

"Was already in the neighbourhood."

"I see," Thomas said, looking puzzled.

Nicholas wasn't about to explain.

Thomas was silent while they got closer to the parking lot. He halted his steps. Nicholas stopped walking and turned to face him. He waited. This was Thomas's show.

"Doc," the detective finally said. "I've always wanted to ask, what makes an army doctor choose pathology as a specialty? Don't you see enough death?"

A philosophical police officer. Interesting. "I was in medical school when I realized that the dead taught us how to live better lives. Once I understood one death, I wanted to understand them all."

Thomas was silent for a while, as if waiting for more. Then he flicked a palm toward Nicholas. "That's it?" he asked.

"That's it, Detective."

He looked toward the pavement, then back at Nicholas and nodded. "Thanks for coming out," he said.

"Am I right in assuming this is out of your jurisdiction?"

"A buddy from the Ontario Provincial Police is working this one. He called me. Our time here is limited."

"You said the victim is from Westbury?" Two uniformed officers parted the growing crowd to let them into the crime scene.

"Yes," Thomas said. "Used to be on staff at Westbury General."

Nicholas nodded.

Thomas led him toward the blue tarp. "I wanted you to see her. A connection to one of our recent victims is rather uncanny."

So far, Thomas said only that the victim used to work in Westbury.

"Anything you can tell us would be helpful," Thomas said.

Nicholas met his gaze. "I'll do my best."

The only car in the lot was parked two spots to the right of the body and a few yards from the entrance. Four people stood close by waiting to attend the body. The two wearing white jumpsuits, complete with hoods and blue booties, carried on a conversation. The other two, wearing green overalls, held folded white sheets, presumably for the body, and some paper bags to secure the hands and feet.

"Detective Barry Reynolds," Thomas said. "Dr. Wade, Westbury Forensics."

Nicholas shook hands with one of the men wearing a white suit. Between the black-framed eyeglasses and the mask with a crimp across the nose bridge, Nicholas couldn't make out his features, except for the acne covering his forehead.

"Good to meet you, Detective," he said.

"Doc." He pumped Nicholas's arm.

"Dr. Wade," the other man offered Nicholas his hand. "Gerald Lisp, City Coroner." Lisp stood about four inches shorter than both Nicholas and Thomas.

"Good morning, Doctor," Nicholas said.

Lisp pointed at the body. "Detective Thomas said you dealt with a case with a similar characteristic."

Nicholas took the question as an invitation to lift the tarp. He snapped on his gloves and stooped next to the body. He pinched the blue plastic between two fingers and lifted it.

The victim was positioned on the back with her face turned away from him. Nicholas noted the similarity immediately. Her arms lifted above her head in a permanent surrender position. Dark purple bruises circled her neck. Her blue scrubs were ripped at the collar, probably during a struggle. Her left leg was awkwardly bent with the knee turned inward.

Jet-black hair showed signs that the victim had the rare hair condition known as poliosis. The Mallen streak above the decease's right eye almost knocked him onto his heels. He stared at what he could see of her face, hoping to be mistaken. He dropped his eyes to her chest. The badge still clung to her breast pocket. Nicholas lifted it with his index finger. He wasn't mistaken. Cold fingers clawed at his neck. He stiffened against the chill. Janet Whateley. How could this be possible?

He touched three fingers to the side of her calf, up from her ankle. The muscle was firm, evidence of long hours on her feet, but not yet affected with rigor mortis. He felt her jaw. The thin face that smiled at Savanna was rigid now.

"She's been dead less than twelve hours," he said.

"Yes," Dr. Lisp said. "My early estimation places time of death between 11:30 and 12:30 last night."

"Was she working?"

"Was scheduled for the graveyard—" Detective Reynolds started to say.

Nicholas looked up at him.

"Ah… midnight shift," he corrected. "But traded with a colleague. Started at 3:00 yesterday afternoon and clocked out at 11:15 last night."

Nicholas turned back to Janet's body. *And dead fifteen minutes later.* Someone had waited for her. He was about to release the tarp, then recalled something else Savanna noted in their other victims. He sniffed the body. *No cortisone.*

He released the tarp and pushed to his feet. "The missing hand is definitely similar to our landfill victim," he said to Dr. Lisp.

Lisp nodded.

"If you don't mind," Detective Reynolds said. "I would love to see your notes on the victim."

"Certainly, Detective," Nicholas snapped off the gloves. He met Thomas's gaze.

Now he must break the news to Savanna.

Chapter 29

The morning after Richard's last performance at the Winspear Centre, Savanna stood on a small wooden deck watching dark clouds roll across the lake. Towering evergreen trees swayed in the wind. Their needles scented the morning air with sweet pine. She felt more contented than she had in the past few months.

Last night, she and Richard mingled at the symphony's after party long enough to shake hands with the conductor. Then Richard whisked her to an awaiting Range Rover.

"Where are we going?" she'd asked.

A mysterious smile was his only response.

"I'm not very good with suspense," she said.

He replied by squeezing her hand and raising her fingers to his lips, then soothed her with a be-patient glance.

Forty-five minutes later they arrived at Spring Lake. High tide crashed against the dock of a tiny log cabin. A roaring fire, chilled champagne and hors d'oeuvres set the mood for a romantic end to their evening.

Richard surprised her with a world removed from her life in Westbury. This morning the wind zipped through the wide armholes in the t-shirt she wore, but now the water had calmed to a trickle between the rocks.

The sun warmed half of her body. The left side shivered from the cool breeze. How long could she bear to stand in the chill, wearing nothing but Richard's t-shirt?

The goosebumps on her left arm reminded her of the childhood stunt that tested her endurance. In minus ten-degree temperatures at Red Mountain Resort in BC where she and her father spent a week every year, she'd lasted an entire minute before her father found her. He wrapped her in a blanket and hauled her back into the cabin to nestled next to the fire.

She rubbed her arm now. Soon, they will tell him about the baby soon. He and Richard were all the family she had. A great-aunt still lived in Brazil. Savanna hadn't seen the woman since her mother's funeral.

To complicate matters, her father had never really warmed to Richard. "Why?" he asked the day she introduced them. "He's so much older than you."

She detected more of a distrustful undercurrent to his reaction. When she prodded him, he'd reached for her hand and said, "You've always got me." For the last four years, she had stood between them. Their love for her was the only common bond.

Savanna breathed in fresh air and pine forest. Pouring their love into a baby could change everything. She exhaled, letting her hopes soar with the wind.

"Marty's expecting us at the hotel for lunch," Richard said from behind her.

She turned her head just as he slipped his arms around her waist and kissed her neck. "I know you like it up here," he said.

She smiled and nodded. "With you, and no crime scenes calling for my attention."

"Hmm. Then tell me, why did I catch you touching the small patch of mould next to the shower an hour ago? Feeling it between your fingers and sniffing it?"

She leaned into him and laughed. "Guilty."

"Can take the girl away from forensics, but…" Richard nuzzled her neck again. "Let's pack up," he said.

"Another hour, please."

"Hmm." He lifted a hand and pointed toward the lake. "See that?" he asked, indicating the darkening clouds. "I'd like to be back in town before it starts."

She frowned, then turned and tilted her face close to his. In the six weeks since she'd seen him, his hair had gotten more silver, setting off his stark blue eyes. He now sported a soft grey beard mixed with dark blonde and resembled Donald Sutherland even more. "Okay," she said. "You win, but only because I hate driving in the rain."

He threaded his fingers with hers and they stepped through the patio door. Cozy warmth crackled in the fireplace and melted the goosebumps from her bare legs.

Savanna took in the cabin's main room. She blushed. Her amethyst evening dress hung over the back of the rustic leather couch. Her stockings dangled from the moose's antlers and her sling-back pumps spent the night on a small coffee table.

She walked around the room retrieving them. "I thought I would strip the spare room closest to our bedroom and prepare it for the baby," she said. "What do you think?"

"Really?" was Richard's only reply.

Savanna grabbed her overnight bag from the floor next to the entrance. "Since you're gone for the next few months, Dad would be more than willing to come down and help me with the project. He practically demoed his house before the reno crew came in."

When Richard didn't respond, she looked up to see him staring at her and rubbing his temples. He dropped his eyes and started pacing.

Her lower back muscles quivered. "What's wrong?" she asked.

He slowed his steps. "We talked about this," he said. "We were going to wait."

"Yes, I know, but I've been trying to tell you for the past few weeks that I can't get the leave in time. Waiting isn't going to work."

"Are you sure? Because I'm not ready."

"I will be too far along by the time I do get some time. It's best to tell him now."

Richard started to move around the small cabin, weaving between the furniture and returning to stand only a few steps from her before he started again. "I need…I need…"

She wondered if she would like what he was trying to say. "Are you worried about the renovations?" she asked.

"What have you told Kenneth already?"

"Just that we want to invite him to one of your concerts."

Richard marched over to the patio door. "I want to talk to you about something," he said. His voice strained and she felt his wall going up.

He kept his back to her.

"What's that?" she asked.

"Well, Marty is talking about adding some tour dates."

Her stomach clenched. "More? How many?"

"There are about six cities, but the number of venues is uncertain at this point." He turned to face her then. His expression was as rigid as his voice.

"Six more cities?" she asked. "How long will that take?"

"A few months, at least. The whole thing could take us into the new year."

"That's five months. You're due home in September."

"Marty thinks the extra concerts will be good for my career. Clayton agrees."

Clayton Bell had been Richard's record producer for his last album.

"And you, Richard?" she asked. "What do you think?"

"Well, this could be my last real shot."

"Last shot?" Her composure was starting to waver. She wanted to shake Richard into reality. "The baby is due in December. If you extend, it's possible…" She patted her belly before continuing. "You will miss our child's birth. Are you sure about this?"

"I think it would be best."

"Best to go away for the entire length of my pregnancy?"

He stared at her for a moment. "I still don't understand why we need to have a child now," he said.

"Sorry, I must've missed something. What the fuck does that mean?"

"Don't swear. It doesn't suit you."

"Then don't tell me shit. What did you mean?"

"I meant this is my life too. Or have you forgotten that?"

"Of course I haven't."

"Then what gives you the right to commit me to this life sentence?"

"Are you serious? Do you think I immaculately conceived this child?"

Richard's nostrils flared. "It's always you, Savanna," he said. "Now you and this damn child are hurrying me into old age."

"Damn child?"

"Do you really think this is what we need right now?"

"Need right now? What changed from a few days ago when you said you wanted this?"

"I said I needed you. I've decided children wouldn't work for me."

Savanna narrowed her eyes, squinting Richard into focus. "You've decided? Wh… What does that mean?

"It means that without so much as a single thought for me, you arranged my future to suit you. Now my life is inundated with responsibility."

She lowered herself onto the edge of the leather armchair and sat with a straight spine. "Where is all this coming from?" she asked.

"Did you once think of whether or not this would work for me?"

"Yes, I thought of you. I'm always thinking of you."

"If that were true, I would come first, not your father, not your job, and certainly not some baby."

Savanna pressed her lips together. She was tired of fighting back tears. Reasoning this out rather than crying would help Richard to see her point of view. "The baby doesn't change my love for you," she said. "And this has nothing to do with my father."

"Can you deny that this child will pull you away from me?"

Understanding dawned on her then. Richard was afraid of losing her to the baby. She pushed from the chair and crossed the room to him.

His chest heaved when she slid her palm down his arm and wrapped her fingers between his. She lifted his hand to her lips. The tears she had forgotten trickled onto his knuckles. "I know," she said. "I know the prospect of raising a child now might frighten you. But we're doing this together. Our child needs you as much as I do."

The deep ridges around his mouth softened.

She smoothed her hand across his cheek. "I've always loved your passion for life. Think how wonderful it would be to share your music and all the hard lessons you learned growing up as a child prodigy with our kids?"

"Don't, Savanna. Rather than patronizing me, I wish you would listen. When did you stop listening?"

"I'm listening, but you need to hear me too. This stage in your life is perfect for fatherhood," she persisted. "Your maturity gives you an edge on parenting most people wish and hope for."

"Come on, Savanna. You know me." He stepped away from her. "I can't share myself that way. What tenderness I have is for my music and you. Your job already intrudes on us too much."

"Is this about my time at the lab? After the baby comes, we can revisit moving to Vancouver. We can talk about it now if you want. I can always get another job there. Something less demanding with a smaller lab."

He studied her for a moment. "Why did you have to break your promise?" he asked.

"What promise?"

"When we lost the first one, you promised you'd always be with me. You promised to let nothing separate us."

"How is bearing your child breaking that promise?"

"The last thing I want… I ever wanted was to share my life and you with a helpless baby. After four years of marriage, how could you not know that I want nothing to do with children?"

"Then why did you ask me to marry you?"

"I wanted you, not the child. We don't need children. Our lives would be better without them."

"That hardly matters now. The baby is here."

"It isn't here, Savanna," he insisted. "This child wasn't meant to be, it's a mistake."

Savanna tried to speak, but her throat clogged. She swallowed and tried again. "You don't know what you're saying," she finally said.

"If you give birth to this child you'd never have time for me ever again."

A fiery ball rose in her throat. "You're… You're kidding right? Do you realize what you said?"

"Yes, yes I do. The child isn't here and it doesn't have to be."

"You don't mean that. I know you don't."

"Like hell I don't. It's not like you haven't done it before."

Blood rushed to her temples, blinding her for a moment. She ignored the faint patter from her heart and closed the gap between them.

They stood close enough to kiss.

She studied his face.

His blue eyes glinted with cold anger, but he said nothing more. *Was he truly the man she loved?*

"Tell me, you son of a bitch," she said. "If you're so sure about what you've always wanted, why didn't you get yourself fixed before we met, and saved us both the trouble?"

Part II

"Our scars make us know that our past was for real."

~ *Jane Austen*

Chapter 30

THE CREW FROM SAVANNA'S flight whipped past her in the busy Westbury airport. The terminal was especially crowded with holiday weekend travellers. Savanna could hardly see past the train of luggage carts ahead of her.

She hadn't decided yet where she would go. If she went home, she might just burn the place down. Maybe she could bend Janet's ear for a few hours, and then bunk on her couch for the night.

Savanna tried to slip past a family of four pushing two carts and a stroller with a whining toddler. She sympathized with the little guy. She felt like whining too.

A space opened up ahead, and she slipped into it. The procession moved slow. She soon found another path and sidestepped the group only to stop dead in her tracks. Oh, great. What was he doing here? Dr. Wade plotted a course through the crowd in her direction. She'd rather not deal with him now.

She dropped her chin and turned away from his path. Having progressed only two steps, she glanced back. He had already spotted her. As a matter of fact, his hazel glare tracked her every step. She might as well see what he wanted.

He reached her and stopped alarmingly close. "Good afternoon,

Ms. Jones." Rather than his usual firm military mien that always, well maybe not always, but mostly looked as though he was rejecting a happy disposition, he expressed concern, attentiveness almost. She didn't mind this calm demeanour.

"Dr. Wade, are you returning from a trip?"

"Not today. I spent a night in Ottawa on Friday and returned yesterday."

"Oh. Still trying to ditch us and get your old job back?" She was kidding, but the frown that crossed his face said he wasn't in the mood.

"Sorry," she said. "That's me, famous for awkward humour. Anyway, what brings you to the airport?"

"You."

"Me?"

"Yes, Savanna. I thought I'd give you a ride."

Savanna? She met his gaze full on. Those all-seeing hazel eyes watched her face grimace from surprise, then frowned from worry. He'd never used her first name before, not even in third-party conversations, at least not the ones she overheard. Why then did he choose now? Her first thought was her partner. "Is it Quinn?" She paused and started again. "Doctor, did you work with my partner this weekend?" Unlike him, she still needed to use their usual formality.

"No," her boss said, "we spoke briefly this morning."

"Is Quinn okay?"

"He's a bit annoyed that I insisted on coming to collect you, but he's fine."

She stared at him. "Surely I don't need to ask why you insisted on collecting me from the airport. Because you would volunteer that information right away since it is so unusual. When one's boss needs to insist on picking you up from the airport out of the blue, said boss should volunteer information as to why." She realized she was rambling, but her nerves were already shot from Richard's ultimatum, and now her boss was on a secret mission that pissed off her partner.

"Is your car here?" Dr. Wade asked.

Her chatter had gone on for some time without his interjection and the first question he could think to ask was about her car? Her unreliable ten-year-old car.

"No," she said. "I took a taxi."

"Good." He reached for her bag. When she wouldn't release it, he took her forearm instead. "That makes it easy," he said. "Like I said, I'll give you a ride."

Savanna went along, letting him guide her since she wasn't sure she would follow him otherwise. When she first spotted him walking toward her, one of the phenomenal things she noticed was how people cleared a path for him. It was that bizarre effect that she took advantage of now.

He was already behind the wheel of the lab's Chrysler and directing them down the spiral parking garage to the exit when he finally spoke.

"I have some disturbing news and I just wanted to make sure you were sitting down first before I told you."

A lump immediately formed in her chest. Notwithstanding the fact that she was a forensic scientist who investigated crime scenes, when it came to bad news Savanna reacted like everyone else. She went mute with dread giving way to the loud thuds in her chest. No, she would not look at the bearer of this bad news.

"I'm ready now," she said.

"I'm afraid your friend Janet Whateley is dead."

"What? No, no. That can't be true."

"I'm afraid it is."

"Stop the car." She wasn't sure where they were in the circular maze of the parking garage. "Stop the car."

"We've already stopped. We're in queue for the machine."

"Never mind then. Keep going. I want to get out of here anyway."

Savanna threaded her hands in her lap, still not looking at him. A cry escaped her throat and she cupped a palm over her mouth. "Are you sure you've got the right person, Doctor?" The question burst from her in a maddening explosion.

He turned his head and there in that single glance sympathy and compassion replaced his usual rigid expression.

"I was at the crime scene," he said. "I saw her."

"Where is she now?"

"In South Huron's morgue. I can take you there."

"Yes. Thank you. Please, take me there." She spoke to Janet on Friday night. They planned to shop for the baby next week. Nicholas Wade had to be wrong. "What happened?" she asked. "Did it happen on the job? An accident or something?" But it couldn't be. He said crime scene.

"Not an accident, Ms. Jones," he said. "We… The police believe she was murdered

Chapter 31

NICHOLAS WADE PULLED THE car into one of the free spots at the main entrance in front of South Huron Hospital. Savanna sat frozen, while the four words—Janet Whateley is dead—registered through her body, weakening every muscle. It was the same feeling that travelled with her all the way from Edmonton.

"I thought the trip would take longer," she said.

Dr. Wade reached for her hand. He wrapped his long fingers around hers. "I'm sorry," he said.

Her breath heaved in her chest. "Do you have a paper bag?" Her eyes stung. "I think I'm going to hyperventilate." She swiped several times at the silent tears rolling down her cheeks, but she couldn't stop them.

"Here," he said. "Let me." He raised his hand to her face with a handkerchief wrapped around his fingers.

The one he offered her in the landfill a couple of months ago still nestled among her clean laundry. She wanted to iron it before she returned it to him. She blinked until her vision cleared to reveal his pained expression studying her.

"We can sit here as long as you want," he said.

If she did, for a bit anyway, she wouldn't be weeping when she saw Janet. The first time they met almost eight years ago, Janet found her crying in the corner of the rape-victim's ward and wiping her eyes with a used tissue.

"Are you okay?" she'd asked and handed Savanna a handful of tissues.

Savanna grabbed them. "Never mind me," Savanna said. "Look after her." She motioned behind her to the teen she and Quinn brought in. Only fifteen and gang raped by a bunch of college students.

"Is this your first rape?" Janet had asked.

Savanna blew her nose and looked up at the nurse. She was older by about five years with a small pointy face, focused blue eyes and black wavy hair. The white lock at her hairline, just over her left eye, was a few decades out of style, but it suited her.

"I'm Janet Whateley, ER nurse."

"Savanna Jones, Westbury Forensics, Criminal Division."

"I've seen you around," Janet said. "Quinn tells me he's showing you the ropes, but I get the feeling it's the other way around."

Savanna smirked. "That's what I keep telling him."

"Look, feeling sympathy for these kids never goes away, but handling cases like this gets easier. You harden yourself against the tough ones. You have to. It's the only way to help them. And the only way to survive."

Janet was always someone's hero. Where was everyone else when she needed help?

Savanna wiped her eyes with her boss's handkerchief again. "No," she said to him and pushed his hand away. Shedding tears wasn't all she would do for Janet. "I'm going in now."

It was another twenty minutes before the technician rolled Janet's body to the viewing window where they waited. The only other time she stood on that side of the viewing window, she was seventeen years old. Her mother had been murdered the same day Savanna flew to Brazil to visit her.

The sheet over Janet's body was already neatly folded to her shoulders. Her face, bruised and swollen, somehow managed to look peaceful, gentle even. *So as we live, so shall we die.* Every time she faced a senseless death, Savanna quoted her father. He kept verses from the bible stockpiled in his head for every occasion.

Savanna wished Janet would wake up and tell her it was all a hoax. But nothing she hoped for, or said, or did, could bring her friend back.

The preliminary exam had already been done. The technician had combed Janet's hair. The white forelock lay obediently in place with the rest of Janet's jet-black waves. The Mallen streak had normally stood out as though she bleached it.

"It has always been that way," Janet had said when Savanna asked six years ago. "And sometimes, I colour it in, but recently, I let it be."

Recently had been after her divorce, which became final around the time she and Savanna started hanging out after work.

Savanna turned away from the window and headed toward the door. She couldn't stand there watching like some bystander. She needed to know what killed her friend.

"Ms. Jones?" Nicholas Wade's voice called from behind her. "Are you ready to leave now?"

"I'm going in there." She kept walking. She sensed him behind her. His unobtrusive manner and military covert training kept his movements quiet.

She opened the door to the adjacent room. The morgue technician, who busied himself on the opposite side of the glass a moment ago, met them at the threshold when she stepped in.

"I'm sorry, Miss," he said. "I can't allow you in here."

Savanna looked past him. She entered and went straight to Janet's body. "Yes, you can," she said. "It's okay."

"We're with Westbury Forensics," her boss said.

But Savanna stopped listening. She stood over Janet gazing down at her. She wanted to stroke the lucky streak of hair. She lifted the sheet from Janet's shoulders and heard the technician hurry toward her at the same time she heard his protest.

"You can't do that," he barked.

Savanna still didn't turn around to look at them. She wanted to fold the sheet down to the waist and search Janet's body as diligently as she had searched Suzette Morgan's and Theresa Filito's. But, how could she? Janet was discreet. Exposing her in the presence of two strange men disrespected her privacy.

Nicholas Wade came to stand next to her. "There is something you should know," he said.

She met his gaze, not sure she wanted to hear any more. In fact, she wanted to start this day over. If there was such a thing as multiple dimensions, she wanted to wake up in another one. She would choose the life where her husband didn't walk away, where her father actually knew about his grandchild, and her friend, the most kind-hearted woman she had ever known, was still alive and embracing her in a hug, rather than lying here on this damn metal table with a brick under her neck.

"You might want to take a look at this," Dr. Wade said and pulled something from his pocket. "I got this off the crime scene photographer."

She released the sheet and took the photo he handed her. It was Janet's body at the crime scene. Her arm had been amputated just above the wrist.

Savanna cupped her hand over her mouth and bolted from the room.

Chapter 32

ICHOLAS FOLLOWED SAVANNA INTO the corridor. She slipped into the ladies' room down the hallway from the viewing room. He waited outside.

That morning he'd practically bullied Quinn into letting him meet Savanna at the airport. Nicholas won the argument because he raised the point that he knew more about what killed Janet, knowing that Savanna would demand details right away. Eventually Quinn backed down.

When Nicholas first spotted her, fighting her way through the congested airport, she looked scared. He wondered then if Quinn had already gotten a message to her. He increased his pace then. Once they arrived at the hospital, he had been glad he coerced Quinn into relenting.

Savanna came from the bathroom looking pale but composed. "Can we go to the lab?" she asked. "I mean… That's where I want to be dropped off."

"The lab? Are you sure? I would much prefer to drive you home."

She stared at her hand, then she started stroking it.

What should he do, or say? He had comforted grieving friends before. Why couldn't he find the right words to help her through this? "Savanna…" he began

She twisted her left wrist, forcing it into an unnatural position. He reached for her hands and folded his fingers around them. "Are you okay?"

She looked at him as though he'd just arrived. "What would it take to cut a hand off like that?" she asked. "So clean in one slice. What kind of force?"

Nicholas studied her puffy eyes that waited for his answer. She could be in shock. He needed to get her out of here. "A sharp blade of some kind, I think," he said. "Bigger than an average kitchen knife."

"What… What about the person wielding it? Strong would you say?"

"Stronger…" He held her gaze. No amount of sympathy could ease the torment in her expression. She tried to mask it with her curiosity, but the anguish trembled in her voice. Yet, if he refused to answer, she would leave him to find her own answers.

He met her gaze again. "With enough force and the right type of weapon," he continued. "Anyone from a strong teenager to an active senior could do it."

She nodded. "I don't think she knew anyone who would harm her in that way."

"How well did you know her?"

"We met when I got the job in the criminal division and started my partnership with Quinn. She was easy to talk to about the job. We could have blunt conversations about the strange and awful things people did to themselves and to other people. Janet always listened—" Savanna's tears started again. She turned her face away from him. "Not just to me," she said, "to everyone. She was a good person. Even her knucklehead ex thought so."

"I'm sorry you lost her," he said though he knew the words couldn't measure up.

She was silent for a while. "Before we head back to Westbury," she finally said. "I want to see the crime scene. Can you take me there?"

"Are you sure?"

"I've already seen her body. I can... I can handle where she died."

Still holding her hand, he led her to the exit.

She looked puzzled when he walked past the car but said nothing.

He took her to the rear of the hospital and into the parking lot. Visitors' parking usually spilled along the tree-lined street behind them, but not today. The police had restricted the area, and only one officer remained. The street was quieter than the last time he was there.

Savanna jerked to a stop when the yellow police tape and chalk outline came into view. She halted and stuck out a hand, blocking him from taking another step forward. "Was an Ident team here?" she asked.

"Yes, of course."

Her hand dropped to her side again and she stood staring at the spot. He couldn't tell if she was crying again. She stood motionless, with her back to him.

After a moment, she walked to where Janet's head would have rested. Savanna stooped and reached out, touching the pavement. Her chin dropped, and her body convulsed.

He hurried over and stood close by, giving her a moment. The time was coming up on 1500 hours. A warm day coming to a slow end. The sun's rays were dimming, but the humidity remained. It wasn't a day for mourning.

Savanna pushed to her feet abruptly. "Can we go to the lab now?" she asked.

"I would much rather take you home."

"No," she said, quicker than he expected. "I can't go there. Not tonight."

"Okay, but not the lab. You can do nothing there now. Let me take you to a friend's then."

"I'll go to Rebec— No. I..." She started to sob again, but stopped, brushing away tears and hardening her voice. "The lab," she said. "It's the only place I can go now." Her chin trembled again.

He stepped close and wrapped his arms around her. She rested her head on his chest. He had been in this position too many times. He recognized the signs. She wanted to run from the pain, turn it into work and make it go away. "I have a better idea," he said.

____

The time was coming up on 7:00 p.m. when Nicholas Wade slowed the lab's wagon in front a row of attractive brownstone townhouses. He skilfully aligned the vehicle into the only free spot on the street and then turned to her.

"Ready?" he asked.

The moment he suggested she spend the night at his house, she welcomed the idea as though it was the only sensible solution to her predicament. Nothing could find her there, not even the reality of her broken marriage.

She nodded.

He swung from behind the wheel. By the time she unfastened her seat belt and climbed from the car, he had already retrieved her overnight case and stood waiting for her. They stood together on the sidewalk with early-July heat sweltering in the air. Screeching laughter came from the children playing nearby. She tried to block it.

Janet loved children, though she never had any. She miscarried during the second year of her marriage and had kept trying. When it came time for Rick to get tested, he insisted that he had no problems and refused to see a doctor. She would have been a wonderful godmother.

A charge surged through Savanna's fingers and up her arm. She looked down to see Nicholas Wade's large fist grasping her hand. The numbness that paralyzed her in the last few hours melted. She clutched his fingers, welcoming their strength.

They mounted the steps to number ten. He held the door open for her. Savanna stepped into the narrow hallway and the children's laughter disappeared behind the closed door. Air-conditioned cool wiped the humidity from her skin.

She stood for a moment taking in the soaring high ceiling, exposed brick and large windows framed in soft, steel grey draperies. The evening sunlight reflected from the wooden rafters and softened the space.

She slipped from her sandals and stepped off the doormat onto the hardwood floor, then padded barefoot into the neatly furnished open-concept living-dining space. A walnut coffee table centred a patterned area rug. She dug her naked toes into it and sank onto the leather sofa that divided the two rooms. It faced a flat screen TV mounted over a gas fireplace.

She looked around for photographs. None were visible, just art. The most personal item seemed to be a worn reading chair positioned to her left with an ottoman stacked with books and some forensic lab files.

She leaned into the sofa. That familiar sandalwood scent enveloped her, and she curled her feet under her. "Your home is cozy, Dr. Wade."

He crossed the room and sat beside her. "I know how you dislike rules," he said. "But they've kept me safe for more than twenty years. So, rule number one, when we're in this house, no last names and no titles."

"Yes, sir."

"None of that either."

"Sorry, I wasn't mocking you—" She stopped talking and dropped her chin when the tears stung again. The eerie distance she felt from everything and everyone around her made her feel off balance.

She blinked away the tears and lifted her chin. "I appreciate your kindness," she said. "Thank you for bringing me here."

He pushed a loose strand of hair from her face and moved his fingers slowly across her cheek. "I'm here," he said.

Her skin flushed under his touch. An arousing tingle surged in her body.

"Whenever you need me," he said. "Just tell me what I can do to help you through this."

"Thank you."

"You and Janet seemed close."

Savanna had been lucky to have two close friends and a partner she trusted with her life. "We were, but in the last year, after she accepted the job in Exeter, we hardly saw each other though we spoke on the phone often."

"Distance can erode a friendship."

"We used to have a girls' night out once a month sometimes with Rebecca. We shared most everything in our lives." Savanna closed her eyes against the tears that trickled down her cheeks.

Nicholas scooted closer and wrapped her in his arms. Her back, where he stroked her gently, quivered under his touch.

She cuddled against his warm, firm muscles. "I need to do something," she said.

"Yes, I know, but not tonight."

She wasn't sure she agreed. Had the police contacted Rick yet? They would have. The spouse, especially an ex, was often the first person of interest in an adult homicide.

Savanna pushed away from Nicholas. "You know how important it is to get the jump on a crime such as this." She was growing angry now. Not necessarily at him, but they were sitting here while Janet's killer could be leaving town.

"I know," Nicholas said. "You know, and so do the police." His voice was calm, his expression understanding. "Let them handle it, especially since this happened outside our jurisdiction."

She got up from the sofa and walked across the room. She tilted her head back. The tears that started again trickled along the side of her face. When she lowered her head, her gaze rested on the two wooden slabs stretching the length of the wall. Nicholas used them as bookshelves.

"Did you bring much of you to Westbury, Doctor?" she asked.

"Not much. It's a long way to move temporarily."

Savanna studied the book titles. Mostly pathology and forensics, even Michael Baden's **Dead Reckoning**. "You must have thought you could catch up on your reading," she said.

"They weren't destined for Westbury."

She faced him at the candour in his tone, but he had moved from the sofa where she left him. Somehow, he seemed taller standing in the archway leading to the kitchen. The sight of his well-built body awakened something else inside her. She slid her gaze over him, clothed in army green cargo pants and a matching t-shirt. His biceps bulged from the cuffs and his pectorals pressed against the thin fabric. Her fingers tingled with familiarity, as though they knew the contours and firm texture of each muscle.

She rubbed her temples.

"Is something wrong?" he asked.

"No, Doctor." Her voice squeaked. "I'm fine."

In a few strides, he stood next to her, searching her face. Satisfied, he swatted her forehead with his lips then moved behind the counter.

Ooh god. She felt that all the way down to her toes.

"What can I make for you to eat?" he asked.

"You don't need to go to any trouble on my behalf, Doc—" She stopped herself from calling him doctor again and joined him in the kitchen. The L-shape layout provided barely enough space for them to move around. "Actually," she said. "To show my appreciation, why don't I make you something?"

When he closed the refrigerator door and faced her, he stood so close the sandalwood scent wafted her way.

She shivered and closed her eyes for a second.

His hands closed over her forearms, now covered in goose bumps. They slid to her waist.

The comforting warmth surged through her body.

"You're not hungry?" he asked.

She felt a yearning and on impulse lifted onto her toes and kissed the lips that had been beckoning her since the night they met in the cheese barn. Yes, she was hungry for him. For his warmth. For his strength. She was hungry to feel his lips all over her.

Nicholas's lips met hers briefly.

She lowered her feet to the floor again.

His finger caressed her cheek and slid down to her throat while he searched her face. His arms folded around her back and he pulled her to him. He lowered his head and touched his lips to hers.

An almost painful urge surged between her legs and a cry left her throat.

She pressed her body to his and parted her lips. He tasted intoxicating. Her eyes fluttered closed as her body swayed into his. She clung to him, trembling and receptive to the gentle flickering and probing that teased her mouth.

Their tongues collided and coiled together. She held on tighter. Every part of her body exploded with a yearning and an arousing need that only he could relieve. She hadn't known it until now, but she longed for him to take her.

Chapter 33

ICHOLAS CLOSED IN ON the point of no return. If Savanna didn't stop kissing him like that—Good god. She tasted so good—He couldn't be held responsible for peeling the clothes from her body and taking her to his bed.

"Nicholas."

His name, seductive and breathless tantalized his longing. "Hmm," he murmured.

"Make love to me," she said.

A growl like a starving wolf left him and vibrated through their bodies. But he was no scoundrel. He couldn't take advantage of her vulnerability. "You'd hate me tomorrow," he said. "You might even hate yourself."

"I'm numb all over until you touch me."

"Hmm." He kissed her again. Suckling at her sweet plump lips.

"Help me feel. I want to feel you inside me."

God. If she kept talking like that, she would finish him. He slid his arms down her back and over her curvy hips his hands never forgot. She was kissing him now, inhaling him with the same hunger he felt for her.

His erection pushed against the cargo pants. She rubbed her stomach against him.

"Savanna." He started to separate their lips.

"Yes, please." She glued herself to him. "Don't stop."

"Maybe we should, just for a moment."

She kissed him again. "Doctor," she said. "Lieutenant. Colonel. Nicholas. Wade. Make love to me."

He needed no more confirmation. He trailed his lips down her neck and rolled the spaghetti straps over her shoulder. His lips followed, and he nibbled the smooth, warm honey skin.

She groaned. Her hands smoothed beneath his shirt. Her soft palms rippled along his abs and along his naked back.

He lowered his head to the soft flesh at the mound of her breasts and trailed his tongue until he reached her cleavage where he buried his face and inhaled.

She leaned back and offered her breasts to him. He rolled the tank top down until her brown nipples, already puckered, called to him. He licked them both. Savanna cried out and pulled her arms from the confining straps.

Nicholas cupped her beautifully shaped breasts in both palms and opened his mouth over the right one first, sucking and licking. Then he repeated the same ravenous greed on the other.

"You smell intoxicating," he said.

She giggled.

He lifted his head. Desire shimmered from her chocolate eyes. "Did I say something foolish?" he asked.

"No. I thought your kisses were intoxicating too."

He kissed her again. "What about that one?"

She answered by sinking her tongue in his mouth and teasing his tongue into hers. She tasted him with a fever he remembered from the night they spent together ten years ago. Her fingers swiftly released his belt. She slid her hand into his pants and grasped his penis over his boxers.

"Aaah." He closed his eyes, throbbing and aching under her touch. His penis threatened to explode under her maddening caress. He pulled her to him and captured her lips.

"I want more of you," she whispered.

He pulled the shirt over his head and tossed it away. Her breath caught.

She met his eyes and bit her lip, then smiled and kissed his pecs, one at a time. Her tongue circled his nipples, then she nibbled them gently.

His groans deepened with every flick of her teasing. He needed to touch her before he lost himself in her caresses. He kissed her deep and passionate, then cupped her behind and lifted her unto his hips.

She wrapped her arms around his neck and he found his way to the bedroom without separating their lips.

He released her next to his bed and stepped back. Her wavy hair cascaded over her naked shoulders and hung seductively beside her bare breasts with the tank top still covering her upper torso. She looked like a goddess. He wanted to ravish her every day for the rest of his life.

She came to him and shoved his pants from his hips.

They fell to the floor.

He hooked his fingers into her skirt waist and pushed it over the lovely curved behind he itched to touch. The skirt crumpled to the floor and the cheek-hugging boy shorts she wore eclipsed his senses. They revealed slender, shapely legs.

He groaned. "You are so beautiful I'm afraid to touch you," he said.

"Touch me. Please."

He reached for her and pulled the tank top over her head. He kissed her lips and dragged his tongue down to her nipples again. He sucked until she cried out and grasped a handful of his hair at the nape of his neck.

"I want to touch you," she said between groans.

He lifted his head then and shoved his underwear over his pulsating penis.

Savanna reached for him and wrapped her fingers around his throbbing erection. She stroked him.

The sensation jolted through him like electricity. In her hands, his restraint waned. He grasped her hand to still her loving caress. He kissed her while coaxing her to the centre of the bed, where she leaned back and greedily dragged her gaze over him.

She smiled and reached out.

He climbed in beside her.

"My turn," she said and threw one leg over him, straddling his hips. His erection pressed against her wet centre and he feared again that it was too much to bear. She leaned forward and kissed him, deep.

His hands glided down her back and over her hips and shapely behind. His fingers explored every smooth contour, up her sides and around her full breasts.

She released his mouth and nibbled kisses along his strong jaw, his chin, and down his throat.

When he groaned and shuddered, she lifted her head and smiled into his eyes. "I like making you shiver," she said.

He grabbed her around the waist and flipped her onto her back. It was his turn and he would show no mercy. He nibbled the firm buds between his teeth and Savanna's hips lifted off the bed as she cried out. He trailed kisses along over the tiny adorable hump in her stomach. He kept going and when he inserted his tongue in the folds of her heated vagina lips, her fingers sunk into his hair.

"Oh god, yes. Nicholas." She arched against him. Her hips shimmied as he stroked his tongue over her swollen petal, sucking it into his mouth and inserting his tongue into her. Her tasty juices flowed into him.

After a moment, he lifted his head from between her legs and covered her mouth with his again. His finger sunk into her wet centre.

She cried out and her hips rose so high, he thought she was already in the throes of an orgasm.

He pulled out again and she ripped her mouth from his.

"No, please," she whispered. "Don't stop."

He groaned and kissed her lightly on the mouth, neck, breasts. His finger drew slow circles around the mouth of her silky heat.

Savanna's legs parted, and her heels dug into the bed.

He wanted to preserve her release for that moment when he buried his throbbing need deep inside her. He wanted her to lose herself, filled with every inch of his power.

She reached for him.

He fitted himself between her thighs. Their eyes locked. The bliss on her face drove him wild and he dipped his pelvis and drove every inch of his penis into her.

Savanna clung to him and lifted her hips to meet his thrusts.

He captured her mouth. They drank pleasure from each other. His desire and passion overwhelming as he made himself one with her.

She moved under him like a woman starved for love.

Her velvet heat sucked his throbbing penis into her and he stroked her over and over and over again. Every maddening plunge propelled him into the intoxicating rapture that captivated him like the first time he made love to her ten years ago.

That night he'd lost all control and drained himself into her only to ache from another craving minutes later. His erection rose again, and they started another round of sweet and mind-blowing sex. Those memories drove him wild for years, just as they did now every time he plunged into her.

She met his stroking fever with a passionate need of her own.

He released her mouth and lifted his head.

Her lips parted in a sweet moan, luscious, swollen berry, then her eyes fluttered open. She cried out and reached for him.

Capable of losing himself in that moment, Nicholas slowed his hips and eased his penis halfway out of her.

She lifted her face to his and nibbled his lips, begging him not to leave her now. Their heat grew intoxicating again. Every kiss, touch, caress, every passionate stroke answered their yearnings for each other.

They moved in slow exhilarating union for sometime. When Savanna's tight muscles grasped his penis, he shoved even deeper. Long strokes of rhythm that encouraged a pleasure that floated them to the height of rapture. She cried out and slammed her hips into his, squeezing her vagina along the length of his penis. Her rhythmic clutching undermined his every effort to control the mounting explosion surging deep in his belly. He pushed onto his palms and answered every clench with powerful thrusts.

A fierce groan ripped vibrations from his throat.

She gasped and the wet heat between her legs rippled and held him even tighter. Her body vibrated into luscious, climaxing quivers. "Yes, oh yes. Nicholas, please. Yes."

Her climax and begging tipped him over the edge. He drove his erection into her and exploded in waves of pleasure he was sure would leave him crippled. The spasm jerked every ounce of energy from his muscles before it deposited him, limp and panting, beside her.

He rolled her into his arms and sighed happily.

She nuzzled his neck and tangled her legs with his and cuddled against him.

No other woman, except Savanna Jones, could reduce him to an exhausted and breathless copy of himself. She owned him, again. If only she knew that he was Ishmael.

Chapter 34

JULY 18, 2002 - VANCOUVER, BC

SAVANNA'S DAYS AS A CAREFREE student would end in twenty minutes. But tonight, she wasn't Savanna Jones, and the handsome man holding her would live on only in her dreams.

A warm Vancouver breeze had rippled against her cheek and she giggled. "Sandalwood," she whispered. "You should have said, call me Sandalwood."

He laughed, sweet and throaty. "Do you know a character called Sandalwood?" he asked.
Her laugh echoed into the night. She felt so silly and happy and free.

"Are you a little tipsy?" he tickled her chin.
"Ah. You noticed," she said and gave him a kiss for that.
"Not a little," she said. "Very." She'd never smoked marijuana before. "Hannibal had something to do with that. He said it would help with the pain from my bruises."
"Hannibal?"

"Yes." She giggled again. "You're very tricky," she said. "No names, remember?"

"Yes, I remember, but you can't blame me for trying." He bent his head and the feel of his lips on hers was like honey. He kissed her neck.

She shivered. "I'm glad I caught you," she said.

"I'm glad you caught me too." His voice was husky and heavy with the same desire pulsating inside her. "Call me Ishmael," he said and entered her.

His name roared from deep within her. "Ishmael," she groaned.

*S*avanna sat bolt upright in bed. "Ishmael?" she said into the dark room. "No, no, no."

The bed shifted under her, but she refused to turn around. Her heart clobbered under her breast. Too afraid to move, she sat still, repeating the words, "He's not the same man. He's not the same man." Each repetition hardly changed the facts of her discovery, but she silently repeated the mantra anyway.

"Savanna."

Nicholas's voice close to her ear sounded so much like the man from that night ten years ago.

"Look at me," he said.

"No."

"Yes."

"You knew?"

"I did."

"All along? You knew and didn't tell me? How long?"

"The night of the landfill crime scene."

"And you couldn't say something? Just one word?"

"I couldn't really believe you didn't recognize me."

"I didn't. How could I, it was one night."

"Was I so different? Why didn't you remember?"

"Because it was ten years ago. Because I lived a lifetime since then. Because…"

"What?"

"Because I was high and wasn't sure what I recalled about your appearance over the next few weeks was real."

"What do you mean? You didn't know what you were doing when you slept with me?"

"That's not what I'm saying." She twisted away from him and tried to leave the bed.

He caught her forearm. "Tell me," he said.

She tugged the sheet up to her chin and faced him. In the dark, she fingered the outline of his jawline and his lip. "I recalled only how…" She stopped talking. Alive and free she felt that night with him.

"How what?" Nicholas asked.

"How safe I felt in your arms."

"You're here again." He wrapped his arms around her. "And you're safe." He pulled her to lie on his chest. "It's okay. We don't have to talk about this now. I found you."

Savanna laid still, her heart thudding in her chest. *Ishmael?* How could she tell him the rest of their story?

Chapter 35

THICKNESS FILLED SAVANNA'S THROAT at the sight of three-year-old Peter Dubai tackling his father. His small arms wrapped around Ben's muscular legs and they both tumbled to the grass.

Savanna left the lab early for the first time in three weeks to join Rebecca and her boys for dinner.

Eight-year-old Nichole had already left for her first away camp. Actually, Rebecca threatened to march into the lab and drag Savanna out by her lab coattail if she didn't show up.

"Yeaaah," Peter squealed. He rolled on top his two-hundred-pound opponent and kicked his legs in victory. "I won, Aunty Savi. I won."

Savanna smiled from the patio deck and flicked Peter two thumbs up.

At thirty-seven, Ben moved with the same agility as Tom Brady, but his mind sped around his global data centres at the speed of fibre optic cable, every bit the athletic geek. Yet, he found time to stay committed to his family first. Driving his young daughter to her first away camp and playing football with his son.

Watching him and Peter, Savanna's heart sank. Why would

Richard say no to this? Maybe one day he would change his mind. But since he asked her to choose, a divorce was her only option. This wasn't ten years ago, and she wasn't an inexperienced college graduate. She had paid for her earlier mistake and she had put it behind her.

Her breath caught in her throat again and salty tears burned her eyes. She picked up the makeshift fan she'd been using to cool the early August heat and fanned them dry.

"Here you go," Rebecca said coming up to her with two tall glasses of bubbly Perrier on the rocks. She placed them on the table and slid Savanna's BlackBerry from her pocket. "You forgot this inside and it has been vibrating all over the kitchen counter."

"Sorry," she said and checked the phone. It was a text from Sally asking if she was free for a coffee tomorrow. Savanna decided to respond later.

"Nooo!" Peter's voice screeched from the yard.

She looked over to see him gesticulating wildly as Ben tucked his son under his arm and planted him in the playhouse.

"Touchdown," Ben said.

She smiled and pressed her lips together to stop another round of tears. Ben and Nicholas would probably get along. She shook her head. What was she thinking? Sleeping with your boss was never a good idea. She felt so good in his arms that night when the world seemed so cold and all she held sacred was gone. Janet's death, and Richard's lack of interest in fatherhood still brought her to her knees, and in those moments, she wanted to crawl into Nicholas Wade's arms again.

Oh God. How was she going to work with him knowing how good he felt, and smelled, and tasted?

"You okay?" Rebecca asked.

"Sorry. I'm a mess. Since Edmonton and Janet, the simplest thing triggers the water works."

"You managed to pile on two of life's biggest stresses in one day."

Savanna's eyes burned and her throat swelled. She hung her head, thinking of Janet's pale corpse under a white sheet. When the image reminded Savanna too much of her mother, she lifted her chin. "Yes," she said. "Janet's death threw me, and I just need to find the bastard who did it."

"I didn't know her as well as you, but she seemed like such a lovely person. Does the police know anything yet?"

Savanna eyed Peter.

The small boy swooped down the slide and charged at his father headfirst. He collided with Ben's legs.

"Not really." She met Rebecca's gaze.

"I know," her friend said. "You can't talk about it."

"It's more than that, but thanks for understanding." She pushed from the chair. "Let's go inside. I don't want to talk about this in front of Peter."

Rebecca stood and looped her arm through Savanna's. "Come on," she said.

They entered the family room. The high ceilings and smooth plum-coloured walls covered in family vacation photos wrapped Savanna in cozy family warmth. She picked up one of Peter's Mega Bloks and a robot Transformer from the oversized single chair and flopped into it.

"What's the name of that lawyer I met here a few months ago?" she asked. "She was a friend of Ben's?"

Rebecca was quiet for a moment while she studied Savanna's face. "Are you sure?"

Savanna sucked in a breath. "Of course I'm not sure," she said. "But I will not force him to father his own child. He asked for his life back, as though our marriage came with a return to sender clause. Then," she hiccupped and clamped her hand over her mouth until she could speak again. "Then he said that he spoke to Charles Covey."

"Who is that?"

"Richard's lawyer."

"Richard is an ass and I think you should sue him for a divorce."

"I've called him worse in the last couple of days." Actually, in her darkest moments, she pictured herself hacking into his chest and searching around for a heart. "How could I not know that he would be so against having a child?"

"Because the bastard didn't want you to know."

"At first I thought he was scared because we lost a child. Then he tells me he never wanted children in the first place."

"That doesn't mean that he should make you choose."

Savanna shook her head. "No, it doesn't." She slammed her fist.

"That's the spirit," Rebecca said. "So, what's your plan?"

She shrugged. "Don't know really. I've never done this before. I'll start with moving out."

"Why add more stress? Since he's going to be gone anyway, you should stay in the house. You're the one having a baby. You need the house more than he does."

"I can't live in Richard's house, sleeping in the same bed like nothing has happened. I've already moved to the guest room."

"You're going to find your own place?"

"I haven't had much time since I got back." In fact, she hadn't had any time. "But when I left the lab for lunch today, I flipped through some online rental ads."

"You can come stay here until you find something you like."

Savanna's heart warmed. While she'd been drifting in a fog for almost an entire month, Rebecca's friendship kept her feet on the ground. "Thanks," she said. "But I wouldn't do that to you. Moving in here with my baggage could off-balance your household."

"The spare room is all yours if you find yourself needing some Dubai love."

"You're the best."

"Have you told Kenneth any of this?"

Savanna picked up the makeshift fan she'd held earlier and flicked her wrist with humming bird-like speed. "No," she said.

Rebecca shot her a puzzled glance. "How come?"

"The opportunity never came up. But I'm planning to explain everything."

"His support is what you need right now so don't let your regret shut him out."

Her father never trusted Richard, but how could he have known Richard would do this? "I'll call him soon," she said.

"There's something else I wanted to tell you."

"What's that?"

"I slept with my boss on the night of Janet's death."

Rebecca's eyes popped from her head. "I didn't think you had it in you."

"That's not the worst of it. I haven't told him that I'm married and pregnant."

Chapter 36

NICHOLAS YANKED OPEN HIS office door on his way to see Savanna. In the last three weeks she avoided him unless absolutely necessary. Since their night together, she prepared reports and sent emails rather than entering his office in her usual unannounced manner. Rather than push her, he stepped back. But he needed to see her now.

According to Miller, Scott Allen was her contact for the army's investigation on a psychotropic drug. Savanna believed it could be the same substance discovered in Moore's victims. Whoever this man claimed he was, he wasn't a second lieutenant working out of the local air force base.

"Doctor." Josie's voice stopped him before he closed the door again.

He turned to see her chewing the corner of her lip. He moved his glance to the hand cupped over the mouthpiece of the telephone receiver.

"Doreen Bellamy is on line one."

"Tell her I'll call the Crown Attorney's Office in half an hour."

Josie held onto the telephone and met his glance. "She said it's urgent."

Nicholas translated urgent to mean I will not take no for an answer. "Put her through," he said. "Thank you." Behind the closed door of his office again, he perched on the corner of his desk and picked up the receiver. "Mrs. Bellamy, what can I do for you?"

"I have some information I thought you should know, since it concerns one of your staff."

Nicholas twisted his body and focused out the window behind him. It was another unusually wet day at the end of July. The rain hadn't let up in weeks. He was starting to see the effect in the glum attitudes around the lab. "What information?" He asked.

"It has come to my attention that Savanna Jones has acted inappropriately with a key witness in the Colton Moore case."

Nicholas's jaw clenched. "Inappropriately? Can you be more precise?"

"Savanna has been impulsive before, but this has gone too far."

"Mrs. Bellamy, are you able to describe Ms. Jones's actions?"

"She told Sally Starr to leave town in an effort to avoid further involvement with the Moore case."

Nicholas pushed up from the desk. "Are you absolutely certain this is what was said?"

"The witness informed me herself."

"And she's sure this is what Ms. Jones meant?"

"Look, Doctor, I'm just the messenger."

A very biased messenger. Nicholas bit down on his lip. If he didn't know better, he would swear Doreen Bellamy and Sally Starr cooked this one up together. The spurious claim was rather insulting. "Thank you," he said finally, then eased the receiver back into the cradle.

He stared unfocused out his office window. With all that infuriated her in the justice system, Savanna's impatience with the legal process frustrated her most, but she was an experienced and talented scientist. She knew that accurate results depended upon a meticulous and thorough process. Though she was willing to ensure that Colton Moore never walked the streets again, Nicholas would never believe that she indulged in behaviour that bordered on reckless.

He rubbed his neck. The investigating team had finally collected and presented viable evidence to satisfy the Crown Attorney's Office. Savanna was scheduled to testify in court on Monday. Maybe now she would talk to him.

SAVANNA SHIFTED IN THE chair trying to fight the frustration riding her. OPP Detective Reynolds refused to answer any questions about Janet's death investigation. When she spoke to Thomas, he sounded just as annoyed as she felt. Well, maybe she could do some poking on her own.

Her lab phone rang, clearly validating her plan. She read the screen and her stomach fluttered. Nicholas. As his assistant, avoiding him was hardly a viable option. She'd need a body double to pull that one off. Instead, her new norm was overt politeness, then scurrying away.

Sleeping with him might have been easier to get over if he hadn't turned out to be Ishmael. And to muddle their situation even more, the sight of him still reduced her to a puddle of lust.

The phone rang a third time and she snatched the receiver from the cradle. "Savanna here," she said.

"Can you come to my office, please?" his voice boomed through the earpiece.

Her heart thumped. "Of course, Doctor," she said, faking calm.

Minutes later, she sat across from his desk waiting for him to speak.

Instead, he pushed up from the chair and stood next to the window.

Her eyes rolled over his sturdy frame. During his weeks in Westbury, his military haircut grew into a more fashionable style. He hardly resembled the army Lieutenant-Colonel she met in the cheese barn three months ago. Gone were the stiff collars and buttoned-down shirts. He still never smiled, well, almost never, if you counted the wistful grin that sometimes creased the corners of his mouth.

Sighing, he shed his blazer and pushed the cotton sleeves to his elbow. His gaze levelled with hers. "Doreen Bellamy accused you of tampering with the Moore case," he said.

"Tampering? What does that mean?"

"She said you suggested to Miss Starr that she should leave town rather than testify at the trial."

Savanna's breath caught, and she wondered if she'd heard right. Perhaps if she left the office and came in again, his tone and the words themselves would change.

"Well?" he prompted. "Did you?"

"Of course I didn't." She watched the stiffness leave his body as a thought occurred to her. She placed both hands on his desk. "Well… not really. I encouraged her to turn to her family for support."

"So how did Doreen Bellamy arrive at her conclusion?"

"Are you saying Sally spoke to Doreen?"

"It would appear so. What did you say to Miss Starr?"

The hair on the back of Savanna's neck prickled. "Sally asked my advice."

"On how to avoid the trial?"

"No. On whether she should get involved."

Nicholas left his position at the window and leaned over his desk. She refused to look away even though having him this close sent a tingling ache through her.

"A witness in an ongoing case, one in which you're testifying, asks your advice and you give it without thinking of the ramifications?"

Would she ever get used to his cut-and-dried thinking? A military man since eighteen, Coroner Miller had said. A man who lived by rules and regulations. She peered closer, looking for the compassion that encircled her like a bubble when he picked her up from the airport the day Janet died. Only duty to Queen and country stared back.

"I thought it best to encourage Sally's cooperation," she said. "I told her that when the Crown's Office got around to charging Moore, they would consider her a prime witness. I suggested she testify willingly rather than force them to subpoena her.”

“It wasn’t your place to suggest anything of the kind.” His rigid tone was back.

“I referred her to Doreen Bellamy.” She scowled and set her jaw. Did she need to consult him on that too?

“What did you say to Miss Starr about leaving town?” he asked.

“She was concerned that testifying again would get her name in the news. She worried that her brother and father back in Brandon would discover the details of her kidnapping and the rape. I suggested she confide in them.” Savanna’s stomach dropped. “Oh, no… Oh no,” she said.

“What did you say?”

“I said she should speak to them in person. Sally misunderstood. This is my fault, I’ll meet with her again and—”

“You’ll do no such thing.” His eyes narrowed. “This case is in court on Monday. You need to cut off any contact with her.”

Heat pounded at her temples. “I will not abandon her now,” she insisted.

“I’m sure she has another support system.”

“I offered my help should there be a trial.”

“And you don’t see that as a conflict of interest?”

“No, I do not.”

“Then let me suggest to you that the defence attorney will.”

That familiar weight of impotence she sometimes encountered on crime scenes surged in her chest. She drew a breath. “Well, he would be wrong.”

“Look, I get it.”

He did?

“She’s alone out here and you want to be there for her, but this could go sideways, so I have to warn you.”

She steadied her eyes on his. “Warn me?”

He leaned forward. “I have no choice. Either you cut your ties with Miss Starr, or I’ll suspend you until after the trial.”

“Did it ever occur to you that Doreen is looking for an excuse to delay the trial even further?”

"That may be, but she's not going to find her reason in my labs. I want confirmation that you understand my warning. Am I clear, Savanna?"

"Yes, Doctor. Crystal." She shot from the chair. "Is there anything else?"

"No, that's all. But, for the record, I didn't believe the accusation."

"Then why the warning?"

The changing colours in his hazel eyes that raged moments ago steadily observed her. "Consider it my attempt to save you from yourself," he said. "You may not be thinking straight at this time."

She'd let him get too close. Now she couldn't hide from that look that knew she ached for his touch. She kept her distance because she couldn't even trust herself in his presence. Now she wasn't sure she could trust him.

Chapter 37

S AVANNA EMAILED ANOTHER APARTMENT rental ad to her cellphone. She would call tomorrow and make an appointment to see if it was half as good as it sounded. She stretched out on the couch and dialled her father's number. It was Sunday after all and he was expecting her call.

Her hand trembled as she raised the phone to her ear.

"Hi, princess." His voice sounded cheerful, but she detected the slightest hint of worry.

"Hi, Dad."

"You're calling early."

Tightness roped in her chest. It was 7:00 p.m. in Westbury. With the Vancouver three-hour time difference, he was probably just having a late afternoon coffee, with dinner a few hours away. "I'm in court tomorrow, so an early night for me," she said.

"Is that all?"

"Yep." She pushed the lie from her lips with curt enthusiasm, then sighed and decided on some version of the truth to ease her into the conversation. "Well, I haven't been feeling myself recently."

"Caught a bug?"

"I might have, but that cleared up last month. Dad, I—"

"Have you been to the doctor?"

Oh, not yet. She wanted a bit more chitchat first. "Yeah," she said.

"And? Is everything all right?"

"Dad. Calm down. I'm fine." She glanced up at the photograph of them last Christmas. As always, his smile calmed her. She had decided to leave that one on the shelf until she was actually leaving.

"I have some news."

"News? Do I need to sit down?"

"Maybe."

"Don't keep me in suspense. Tell me."

She giggled as nervousness feathered her stomach. "Congratulations, you're going to be a granddad," she said.

"You're pregnant?"

"Yes." She choked out the word with a tight quiver.

"Oh, Savanna. That's marvellous. Really marvellous. I wish I was there to give you a big hug."

Her eyes stung, and tears blurred her vision. "Me too," she said. It's the response she had been hoping for. If only she had gone to Vancouver after she left Edmonton. Now she wanted to tell him everything.

"How far along are you?" he asked.

"I'm just about nineteen weeks." She leaned back and rubbed her stomach. "The doctor called me on the anniversary of mum's death. I was already five weeks along."

Not a sound echoed from the other end of the line.

Her hand holding the phone shook. Savanna knew her father heard what she said. She also knew she'd hurt him. She bit her lower lip as she waited for him to speak. Her blurry eyes stung with her regret.

"Savanna," he finally said, "I spoke to you the very next day."

"Sorry, Dad." Her voice broke.

"Does he know?"

Her father's bitterness scorched through the pain already riding her. Not using Richard's name was his way of noting her husband's absence. Her stomach burned. She sat up and slid off the sofa. "He knows," she said. "But it was my decision not to tell you."

His sharp intake echoed in her ear. "Why would you keep your pregnancy from me?"

"I thought it would help Richard if I didn't say anything for a while. I'm sorry. I see now how wrong I was."

"Yes, you were wrong. How many times have we spoken since then? And not one word, not even a hint."

Savanna imagined his shoulders sagging as he sat on a stool in his new kitchen, his head hanging low into his chest. "I was foolish," she said, then swallowed. "Dad I…" She broke off, reluctant to tell him about the divorce over the phone. She cleared her throat.

"Dad, when my mother carried me," she said. "Did she have much of a baby bump?"

"You mean how much she was showing?" The nostalgic in his chuckle eased her distress.

"Yes. When did she start to show?"

"You know, she got through the nine months without most of the normal symptoms. No morning sickness, no swollen limbs, just multiple visits to the bathroom. It seems you liked pushing against her bladder. When her water broke, we arrived at the hospital before our doctor. They put us in the waiting area, saying her labour was a false alarm. By then, the bump, as you called it, looked like she'd just entered her fifth month."

A sigh popped from Savanna's chest.

"Something wrong?" Her father asked.

"No, not really. I'm not really showing. Not much anyway and I was a little worried."

"What does the doctor say?"

"That I'm within the normal weight range and the baby is growing well."

"Good. So stop worrying."

"I'll try."

"I want to see you. Why don't I come for a visit?"

"Oh, Dad. Do you mean it?" She squealed, instantly breathless with excitement.

"It's been some time," he said. "And you shouldn't be there on your own anyway."

Savanna pressed her lips together, knowing that her father was from the old school of thought. Women should be waited on hand and foot during pregnancy. She stumbled against one of the boxes she stacked in the corner of the room. In her excitement to see him, she forgot that her life had changed.

"Dad, why don't I come to you?"

"That's sounds even better. This weekend?"

"Ah… I may have to get back to you about the date. The Moore case is going to trial and… Well you know how it gets."

"Are you sure you don't want me to come out there?"

"I would love it, but I wouldn't be able to spend time with you if I'm working. And Vancouver is so lovely this time of year."

"Okay. You've convinced me. Let me know soon when you can come out."

"I will for sure." She still felt guilty. "Dad," she said.

"Yes."

"Do you forgive me for keeping the news from you?"

"Not so fast, young lady. That will take a little more time, but I'm getting there, and the visit certainly will help."

A little forgiveness was better than his disappointment. The knot in her stomach loosened a little. His warm tone soothed her, and she closed her eyes, picturing them together when she was younger. She needed to hold onto that image even when she told him about Richard.

Chapter 38

____

DEFENCE ATTORNEY, CHARLES DENTON stretched his long
arms to grasp the lectern. "Savanna Jones," he said. "You
testified here today that you have been with Westbury Forensic
Services for ten years. Is that correct?"

A tall and slender man, he presented an impressive figure in
front of the jury, but his apparent poise was a sham. Savanna knew
what was coming.

That morning, before Nicholas derailed her focus as she entered
the courthouse, Savanna had planned to handle Denton in the
regular fashion: keep her answers short and avoid his traps.

"I have some news that will impact your testimony this afternoon," her boss had said.

Will impact? Not, might, but will.

The concern tightening his expression silenced her for a
moment. She watched him wondering what this was about. "What
news?" she asked she found her voice.

"I had to inform the Crown Attorney's Office this morning that
we found your DNA on Suzette Morgan's remains."

Savanna's heart seemed to stop in that moment. Clearly her
brain was short-circuiting since she had to ask him twice to repeat

himself. Up to the minute she walked toward the witness box, she kept thinking that somehow, someone in the lab made a grave mistake.

Denton scowled at her. His question, though seemingly innocent, held the potential to destroy every piece of evidence they'd collected. "Was that your testimony?" he asked.

"Yes," she said. "That's correct."

"You've also testified that you trained with the Westbury Police Services Forensic Identification Section for eighteen months before you qualified as a forensic identification investigator working with the Police Criminal Investigation Division. True?"

"Yes."

During the first five minutes on the stand testifying for the Crown, Savanna had outlined her ten-year forensic career in Westbury. Why Charles Denton needed a repeat of the same information was beyond her. But she kept her cool.

"During that decade, how many deceased bodies have you investigated?"

"Many. I never counted."

"Could you hazard a guess? One hundred?"

"More, Mr. Denton."

"After ten years, you've probably investigated all manner of crime scenes. Is that right?"

"Yes, I have."

Denton looked down at a notebook. After a few seconds, he looked up at her. "Ms. Jones, in the interest of time, would you say you've investigated 500 or more death scenes since you joined Westbury Forensic Services?"

"That's sounds about right."

"Have you ever thrown up on a crime or death scene while collecting evidence?"

Savanna's throat constricted. She swallowed. *Here it comes.*

She flicked a glance at Colton Moore in the accused box positioned behind the attorneys' tables.

Moore's apathetic stare met hers as a smirk stretched his wide mouth into a stained-tooth grin.

Her scorn for him far outweighed his intimidation tactics. She glared as though he emitted a bad smell and then returned her focus to his lawyer again.

"On a crime scene?" She repeated. "No."

"Not even when you were a rookie? Or working an especially unpleasant environment? One that might cause most of us to suffer from its effects?"

"No, never."

"If we may, I'll like to take you back to the night of May 16th, when you were called out to investigate the body discovered in the McGuire Landfill. Do you recall that night?"

For the first time since she took the stand, Savanna lifted her glance to the back of the courtroom where Nicholas sat. That night, the smell of his cologne filled her nostrils and blocked the scent of the landfill. She moved her gaze back to Denton. "Yes, I do," she said.

"Did you throw up on the McGuire Landfill crime scene while collecting evidence?"

Savanna settled into the seat, her method of projecting calm under pressure. She knew where this line of questioning was going. Should she wait for Denton's trap, or lessen the impact of his bomb by speaking up? She was the Crown's witness after all. Turning the tables on Denton would offer the defence inflammatory testimony, and Doreen would have no grounds to object.

"I did not throw up on the crime scene," she said. "No."

"Did you or did you not vomit while carrying out the investigation, Ms. Jones?"

"I threw up in the McGuire Landfill. At the time, I believed I had cleared the immediate area of the crime scene."

"Did you?"

"For the most part, yes, but minute traces of my DNA were found on the victim's scarf."

Denton paused for effect before continuing.

"Anything different about the night that caused you to lose control?"

Numbness started in Savanna's big toe. She tapped the tip of her right shoe. "Well," she said. "The McGuire Landfill remains one of the most decaying pieces of property in the city. I suppose I succumbed to the stench."

"Is that your excuse for contaminating evidence, Ms. Jones?"

Though the traces of her DNA were hardly enough to be considered contamination, or even relevant, Denton intended to push until he could prove grounds for a mistrial.

"Objection, Your Honour." Doreen Bellamy leapt from her seat, and the defence counsel sat down as though they played an angry version of musical chairs.

The Honourable Horace Kaufman presided over Moore's first trial as well. He peered over his thick black frames at the lawyers. "Objection sustained," he said.

Counsel and prosecutor returned to their original positions.

"Did anyone else at the scene suffer with a queasy stomach that night?" Denton asked.

"There was one other officer."

"Officer Merton?"

"I believe that's his name."

"As I understand it, Officer Merton was straight out of the academy, his first day on the job."

She waited for the real question.

"So, no one on the experienced investigating team vomited that night? Not your partner, not the detectives, just you. A seasoned, highly skilled forensic scientist didn't know enough not to enter a volatile crime scene when she was feeling queasy. What were you expecting to achieve, Ms. Jones?"

"I was there to do my job as always, Mr. Denton. To process the crime scene for the purpose of collecting and securing evidence."

"How were you feeling before you received the call?"

Her throat burned under Denton's challenge. She preferred not to recall how she felt that night. She reached for the glass next to her and sipped some water. The liquid hit the soft flesh in the back of her throat. Her eyes moved around the courtroom and landed on Nicholas. After spending a night in his bed, she still couldn't penetrate the mask he sometimes hid behind.

"Before my partner called me," she turned to Denton again, "I was already in bed, asleep."

"Was it an early night for you, Ms. Jones?"

"No, I left the lab rather late that night."

"How late?"

"It was almost midnight."

"How were you feeling before you went to bed?"

"Tired."

"Your Honour, really?" Doreen pushed to her feet. Her sharp grey eyes shot to Kaufman. "I don't see the relevance of this line of questioning. Ms. Jones isn't a suspect in this case."

Denton was already seated and stood to address the objection. "I intend to make it all clear shortly, Your Honour," he said. "If you'll just allow me a bit of latitude."

"Get to the point," Kaufman said. "Or move it along, Mr. Denton."

Doreen shot Savanna a glance laced with irritation before she returned to the Crown's bench.

With her pregnancy at the forefront of her thoughts, Savanna stared back at her, knowing the Crown prosecutor intended to leave as much as possible for Savanna to clean up.

Denton took his place at the lectern again and shuffled his notes. "Ms. Jones, have you thrown up since May 16th?"

She squirmed on the hard chair. "Yes, I have," she said.

"Would you tell the court why, Ms. Jones?"

"If it were relevant to this case, I would."

Denton's chin jerked forward. From the lectern, his eyes penetrated her determination. Then a smile flickered across his thin lips. He dipped his chin to his notes and posed his next question. "Are you pregnant, Ms. Jones?"

Savanna felt the blood drain from her face as Denton's surprise throttled her. As a wave of shock rose in the gallery, her eyes shot to Doreen Bellamy and met raised eyebrows beneath a wrinkled forehead. Apparently, the revelation of Savanna's pregnancy prevented the Crown Prosecutor from objecting to the totally inappropriate question.

With no objection raised, the weight of the question sat on her chest and stifled her breathing. She finally tugged her gaze toward the bench in the back row where Nicholas watched the proceedings.

If the news of her pregnancy shocked him like it did the rest of the courtroom, he had already recovered. His blunt stare registered only indifference. Savanna had seen that expression enough to know what it meant.

"Ms. Jones." Denton demanded her attention again. "Are you pregnant?"

Savanna broke her gaze with Nicholas and focused on the defence lawyer again. "What does my personal health have to do with your case, Mr. Denton?"

At that moment, Doreen seemed to recall her role and leapt from the bench. "Objection," she said.

Denton sat down.

"Your Honour," Doreen said. "Mr. Denton is violating the rights of this witness without grounds."

"This witness just testified that she contaminated a crime scene," Denton said. "We should be allowed to hear the reason it happened."

"Objection overruled." Judge Kaufman said and the chatter in the gallery rose even louder. He banged his gavel on the block once. The room went silent. "The witness will answer the question," he said.

Like any seasoned defence counsel, Denton broke no rules in his cross-examination. He knew the answer to every question he posed.

"Thank you, Your Honour." Denton turned to her again. "Are you pregnant, Ms. Jones?"

Savanna's cheeks burned, but she kept her eyes on the defense counsel. "Yes, I am," she said.

Again, he paused before questioning her.

She worked hard to keep her breathing even since she had no intention of caving under Denton's obvious pressure.

"Do you remember investigating and testifying in the trial against my client a year ago?" he asked and pointed at Colton Moore.

"Yes," she said. "I remember."

"Are you acquainted with Sally Victoria Starr?"

"Yes. She's the woman your client kidnapped, raped and—"

"Mr. Moore was convicted ten months ago for his crimes against Miss Starr,," He quickly interrupted her. "How well do you know the victim?"

"Not well. I first met her on the night she escaped from your client's captivity."

"Do you socialize with her?"

"Since the trial, we've met for the odd coffee."

"Odd? How often would you say you've met with this witness since her unfortunate circumstances?"

"I don't know. A few times."

"Would you say that you and Sally Starr have become friends?"

"Friendly would be more accurate."

"The local media reported that your friend, Miss Starr, believes that my client and I quote, 'is getting off Scot-free for what he did to me and should pay with his life.' Would you say that you'd do anything to see Miss Starr justified in her thinking?"

"Objection." Doreen was on her feet before Savanna could respond.

"The witness will answer the question," Judge Kaufman said.

Doreen sat down.

"Ms. Jones?" Denton prompted. "Would you do anything to see this man pay with his life?"

Fire burned in her veins. She hated the way this lawyer handled the truth, like it was a bad hand in a poker game. Now he accused her of tampering with evidence. "Are you suggesting that I purposely threw up on a crime scene in order to frame your client?"

"Did you?"

"As you pointed out, Mr. Denton, your client has already been convicted for his crimes. We are here to find justice for another one of his victims, Theresa Filito."

"Alleged victim, Ms. Jones. Alleged."

"With his DNA all over the victim, we are beyond alleged, Mr. Denton."

"I have no more questions for this witness at this time. However, I reserve the right to recall Ms. Jones."

"Noted," Kaufman said.

Denton gathered his notes from the lectern then raised a smile to her. "By the way, Ms. Jones," he said. "Congratulations."

And just like that, her secret was out.

Chapter 39

S AVANNA'S GAZE SWEPT THE gallery as she zipped past the
attorneys' benches. The reporters had already left. *Damn.*
She should have seen Denton's questions coming. She neared the
door and a sideways glimpse told her that Nicholas, too, had left the
courtroom. Avoiding him right now eased the tightness in her chest
a little.

The night they spent together, making love, every time she
thought of revealing her condition, she froze. She'd woken up the
next morning and bolted to the bathroom with her usual morning
sickness churning in her stomach. She had sat back on her heels
knowing then that she would need to explain.

He was a doctor, after all, and puking first thing in the morning
wasn't the general response to excellent love making. The night
before, his tender hands and tantalizing kisses kept pushing the truth
from rising up between them.

She wrapped his robe around her and followed the sweet
cinnamon scent to the kitchen, but rather than finding Nicholas, she
found a warm bagel, peppermint tea and a note.

I left the keys to the wagon for you. Take as long as you want.
She could have told him when she got to the lab that morning.

Instead she let the discovery that he was Ishmael scare her into silence. Now she had no choice.

The twenty minutes it took her to reach the lab offered no explanations, theories or plain-as-day justifications for why she kept the truth from him. She arrived at his outer office and stood watching Josie's plump fingers at work. They flicked through a three-inch high paper stack, then came to her mouth for a lick.

"Go right in," Josie said. "He's expecting you."

Of course he was. She straightened her shoulders and knocked lightly on the door. The brusque "come in" was all she needed.

"Savanna." It was Miller standing in the middle of Nicholas's office. He ran his hand through his curly white hair and stared at her from sunken eye sockets. "What have you done to the case?" His direct glare was as accusing as his question.

Savanna looked toward Nicholas. He stood behind his desk, his gaze on her and his fingers resting lightly on one of his well-ordered paper stacks. The softness in his expression distracted her for a moment, then vanished. His jawline hardened, and his attention flickered from her to the coroner.

So, this was her mess. She turned to Miller again. His tall frame sagged as he waited for an answer.

"Denton's claim that I purposely contaminated the evidence would never hold up in court," she said, feeling a lot less confident than she sounded.

"How sure are we about that?" Miller asked.

"The contamination was minuscule, Coroner." Nicholas finally spoke up. "Doreen Bellamy said we shouldn't worry about it."

"Perhaps if you had disclosed your pregnancy earlier," Miller said, "the Crown could have shut down Denton a lot sooner."

"Excuse me, Coroner, but my pregnancy is my business and not part of this trial."

"You're right, but it becomes an issue when it interferes with your job." He turned to Nicholas. "Let's see what we can do to clean this up immediately."

Nicholas opened his mouth, but Miller cut him off. "Maybe it's best if you backed off the case for now. Until it's sorted out."

"You can't be serious."

"I agree," Nicholas chimed in.

Savanna pivoted to face him. "You do?"

"I'll let you two figure out the details." Miller was already heading for the door.

"Coroner, I don't think this is—" Savanna began.

"Ms. Jones." Nicholas said. "I'm sure you agree that justice for the murdered women is what we're after here."

He really said that to her? She was so stunned on both counts and couldn't find the words to tell him to go to hell. She stood there staring into his accusing face.

Miller pulled at the door. "Keep me up to date on this," he said, then he was gone.

Savanna headed for the door. She couldn't handle this now.

"What happened on the night of the McGuire Landfill investigation?" Nicholas asked. "Were you aware of your pregnancy even then?"

This time she heard the disappointment in his tone. *Or was that scorn?* She turned to face him. "Yes, I knew. As a matter of a fact, I found out an hour before I met you in the cheese barn."

He was silent, his expression unreadable. Only the slight stiffening in his fingers resting on the stack of papers indicated his surprise. Or was it disappointment?

She waited.

"Are you saying you were aware of your vulnerability to the landfill conditions?" he asked.

"I'm not the only one who couldn't handle the scents floating around that crime scene. Sewers smell better than the McGuire Landfill, and you know it. What I don't understand, is why you want to talk about this now."

"What should we talk about?"

"Us. What happened between us."

"What about us?"

"You didn't know any of it. I didn't… Well I should have said something. I'm sorry."

"What are you sorry about, Ms. Jones? That you've made me an adulterer?"

Ms. Jones? That wasn't just for Miller's benefit? Well, if he was going to be like that, then she too would pretend that it meant nothing. "Look," she said walking closer to his desk. "You're a big boy."

"Not that big."

"I didn't force you into this."

"Nor did you tell me what I needed to know before you enticed me between your sheets."

"Enticed?" She snorted. "First of all, they were your sheets. And as I recall, you were the one who started this, dangling yourself in front of me like man candy. Don't go blaming me if I accepted."

"Why did you agree to stay? Were you planning this all along? Should I expect some sexual harassment suit now?"

"If you keep acting like some spurned school boy, then yes."

"I looked up your husband after I left the courthouse. He's on tour."

"What of it?"

"Is that what you do when he's gone? Jump into every available bed?"

Dammit. That hurt. "How dare you?" she snarled and balled her hands into tight fists.

"I dare because you dragged me into this. Perhaps if you behaved like any decent married woman rather than bedding every newcomer, then I would have known you were someone else's wife."

Her pulse spiked, and she folded her arms. *Just when you think you know someone.* Served her right. She should have never let him talk her into staying.

"You're right," she said. "We should talk about the case. If you must know, that night in the landfill, I wasn't sure it was morning sickness that upset my stomach. I thought I would feel well enough to work if I took Tums or something. Most of all, I knew the landfill's conditions and the difficulties working there. I couldn't let Quinn spend the night there alone. I did my job and I cleared the crime scene before I became sick. But please, feel free to call it what you must."

"Regardless of how we frame this, the coroner wants you off the case. So, you're off the case."

"Just like that? Even though we're short-staffed? Even though my explanation is completely rational?"

"Again, this is not about you. The decision stands. You can dispute it, but I would prefer if you just trust me for now."

Trust him? "You really don't expect me to sit on my hands while Denton decides my fate and the fate of this case, do you?" she asked.

"No, but doing something rash would make matters worse."

"What about the consequences of your decision?"

"What about it?"

"Have you considered that I would appear guilty if you take me off the case?"

"I have a responsibility here. And the perception would be the same if you were suspended, so take your pick."

Is this how he expected her to trust him, by controlling her every move? "I get that you're responsible for what goes on in these labs," she said. "But I intend to take responsibility for this setback and I'll do whatever I can to resolve it."

Chapter 40

ONCEALED IN BLACK LEATHER, Nicholas switched off the engine and rolled the bike between rows of leafy red maple trees. He plucked binoculars with night vision from his saddlebag, removed his helmet and crouched down with an unobstructed view of the cheese barn.

This wasn't his only visit. Forty-eight hours after meeting Savanna there, he had returned in the lab's wagon. He had parked next door in the plant nursery lot as Savanna had done and watched the building for four hours. By the time he left at 0130 hours his injured leg had started to cramp and throb. Still no one had attempted to enter the barn.

Since then, he'd driven out often, at varying times. The spring rain showers had continued into June and even sporadically in July. His career had taught him how to be patient. During his three months in Westbury, he depended heavily on his endurance. Finally, in the middle of summer, a clear and warm night. He was going in.

This time he'd be more quick-witted. Back in May, he let the cheese aroma distract him. His leg had healed since then and though he walked without a limp, a residual spasm sometimes surprised him. Still, he had the flexibility should he encounter someone.

Whatever activities he and Savanna interrupted three months ago, he wanted the perpetrators to relax into complacency again. Hopefully Savanna hadn't returned. She would have told him if she had, since she believed they were trying to solve the same crime.

That was another kettle of fish he wanted to leave untouched, but she insisted that they were searching for the same drug. He wasn't convinced. Moore slipped the women he kidnapped some version of a date-rape drug. The high-performance psychotropic substance Nicholas found in the soldiers he'd autopsied was a far cry from the run-of-the-mill roofies. At least that's what the evidence showed until yesterday.

Nicholas pulled his cellphone from his pocket and accessed the camera. If he tried snapping photos, the flash would alert anyone already in the area or approaching. He chose the binoculars instead.

Likely, no one hung around this area after business hours. It wasn't really a neighbourhood. More like an industrial strip. Manufacturing companies lined the street. He peered into the open area surrounding the barn. If anyone was out there, he couldn't see them.

He checked the time. 0145 hours. It shouldn't be long now. He pulled a metal object from his pocket. He'd found it the night he waited on the floor for Savanna to return with her first aid kit. He spotted it when he tried moving toward the stairs with a piece of metal stabbed into his leg. The small object was about seventeen millimetres in diameter, and about twenty-eight millimetres high, but its most interesting feature was the shape. It was a lightning bolt.

He had sent a photo of the object to Fraser McDaniel, his old professor and life-long mentor. McDaniel came back with an answer that astonished Nicholas. "It's a pill die for a tablet press," he'd said.

Nicholas had sealed the die in an envelope and walked it to the toxicology department. He instructed the toxicologist, Jenny Gupa, to swab and test the tiny hole in the centre as well as any substances she retrieved. The chances of collecting enough for testing were slim, but finding the single die was a stroke of luck not to be squandered.

The die was another link indicating that the cheese barn was somehow a drug-manufacturing site. It was enough evidence to pursue his investigation.

Using this location was genius. Concocting psychotropic products required a clean room to prevent impurities. The last place the authorities would look was a cheese barn, which meant there had to be a hidden section.

Nicholas peered around the perimeter through his binoculars. He was definitely not alone, but the scurrying night animals with glowing yellow eyes weren't interested in him.

He crept along the compound's perimeter, slipping into the shadows for cover. With two months of rain, the trees lining the gravel lot had transformed from mere sticks with budding blossoms into full blooms. They provided a perfect camouflage.

He hopped over the four-foot rock wall separating the two properties and ducked behind a tree when he thought something moved in his peripheral. He listened for footsteps on the gravel, but silence pervaded.

He scaled the rickety steps and picked the lock, like he'd done before. By the time he entered the barn, he was prepared for the odour. The impact was less severe than the first time he was here. He waited for his eyes to adjust to the dark, then crept down the wobbly stairs leading to the barn floor.

A solid cedar panel divided the front office from the storage area. It supported two six-foot shelves. These were lined with pyramid stacked cheese rows. The distinctive odour of mouldy earth mixed with freshly turned soil penetrated the mask he brought from the lab. In the centre, a metal rack reaching his chin housed boxes and cartons.

Nicholas retrieved a small penlight from his pocket and spotted it along the seams in the wooden panels, searching for open creases between the wood. He'd studied the building on his multiple visits. The exterior layout differed from the internal space he observed the only night he gained access.

Yet now his search revealed no open joints, or any other evidence of a hidden door. Without the overhead light, he couldn't discern a colour or shade difference in the wall. The unpainted wood looked the same wherever he spotted the light. He held onto his theory that another room existed between the front office and the back storage.

He pushed on the panel, hoping it would give. Nothing. He stood in front of a metal rack directly facing the stairs that led to the exit door. Nicholas turned and focused behind him for a moment. Often, doors aligned with doors. He shoved the rack aside and shone the light along the wall. He stooped following it to the bottom where the panels stopped a quarter of an inch from the floor. He stood upright again. No locks, no latches, no bolts. He pushed along the side. A click released and a section in the panel gaped open an inch. *Bingo*.

He eased the door open, listening for sounds on the other side. Silence. When he pulled the door wider, he understood. He'd found a closet. Damn. He turned, about to check another area, but pushed on the dark panel lining the back of the closet instead. The divider moved. He pushed harder and it buckled into a folding door.

Nicholas stepped through the parted wall. The air changed from pungent, old cheese smell to heavy ammonia. He wrapped his left arm around his face and felt the wall next to the door until he found a switch. The overhead light flooded the room. "Holy crap."

Two feet into the room, something rustled in the air behind him. He shifted to the side and turned. A hand gripping a lengthy pipe swiped at his head. He ducked to the left and avoided the full impact of the blow. The edge caught him on his upper left arm. Another body shifted in his peripheral just as the first man came after him again. Nicholas twisted sharply and kicked the first assailant in the knee.

"Aargh." The man went down, and Nicholas followed up with a kick to his large head that landed squarely on his ear. The first assailant tried scrambling to his feet, but he stumbled off balance.

Nicholas repositioned to get eyes on both men, but a foot came out of nowhere and tripped him. He hit the floor. He was on his feet in no time, but the men staggered from the room, hitting the light switch on the way out. Nicholas ran after them. He pounded up the steps. The door slammed ahead of him. He kept going. A step broke and he lost his footing. By the time he reached the door, a car swerved and spun its tires, then gunned out of the driveway. He lost them. He pulled his cellphone from his pocket and called Detective Reynolds from the OPP.

Chapter 41

S AVANNA TRIED SECOND LIEUTENANT Scott Allen's cell number one more time. And again, the voicemail picked up immediately. She hung up. What was the sense of leaving another message?

She hadn't heard from him since they met in the coffee shop back in May. Her investigation on the drug side had dried up. She wondered if the army had any better luck. But he hadn't returned any of her five calls.

The sooner she cleared this case from the lab's roster, the sooner she could get on with her life. Such as it was. She picked up her lab phone and dialled. "Dave, are you available?" she asked when he answered.

"Well, I'm just getting back to the precinct. What's on your mind?"

"Colton Moore. I need your help sourcing some information."

"I'm heading into an interrogation. Does it have to be now?"

Moving this case along was like hauling a brick through quicksand. "This is important too," she said, frustration riding her short fuse.

"Weren't you taken off the case?" he asked.

She rolled her eyes. "Can you see me or not?"

"You got fifteen minutes."

Three weeks into the trial and the evidence trail on Moore's accomplice ground to a halt. Yes, she had been taken off the case, but that didn't stop Denton from recalling her a week later. Right now, the team needed answers, and she would get them. Savanna shrugged from her lab coat and grabbed the list she had been working on in the last two weeks.

When she entered the homicide squad room, she spotted Dave perched on the corner of a desk, holding a coffee mug with an icon of Inspector Gadget.

"Hey," he greeted her and headed down the hall. They entered a small, grey room, brightly lit with a single wooden table and two metal chairs.

"Just as well you came by," he said as soon as she closed the door behind them.

Savanna took the chair closest to her. It rocked slightly on three legs when she sat down.

"Thought you might want to know that Lamons Street, Moore's house where you found the severed hand and the two boys, is still very popular." Dave sat across from her. "Especially for the transient-minded," he said.

"How so?"

"Found a homeless woman camping there. A junkie. We brought her in for questioning, but she didn't seem to know anything. She was a mess and not easy to look at."

"What do you mean?"

"You know the type, could use a good nutritionist. Oblong face, pointy chin, skinny as a rake, with pock-marked skin."

"What's her name?"

"You know someone fitting that description?"

"No, just curious."

"Margaret Ross. Goes by the nickname Molly."

"Doesn't sound familiar. Do you have a file on her?"

"Yep. I can get you some details. Now, what can I do for you?"

She tried to steady the chair. "Any news on Sally Starr's necklace?" she asked.

"The one from the photo? Nothing yet, but she shouldn't hold out hope."

"Nothing from the pawn shops?"

"Not yet. It might have been sold already, which means the shop owner isn't inclined to tell us the truth."

"Hmm." Savanna scratched her fingernail on the tabletop.

"What's on your mind?"

"Up until his capture, Moore had only used two locations, his own house and his mother's. His profile mentioned nothing of a souvenir collection, yet someone ripped Sally's necklace from her neck. Perhaps the accomplice collects trophies."

"You've really got your teeth into this one."

"Maybe you're right." She straightened in the uneven chair again. "What about the van? Any leads yet?"

"Nothing yet."

"How come? It's been weeks now."

Dave studied her, concern gathering around his furrowing brows. "Is this about Charles Denton's cross in court?"

Savanna rocked in the chair. She reminded herself that Dave wasn't the enemy. She needed to keep this professional. "I need to leave no doubt about the lack of contamination on the evidence," she said. "Plus, there's an accomplice out there who deserves an adjoining prison cell with Moore."

"Denton used his regular shadows and mirrors. He targeted you because he had his goons follow you around town."

"Maybe, but you can't deny that he knows juries, and he knows it doesn't take much."

"Most jurors are dim-witted, but not that slow. They'll see through his distractions. Moore's been convicted once already. It doesn't take much of a leap to get him for this one too."

"That's Denton's point exactly. So, he discredits the evidence and creates reasonable doubt. It's enough and all he needs."

Dave turned his pensive brown eyes on her again. "I suppose you're right. Is this keeping you up at night?"

Heat flushed through her. "We would all sleep better if we at least had a lead on this person, or a place to start looking."

"Amen to that."

She sighed. If only she could see two feet in front of her. "I watched your taped interview with Moore," she said. "There's nothing glaring, just what you and Fontaine pointed out in your notes."

Dave adjusted his tie and nodded. "We got nothing out of him that afternoon. I can't imagine why he agreed to talk to us without his lawyer present. Maybe to find out what we knew."

"You don't think he recognizes the van either?"

"No."

"Something about your questions got his attention though."

"You got that?"

She tensed as the image of Moore shackled to the table came back to her. "He looked… curious," she said. "Like he had his own questions about the van."

"Then why not give up the accomplice? Unless he's gathering information of his own."

"That brings me to the reason I wanted to talk to you."

"Yeah?"

Savanna unfolded her list. "I need to collect some extra samples, but since Nicholas… um, Dr. Wade took me off the case for the time being, I'm committing a cardinal sin even discussing it with you. If you prefer not to get involved, I'll understand." Without Dave's help, she would take one of those impetuous actions her boss warned against.

"Why not ask Quinn?" Dave asked

"This is your case. I thought I should come to you, stakes and all. Plus, I don't want Hannigan going after Quinn too."

Dave's head jerked back. "What, you don't mind him coming after me?"

"I figured you could handle the heat."

"Uh huh. What are you working on?"

"I need clean samples to run some tests. Is this going to be a problem?"

"When has it ever been a problem? Just let me know when and what."

"Okay. Here's what I need." She handed him the paper. "If I think of anything else, I'll email you."

His eyes scrolled down the list. "What do these check marks mean?"

"Material I collected myself."

"All this even though you're off the case?"

"Off-duty hours don't count."

Dave grinned. "It's Friday," he said. "Can this wait until Monday?"

"Why, you have a hot date lined up?"

He grinned. "We all don't have Richard's luck."

Savanna dropped her chin feeling embarrassed. What would Dave say if he knew she slept with Nicholas? "Monday is fine," she said, skirting the subject altogether. "I'll work with your timeline. Just let me know when, and I'll come out and meet you." Now she just needed to insert the extra testing into her colleagues' schedules, and hope that Nicholas wouldn't notice. Since her court appearance, he went out of his way to avoid her, which worked well for her under the circumstances.

She pushed from the chair, but lagged.

"Something else on your mind?"

She gripped the chair. "Yes," she said, her voice softer now. "It's been seven weeks since Janet's death. Did Detective Reynolds come up with anything?"

"I thought Wade would have told you."

Prickles rose on her arm. "What?"

"Reynolds believes her death is connected to a lone perpetrator they have been trying to track for the last few months. Maybe close to a year, off and on."

"What do you mean?"

"They received reports of a large man, bulky sort, beating up on women outside a couple of clubs in Exeter. Detective Reynolds said they checked it out and came up empty-handed. Then a few months later, another report surfaced. Same thing happened. They checked it out and couldn't get so much as a skin colour consistency, just that it was a guy and he was bulky. Maybe Janet tried to run interference and got caught in the crossfire. Then there was the drug operation in the cheese barn Dr. Wade called in."

"What?"

"So he really said nothing to you about this?"

"Not one freaking word." Well, two can play at that game.

Chapter 42

$\mathcal{I}$T WAS TUESDAY AFTERNOON the following week when Savanna walked into the trace evidence lab with the samples she and Dave had collected. Senior technician Terry Allen lifted his head from the stereomicroscope and smiled. Then his eyes zipped to the box she carried. He scowled and lowered his head to his test again.

She expected resistance, but she was determined to persevere. "Hello Terry," she said. "I promise it's not as bad as it looks."

"Huh. Whenever you come down here, I'm looking at unauthorized extra work. What is it this time?"

"But our collaborations are always a success."

"You want another favour?"

"I have some samples I need tested. Just a few."

"Oh really?"

"It's crucial evidence in the Moore case."

"Everyone comes in here with a box of crucial for something."

"The results would help the police in their search. They would also change the tide in Doreen Bellamy's court case. She'll appreciate any extra help right now." Savanna hoped she didn't sound too desperate.

"What's that gotta do with me?" Terry asked. "Besides, I haven't heard the one name that should matter most."

"Who's that?"

"Wade."

Darn. Doreen was Savanna's trump card. She had hoped to aid Terry's cooperation by appealing to his crush on the assistant Crown attorney. He'd been so smitten with her, he never neglected to show favouritism when pushing through evidence in her cases. It was the only way to sidestep authorization from their chief.

"Okay," she said. "I don't want to cause trouble for you." She reached for her box.

"Did you say Doreen wants this evidence?" Terry asked.

"It's important to her case."

"Fine, but if Wade asks, I'll let him know you coerced me."

"No problem. I'll take the blame."

Savanna stuck to Dr. Wade's procedures with one minuscule exception. Her boss had no knowledge of the recent investigation she pursued. She bent the rules and enlisted the help of her colleagues without his consent, hoping that the weight of her results would soften her insubordination.

"So, what do you want anyway?" Terry asked.

Savanna reached into the box. "Pile 'A'," she said. "Is compiled of unidentified materials collected at the time of the Moore investigation. Pile 'B' is a set of recently collected samples with known origins. I want to know if any fibres from pile 'A' matches pile 'B'.

"Can I ask where this new evidence came from?" Terry scrutinized her labeled samples.

"Well, I—"

"Know what, never mind. The less I know, the better. Except, what are you hoping for?"

"A match."

"I'll let you know what I find." He pushed the box aside and lowered his head onto his microscope again.

"So," Savanna said. "When can I have the analysis?"

"I'm sorry, lady, but you don't scare me as much as the man upstairs who checks my roster on a regular basis."

"Fine, but I would be grateful if you can squeeze me in as soon as possible."

"I suppose I shouldn't even ask how come Wade isn't all over this?" Terry chuckled at her blank stare. "He doesn't even know about it, does he?" he asked.

"He will when I complete my report. Thanks, I owe you one."

Terry's gaze moved over her face and then down to her stomach.

"How about naming your first born after me," he said.

"I don't think he'll survive in the shadow of your brilliance."

Terry showed up at her table two days later. Her face went numb when he entered the serology lab with her box clutched under his arm. Nicholas probably discovered her little side project and burnt it. She reminded herself that this wasn't Terry's fault.

His plump arms dropped the box on her worktable like a burden he longed to release. "There you go," he said. "I hope this is what you were looking for."

Savanna's eyes widened. "You didn't?"

"I did. You said it was for Doreen. Now you owe me."

"Anything," she said, but she had already started digging into the box.

"How about those Glosettes for starters?" He pointed to the chocolate-covered raisins on her desk.

"All yours," Savanna said and handed them over. "Thank you," she said.

"Nice doing business with you."

"Until next time."

Terry scurried from the lab shaking his reward.

Savanna plucked the single sheet of paper from the box and held her breath. She scanned the comparison notes. Then she sat back with a smile. All the proof she needed to convince Nicholas Wade existed in Terry's fibre analysis.

It took her ten minutes to plug in the findings and re-read the report she started on the weekend. Now to see Dr. Wade. She slid off her stool and exited the serology lab. Unhurried steps took her closer to his office.

She suspended every thought that entered her head, ignored rehearsed speeches, and dismissed excuses for working on a case no longer on her docket. Even the results she clutched between her fingers took a back seat to the ramifications of what they meant.

Strolling past Josie with a slight wave, she knocked on his closed door.

"Come in," he said brusquely.

Her eyes found him behind his desk and her stomach fluttered at the sight of his eyes dipping to her now visible stomach. Maybe she should come back. He did look busy. After avoiding him in the last three weeks, seeing him this close muddled her thinking.

"Ms. Jones, I was just about to call you. I wanted a quick word."

So we're back to Ms. and Dr.

His eyes moved past her. "That's all right, Josie," he said. "I'll see Ms. Jones."

"Yes, Doctor." Josie closed the door and left them alone.

Her boss rocked back and closed the folder in front of him.

"I need only a few minutes of your time," she said. "I'll get straight to the point."

"I'm listening."

"I have some new evidence in the Moore case."

"The Moore case?" His face lost all expression and his eyes zipped to the folder she held. He reached out his arm without another word.

She handed it over and followed his eyes moving across the page. She waited for the contents to reshape his expressionless face.

Almost on cue, unreadable squinted to uncertainty. He turned that questioning gaze on her. "What makes you think the accomplice is female when the police are searching for an unidentified male?"

Savanna silently reminded herself to keep breathing. "Do you mind if I sit?" she asked.

He nodded toward the upholstered chairs in front of his desk, and she quickly pulled one out and took a seat.

"Well, the local database produced nothing on the only unidentified evidence in the case," she said. "That's when I reached out to a contact at the RCMP."

"Who's that?"

"Ben Folly. We worked on another case a few years ago."

Nicholas read from the file, then glued his eyes to her face again. "Folly came back with Margaret "Molly" Ross."

"Yes. She moved to Westbury from Halifax four years ago, after an arrest for prostitution earned her permanent status on the local database back home. Detective Thomas mentioned a few weeks ago that he found a drug addict loitering around the Lamons Street location. He said her hair was blue at the ends."

Nicholas's upper body jerked backward. "Blue?"

"You may recall that we found similar unidentified hair fibres among the Moore evidence."

He nodded.

Of course, he remembered. He didn't forget much.

"But that would mean you knew of this connection for weeks," he said.

"I speculated, not knew."

"Are these the fibres Terry analyzed?"

"Yes."

"Not only have you proven resourceful with other agencies, you've been using my staff quite liberally, Ms. Jones."

"I have, Dr. Wade."

"According to Terry's report, all the matches are negative."

"I expected that."

"Then why have the tests done? You didn't waste the time and resources of this lab on a hunch, did you?"

"I needed the proof, not just—"

"Proof of what?"

Savanna bristled. He intended to hold her accountable for every minute of manpower she used without his consent. "I believe there is another location," she said. "None of the new fibres matched the fibres found in our evidence."

"New fibres?"

"Yes, new samples collected for the purpose of this analysis."

"From where?"

"The samples were taken from the victims' homes, cars, and places of employment."

"When?"

Her face muscle twitched. She braced herself for a battle. "Last week," she said.

"And which member of my staff did you direct to gather these samples?"

She straightened her back against the soft chair and uncrossed her legs. "I got them," she said.

"Sorry, Ms. Jones, I must be mistaken. I thought I heard you say that you collected the samples yourself." He tossed the file onto his desk and the pages slid from between the folder.

She flinched.

"But that would mean you worked on the case, ignoring a direct order," he said. "So please tell me that I heard incorrectly."

Her pulse galloped. Was that a bulging vein crawling along the side of his forehead? She was becoming very familiar with that one. It appeared only when he strained to hold onto his restraint. "The evidence is still real," she said.

"You promised to stay off the case until we work out Denton's accusations."

"I never promised you that."

He vaulted from his chair and, once again, she faced his hardened jawline.

"I recall saying that I would do everything I could to turn around Denton's insinuations before they got any further," she said.

"You believe your actions have done that?"

"My report implicates Colton Moore in Morgan's death. The evidence also shows a third location, pointing to an accomplice. I would say that this report more than responds to Denton's attempt to discredit the evidence. It's clear proof his client is guilty."

"You collected and processed all this evidence."

"With the help of the police department and the scientists here."

"You have been taken off the case."

"I still work for the Westbury Forensic labs, and I collected the evidence with the help of a detective on the case."

"Which one did you persuade to help you?"

"I didn't need to persuade anyone…" She paused. With one exception, she thought, and met his glare. "The police want this case closed as much as we do," she said. "What difference does it make anyway? Rather than chasing our tails, we have a name to investigate."

"Is that how you see everything in life, Ms. Jones? The ends justify the means?"

Savanna pressed her lips together. This was more than a little disappointing. "You meant it, didn't you?" she asked.

"What are you referring to now?"

"You wanted me to sit on my hands and do nothing; to wait while the wheels of the old boy network slowly turn and decide my fate and the fate of this case?"

He twisted his chin away from her. "Yes," he said. "If that's what it took."

The words struck Savanna like a well-placed slap across her cheek. She drew into the chair. What had she expected from him? A declaration of her value to his staff? —*Don't be absurd. You and every woman who work in this lab are valuable members of my team*—

She met his eyes again. "What it took was actual evidence," she said. "And the will to find it."

"Since the situation is already volatile, it might have been better if you had informed me about your actions."

"Why? Don't you trust me now?"

He stared for a moment. "I could have worked this new angle with you to at least discredit any hint of impropriety."

She exhaled hard. Whether she liked it or not, he made some sense, even if she didn't intend to admit it. "So, should we just ignore my discovery of a more than plausible lead?" she asked.

He moved to his desk and sat down again. "I suppose you want me to sanction this before taking it to the police and the Crown attorney?" He opened the folder again and started reading.

"That's the idea," she said.

"I will pass on your report, but I don't expect a response until sometime next week."

She suppressed a smile when he flicked a measured glance in her direction. She pushed from the chair, ready to strut from his office when he spoke again.

"I'm surprised you didn't just go over my head and hand it off yourself," he said.

Now why did he have to go and spoil her enthusiasm? "Unlike you, Doctor," she said. "I share my discoveries."

Chapter 43

SAVANNA HEADED FOR THE DOOR. She'd leave him to mull over the report for a while before he admitted that she was right.

"Is that supposed to mean that I don't?" he asked before she reached for the doorknob.

She turned to him again. "Since you're asking," she said. "Just over a week ago, Dave Thomas told me that you found something in the cheese barn."

Nicholas tipped his head away from her and pinched his nose bridge. "The cheese barn?"

Savanna couldn't tell if it was surprise or relief in his tone. "Yes," he said.

"Dave also said that Detective Reynolds thinks whatever you found there could be a clue to Janet's death."

Nicholas's face softened.

"You could have said something," she accused.

"You're right," he said. "I should have mentioned it."

"So why didn't you?"

"I intended to, but they had nothing really. And I was waiting for some test results."

"Of what?"

He studied her for a moment. When he spoke, his tone was less constrained. "Let's start at the beginning," he said. "Both our leads about that place were right. A full-on drug distribution operation is housed in the barn."

"What made you go back for a second look? Did you find something the night we were there together?"

He cleared his throat. "Yes."

She closed her eyes for a moment. "What was it?"

"A pill die. It was among the rubble that fell from the rack."

"Why couldn't you tell me about that?"

"Maybe because I didn't want you going back out there."

"Sharing the info with me might have guaranteed that."

"I think it would have guaranteed the opposite."

She stared at him. He was probably right. The only reason she hadn't returned was because she promised Quinn she wouldn't. She dropped her gaze when she realized she was staring at Nicholas's lips. Best to keep her anger seething.

"So what kind of equipment did you find that prompted you to bring in the police?" she asked.

"Enough to indicate an entire operation." By the time he was done explaining how he found the secret room, she was sitting on the edge of the chair. This was incredible. How could she have missed an operation right under their noses?

"Did you find any drugs?"

"There were a few samples. And the rest of it."

"Like what?"

"Foil blister packs, a blister packing machine, shipping boxes, packing tape, et cetera."

"What about the drugs? Do you have the tests back yet?"

"As you well know, these things take time."

"How much time?"

"I had to send it away since we don't have the equipment here."

"What kind of equipment?"

"A performance liquid chromatography machine. The funny thing is, running their operation, they would have needed one to test the integrity of the raw material and pass it off as a regulated product."

"How do we locate the one they used?"

Nicholas pushed from the chair. "We don't," he said. "I do."

"This is as much my investigation as it is yours, so don't shut me out." Savanna dragged her hands over her face. This was frustrating.

"You never told me why you were in the cheese barn in the first place," she said. "Does this investigation have anything to do with removing the cloud from over you and getting your old job back?"

His head twitched as though he didn't expect the question, but the startled expression lasted for only a moment. "Cloud?" he asked.

"The way I heard it, you're on leave under a cloud. As you could imagine, the cheese barn was the last place I expected to find you."

"You know that I'm under sanction for one year."

"What for?"

"You really don't know anything about it?"

"Why would I?"

"With the help of Google, you could discover just about anything."

"Oh." Though she sometimes wondered about his life since they last saw each other, it never occurred to her to investigate him that way. "Not everything," she said. "Why are you under sanction?"

"Do you know the magazine Global Research?"

Know it? Her father was a contributor. "Yes, I do," she said.

"Early this year, I spoke to them about the army's rampant drug use. A few generals didn't like what I said."

"What did you say?"

"That the army's lack of action against drug use and the aftereffects is evidence that they condone substance abuse."

His answer triggered memories of her mother. Savanna knew little of her mother's life as a soldier in the Brazilian army, but she knew what the authorities did to soldiers turned whistleblowers. Nicholas Wade got off lightly.

"And they sent you here?" she asked.

"Not at first but eventually. The article is due out in a matter of weeks. Upper brass wanted to make sure I'm not available for further comment."

"Where does the cheese barn come in?"

His expression darkened. She waited as his eyes narrowed and glared at a distant fury. "In the last year, I performed autopsies on six soldiers who overdosed. They all tested positive for Ecstasy. A narcotic generally popular with the military. But recently the supply making its way through the army units has been cut with ketamine. I've been tracking a lead."

"What lead?"

"Just something from a friend."

"He gave you the cheese barn location?"

Still wearing his solemn expression, Nicholas nodded.

"Can you speak to him again? See if he remembers anything else?"

He pushed from the chair. "No, I can't speak to him."

"Why not? He obviously knew more than you did."

"He's dead, Savanna."

"Dead?" She certainly didn't expect that. "Sorry. I didn't mean to…" A shadow of dread crept over her. Six dead. Add Suzette Morgan, Theresa Filito and Janet. There were probably more. None of them deserved to end up in a landfill, or trash heap, or a drum at a loading dock. And Janet…

Savanna looked up at Nicholas. She shook her head. "Sometimes," she said and paused. "Sometimes I think forensic pathologists are the true witnesses of human self-destruction."

He came to stand next to her. "You really think that?"

That wasn't all she thought, but she was determined to put what she felt for him behind her.

"Pharmaceutical companies use the machine you're looking for," she said. "It measures the active pharmaceutical ingredient, also known as API, in the products as required by Health Canada. The test proves that the drug matches its accompanying Certificate of Analysis. For an outfit that operates under the illegal guidelines, they use the machine for the same purpose."

"You're saying that the machine is used to produce designer drugs that skirt Health Canada's regulations?"

"In the hands of illegal manufacturers. That's our tax payers' dollars at work."

Nicholas crossed the room again. "You're saying this could either be a rogue army outfit, or a legit pharmacy?"

"Very possible."

"Who do you know would have access to a machine like that or connections to a lab that housed one?"

"Well I would."

"You?"

"Yes, and every scientist in this building."

"Where is it?"

"Exeter."

They both went silent. Then Savanna thought of her last conversation with Scott Allen. "Nicholas."

He met her gaze, his hazel eyes softening. She squirmed, then cleared her throat.

"Do you know Second Lieutenant Scott Allen?"

"No. Who is he?"

"He said the drug most popular with soldiers is one that Health Canada approved for a very specific use. He said it's the same one that the army is trying to track down because—"

"Have you met this man?"

She should have told him sooner. "Yes," she said rubbing her neck.

"When did you last speak to him?"

"Back in May?"

"May?"

"The Monday following the McGuire Landfill murder. He knew details that hadn't been released"

"Did he say how he knew?"

"A friend on the OPP force filled him in after he mentioned he was thinking of joining the department after his next tour."

"Did you believe him?"

"I didn't at first, then I did, and now I'm not so sure."

"What's your gut instinct about this guy?"

Her instincts weren't working that great these days. In fact, she couldn't remember a time when they steered her right. She shrugged. "I've learned to trust only what's in front of me. I don't know. Not for sure."

"But if you had to say what you think of him, what would that be?"

"He's hiding something, which I thought was natural because of the nature of the case."

Nicholas looked thoughtful for a moment. "What does Allen look like?"

"He's a bit taller than you, thick torso…" She paused. "Thick everything really. Solid. Reminds me of a tank. Oh, there's something else I noticed. He has a lightning bolt tattooed on the inside of his wrist. Hardly noticeable, but it's there."

Nicholas's expression darkened. He leaned back and pulled his desk drawer and took a file. He opened it to reveal a few photos of soldiers. He chose one from among the stack and handed it to her. "Is this him?"

"Why do you have a picture of him?"

"Savanna, is this the man calling himself Second Lieutenant Scott Allen?"

"Calling himself? Do you mean…? Yes, that's him."

Nicholas sat back. For the first time ever, blood drained from his face.

"What's wrong?"

"He's a captain, not a second lieutenant, and his name is Gerald Brock."

Chapter 44

$\mathcal{N}$ICHOLAS PUSHED BACK HIS chair and stood. Brock was in Westbury. Talking to Savanna about a psychotropic drug. He lied to her about his rank, and his name to gain access to a police investigation. Not to mention that the tattoo he wore was the same shape as the pill die Nicholas found in the cheese barn. Together, all these pieces can't be mere coincidences. What else was Brock up to?

Nicholas turned to Savanna. The only sign that she was alarmed was how unnaturally still she sat, her eyes fixed on him.

He leaned over with his palms pressing into the desk, his face inches away from hers. "Brock is a sociopath," he said.

"Is that why you have a file on him?"

"He came up in my investigation."

"The cheese barn investigation?"

"That's right."

"He lied about his identity. Does that move him up on your list?"

"You can't meet with him again."

"I think breaking contact is a mistake. He would know that we're onto him."

"If he knows I'm here, then he already knows something."

"He doesn't know your role. Not for sure."

Why does she always have to make such good points? "It's not worth the risk," he said.

"Refusing to see him again might spook him. He could run."

Nicholas wasn't concerned with Brock leaving. He feared what the man would do if he felt Savanna had been deceiving him. "He has already lied to you to get this close. And he's using you to monitor the investigation from the inside."

"Then tell me what I should say to him. I'll feed him information that only he can act on and that way we would know for sure."

"Aargh." Nicholas pushed away from the desk and started pacing again. "You're not listening," he said.

"Yes, I am, and I know you're hearing me. You know what I'm saying makes sense."

"For you to put yourself in danger?"

"I'm the only one in contact with him."

He tilted his head to one side and considered her expression. Why was she so calm about this, sounding so rational?

"If anyone else tries to meet with him, he might bolt," she said. "And we wouldn't have the slightest clue how to get close to the drugs again."

It's true. Finding the location of the drug operation hadn't really brought them any closer to the people who ran the outfit. The Ontario Provincial Police thanked him sincerely for his find and threatened to arrest him the next time he trespassed on private property. If Detective Reynolds hadn't shown up at the cheese barn, he might be having this conversation with Savanna from a jail cell. He checked every couple of days for an update but got the brush-off.

"Brock may know something that would lead us to whoever is manufacturing these drugs," Savanna said. The determination in her voice pulled him back to their conversation. He stopped pacing. Something else other than the way she sat riveted spooked him. This time she wouldn't meet his gaze.

"I can't agree with your idea," he said. "More than that, I absolutely forbid you to meet with him again."

Fire blazed in her eyes and he knew the jig was up now. Whatever she was feeling about Brock's deception was about to surface.

She shoved from the chair with such force, it rocked on its back legs before settling again. "Forbid me?" she asked. "Listen here, Lieutenant-Colonel Wade. You're not in the army now. Out here in the civilian world, women are allowed to follow a trail of evidence not drilled into our brains by a commanding officer."

He raised an eyebrow. *Did she just call him sexist?* He was trying to keep her safe and she insulted him. "Like I said when we first met in Exeter." He smoothed his tone for her benefit. "You are over your head. You have no clue what you're getting into."

"Well, you're wrong. I may not know Brock, or Allen, or whatever he calls himself, but I know he had something to do with Janet's death and I will find out what."

Janet's death. He exhaled. He should have seen that. "Look," he said, feeling like an ass for not making the connection. "I understand how important this is to you, but we have to trust the system." He kept his voice even.

"Really?" she asked rather smugly and sat down again. "Is that what you did when you went to the cheese barn the first time? How about when you returned, did you trust the system then? And what about now? Do you intend to give the OPP detectives whatever you know about Brock?"

Nicholas pulled his chair and plopped down into it. "You fight dirty," he said.

Savanna crossed her legs and sat back. "Are you ready now to talk about your investigation," she asked. "Or are we going to go our separate ways again?"

He darted a glance at her. She outwitted him. He might as well admit it. He leaned back in his chair. There was no escaping her determination to argue her point. And she was winning too. He was the one blind to the connections. If he had shared his information with her earlier, they might have been way ahead of Brock. *Crap.*

He twisted his mouth to one side. Savanna dropped her gaze from his eyes. He smiled, slowly. Her lips parted.

"How are things with the baby?" he asked.

"Don't change the bloody subject."

Her snap was so sudden, he startled. Now he was the one feeling disarmed.

"I may be pregnant," she said, "but I'm certainly not barefoot and empty-headed. What do you intend to do with this new information?"

There was only one way to ensure that she never met with Brock again. He'd have to include her from now on. "Do you have any suggestions?" he asked.

"Yes. Well maybe it's not a suggestion."

"Then what is it?"

"From our discovery that Allen and your Brock is the same person, I believe they're working together?"

"Who?"

"Colton Moore and Gerald Brock."

"All we need is evidence that they know each other," Savanna said. The thought crossed her mind before. It had to have. She remembered thinking it when Brock brought up the landfill victim, but the possibility was too flimsy. Nothing but a fleeting thought connected the two men and she dismissed it. Now here it was again and this time the idea seemed more than possible. It was even probable.

"What makes you think they know each other?" Nicholas asked.

"Maybe it was something Scott… I mean Brock said that I didn't think was relevant at the time."

"Let's put that thought on hold for a bit. First, let's figure out Brock's connection to these drugs and that might lead us to what you remember."

"Okay." Savanna rubbed her stomach.

Nicholas's eyes followed her hand. "Are you all right?" He asked.

She should eat. When was her last meal anyway? "Yep." She looked at her watch. "I have to go. I could do some research tonight at home." With no food in the house, she needed to stop at the market.

"Are you sure?" Nicholas asked again. His face scrunched as he watched her still rubbing her stomach.

"I don't suppose you have a candy bar in your desk drawer?" she asked.

"You're hungry."

"I could eat."

"I would say it's more than that. Come on, we can continue this at my place while I make us dinner."

A boulder dropped somewhere in her stomach. She just hoped it missed the baby. "Your place?" She vowed never to go back there, especially feeling the way she did. As horny as a—Was there anything else hornier than a jackrabbit? Maybe just her, and knowing he could do the job in spades meant staying away from—

"Yes, my place," he was smiling down at her.

Was she drooling or something? "We can work on this separately."

He started packing up. "Don't you think that's a waste of time? You've already proven this evening that pooling our resources works better."

Did he just admit that she was right? "Sorry, I didn't hear that? Are you saying that I had been right from the beginning?"

"I don't remember saying anything remotely close to that but let's discuss it while we work."

"I don't know," she said. Besides grocery shopping, she had thought about calling an apartment listing she found before she left the lab. "I have to make a stop on my way home."

"Ms. Jones," he said underscoring the level of disgust evident in his expression. "Are you afraid you wouldn't be able to keep your hands off me?"

She snorted to hide the rapid heat flash. How did he know what she'd been trying to push away from her thoughts? She looked away from him without answering.

"If you lower the shields a little," he said, "we might find trust a bit easier. I have no intentions of seducing you again, but if your errand takes precedence over this case, then by all means, let us go our separate ways."

What the…? She opened her mouth, but the words wouldn't come. She pushed from the chair and marched toward the door. "I'll see you at your place in half an hour," she said. "And for the record, I'm the one who did the seducing the last time." She yanked the door open and left. Only when she arrived at her table in the serology lab, did she realize that he played her, and she gave in just to prove that she wasn't afraid of being near him, which she was.

Chapter 45

SAVANNA RUBBED HER KNEES together under Nicholas's home office desk. A modern L-shaped fibreglass built-in. The soft white keys under her fingertips responded effortlessly. Zero lag time in the Safari browser showcased on the screen of the eye candy in front of her— a 2012 iMac. *Beautiful.* The Magic Mouse though, well, all she could say was, there was nothing magical about it. She cupped her palm over the thing, and it zipped all over the screen. Where was the bloody wheel for her index finger?

"A running commentary of your thoughts would keep me in the loop," Nicholas yelled from the kitchen.

Savanna grinned.

The sounds of kitchen utensils connecting with the counter echoed into the small office. He insisted on making sandwiches or something for her to eat. So long as they weren't cucumber and salmon paste, she was fine. The man probably forgot she carried another human being inside her, and one that liked to eat, she was discovering. At nineteen weeks pregnant, she ate like a college linebacker.

"It's 2012," she said. "Just about everyone showcases their talents on the Internet these days. It makes life a little easier."

"That's true, but what's your point?"

"We don't only do business on the Internet with people in our own backyards and halfway around the world." She brought up a Google page. "We air our dirty laundry and we get cocky and don't consider our own security. Brock strikes me as the efficient type, and a bit of a show-off too. He does it for the creds."

"I've had that same thought. I searched Google and got nowhere. So now I'm perusing the military chatrooms for threads that might open a lead."

Resourceful guy. "What are your search terms?"

"I have only one."

When the silence lingered, Savanna pushed back in the chair, but still couldn't see him from her position. She waited. *Not a word*. "Still keeping secrets, Doc?" she asked.

"Excuse me if I seem apprehensive. I'm just not sure what you can do that I haven't done already."

What's that supposed to mean? The man's hubris was astounding. "I'm happy to show you," she said. "But you've got to trust me."

"Vader." Nicholas yelled into the office.

"Really?" she asked. "As in Darth?"

"Brock has the Star Wars tattoo on his neck. I thought it would be a good place to start."

A savoury scent wafted in from the kitchen. Savanna rubbed her stomach. Hmm. Not exactly tea sandwiches. It certainly smelled like the man possessed another talent. On her way to Nicholas's place, she devoured a Snickers bar that soon had her mentally bouncing off the walls. But a crash was imminent and on its way.

She started typing again. "What smells so good?" she asked.

"It'll be ready soon."

In Google, Savanna started with a basic Star Wars reference. Wasn't Vader too obvious? Then again, most people didn't look very smart on the Internet. Still hoping to cover all the bases, she typed Sith Lord. The regular Star Wars craze filled the screen. Darth. More of the same. Lord Vader. Every listing from face, appearance, death, quotes, voice, unmasked, but no usernames. Vader username. What's this? Vader Stream. Not the same thing.

She sighed. Would they ever find this guy? There must be something that would get them into his inner sanctum. She touched the mouse, but the cursor seemed stuck. What the heck was wrong with the thing? She picked up the mouse and twisted it.

"You're not going to eat it, are you?" Nicholas's voice said from the doorway.

She startled and turned to see him leaning against the doorjamb with a plate of something in his hand. *Did he have to sneak up on her? And then stand there looking like that?* Apron wrapped around his hips, shirt unbuttoned, showing off the rise in his pecs and that lazy, sexy expression on his face. No man who refused to sleep with her again had the right to look like that.

"What's that?" she asked.

"Dinner will be another twenty, so I thought I'd bring you a little snack. And just in time, too, I see." He set the plate down beside her. "I think you need a break."

She reached for the food. Devilled eggs. "You made these?"

"Uh huh."

"I love devilled eggs."

"Good. Better protein source than…" He reached over and wiped something from her cheek, then tasted it. "Chocolate?" he asked.

Her centre warmed. "Thought you said no seducing?" she asked and bit into the appetizer.

"Not to worry. I mean to keep my word."

What a shame.

"I see you're having as much luck with the search as I did." He motioned to the screen.

"I'm just getting started," she said. "I have a few more tricks up my sleeve."

"Show me." Nicholas came to stand next to her.

She stuffed the last half of egg into her mouth and looked around for a napkin. She didn't have one.

"Here," Nicholas said, offering her his apron without removing it. "Use this."

She took it slowly and wiped her hands, being careful not to touch him. That didn't stop her mind from recalling what he looked like under the pair of slacks that hid his well-formed lower body. She knew there was a set of cheeks in there and two ripped thighs that were enough to make her drool. Then there were the other injuries. She'd rather not think about those.

"How's the wound?" she asked. "Do you have a scar?"

"A little one?"

She dropped the apron, wondering if she'd ever get to see the mark. Then admonished herself for wanting to get into his pants again. "Let's get started." The words came out hoarse. She cleared her throat and avoided looking over when Nicholas pulled up a chair and sat beside her.

"I tried it your way," she said and pointed at the search terms she scribbled on the page. "And you're right, I came up blank. Do you have anything other than Vader?"

"I have another phrase. I believe it's the name that Brock uses to refer to his drug." Nicholas went silent again.

She met his gaze and had to steel herself from leaning over to kiss him. "Don't you think it's a little late to keep the information to yourself?" she asked.

"Major Mac."

In a new Google tab she started typing:

+major mac +vader -mackenzie. Then she pressed the 'return' key.

The screen filled with results. The first page listed no references to their search, but Savanna clicked to page two. On the third option down, she spotted an interesting link. "What's this?" She whispered, mainly to herself. "Oh my," she said a bit louder. "I think we have something."

"What?"

"Here." She pointed to a post.

'https//reddit/r/darkmarkets/ships_fast

Need directions to Major Mac! Finding Lord Vader'

"What is it?"

"This is a string in a chat forum where someone replied to a searcher looking for Major Mac. They even supplied the darkmar-ket's URL."

Nicholas leaned closer and his breath heated her face. "Can we go there?" he asked.

"Uh hmm." Savanna copied the URL and pasted it into another tab. The page opened up and she scrolled down, but the chat listed multiple responses. She typed Vader into the 'find on this page' window. She got a hit. One user, going by the name *Idol*.

"Here is a reply that might match," she said.

'Follow the Silk Road! Look for Lord Vader Billboards'.

"Silk Road? How do we get there?" Nicholas asked.

"You need separate software, called TOR. It's free and enables anonymous Internet chats. Once you have the software, you can set up an account on Silk Road and buy anything from drugs, to weapons, to stolen bank accounts."

"The Dark Web? Is that a joke?"

"Not a joke. It's as real as you and me."

"Then I need an account."

"I figured you would say that. So, you would need to go here." She started typing the website for TOR.

"How come you know all this stuff?"

Savanna grinned. "My father is a computer scientist, a genius really, and before my mother's death, I intended to follow in his footsteps. Though I switched from computer science to forensic science, I never gave up my fascination for technology."

"That sounds like an interesting story."

"It is," was all she was willing to disclose.

"How did you get to the information so fast?"

"You told me what to look for. With the billions, even trillions of search terms, it could have been anything. Your friend gave you a valuable piece of information."

Nicholas spun the chair and offered his hand. She met his gaze that suddenly seemed haunting. The honey flecks that softened to a warm brown the night they made love lost their light. She took his hand and let him pull her to her feet.

A smile creased his stubbled face, but the sadness lingered. In all this, she forgot he, too, lost a friend. She touched her lips to his, wanting to ease the pain. Tension stiffened his arm holding hers and he stared into her eyes.

Her heart stopped. *Crap*, she did it again. "I'm sorry," she said.

He didn't speak for a moment then he cupped her face and lowered his lips onto her. She moaned and slid her tongue along his lower lip. He rumbled deep in his throat and kissed her harder, deeper. She wanted him so much, she might lose herself before he stopped kissing her.

After what seemed like a long sweet forever, he lifted his head, then nibbled her lips one more time. "You're hungrier than I thought," he said. "Let's eat."

Chapter 46

CREATING AN ACCOUNT ON Silk Road wasn't as easy as typing in his preferred alter ego. Nicholas needed an invite code. In other words, an invitation from a legitimate criminal. For that, he needed to contact one of his colleagues at the Canadian Security Intelligence Services. He sent Pat Ryan, a senior intelligence officer and long-time friend, a quick message through Signal asking him to get in touch.

What Nicholas and Savanna discovered still didn't prove a connection between Brock and Moore. Nor did it prove that Brock was the distributor of the drug they knew only as "Major Mac". Nicholas knew he needed hard evidence. They need proof that Brock used the nickname Vader to traffic the drug to various Canadian Army bases around the world.

If Brock and Moore worked together, then they must have had a prior connection of some sort. Moore must have experience in drug distribution. That kind of qualification would have interested Brock from the start.

Savanna was continuing her search into Moore's background. She had access to his police file as well as his school and employment records.

Nicholas was on Brock's case. What brought him to Westbury lying about his identity? Nicholas logged onto the local air force base system using the profile Brent set up for him, Captain Ishmael. With credible access, he made his way over to the main system in Ottawa. The level of clearance Brent provided was enough to get him into the personnel database at the tier two level.

Steven Gerald Brock was a thirty-five-year-old from Sydney, Nova Scotia. Between the ages of seventeen and twenty-one he had a few near brushes with the law, where he was cited for fighting in public parks as part of a fight club. He never spent any time in jail. After joining the army at twenty-five, he went by his middle name.

In training, Brock moved up quickly. He excelled in team training missions, both local and international. In individual assignments he maintained a top five rank. As a private, Brock tested positive for steroid use more than once. He had been warned, but the army's policy wasn't as stringent as, say, an athletic council's.

If the soldier wasn't showing signs of abuse, then the warning persisted without action. Brock either benefited from that practice, or his better than average service record helped. Maybe it was a bit of both. But neither Brock's talents nor his abilities saved him from his temper that soon got him either pulled, or grounded, from various Canadian missions in the last two years. His fighting had graduated from street brawls to drawing his weapon on a fellow soldier. In his last altercation, Brock gave a soldier a beatdown so severe, the other man's jaw was wired shut for weeks. The corporal pressed charges.

If Savanna was right about Brock and Moore, then the two men would have known each other for some time before Moore was arrested.

In her background check on Moore, Savanna provided information that Moore had been unemployed for the last three years. Yet, before he was incarcerated, his lifestyle didn't suggest that he was unemployed. He owned the house on Lamons Street and frequented bars around town, buying multiple drinks for his friends. Where does an unemployed thirty-two-year-old get the money to maintain such a lifestyle? Savanna might have an answer for that now.

Nicholas laughed and shook his head. Yesterday she sat in this same chair working her magic to track down "Major Mac", the key to this whole mess. She was good. What if she'd decided to follow in her father's footsteps? Would they have met that night at UBC? There would have been no reason for her to move to Westbury immediately after university. She probably would have gone all the way, like her father, and acquire her doctorate in computer science. That would have taken her anywhere in the world, even right here. *They should have kept in touch.*

He squirmed in the soft seat. He certainly hoped she meant *professionally* when she talked about separating. Whatever was going on in her life seemed stressful. The cords in his neck tightened. His plan to distance himself from those overwrought feelings he carried around for her disappeared the minute she came close.

None of it mattered now. She was married. *Then why the hell did she sleep with him?*

Chapter 47

SAVANNA SPENT WEEKS TROLLING the rental ads and viewed some of the most unsuitable apartments she had ever seen. Was it too much to ask for a bug-free, leak-free, clean-smelling place to live?

The thought of renting an infested hovel had her considering Richard's house until she left on maternity leave. But she was already sleeping in the guest room. On her first night back, she tried the couch. She didn't make it through the night. The bed in the guest room wasn't much better, but it worked. She no longer belonged in the house.

She drove up to the address she had called that afternoon and breathed a heavy sigh when she pulled into the driveway. The refurbished two-storey Edwardian should have had her smiling with enthusiasm, but her heart sank at the midnight blue Mercedes. The last few places she viewed with Rebecca were owned by Mercedes-driving landlords. In both, they scurried faster than the roaches to reach the front door.

She parked beside the Mercedes and climbed from the car. The apartment advertised, occupied the main floor. A long set of stairs on the side led to the second floor. She eyeballed the black and white structure, and then with a promise to turn and run at the first sign of any creature smaller than a cat, she moved toward the porch steps.

"Hello there," a voice said from the opposite side of the house.

Savanna turned and saw a man coming toward her. Thick globs of plaster hung from the white overalls he wore. Rich dark hair, pulled back in a ponytail, displayed his round face.

His mouth stretched into an easy grin. He wiped his hand with a small white towel, then offered it to her. "I'm George Newman," he said. "You must be Savanna Jones."

His infectious smile and affable manner charmed her right away. She took his hand. "I am," she said, a little taken aback. He was the famous artist George Newman. The Westbury Art Gallery displayed many of his sculptures.

"I didn't realize from the ad that you owned the home," she said. "But I guess that was the point."

He laughed. A small goatee added a good-natured humour to his ageless appearance. From what she knew of his career, she guessed he was in his early forties.

"Come on inside," he said.

Savanna had only a few requirements. She needed a clean and safe place with an extra room to set up a nursery. If this place fit the bill, she could sublet it while she was in New Westminster with her father for the last few weeks of her maternity leave and a few months after the baby's birth.

George unlocked the door and stepped back to let her enter first.

"Oh, my." She stepped onto a smooth marble floor in the foyer that soon transitioned into warm cherry jojoba hardwood. The fancy crown moulding, baseboards, gilded ceiling, and floor-to-ceiling bookcases flanking a wood-burning fireplace told her she couldn't afford the rent. She grinned sheepishly at George Newman, feeling silly for wasting his time.

"I think I made a mistake. I must have mixed up the rental amount with another location," she said.

"You don't like what you see?"

"Yes, I do, but it's bigger than I thought and clearly out of my present budget."

"Why don't you take a look before you make that call? Plus, the amount was never listed."

"I don't want to waste your time."

"You're here already. I'll wait here if you have any questions."

"Okay." She nodded and took the tour as George suggested. The fabulous contemporary kitchen, with its marble-top centre island, stainless steel appliances, and a view of the beautiful back-yard, confirmed her fears. What would she do in a kitchen like that? Spaghetti and the whole chicken she sometimes chanced would never do justice to such a beautiful space.

That thought vanished when Savanna entered the bedroom, a room fit for royalty with its fluffy white carpet, a king-size bed and walls of vanilla cream with a deep plum accented panel behind the headboard. Her head tilted upward to the soaring ceiling adorned with a sparkling crystal chandelier. Her spirits rose.

She wanted to stay.

She walked through to the bathroom. White marble with grey striations tiled the floor and covered the double sink vanity top. The wall concaved into a crescent shape to hug the flotation tub. A glass shower stall stood on the opposite side of the room. Savanna smiled at the luxury of beginning and ending her days in such a space.

Shaking her head, she returned to the living room where George waited. He smiled and rose to greet her.

"You are aware that I want to rent only for three months?"

"Yes. Short-term is okay, but if you desired a longer period, we could discuss it." He handed her a paper.

She read it. Choked. Then sputtered. "What's the catch?" The amount was so low she started looking around for roaches.

He dropped his gaze then looked toward the window.

Savanna's annoyance flared. *Too darn good to be true*. She turned and headed toward the door without another word.

"It's the cemetery," George Newman's voice reached her.

Her hand was on the doorknob. She faced him again. "The cemetery?"

"You might have seen it on your way in. There's only a metal fence separating the two properties. The price is so low because we back onto a cemetery."

The tight muscles in Savanna's stomach relaxed and she grinned.

"People are superstitious," George said. "When I bought the place, my real estate agent warned that it would be hard to rent. I dropped the price twice and still no takers. To add mystery, I removed the amount from the ad, but people in this city don't want to live near a graveyard. You're the first person in about three months."

"Is the cemetery the only reason for the low rent?"

He turned, squaring himself to face her. "I've owned the house for many years. I live alone on the second floor, accessed by the long set of stairs you may have noticed. I work in the basement. It's my studio. The renovations were completed almost a year ago, that's how long I had it up for rent. I thought the place would have been occupied within the first month. What you see is what you get. There are no problems."

She looked around again, then grinned. The spacious two-bedroom apartment was lovely and tastefully furnished in a modern style. It offered her privacy and solitude. She couldn't ask for better neighbours. "When can I move in?" she asked.

He studied her for a moment. "You don't mind the graveyard?"

"I like quiet neighbours," she said.

He grinned and lifted his hand and a set of keys from the counter and came toward her. "We'll sign the necessary papers once you're settled," he said. "Move in when you like."

Savanna took the keys. She hadn't meant to take this long to choose a place, but since she needed a home for her and the baby, she wanted as many comforts as she could provide.

"How's this weekend?" she asked.

Chapter 48

SAVANNA TOOK ADVANTAGE OF George's offer to move in right away. She didn't need much since the apartment came furnished. On Friday, she rented a cube van. Ben volunteered to help her load it up with the boxes she'd been packing since she returned from Edmonton. Then he drove it over to her new place and offloaded them.

Rebecca helped Savanna rustle a small desk and chair from storage. By Saturday, not much of her was left in the house she shared with Richard. took the kids to the park, while Rebecca returned to help Savanna unpack her clothes and linen.

Sunday morning she moved a bit slower and by the afternoon, she had collected her forensic gear into small boxes and stacked them at the front door.

She had been so busy concentrating on steadying the pile, she hadn't realized that the motorcycle engine she heard emanated from her driveway. She turned and almost dropped the box she held at the sight of Nicholas Wade dismounting.

He removed his helmet and stood there staring up at her. *Hmm. He sure knew how to make an entrance.*

His weekend mode, visible muscles, two-day stubble and the

bike helmet tucked under his arm sparked that longing to taste him again.

"Are you getting a jump on your next spring cleaning?" he asked.

She reeled in her lust and met him in the driveway. Under clear blue skies, a warm breeze filtered barbecue scents around the neighbourhood and the beaming sun heated her bare shoulders.

"Dr. Wade?" she asked. "Why are you here?"

"Do you think we should be that formal? Two people who know each other so, intimately?"

The heat enflaming her cheeks was so hot, she thought the skin would peel from her face. On Thursday night after they kissed, she wanted to leave his house before dinner. He insisted that she stay. After he had gone through all the trouble to prepare the hamburger sliders and crisp tossed salad, she couldn't just leave. Plus, her mouth watered and her stomach growled at the tantalizing smells coming from his kitchen. After they ate, she refused the foot rub he offered and made tracks for her car.

"Why are you here?" she asked.

He met her irritation with a wistful expression. "I have some questions."

"About?"

"Number one, I wanted to follow up on your search on Moore. Number two, I thought we should talk about us."

"There's no us. You've made that quite clear and—"

"We should take this inside, don't you think?"

She glared at him and entered the house, then waited for him to follow her before she closed the door. She led him from the foyer and into the living room. *Did he really need to bring this to her now?*

"Can I get you something to drink?" she asked a bit testy and stood on the other side of the room to put some distance between them.

He looked around at the pale green walls before he settled on Richard's piano. "No, thank you," he said. "I'm here because I didn't have you down as the disloyal type, so I'm having a hard time figuring out why you went to bed with me."

The serious expression seemed more pronounced in his tanned complexion. "I thought you were content to leave things as they are," she said.

"I'm not."

The night he sheltered her during lonely hours of grieving for Janet, she made no attempt to tell him that she was married and interested only in a fling with her boss. Now she owed him an explanation. Plus, having him believe that she was a liar and cheat didn't sit well with her.

"Did you know I would be still in Westbury when you planned to come here?" she asked.

"No."

"Is that why you came?"

"I had no choice in the matter. My commanding officer changed the assignment at the last minute."

Her stomach quivered. *He hadn't come looking for her.* "Maybe if you had said something when you discovered who I was, we wouldn't be here now."

He came to her and his face settled into a gentle expression. "But we are," he said and lifted strands of hair from her cheek. "At the end of June, I spent the most electrifying night with you."

She didn't move.

"Weeks later I found out that you were married and pregnant," he said. "What's going on?"

"Doctor—."

"Don't call me that, not now. Talk to me."

She stepped away from him. "I'm not spring or summer cleaning," she said. "I'm moving out."

"Because of us?"

"No, my decision to leave my marriage happened hours before the night at your place."

"Only hours?"

"Well it might have been months, perhaps years in the making, but yes, hours."

He watched her in silence for a while, then asked. "What could have happened to make you end your marriage while you're pregnant?" He frowned. "Is it—?"

"His?" She cut him off before he believed anything worse about her. "Yes, it's his," she said. "You're the only other man I kissed in more than four years."

That confession erased the disappointment in his expression. "That was more than a kiss," he said. "Now we're in an unusual position. But that still doesn't explain why your marriage is ending."

"It's simple really. I'm pregnant. My husband doesn't want children."

Nicholas's disgusted expression was back. "So, he left you?"

"Technically, I'm the one doing the leaving."

Nicholas sat on the edge of the chair behind him.

She'd never seen him look so bewildered. "I didn't think anything could shock you," she said and sat across from him.

"You found out that weekend?" he asked.

"That very morning."

"Must have been hard to deal with Janet's death after."

"It was."

Silence lingered while he stared at her. "Why me?" He tossed the question on her.

"What do you mean?"

"Was I just convenient? If someone else had picked you up from the airport, say Detective Thomas, would you be having this conversation with him?"

She pushed to her feet and picked up an empty box. She started dropping items into it. "What do you want from me?" she asked.

"The truth."

Really? Her brain flickered between the past and the last two months. She faced him and the uncertainty in his expression reminded her of the handsome doctor-soldier who she spent the night with ten years ago.

She tried to meet his eyes, but her courage waned. She focused on his lips instead. What truth did he want? That she fell in love with him as they worked together. Her stomach twisted now with older memories. She might have forgotten what he looked like, but she couldn't forget that, three weeks after he brought her to multiple mind-blowing orgasms, she discovered she carried his child. Telling him about the baby now would change their relationship in ways she wasn't prepared to handle.

"The truth is that I have a different life and so do you."

"I accept that, but I have been wondering all these years." He cocked his head and scanned her face. "Why keep your name a secret, even after you gave yourself to me that way?"

Savanna bit her lip. How could she tell him she'd stopped herself short of knowing him, a soldier who would leave her side and walk into a war zone in the next few hours? "It was a long time ago," she said.

"Is that all I am to you? Just a one-night stand?"

His words pricked beneath her skin. "What should I say now? That I wish we had exchanged names and promised to wait for each other? How long would I have waited, living from one anxious moment to the next, living in agony until I heard from you again?"

"Our lives didn't have to be about waiting. I would've found you sooner, the first time I came to Westbury—"

"The first time?"

"Yes, three years after that night in Vancouver. I spent two days looking for you in all the wrong places. Without a name, it was next to impossible."

"Did that night mean so much to you, Doctor?"

"What did it mean to you?"

"It was a long time ago." Guilt tightened her chest.

"We spent weeks working together and not once did you recall a single minute of that night. How long did it take you to forget what we shared?"

Savanna winced. "I never forgot."

"You forgot what I looked like."

"I never really trusted what I remembered anyway. Like I told you in June. That night I wasn't myself, wasn't in control of my faculties, whatever you want to call it." She looked over at him and her resistance wavered at his wounded expression. She put down the picture frame she held.

"What is this about?" she asked.

"I told you, I want the truth."

She shifted her gaze away from his. "You have it. Anything else?"

"I want to be here for you."

"You hardly know me. Why would you want to do that?"

"You think we're here now because I didn't tell you who I was when I got to Westbury?"

"You don't think so?"

"If we had exchanged information that night, our lives would have been different."

"That's a reach, don't you think?"

"From the very first moment I set eyes on you that afternoon in Vancouver, something drew us together and whatever it was never let go."

He was right, on all counts. But how could she tell him what connected them weeks later? She focused on the stubble framing his jaw and grazing his chin. She wished she hadn't remembered him. She wished he remained buried in all her grief. But that was her fault. The day her life turned upside down, she lost her hold on reality. He came to her rescue and she let herself give in to the only thing that felt real. His arms.

"Why did you kiss me that night?" he asked.

"The night in your kitchen?"

"The first time in Vancouver. Did the marijuana have anything to do with it?"

He wanted to know this now? "I'm sure it did. Isn't that what drugs do? Free your inhibitions, leaving you to do the things you wished you could do?"

"What were you wishing for?"

"I fell for your lips. I wanted to know what they tasted like."

He swallowed but remained seated. "And the night in my kitchen? What happened then?"

Rather than meeting his eyes, she focused on his lips again. "I told you then. I was numb. I couldn't feel anything until… Until you touched me." She tried turn away. "I was afraid I would disappear if you stopped."

He closed the distance between them and searched her eyes. When his hot breath scorched her cheek, her lower lip trembled for the feel of his mouth on hers. Instead, he took her hand in his and kissed her palm. The familiar sensation pulsated between her legs and she lost herself in the feel of his mouth brushing lightly over hers.

He pressed his lips to hers, soft and comforting as though he knew she ached for tenderness. Her mouth parted in sweet surrender. His arms folded around her lower back and urged her closer. She groaned and swooned into him. The kiss soothed the desolation that had agonized them both since she begged him to make love to her two months ago.

Savanna trembled in his arms. Each maddening second weakened her will. He was right. Since she smiled at him ten years ago, she had never let him go. Her desire and yearning for him now violated every tenet of their working relationship. Yet, she wanted to belong to him. His delicious tongue explored her mouth and wrenched another memory from its safe haven. She rose onto her tiptoes to get closer, but her baby bump kept them separated.

Savanna eased her lips away from his bone-melting kiss. Her palms slid down his chest against his thundering heartbeat.

"Nicholas," she murmured.

"Say it again. I like when you say my name just like that."

"Nicholas," she said breathlessly against his lips.

He groaned and kissed her again then lifted his head. His hazel eyes drooped with desire.

"We can't do this," she said.

"Why not? I'm here. You need me."

She quivered.

"Savanna," he touched her chin. "I mean it."

Who was this man, showing up when she needed him most and offering her, *what*? *Friendship with benefits*? She had enough complications for one lifetime.

"Don't look so shocked," he said. "I'm capable of making up for lost time."

How could she let him care for another man's child when she'd aborted his? She stepped back and detached their fingers. "That night at your house was special. I… We can't do this."

"You're alone now. Why can't we? I can come to a Lamaze class. Drive you to a doctor's appointment—"

She twisted her mouth. "A Lamaze class? Soon you'll be offering to pack my suitcase for the hospital."

"And drive you there, and wait outside for you and—"

"Whoa there, buster. Right now, I just need to get these boxes into that car and over to my new place."

"And when we get there. . .?"

She met his eyes and bit her lip.

He grinned and kissed her.

She obliged, ignoring for the moment that nothing he offered her could ever happen. When he lifted his lips from hers, she steadied herself with a hand on his chest, then stepped back.

"Remember your number one reason for showing up here?" she asked. "When we get there, we can talk about Colton Moore."

Chapter 49

$\mathcal{N}$ICHOLAS FOLLOWED SAVANNA TO her new apartment. He liked this place better. He had tried to imagine her living in the 1950s two-storey side split she had shared with her husband. He couldn't. Except for the small garden edging the front landing at the old place, the wide property surrounding the house wasn't her.

He strolled around the main floor Savanna would occupy, taking her directions for where the boxes should go. Not usually interested in architecture, he was surprised how taken he was with the house the moment he swung his bike into the driveway. The wraparound porch reminded him of his grandfather's home in Edmonton. The interior had a calming effect on him. He walked around admiring and touching the new furniture. "When did you get this place?" he asked.

"Got the keys on Friday afternoon," she said.

"It suits you."

"Thank you."

"Was this the errand you mentioned when you were in my office?"

"One of them." Savanna shot him a quizzical glance and headed to the front door.

He followed the hallway and found a two-piece bathroom on his right. A small vanity with a fancy glass bowl sink centred a single-pane window looking onto the driveway. He turned and pulled the door facing the bathroom. A linen closet. A few feet ahead, another room with the door slightly ajar faced the hall. He'd only stuck his head around the door and took in the king-size bed when he heard Savanna behind him.

"Taking a tour, Doctor?"

He made an about turn and headed toward her. "Sorry," he said. "I guess that's your bedroom."

"Uh huh." She was grinning at him as though she caught him doing something mischievous.

"It's nice," he said awkwardly.

She grinned. "I like your place too," she said. "I remember thinking that it looked like the perfect man cave. The updated kind."

The narrow hall was barely enough for both of them to face each other without touching. He kind of liked it that way. With her hair in a sloppy bun, and her short overalls fitting loosely over a tank top, she almost looked too young to be pregnant. "Do you like it here?" he asked.

She nodded.

"I noticed the cemetery next door. That doesn't bother you?"

"Are you concerned with the company I keep now, Doctor?" She stretched her neck.

He dropped his glance to the smooth skin under the loose tendrils and took in her barely covered shoulders. Her breasts tented the overalls and her belly sloped in an almond shape. When he met her gaze again, she tilted her head toward him. The seductive blush that welcomed him the night they made love at his house, drew him closer now.

He'd tried to stay away, but here he was offering to take care of her. She was on the rebound. How long would she keep him around? Something in him didn't care, just so long as she wanted him. He leaned over and kissed her. Her skin was warm and supple next to his. He lifted his head.

"Just want to make sure you feel safe," he said.

"I'm safe." She kissed him back. "Thank you for helping with the boxes."

"Hmmm. You're welcome." He ached with the need to taste her again. He groaned.

"Didn't you want to talk about Colton Moore?" she asked.

"Right." He leaned back. "You still have boxes in the car. I'll get them." He needed a minute to switch gears and headed out the open front door.

He carried the boxes stacked on top of each other. The strain was enough to get his mind off Savanna naked and panting on top of him. "Where should I put these?" he asked.

"In there." She pointed to her bedroom.

He eyed her. So much for calming his loins. "Are you saying I'm allowed?"

"You've already seen everything I have to hide." As soon as the words were out, she bit her lip and looked away.

So, he wasn't the only one needing to reel it in. He headed into the room and placed the boxes on a chair next to the door. The ten-by-twelve-foot European-style space was bright and calm at the same time. He pictured Savanna curled under the sheets in the middle of winter, warm by the glow of the gas fireplace with the baby asleep in the other room. He wanted to curl up with them. That thought jolted him, and he turned and scurried into the hallway.

"The history I found on Moore offered nothing glaring," Savanna was saying from the kitchen. "He was born and bred in Westbury. Attended Jack Chambers Elementary School from age four. His middle school was Cleardale Public. His father travelled for work, so his mother stuck him at an all-season camp not far from here during the summer. It's a large remote property on the Exeter-Westbury border. After he graduated high school, he attended Conestoga College and studied chemistry. Squeaked out a B average after three years.

"Did you say chemistry?"

"Uh-huh."

"From what I saw in that cheese barn warehouse, it's possible that Moore was Brock's cutter. Has Moore ever been arrested for drugs?"

"If he was, it's not listed in his record. The teachers there remember him, though not fondly. It's hard to tell how much of the hostility over the phone is connected to what they now know about him, as opposed to any vibes he might have given off during his academic years."

"What about work? Anything there?"

"He worked as a stock boy at the Shoppers Drug Mart pharmacy in Hyde Park Plaza for a while. Nothing spectacular."

Savanna handed Nicholas a stack of plates.

He took them and at her direction, placed them in the cupboard next to the stove. Then he prompted her to continue with her summary of Moore. Nothing she said so far connected to the information he found on Brock. But there had to be something linking those two.

"I happened to be in there on Friday night," Savanna said.

"Where?"

"At that particular Shoppers."

"Just happened to be there?"

"Ran out of folic acid. Anyway, I spoke to the pharmacist, Donna Rifkin. She remembered one incident, but she'd already told the police about it during Moore's first trial. She overheard one of the store clerks discussing Moore with another employee. Said she went out with him and they had sex. He was rough with her and she played along to calm him down and get it over with. She was afraid to go to the police because she consented. Thought they wouldn't have believed her."

"That's all too common."

Savanna bristled. "What particularly are you referring to, Doctor?"

"That wasn't a slight against your colleagues. Just my observation that women are too often afraid of being judged."

"Sorry. You're right, of course. I wish it were different, but the stereotypes are baked in."

He touched her cheek with an index finger.

She looked over and smiled.

Good. He didn't want anything spoiling the day. "Moore must have started at Sunrise Records soon after that," he said.

"Yeah, he left the pharmacy after a couple months. He'd worked there for a total of eight months before the job at Sunrise."

"How does selling old vinyl records fit in?"

"I don't know. Can't stalk your prey when you're stuck in the stock-room?" Savanna twisted her mouth in a sarcastic grimace.

"Did you talk to Sunrise?"

"Didn't need to. The police started there when Moore was arrested. All the interviews are in the file."

"From what I recall, he worked for them for two years."

"Yep. Took what he learned at Shoppers and made the job his own. He climbed the promotion ladder fast, and in no time, he was streamlining the inventory process and training staff for all the stores around the country."

"In your report on Molly Ross, you noted that her hometown is Brandon, Manitoba."

"That's right."

"Sunrise has a branch in Manitoba. Is it possible that it's in Brandon?"

"Sorry. Two branches in Winnipeg. Nothing in Brandon. That would have been too easy."

He took the box from her and collapsed it.

"Anything match what you know about Brock?" he asked.

"Afraid not, but I'm not done digging."

Chapter 50

$\mathcal{N}$ICHOLAS COLLAPSED THE LAST of the boxes, then followed Savanna into the living room. She had flopped onto the couch. The circles under her eyes revealed her exhaustion, though she kept up an impressive front. How devastating her husband's narcissism must feel. Not to mention embarrassing and overwhelming. Yet she juggled her life without missing a beat.

"Did you move all this other stuff here in such a short time?" he asked and pushed the coffee table away. He wedged himself at her feet and removed her loafers.

She lifted her head from the back of the couch, her eyes widening. Whatever objection she was about to utter, she changed her mind. "The furniture is George's," she said.

"How did you get so lucky?"

A painful expression crossed her face.

He wanted to punch himself. What was so lucky about having to end your four-year marriage because your husband found out you were carrying his child. *You're an ass, Wade.* "I'm—" he started to say.

"Either we both are lucky since you got the same deal, or there's a market for people with our particular needs," She cut off his apology.

"Sorry. I didn't mean to make light of your situation."

She squinted at him for a moment before she forgave him with a weak smile. "George sweetened the deal with furniture," she said. "The cemetery is a hard sell to most."

"Yet it doesn't concern you."

"Most days I carry a morgue full of people in my head. Six feet underground is lightweight."

He started rubbing her feet, encircling her ankles and running his fingers along her Achilles' tendons. She arched her back and squirmed.

"You'll never benefit from the massage unless you relax," he said. "It doesn't torture, you know."

"Speak for yourself," she said and wiggled her toes one more time, then settled back and closed her eyes.

Nicholas worked his fingers up the back of her calves and then down again with slight pressure. He meant to ease her tension but touching her silky skin like this increased his.

When a soft murmur escaped her throat, he glimpsed the sensual woman he met ten years ago. She bit on the inside of her bottom lip. He liked that. How was he to keep himself safe from her when he couldn't keep his hands off her body?

He slid his hand up her outer thigh and hoisted himself onto his knees between her legs.

She opened her eyes and sat up, then reached for him, encircling her arms around his neck. "I can't tell you how good it felt having you around this afternoon."

"Anytime. You shouldn't do it all yourself."

"But I didn't. Ben and Rebecca helped, even Max offered."

"Max? Who's that?"

"Kickboxing instructor."

"You kickbox with the baby?"

"It's not such a big deal since I've been doing it twice a week for eighteen years."

He looked down at her legs in the shorts. No wonder they were so shapely. "And your doctor is okay with this?"

She grinned. "My doctor? He feels better about the slight modification Max and I made to the workout."

"What's that?"

"No kicking. Just sparring. Most days when I leave the lab I need something to punch." She was grinning again.

He caressed her arms still linked around his neck. "Not sure what to make of that," he said.

"It's been some time since you were that thing I wanted to punch."

He laughed out loud.

She looked at him with a sweet smile, then kissed him.

As much as he wanted this to end in that fancy bedroom, he had something else in mind. "You're probably hungry now," he said.

She laughed. "Still afraid I'll seduce you?" She asked.

"I'm hoping you would."

"Then why shove food at me when I kiss you?"

"Because, when you start, I don't want you to stop."

She bit her lower lip.

His pulse raced. "I'll check your fridge," he said, "and see what you have, then you can invite me to stay for an early dinner."

"Will you do the cooking?"

"You like my cooking?"

"Janet always said a man should have at least two talents." She didn't move for a moment, then her eyes glistened with tears.

Nicholas slipped his palm under the hair at the back of her neck and pulled her head onto his shoulder. "I'm sorry you lost her."

Savanna pumped both her fists against his chest in short taps and shook her head. "I'll be all right," she said. She lifted her face to his. There was more anger there than sadness now, and he knew that's what drove her determination. "I'll be fine."

"It's all right to take some time to grieve." He held a finger under her chin.

She blinked the tears back.

He kissed them. "Like I said, I'm here for you."

"Okay," she whispered.

He pushed to his feet and offered her a hand. Savanna took it and followed him to the kitchen. She plucked a couple cans of orange flavoured San Pellegrino from the fridge. She handed him one and popped open the other for herself. Already, they were behaving like old lovers.

"You have an excellent kitchen," he said and pointed to the fridge. "May I?" he asked.

"I see your mother raised you to always say please. Nice."

His scalp pricked. He put the can to his mouth and washed down the sheepish discomfort that rose from her teasing. Usually, his knee-jerk reaction would have him finding an excuse to leave. With Savanna, he didn't mind letting his guard down just a little. "Is it that obvious?" he asked.

She poked his rib and smiled. "You're the cook, feel free to check things out."

He pulled the fridge door and reached for the brown paper package. "What's this?" he asked.

"Fish."

He unwrapped the package and smiled at the two pieces of meaty white slabs, wondering what Savanna intended to do with them.

"Can you cook that kind of fish?" she asked.

"It's cod. Nice ones too."

"Is that what they are?"

He laughed and turned to look at her. "You didn't know what you bought?"

"My father said to make sure to ask for the catch of the day. He said it was the only way to buy fish."

"I see."

"The guy at the market said they were easy to prepare. He even gave me instructions."

"What were you going to do with them?"

"Oil, salt, onions, oh yes and dill. Got some in there too. Maybe I'll plant the rest of it. Seems like too much for the fish I have."

"You never learned to cook?"

"I did. Just not as good as you."

He turned to look in the fridge again. It was empty. "Any more food in the boxes?"

"That was the other errand I needed to do the night you dared me to come to your place."

"Oh." He actually thought she was trying to avoid him and was very pleased with himself when she chose to show him how wrong he was. That night, they had enjoyed his homemade sliders and Savanna went home with a doggy bag. "I'll run out and pick up some stuff," he said.

"I'll come too since I obviously need to shop." She tossed him her car keys. "You can drive while I write my list."

"You have a deal."

Chapter 51

<hr>

THE FIRST ITEM SAVANNA purchased when they arrived at the market was a freshly-squeezed veggie juice. The nutrients satiated her ravenous appetite.

Nicholas lagged behind, reading labels and meticulously choosing items. He was so attentive, she almost forgot he was her boss.

Forty minutes later, they were back in her kitchen and the savoury herbs and spices that flavoured his food deepened her attraction for him. She chopped vegetables, trying to stay on her side of the counter. Nicholas rinsed and seasoned the two fillets, but every time she got in his way, he pulled her close for a kiss.

"If you keep up those mind-bending kisses," she said, "you might get your wish."

He wrapped her closer and rubbed his nose against hers. "Then it's working," he said.

She smoothed her hands over the ripples on his chest. "Your herbs aren't helping, either. They smell amazing. Makes me think about that other talent of yours."

"Which one is that?"

She swiped her tongue over his lips. "The one where you make me call you a god."

He picked her off the ground and deposited her on the only empty space on the kitchen counter. "How did you get so naughty?" He slipped between her legs.

"You inspire my imagination."

"Now when did I start that?"

"A long." *Kiss.* "Long." *Kiss.* "Long time ago."

"And are you hoping to experience my other talent right here?"

"No pressure, Doc. I'd understand if you can't swing…"

His tongue flicked across her eager lips, quieting her taunts. He captured her mouth when she pulled him closer and her entire body opened up.

She groaned and wrapped her arms around his neck. For the last twenty minutes, his teasing and kisses left her creamy and panting to feel him inside her. She pressed her knees against his hips. Her pregnant belly rested between their need to get closer.

Nicholas kissed her deeper.

She held him closer, relishing the long and hungry exchange.

When he released her lips and jerked away, she grumbled her complaint. He leaned toward the stove behind him.

"Babe," he said. "The pan is ready."

She reached for the bulge in his pants. "So am I," she said.

He was between her legs in no time.

She sucked on the space beneath his Adam's apple.

"Hmm." He murmured. "I…hmm."

She couldn't stop now. Her fingers loosened his belt buckle. She wanted him more than she wanted the food. When her hand closed over his penis, Nicholas groaned deep in his throat.

"Oh, hell," he said and reached behind him with one hand. He slid the pan from the heat and turned off the burner.

She pushed his pants over his hips and they dropped to his ankles. His fingers had already released the metal hooks on her overalls. He cradled her in his arms and whipped them off along with her panties.

"Oh," she screeched when her bare flesh touched the cold

counter. His hands sliding up her inner thighs distracted her from the mild shock. She pushed his hands away and wrapped her feet around his legs, pulling him closer.

He understood she was ready for him. He entered her with a quick and forceful joining. The movement ripped a chorus of pleasure from them both.

Savanna surrendered to the wondrous feel of Nicholas's throbbing heat inside her. He held onto her hips and stroked such gratifying pleasure into her she thought she would lose her mind. Just as she whispered his name and caught her breath, he entered her again and the world spun out of control.

"Nicholas," she moaned and rolled her hips to feel even more of him. He buried his penis deep inside her. "Oh god, Nicholas."

His sensual strokes elevated her desire for more. With every thrust, she yearned and ached and begged and craved. Nicholas gratified her lustful longings. He took her soaring in raptures of ecstasy. Together they climbed higher and higher and higher.

Nicholas's sensuous whispers willed her to come with him. She did. He kissed her and buried himself inside her. Savanna's head swam, and she lost touch with reality. An explosion erupted between her legs. She soared in wondrous, dazzling pleasure.

Nicholas' strong arms held her close. His throbbing masculinity filled her. In one thunderous roar, her name ripped from his throat, and he pulsated even deeper into her soft flesh. His body erupted in a series of gasping shudders. He buried his face in the curve of her neck. She slid her fingers into his hair and caressed his scalp. They held each other in silence.

Just when she thought she would wrap her legs around him and fall asleep, he moaned against her neck.

"You were supposed to cut the vegetables," he said, his voice heavy with desire. "Not seduce me."

She licked his lips. "Too late," she whispered. "Cooking was never my thing."

Chapter 52

Savanna jerked from a dream and flipped over in bed. Her body quivered with sudden wakefulness while she tried to discern her surroundings. She released a breath. Since her pregnancy, her dead mother visited her more in her dreams. What would Ana think of a grandchild if she was still here?

Savanna's eyes drifted closed again and she touched her stomach. Her father said her mother stayed in Brazil to protect them from her dangerous work. But if she had lived, would the promise of a new beginning compel her to change her mind? Savanna missed out on so much growing up without a mother. Then when Ana was gone, all Savanna's hopes of reuniting died with her. The only memories that remained were recorded in Ana's handwritten letters. Her last one was in celebration of Savanna's seventeenth birthday.

Happy birthday, my sweet. Remember to always trust your heart. It knows more than your head does.

Savanna sighed. *Shouldn't she be thinking of her future?* She opened her eyes and listened into the silence. Nicholas was gone. She sat up hoping to hear him. Stillness outside the bedroom told her that he'd already left the apartment too.

A couple short buzzes pulled her attention to the BlackBerry on the bedside table. She lunged for it. A text from Dave flashed on the screen.

Hannigan wants to talk about the suspect in your report. Can you come to the station?

She typed the letter 'k' and pressed 'send'. What time was it anyway? She tapped the phone again and the screen lit up. 8:55 a.m. "Crap." She slept in? She smiled. It was an exceptional night. After hours and hours of glorious lovemaking, no surprise she had to drag herself out of bed.

She entered the bathroom and emptied her bladder. She peered at her face in the mirror over the sink. Her cheeks still blushed and her lips were swollen from Nicholas's kisses.

The memories of them together tingled between her legs. She shook her head and tried to focus on work. A cold shower, that's what she needed. She pulled the glass door and halted when the doorbell shrieked through the apartment. She grabbed the bathrobe. By the time she reached the front door, she'd wrapped it securely around her naked body.

George stood on her doorstep with plaster clinging to his white apron, and a newspaper in his hand.

"Good morning," she said. She hadn't seen him since she signed the lease on Friday night when she started moving in. "Come in." She stepped away from the door and passed her hand over her hair.

"It looks like I woke you," he said without entering. "Sorry about that."

"No, it's okay. I should get to the lab anyway. Is something wrong?"

He shoved the newspaper at her. "I just wanted to drop off this. I thought you looked familiar when we met, but I hardly read the entertainment section, even when it features my art."

Savanna took **The Westbury Gazette** from his outstretched

hand. Perhaps Richard finally announced the divorce. Well, that took longer than she expected. "Thank you," she said.

"I'll leave you to it. Just remember, there's no such thing as bad publicity. Take it from an old pro." He flicked her a sympathetic look and turned toward the side of the house for his studio.

Still dragging her feet, Savanna closed the door and headed into the kitchen. She tossed the newspaper on the counter. A note stuck to the fridge door stirred the butterflies in her stomach. She couldn't hide from the truth anymore. She had fallen in love with Nicholas. She read the note.

Smoothie in the fridge. See you later. N

She smiled. The first time she laid eyes on him ten years ago, she was so smitten, she slept with him and didn't even know his name. Now years later when she had every reason to keep her distance, she couldn't get enough of him. He made it difficult for her to refuse by showing up and offering his amazing self.

She pulled the refrigerator door and grasped the beet-red smoothie. A sip chilled the heat rising in her body. Good, but too cold. She left the glass on the counter with the newspaper and headed into the bathroom.

Fifteen minutes later, she reemerged, wrapped in a towel and started on the smoothie while she prepared eggs and toast. With no time for a leisurely breakfast, she dressed while she ate. The newspaper George left caught her attention as she hustled to leave the apartment. Maybe she was purposely avoiding Richard's face and reading about her life in the media. She was moving on. Richard's manipulations were part of her old life.

Fully dressed, she snatched her purse and car keys from the counter, then decided to take the newspaper too. If Hannigan wanted to discuss Molly Ross, that meant he read her report. He probably needed details for a search warrant.

The front door self-locked when she pulled it shut. It was a beautiful day. Already sunny with a promise of heat. George wasn't much of a gardener. He planted yellow hostas and evergreen cedars that scented the morning air with sweet pine.

Savanna headed to the side of the house where Nicholas parked her car. She climbed behind the wheel just as her BlackBerry rang. She plucked it from her pocket to see Rebecca's strawberry curls filling the small screen. She connected the Bluetooth speaker to her visor and started the engine.

As usual, Rebecca spoke first. "I'm your best friend and this is how I find out that you're still sleeping with your boss?"

Savanna's foot hit the break. Her body lurched forward. She nudged the gear to park and shut down the engine. "What are you talking about?" She practically growled the question into the phone.

"You haven't seen the *Gazette*?"

Savanna reached for the newspaper in the passenger seat and extracted the entertainment section.

The picture on the front page stopped her heart. She and Nicholas kissing in the baby aisle plastered the page. She gasped. "Oh my god," she whispered.

A scandalous affair was the last thing Nicholas needed. The photograph violated the terms of his sanction, revealing his location.

"This is outrageous." She was panicking now.

"No kidding. That's some way to announce your divorce."

"You think I had something to do with this?"

"You didn't?"

"Of course not. He was giving me a hand with the rest of the move yesterday. This could ruin things for him."

"Both of you should have thought of that before you started necking in public."

Savanna banged on the stirring wheel. Rebecca was right. They should have been more discreet. Considering the fact that her marriage was over, she needed no one's permission to fall in love.

"How will you clean this up?" Rebecca asked.

"I don't know." She never meant for this to happen. "I have to go," she said. "I'll call you later."

"Wait," Rebecca yelled before she disconnected. "What are you going to do? Don't go charging in there and do that thing you do."

"What thing?"

"You know, where you act first and think later."

"Are you calling me impulsive?"

"That's my Savanna."

"Well, in a case like this it just might work."

Chapter 53

NICHOLAS SAT FORWARD IN his chair and held the telephone away from his ear. He expected this call, but not so soon. He brought the receiver closer to his head again.

Major-General Corbett growled through the phone line. "Lieutenant-Colonel Wade," he said, "you've failed your mission. I'm recalling your appointment. I expect you in my office tomorrow at 1300 hours."

"With all due respect, sir, I cannot end my appointment and return now."

"This is not a request, this is a direct order."

"I understand, sir, but I cannot walk away from my obligations here."

"If your obligations have anything to do with the celebrity's wife you've been photographed with, then I suggest you let this woman know that these are measures beyond your control."

Nicholas exhaled away from the receiver. "Leaving Ms. Jones to face the media without support when I was clearly a party in this scandal is not how I operate, sir. But that's not my only concern. I've made… We've made progress in the investigation and I intend to see it through."

The line was silent for a moment. "What you call an investigation was a farce to begin with. You are chasing a phantom and you are involving the army's reputation. I hope you intend to take responsibility for the turn your career takes."

Corbett meant every threat he insinuated. Yet, Nicholas knew that protecting his own legacy while McBride and the other soldiers' deaths went unanswered wasn't something he could live with for the rest of his life. Obeying Corbett's orders wasn't an option.

"The answers to this investigation are here, sir. I'm staying until the people responsible are brought to justice."

"Sounds like you're prepared for the unpleasant consequences, Lieutenant-Colonel." Corbett ended the call without another word.

Nicholas hammered his fist into the newspaper spread across his desk. Six months into the year without a single mention of him in the press. Now some gossip columnist revealed his location. And just like that his status and possibly his investigation were in jeopardy. When he was with Savanna yesterday, discretion never crossed his mind. Maybe it should have. *What a freaking mess.*

He closed his eyes. A slow, steady breath held his emotions in check. If Corbett believed Nicholas had been on a hopeless pursuit all this time, that was the man's prerogative. Nicholas emailed the report he had been preparing all along to his CO, and the members of the committee who had rubber-stamped his sanction. The unfinished investigation should prove that his stay in Westbury involved more than being close to Savanna.

He loved her. Their time together told him she cared for him, yet, he had no way of knowing how she would take this burgeoning scandal. He tapped the telephone. No way she was still in bed. The gossip had probably reached her already. He lifted the receiver.

"Dr. Wade." Josie appeared in his doorway.

He froze with his finger on the first digit. His secretary never entered his office unannounced.

"Savanna Jones is here to see you," she said.

His chest tightened. Only the worse can come from Savanna waiting outside his door. "Thank you," he said and replaced the receiver. "Show her in." He released a breath.

Savanna walked toward him with a pair of sunglasses perched on top of her head. Her tight expression monitored him, and her stiff right hand grasped a newspaper to her side.

So, she'd read the article. He stepped from behind his desk.

She stepped back.

His shoulder spasmed. "I was just about to call you," he said. "It's perfectly okay for you to sleep in sometimes, you know."

"I did, but don't tell me you're ignoring this?" She raised the newspaper.

He cast a quick glance at the paper.

"I'm so sorry," she said. "You shouldn't be caught up in this senseless gossip."

The strain in her voice pained him. "I can take it," he said. "Are you okay?"

She shook her head. "This isn't about me, not really," she said. "When this hits Ottawa, your life will be turned inside out." She looked away. "Maybe I can leave town for a while. Go visit my father or something."

The idea slowed his response. "If I didn't know better," he said. "I would think you're leaving me in the lurch here."

"That's not it at all." She dismissed his attempt at humour. "I don't know. We need to do something."

"Running away isn't the answer. I can find a way to fix this that doesn't include you leaving." He had no idea what.

"How? When this gets to Ottawa, your CO will probably have an MP squad here in a few hours."

If she was this afraid for him, she shouldn't talk about leaving. He went to her.

This time, she waited and resisted slightly when he wrapped his arms around her. He stroked her oval belly. She released a sigh.

"The next few weeks may be hard," he said. "But I can handle Corbett." Nicholas pressed his lips against her forehead.

"You have to convince him that it was an unfortunate mistake," Savanna said.

Her words slammed into his chest. "You know explanations do more damage than good," he said, and tugged her closer. "I've faced the press before and though Major-General Emmanuel Corbett has lungs more powerful than a newborn, his bite is tolerable." He soothed her belly with soft strokes.

Savanna leaned her head on his shoulder.

A slight movement under his fingers sent a shudder up his arm. Nicholas gasped. "The baby kicked," he said. The emotion in his own voice surprised him.

Savanna lifted her head and her smile softened the worry around her mouth. "This little one likes when you're around," she said.

"The feeling is mutual, so don't go anywhere. By tomorrow something more important will replace that photo of us."

Savanna pulled back and inspected his face. "By then, the damage will be done," she said. "If we're not seen together, you might have a chance to explain the photo."

"What can I say that would change what that photo depicts? In this case, the picture says it all. Maybe this is the best thing that could happen."

She shoved away from his embrace. "You can't be serious. Have you read what the columnist wrote? Without public knowledge of my divorce, you'll have this stain hanging over your head."

"It won't matter when the truth comes out."

"The truth?" She turned away from him. "Why would you want to wait around for a truth that will raise more scandal?"

"I can handle it. Plus, when everyone sees that I didn't run away because I'm afraid to get my morals soiled, they'll back off."

"You want to put your reputation through a public scandal to satisfy gossip?"

"No." He went to her and wrapped himself around her again. "To show my love for you," he said. "I love you."

Her body went limp in his arms. She stared at him with her mouth open. "You love me?"

He didn't expect the bewilderment. "That doesn't surprise you, does it? I don't just kiss anyone like that. I want you and the baby in my life. I should have said so last night, to let you know that you don't need to go to Vancouver when you've got me."

She shivered. "The baby? You want my baby?"

He pressed his lips to hers.

"Nicholas," she whispered and let him kiss her. The passion they shared last night resurfaced and he nibbled her ear.

Her expression softened. He knew she thought of them together. "It wouldn't work," she said.

Something heavy and hard clobbered Nicholas's chest from inside. He stared at her, unable to speak for a moment. "Why not?" He finally asked.

She was silent for a while and stood there not looking at him. "I've told you that my mother was a soldier," she finally said.

He winced. "What does that have to do with us?"

"Things between us have been getting pretty close and you are a soldier too, and that life scares me."

In spite of his efforts to remain patient, his anger mounted. "What is it with you? I'm good enough to sleep with but not good enough for you or your baby? You don't think I can make you happy?"

She responded with a simple shrug, one hand covering her stomach. "You think you know me, Doctor, but you don't. I'm not the person you think I am." Her eyes, hard and steely, glared at him. She turned toward the door. "I'm a better judge of what makes me happy," she said.

He didn't want this to get out of control before they had the opportunity to talk about it sensibly. "Savanna, wait. Don't go like this."

She turned to face him.

"Can we talk about this later?" he asked.

She looked away and said nothing for a while, then her entire demeanour changed. "Do you still have that photo of Brock?" she asked.

Not what he expected. "Ah… Yes."

"May I borrow it?"

"Why?"

"I'm heading to the station now to speak with Hannigan about Molly Ross."

He pulled the desk drawer. He'd already spoken with the OPP and sent them a scanned copy of the photo, but local law enforcement should have one too. He should have sent it over already. He handed it to her.

"Thank you," she said.

"Fill me in when you get back?"

"Sure." She was gone before he said another word.

Part III

"The first step toward change is awareness. The second step is acceptance."

~ *Nathaniel Branden*

Chapter 54

*N*icholas yanked open his office door and hurried past Josie's empty chair. When he reached the outer hallway, he came to an abrupt stop. His heart, which had been banging like a battle drum slowed at the sight of the two people talking a few yards away.

In fact, they weren't just talking. Brent and Savanna stood there holding hands and smiling at each other. Hers was weak and polite. As usual, Brent beamed with all his affability. He covered the hand he already held and laughed even louder. Only moments before, Savanna stormed from Nicholas's office refusing to talk, and she certainly wasn't smiling.

Nicholas convinced his feet to walk again and hurried to reach them.

Savanna spotted him. She offered Brent another weak smile then fled.

Nicholas watched her until she disappeared around the corner. Was that his fault? Did he offer her too much too soon? Maybe tonight they could sort it out together. He sighed and slapped Brent's shoulder. "Welcome back," he said. "What brings you here?" He had a pretty good idea but asked anyway.

Brent turned in the direction Savanna had stalked away. "I couldn't believe it when I saw the bloody paper this morning. Now that I met her, I get it. She bewitched you, didn't she?"

Nicholas could always trust Brent to speak his mind. "Let's take this to my office," he said.

Brent entered ahead of him and dropped onto an armchair with a distant gaze, apparently still recovering from his conversation with Savanna. Maybe he had some advice. Brent knew more about relationships than Nicholas. He would know the right words to persuade her they belonged together.

"She didn't bewitch me," Nicholas said.

"Then how the heck did you end up on the front page of a newspaper kissing her?"

"It wasn't the front page. People should mind their own business."

"You're not serious. You kissed a pregnant, married woman in the baby aisle at the grocery store and expect no one will take notice?"

"I don't expect people to follow me around taking photos of my personal business."

"Your girlfriend is a beautiful woman. Her husband is a celebrity, and she's not shy about making her opinion known when it comes to crime in this city. Whatever she does, people notice."

"None of what you're saying condones plastering someone's personal life in the media."

"How did you get mixed up in this spectacle, anyway?"

"That's my business, don't you think?"

Brent studied him for a moment. "You're starting to lose your cool," he said. "If you don't watch yourself, it'll be hard to convince anyone that it was just an innocent kiss. You wouldn't be able to deny the accusations."

"I'm not denying anything."

"What's that supposed to mean?"

"What I said."

"You're sleeping with her? Good God. I should have guessed. Now I know you've lost it."

"You're the one who said I should meet someone."

"So now this is my fault? Jeezus. No wonder you didn't warm up to Marie's matchmaking efforts."

A slight irritation pricked Nicholas. He waved Brent's comments away. "Savanna deserves better than a husband she can't count on."

Brent pushed from the chair and came to stand directly in front of Nicholas. "Listen, old man," he said. "Until she says different, she's got what she deserves. Warming her bed while her husband is away isn't going to make one heck of a difference."

A knot twisted in Nicholas's stomach. The painful truth he avoided since the first night he brought Savanna back to his house clobbered him like a bully on the playground. Until she shared his feelings, what he wished or hoped for didn't matter. "They're getting a divorce," he blurted out.

"What? But she's pregnant." Brent threw him a glance. "Tell me it's not yours."

"It's not, though I wish to God it was."

"Have you replaced your common sense with a lethal dose of stupidity?"

"Back off, I've had enough stress for one morning."

Brent raised a hand. "You're right. This is none of my business." He crossed the office and leaned against the window. "That's not the only reason I came to see you," he said. "What is this 'Major Mac' anyway?"

Glad for the change in subject, Nicholas perked up. "Why? You heard something?"

"Not really. Just want to be in the know in case the drug shows up at my base."

"Major Mac is Ecstasy cut with ketamine. Short term, the effects range from drowsiness to slurred speech. Long-term it gets more fucked up. Hallucinations, delusional thinking, aggression, and panic. Not a good mix when weapons are involved. You know anyone with those symptoms?"

Brent's forehead creased. "Not really." After a moment his head jerked up. "Did you get any hits on Silk Road?" he asked.

Nicholas knew Brent would come to him if he needed to talk.

He wouldn't push, but he didn't intend to watch from the sidelines again. "Not yet," he said. "I'm starting to think that Brock's onto me."

"Well, you may not need it." Brent pulled a folded page from his breast pocket.

"What's that?" Nicholas asked.

"I helped Private Kyle Webber with his application last year. Ever since then he's been itching to return the favour. I needed someone with systems admin access to the army's mail server and he was my man."

Email. Now why didn't he think of that?

"Webber searched Brock's inbox," Brent continued, "he got diddly-squat. He even checked the man's trash folder. Though there was some disturbing stuff in there, nothing to implicate Brock in anything we were looking for. Then Private Webber, the little genius, had an idea. He checked the sent messages folder, and what do you know? There it was: an email from *silkroad@tutanota.com*. Looks like Brock locked himself out of his account and requested a password reset. He supplied his forces.ca email address. That could have been his first slip up."

"How's that?"

"The way Webber explains it, an email from *silkroad@tutano-ta.com* landed in Brock's forces.ca account at 07:42:20 and was gone by 07:42:31. Because of the length of time the email was there, Webber thinks that Brock meant to use another address. A web address maybe, one he could access from anywhere. When he realized his mistake, he forwarded the message to another address: *brock77@hushmail.com*."

Nicholas took the page. "Hushmail?" he asked.

"It's one of those email services where some dodgy characters hang out. This one is Canadian."

"After forwarding the message here, Brock deletes the original from his forces.ca inbox?"

"And even from the trash. At that point, either he forgot, was distracted, or just plain got cocky. Whatever it was, he left the copy of the message he forwarded in his sent box. And that's where it is today."

"Can he figure out that you've been searching his mail?"

"Not unless he has server access too. And I doubt that."

"So, what do we really have now?" Nicholas took the paper from Brent and leaned against his desk.

"What you have here," Brent said. "Are the contents of the email."

Nicholas read down the page: username: *vader1977*; password: *LockAndLoad93*.

"And if I'm not mistaken," Brent said. "As further proof, I believe 1977 is the year he was born."

"You're right. April 25, 1977. From this, we know that this Silk Road account that sells psychotropic drugs to whoever contacts him here is run by Brock."

"Hands down."

Nicholas jabbed a fist in midair. "We've got him," he said. He knew Brock sold the drug. It was possible that Moore was his cutter. Still, one gaping hole was left in their investigation. How did Brock and Colton Moore meet in the first place?

Chapter 55

Savanna pulled into a spot at the rear of the parking lot. She took her time climbing from the car. A slow walk to the building afforded her a few minutes to calm down before she faced the people behind those doors.

It was almost 11:00 a.m. Heat from the sun stung her forehead. She wished it would scorch out her thumping headache. Maybe she should have come here first. Now all she could think of was Nicholas's promise of forever.

He wasn't supposed to say those things. When she told him that their relationship could ruin his career, he was supposed to agree. He wasn't supposed to say he loved her, that he wanted her and the baby.

She loved him. She should have told him that rather than run away. But what if he didn't really love her? What if he said those things because he'd gotten so used to rescuing her? *Oh, god. Oh, god.*

Richard had said he loved her too, but he abandoned her when their marriage no longer resembled the fantasy in his head. Nicholas was nothing like Richard. Nicholas offered her and the baby his life. He kept saying he could handle raising a child that wasn't his. Would he feel the same when she told him about his baby? She had

310

to tell him. There was no other way. She had to risk that he might never forgive her.

Her knees weakened when she mounted the steps. She was far from ready to face the comments inside. Likely they all saw the same photo. She grasped the stainless steel handle and pulled the door. Cool air jetted from the vent above the entrance. It sucked the heat from her body.

Regular police activity bombarded the sergeant's desk. Savanna stepped away from the forced air and approached the counter. Usually, the daily timesheet was clipped to a board with a pen. Today nothing.

Sergeant Davis, tall and balding, removed his glasses to talk to a woman who demanded to see someone in charge. "Lady," he said, his voice stern, "I've already called a detective. Wait over there and he'll be right with you." Glasses went on again.

The woman turned away, grumbling.

Savanna took her place and spotted **The Westbury Gazette's** entertainment front page on the counter.

Davis followed her gaze and snatched the page away. "Morning, Jones. You're looking for this?" he asked and handed her the clipboard.

She held eye contact, giving him the opportunity to get whatever he wanted to say off his chest.

A flush blotched his cheeks He fidgeted with his glasses.

Rather than prolong his embarrassment, she signed the sheet and handed back the clipboard.

The detectives' squad room was quieter than the first floor but just as busy. Savanna headed toward the homicide table. She garnered a few stares, silent nods and quick eyes down. When two uniformed officers turned to whisper, she flushed and kept walking. As she continued on, the room went silent. She could almost feel the judgments poking her from behind. Though she thought she would crumble, she held her head high.

"What are you staring at, you ignorant pack of wolves?" Quinn's voice startled her. He grabbed her elbow and chucked her into the nearest interrogation room, then slammed the door.

Her whole body shivered. She searched Quinn for a trace of the curious innocence that wiped away all judgment. He stared back at her tight-lipped and tossed the newspaper on the table. "Sit down," he finally barked.

"You sit down."

He glared at her. "Imagine my surprise when I picked up the newspaper this morning. I suspected something after your return from Edmonton, but not this. Is it true?"

"What if it is?"

"You're married, pregnant, and having an affair with your boss. What do you think? This city would have a field day with something like this."

She gripped the back of the chair. "It's bad. I know. I'll do something to fix it."

"How can you fix this? It's already in the wind."

"This shouldn't matter," she said. "I'm divorcing Richard."

"What? You've lost your mind. Do you care to explain?"

"Back in June, he decided he wanted me without our child. I refused and he, well…."

"Jesus Christ." Quinn pulled the only other chair in the room and dropped down on it. "Why didn't you tell me?"

Savanna shrugged.

"We're partners, for Christ's sake. We talk. You should have told me." He flicked a dismissive hand when she said nothing. "So, what's happening now?"

"What do you think is happening? I've already moved out."

"You're living with Wade now?"

"No, I have my own place. Why are you interrogating me?"

"Because this was stupid. Idiotic." He jabbed the newspaper.

She released the back of the chair holding her upright and sat on it.

"You, who can always spot trouble a mile away," Quinn said. "Couldn't see this coming?"

Maybe she didn't want to see this. Maybe she was too lonely and hurt to recognize a catastrophe of her own making. "I didn't mean for any of this to happen," she said.

"But it did, and you'll be lucky to have a job, much less a career, in a week. You know how stuff like this plays out. Wade gets to go on his merry way, and you become a pariah."

Damn. She stiffened against the tears that stung her eyes. She wasn't the first woman to have an affair with her boss, and she wouldn't be the last. "This has nothing to do with my job, and it's certainly no one's business," she said.

"You've made it everyone else's business when you smooched with your boss in the middle of the bloody grocery store."

"I didn't point that camera at myself, and I didn't tweet details of my marital problems. I can do nothing about someone else's actions."

Quinn glowered at her. He shook his head slowly and slumped in the chair. "You were always my moral compass. I figured if you didn't disagree too much with my dalliances, then I hadn't yet crossed the line. Now you can't even see your own lousy judgment."

She flinched. His disappointment landed between her upper ribs. "Still," she said, "that's my position." Frankly, she'd had enough of his tough love. "Now if you'll excuse me," she pushed from the chair. "I'm here to see Hannigan. Are you coming?"

Chapter 56

Savanna left the interrogation room, leaving Quinn behind. She leaned against the closed door and took a breath.

"Jones." Dave's voice reached her from a few paces away. "I heard you were here." He walked past her. "Coming?" He asked.

She fell into step with him. "Before you say anything," she said. "It's—"

"I don't want to know. No offence, but I stuck my mouth in your business before. I don't intend to make that mistake again."

She nodded a grateful thank you.

They stopped in front of DS Hannigan's office. Dave knocked and pushed the door.

"Good morning," Savanna said when the door closed behind them.

Hannigan tried to slam the file cabinet he'd been searching, but the excess paper bulged out the top. He shoved them in and tried again, this time closing it with a click. He turned to her.

"I bet you've had better mornings," he said and eased into the chair behind his desk.

She shifted her glance away from him and landed on Fontaine's direct stare. He stood on the opposite side of Hannigan's desk with his arms folded across his open suit jacket.

"Detective," she greeted him.

"Jonesy." He touched his forehead in a mock salute.

Dave took the chair in the corner of the office.

A few seconds of quiet stilled the room. Savanna felt like she had walked into another ambush.

Hannigan pointed at the chair in front of his desk and sat back like an unimpressed school principal. "Jones," he said. "Do you know what the public would do to this police department if we started mixing up victims and suspects?" He referred to her as though she counted among his squad of constables and detectives. She liked him and thought the reference meant he respected her.

She exhaled. "Sounds like you're concerned with the evidence in the report, Lieutenant."

"You bet I'm concerned. Wade tells me it has all been retested."

"You have an updated report?" she asked.

"Wade said there's nothing to update. But I don't see how, since what you have here isn't pointing one way or the other."

"I get that," Savanna said. "My lab needs a DNA sample from Molly to prove if she is your perpetrator or another Moore victim."

"Lieutenant," Dave said. "Whether Ross is a perp or not, she can help move this case along. She could be the missing link. It's possible she's the reason Moore is laughing at us."

"Why are we looking at this woman?" Fontaine asked. "We're searching for a male partner."

"And maybe that's the problem," Dave suggested. "Every time we pull Moore in, we keep saying the same thing. 'Tell us who *he* is'. And all this time, Moore knew we had nothing on his accomplice because he wasn't working with a man. But Ross might know something about the man driving the blue van."

Savanna gasped. Actually, she was trying to inhale. The man driving the van. How could she have missed it?

"None of the evidence," Dave continued, "with the exception of Colton Moore's…" He trailed off when Hannigan raised a hand.

"You got something, Jones?" Hannigan asked, still holding his hand up to Dave.

"I think I know who he is. The man driving the van."

Dave was out of the chair and crowding her. "What?" he asked. "What do you mean you know?"

"I believe I know." She grabbed her purse that hung on the back of the chair and slid out the photo she took from Nicholas. She handed it to Dave.

"Who's this?"

"His name is Gerald Brock. He's an army captain stationed in Petawawa. We believe——"

"We?"

"Nicholas. But actually, I believe he murdered Janet Whateley."

"And we're hearing this now?" Dave asked. "Shit, Jones. What the heck is going on?"

"Well, after you told me what Dr. Wade found in the cheese barn, I told him about a man that contacted me in the spring. He said his name was Scott Allen. It turned out he was Captain Gerald Brock."

"In the spring?" Fontaine asked and drew closer. He stood on her other side.

She was surrounded. Her heart pumped twice its normal rate. She wasn't sure where to start and decided to begin with Jimmy's tip. By the time she finished the entire story, minus the times she slept with Nicholas and Richard's betrayal, the three men stared at her dumbstruck.

"And you told me none of this?"

She startled at Quinn's voice behind her. She hadn't heard him enter the office. "Sorry," she said. "It seems stupid now since we are all working the case, but——"

"Ya think?" That was Dave. He was still staring at Brock's photo. "You could have brought this to us weeks ago."

"Calm down," Hannigan said. "OPP has a copy of the photo and Reynolds received a rundown from Wade about the man. Looks like Wade is trying to find something concrete against him and we've been asked to stay clear in case he gets wind and bolts."

"Detective Superintendent," Dave turned on Hannigan. "This is our case. We should have had these details."

"We did," Hannigan said. "I did."

"I'm sorry, Dave," Savanna said. "When we collected those samples for this report I didn't know that Allen wasn't who he was and—"

"You could have mentioned that you were talking to the army."

"He had nothing. Just wanted information and it all seemed like forensic stuff anyway."

"Still. We're a team. You don't just leave us out of the loop because someone new comes to town."

That was exactly what she did. Whether she meant to or not. She excluded the team. She just thought she could do this on her own and get her leave of absence. Everything she learned and worked for over the last ten years she had pushed aside, along with the people who'd always been there for her.

She pushed up from the chair. "You're right. All of you. I'm not sure how this happened. My head was too far down in my own problems. I… I guess I thought only of my selfish needs. I'm sorry." She waved at the report. "It's all here. Everything, except for the connection between Brock and Moore. And I believe you'll get that from Molly."

She kept her chin down and started for the door.

"Where do you think you're going, young lady?" Hannigan barked.

"Well. It's…" She looked around at the grim faces. The two detectives and her partner, all disappointed in her. "It's all there," she said again. "You don't need me."

"Like hell we don't," Hannigan growled. "You have a theory. I want to hear it. Sit your ass down and explain."

No one spoke. They just waited to see what she would do. *Was that her forgiveness?* They trusted her. She had let them down, but their faith in her work held up.

She approached the desk again, leaned over and opened the file folder. She started to explain. "The unmatched carpet fibres our pathologists lifted from the victims during the post-mortems don't match the new material Dave helped me collect from the victims' frequented locations." She paused and looked up to make sure everyone was following.

They all met her glance.

Dave nodded. "Go on."

"If our controlled samples match any evidence at Ross's home, then it can be used as evidence against her."

"You're forgetting the cat," Fontaine said. "You listed cat hairs among the unidentified fibres found at the crime scene. A stray could've brought these fibres from anywhere."

Savanna nodded. "That's very possible, but—"

"Just a minute," Dave said. "I get the hair evidence, but how are we planning to tie the unidentified fibres to Ross?"

"We need a connection to persuade Judge Kaufman to sign a warrant." Hannigan was still not convinced.

Savanna thought for a moment. Without a judge's signature, she would have wasted everyone's time. This was a solid lead. If they lost it, Moore would get away with murder.

She looked up at Hannigan. "Since Dave found Molly Ross squatting at Lamons Street," she said, "we'd need to rule her out as the owner of the unidentified DNA."

"So we pull her in to volunteer her DNA?" Fontaine asked. "What if she lawyers up?"

"That's a chance we'd have to take. But the police have cause to question someone you believe is hiding something."

"Normally, we would, but in this case, we have nothing on her."

"Molly Ross is hiding something," Savanna said. "Why was she squatting at Lamons Street? Which is a crime, by the way. She lives in her aunt's house over on Petterville Corner behind the Claymore factory."

"You've been by her place?" Dave looked alarmed.

She threw him a nonchalant glance. "A mere drive-by. I wanted to see if it was an actual residence. And it is."

"Well, this could be it," Dave said.

"But is it enough to obtain a warrant to search her place?" Fontaine asked.

Dave handed Savanna back the photo of Brock.

She slipped it into her pocket.

"Squatting at a crime scene is illegal," he said. "Maybe something went missing and we're trying to locate it."

Hannigan dropped his heavy frame into his chair again.

Savanna met his direct stare and waited for him to speak, but he studied her without a word.

"This could get you your judge's signature, Lieutenant," she said. "The warrant admits the detectives into Molly's place, and her lie gets us access to her DNA, and a chance to question her."

Hannigan slapped the desk. "What do you need, Jones?" he finally asked.

"An uncompromised sample of Molly's hair, preferably with roots attached, and a saliva swab would tie things up nicely."

"Then you're with them." He flicked a thumb toward the two detectives standing next to her.

"Got it, Lieutenant." Savanna turned to leave and bumped into Quinn. He didn't look at her. He stepped aside to let her pass.

"We'll call you when we have a warrant on the way, Jonesy," Fontaine said.

"I'll be waiting."

Chapter 57

*P*etterville Corner was a narrow dead-end street with a line of run-down homes on both sides. The only blooms surrounding the houses topped extra-tall dandelion plants. Lawns grew wild and long.

As Dave drove the unmarked squad car down the street, shouts rang from one of the wide-open front doors. Seconds later, someone ran from the house and climbed into an aged Ford truck and sped away.

Number thirteen was the last house on the right. Like the other properties, paint peeled from the siding. Windows, covered with taped-on black garbage bags, needed repair. A ten-storey apartment building rose at the end of the road. Two dumpsters stood to one side, overflowing with garbage. When they pulled up to Molly's house, flies buzzed from the trash and hovered around her windows.

Dave stood on the single, weather-beaten step at the front door and pushed the doorbell.

Savanna focused on the metal framed door that lost its screening at some point. More than usual adrenalin pulsated through her bloodstream and she switched from one foot to the other.

When no one answered, Dave tugged the screen door. The

hinges squeaked. He banged on the hollow white door and stepped back.

After a few seconds, a face appeared behind the octagonal glass panel and the door swung open with a casual air. "Detective Thomas." A woman barely out of her teens addressed Dave. "I thought you said we were done."

Savanna stared. A tingling sensation emanated from her forehead. This couldn't be Molly Ross, Moore's accomplice. The girl's short dark hair clung to the face Dave described months ago. A defiant cerulean blue coloured the ends of her hair. Molly Ross didn't look at all like Savanna imagined.

A small, peevish mouth punctuated her disappointment at the three people standing before her. Despite her dismay, her beady grey-blue eyes danced ever so slightly, as though she was delighted to have visitors.

"Margaret Ross," Dave said holding up his badge. "This is my partner, Detective Ronald Fontaine, and Savanna Jones is from Westbury Forensic Services. We're here on a related issue. May we come in?"

Savanna and Fontaine lifted their badges for Molly's inspection.

She focused on Savanna's while fidgeting with the pants that slipped from her tiny waist every few seconds. Her eyes moved down Savanna's body, and her pockmarked cheek tightened. A puff of air left her pursed lips. "If I say no," she said, "you'll barge in anyway." She stepped back and a flick of her fingers consented to their entry.

Savanna followed the detectives into the small living room. A strong scent of marijuana assaulted them. She scanned the area, but nothing to connect the scent was visible. A daytime talk show blared from the flat screen television set behind them. Detective Fontaine turned it off. Molly cut him a razor-sharp glance.

Savanna darted glances around the room that looked as though it hadn't been dusted in months. She inhaled short quick breaths trying to block the marijuana. The constriction gathered in her chest and brought on a touch of claustrophobia.

"You're pregnant." Molly's voice stopped her short. "I thought there was something about you."

"Miss Ross," Dave said. "We're here on—"

"Did you know she was pregnant?" Molly demanded.

"Miss Ross." Dave tried again.

"What's all this Miss Ross business? I'm Molly."

"Molly, as I was saying, we are here on official police business."

"Okay."

"We have reason to believe that you were a victim of an unreported crime."

"That's rich," Molly said and laughed out loud. "Don't tell me, you're concerned for my welfare?" She stood next to a rusting metal table with her arms folded over her flat chest.

"The crime took place at 24 Lamons Street," Dave said.

"I haven't been there."

"We both know you have."

"I mean not since we ran into each other."

He handed her the warrant. "Because we found you loitering at that location, this judge's warrant gives us permission to search these premises."

Molly's trembling fingers took the sheet of paper, while the other hand tugged at her pants yet again. She tried handing back the warrant.

Savanna's gaze followed Fontaine when he entered they kitchen and stopped in front of the stove. The thing looked at least twenty years old. It was piled with pizza boxes and fast-food containers. Not a pot in sight. Fontaine pulled a pair of gloves from his pocket and shoved his hands into them. He started opening cupboard doors.

"What are you looking for?" Molly asked.

"Did you take anything from Lamons Street?" Dave posed his questions while ignoring the warrant Molly kept shoving back at him.

"How could I? You searched my shi … stuff, didn't you?"

Dave led her to the kitchen and pulled a chair from under the table. He invited her to sit.

Molly did as he asked.

Savanna set her kit on the dining room table and opened it. The latex gloves she needed and her camera lay on top.

"My partner and Ms. Jones will conduct the search while we chat," Dave said. "I would like to ask you a few questions about the assault."

"I don't know nothing about that." Her eyes darted from Dave to Fontaine. She tilted her chin and her nervous glance met Savanna's. She dropped her stare to Savanna's belly again. "I had nothing to do with anything," she said. "How long is this going to take? Maybe I can make some tea like on those British TV shows."

Savanna studied Molly for a moment. She seemed so young, maybe twenty. Her flippant responses came off rather naïve and underscored an innocence beneath the bad girl facade. Molly wasn't just nervous, she was scared.

Savanna entered an open door just off the living room. It was Molly's bedroom. The smells of sweat mingling with marijuana greeted her. Already wearing latex gloves, she opened the toolkit on the once white carpet. The single bed swallowed half the room. The ruffled sheets and an oversized comforter piled in the middle seemed the source of the smell. A three-drawer yellowing chest against the outer wall and a mismatched nightstand completed Molly's furniture. The ten-storey apartment building next door blocked the room's only window.

Savanna snapped photos capturing the room before Fontaine searched it. She pushed candy wrappers, clothing, and other debris aside on the carpet and tweezed fibre from various areas. She bagged and labelled each sample, then recorded the time.

Fontaine appeared at the door.

"What's going on in there?" Molly's voice shrieked from behind him.

Savanna turned to the narrow bathroom just off the tiny bedroom. Judging from the state of the apartment, she held her breath, unsure of what she would find. She paused inside the door. The scent of Vim disinfectant rose to meet her. The moss green pedestal sink and porcelain bowl sparkled. Either Molly expected an overnight guest, or she hated dirty bathrooms. A small green mat lay fluffed at the base of the sink and another hugged the toilet.

Savanna collected fibres from the mats and shoved Molly's

toothbrush and comb into separate evidence bags. She returned to the bedroom and found Fontaine wrestling with a drawer in the chest. It came loose, and he placed it on the floor.

A pink children's blanket lay on top.

Fontaine lifted it carefully. Underneath, a framed photograph of a woman with shoulder-length dark hair showed the family resemblance of high cheekbones and a long face. A newspaper-wrapped package tucked neatly into the corner. Fontaine picked it up and pinched the folds open.

Savanna waited, trying not to fidget. She wished he would hurry but understood his caution. The contents were still hidden from her view when he peeked inside.

"What is it?" she asked.

Fontaine spread the newsprint and exposed two items.

Savanna's breath caught. "I've seen that before." She pointed at the piece of jewellery.

Fontaine picked up the ivory moon face pendant set in sterling silver. It dangled from a braided silver chain.

"It's Sally's necklace," Savanna said. She reached for the second item, a vintage WWII cigarette lighter and flipped it over. An inscription, *David Morgan, 1941*, was engraved on the back. "David Morgan," she said. "Related to the McGuire Landfill victim, Suzette Morgan, perhaps."

Savanna photographed the items on the newsprint, then dropped the items into separate evidence bags.

Fontaine pulled out another drawer. A noise from the bed startled them.

"What was that?" Savanna asked.

They both turned at the same time.

A tabby cat leapt from between the sheets. Fontaine shot her a glance before he scampered into the living room after the feline.

The cat hairs Savanna found among the unidentified evidence could belong to Molly's cat.

"What the hell?" Molly yelled. "Leave him alone."

Savanna prepared her tweezers for the unsuspecting animal.

Fontaine returned cuddling it in his arms. "It's okay, kitty," he said. "We just need a few hairs."

Savanna plucked the hairs from its head. The cat yelped and released its paws. "Okay," Savanna said. "That should be it."

"That's a good kitty." Fontaine rubbed the cat's ears. It purred and nudged against him.

When he lowered it to the floor, Savanna turned and watched it scamper from the room. She hated having to hurt the poor thing. Yet, if the evidence matched, it held proof that Molly was present at the victims' deaths. Maybe even helped him. Did she agree to the horror Colton Moore inflicted on the women when he violated, then killed them?

Savanna's rage mounted. She tucked the samples into her case. The victims' faces floated before her. Sally, Suzette, Theresa. He might not have killed Janet, but her death was connected somehow. If she was right and Brock drove the van that transported Theresa's body to the dockyards, then Molly knew Brock too.

Chapter 58

_A_fter five months of searching, Savanna finally held the missing necklace in her hand. She recalled the photo of Sally wearing the ivory face against her flushed skin. How happy she'd been then. Since her escape from Moore's capture, with a shattered self-esteem and impregnated by rape, she would never be the same. Yet, Molly hid away here, waiting for Colton Moore's release. Maybe they planned to murder again.

Savanna left Fontaine in the bedroom and marched into the living room where Dave still interviewed Molly.

The detective's head snapped up when she approached. "What's going on, Jones?"

Savanna ignored him.

Dave raised a finger at Molly. "Don't move. Jones, you have something you want me to look at?" When she disregarded his question, he blocked her path and placed a hand on her shoulder.

"It was her," Savanna snapped.

"You got something?" Dave insisted.

She stared past him at Molly. "Look at this," she said and gave him the evidence bag.

Molly leapt to her feet. "What were you doing in my bedroom?"

"Sit down, Molly," Dave ordered, "I have a few more questions." He inspected the bag, then handed it back to Savanna. "I'll handle this," he said.

She stepped back.

"Molly, do you know Colton Moore?" he asked.

Molly lifted her chin and twisted away from him. "I don't know who that is."

Savanna groaned. Dave shot her a glance, but she ignored him and concentrated on Molly.

Molly met Savanna's gaze. She swallowed, then bit her lip.

"You know him, don't you?" Savanna asked. "You know him, and you know his friends."

"What are you talking about?" She swivelled to Dave again. "What is she talking about?"

"Jones, I'm asking the questions here," Dave warned. "

"At least have the guts to admit it," Savanna snarled.

"Yeah, I do. What of it? He's an okay guy."

Savanna stared at Molly. "How do you figure? He's a rapist and a murderer."

"People like you would never understand us," Molly said.

"What's to understand? He hurts women, and you help him."

"So what if he wanted to sleep with other women? They all wanted him anyway, and I love him."

"Is that what attracts you to him? You watch him hurt other women? Is that why you love him."

"He saved my life. That's why I love him."

Savanna jerked back. "He saved your life?"

"It happened two years ago. I was pregnant. When I told my boyfriend, he twisted my arm behind my back, and said he would pull it from the socket." Molly crossed her right arm over her breasts and rubbed it. "Then he shoved me to the ground and started kicking me. Colt pulled him off me. He took me to the hospital when the bleeding wouldn't stop." She looked over at Savanna's stomach again. "I lost the baby," she said, "but that's okay. I didn't want his kid anyway."

The words chilled Savanna. Then the connection that eluded them dawned on her. "Who was your boyfriend, Molly?" she asked.

Molly sunk into the ratty couch. "I don't see him anymore. I don't know where he is."

"Is that true?"

"What is this about, Jones?" Dave asked.

"Molly knows something she wants to tell you. Don't you, Molly?"

"I told you the truth." She spoke with her chin tucked into her chest, while her glance darted away from Savanna.

"You've seen him recently, haven't you? Savanna asked. "He was here?"

"Where are you going with this, Jones?" Dave's impatience rose again.

She looked over at him. He needed to know this as much as she did. "Molly, why don't you tell Detective Thomas your ex-boyfriend's name?"

Molly kept her head down, nervously squeezing her hands in her lap. "His name is Gerald."

"Gerald?" Dave stepped toward her. "Gerald who?"

"Gerald Brock."

"When did you last see him, Molly?" Dave asked.

"Yesterday, all right? He was here yesterday. He wanted my help, but I didn't want anything to do with him after the way he treated me. He said if I didn't help him, he'd tell the police it was us."

"What was he threatening you with?" Savanna asked.

"You think Colt killed those women, but it wasn't him. Gerald did it. He cut off Suzette's hand because she stole from him."

Savanna squeezed her eyes closed and dug her fingernails into her palms. She was afraid to ask the next question, but she had to. "Molly, what about—"

"What did he want help with?" Dave interrupted.

"Dave, she knows if—" Savanna started.

He gripped her shoulder and propelled her away from his suspect. "Molly, what did Gerald Brock ask you to do?"

"He had a bag with him. A large one, with a lock. I asked him what was inside. He said it's none of my fucking business."

"Where's the bag?" Dave asked.

"In there." Molly gestured with her chin. Both Dave and Savanna turned and stared at the stove.

"Where?" In a few steps, Dave stood in the kitchen.

"In the oven," Molly said.

Savanna wanted to pounce on the stove and rummage through whatever bag was inside. But at the same time, she practically twitched from the urge to force Molly to tell her why Brock killed Janet. She eyed Dave, and then started for the stove.

"Just a minute there, Jones." Dave put his hand out to block her and looked over at Fontaine who watched the entire exchange from the kitchen door.

"I'll do the honours," Fontaine said.

Dave positioned himself between the door and Molly.

Fontaine marched toward the stove and looked it over. He reached out to grasp the handle.

"Wait," Savanna said.

He pivoted toward her. "What the heck, Jones?"

"I should dust it for prints first," she said. "I'll grab my kit." The grime on the oven door handle preserved imprints of whomever touched it. Whether she would get a clean and usable print was another story.

When she had dusted and transferred every print she found, Fontaine yanked the door open. He grasped a black and green camouflage duffle bag and pulled, but it wouldn't budge. He stooped in front of the oven and heaved the bag out.

"Holy crap," he said, "what's inside this thing?" He slung it onto the counter top. A small padlock held the double zippers together.

Savanna photographed the bag while he pulled a penknife from his pocket. She nodded at him when she had enough shots.

Fontaine cut into the bag.

Small Ziploc sacks containing about fifteen pills each tumbled from the sliced hole. The small red pills were shaped like a lightning bolt. They had found Brock's stash, but were there only pills?

"Wait," Savanna said.

"What is it?" Dave asked.

"I need to check that bag."

"Why?" Fontaine asked. "It's full of pills.

"Then why is it so heavy." She tentatively inserted a gloved hand and poked through the multiple small packages.

Her fingers connected to something solid. She tried grasping it but needed both hands. When she hefted it from the bag, they all stared at a block securely wrapped with packing tape and weighing about fifty kilograms. "This," she said, "is worth the entire search."

____

Chapter 59

With Molly's evidence released from police custody and booked into the forensic lab, Savanna headed for the gym. Her emotions surrounding the case and Nicholas's confession had her tangled in knots. She needed a release.

By 6:15 p.m., she was standing in front of Max at the Red Fox Gymnasium, looking to find her way to clarity.

His youthful complexion wrinkled into a worried frown at the sight of her.

She extended her hand and he wrapped it in protective gauze.

"Flex your fingers," he said.

She did.

"So, where are we now?" He grabbed a bulging red boxing glove and fitted it over her left fist. "Push."

"Twenty weeks," she said and stiffened at the shoulder to shove her bonded knuckles into the glove.

He laced the string and affixed the second glove. "Any cramps?"

"No."

"Any unexplained spikes in temperature?"

She could explain every one. She shook her head. With the

gloves weighing heavily on her wrists, she lifted her head to meet his dark blue eyes.

"We'll stop after ten minutes for a check and go from there," he said.

"Okay."

"Ready?"

She nodded again.

He raised his palms and motioned for her to punch.

She lifted her arms into position. The oversized red fists bulged next to her chin.

He motioned to her again.

Savanna's feet dragged as though she wore lead rather than Nikes. Twenty minutes ago, when she left the lab, she'd toyed with the idea of cancelling her sparring session. She'd had enough with confrontation for one day, but anguish rode her.

Max called to her.

She stretched her right fist toward his left palm. Her left followed in a crossover angle.

"Come on," he said.

She repeated the motion, not quite reaching him. Her eyes focused on his foam targets, but her brain lagged.

"Come on, Savanna." Max broke into her thoughts. "I know you've got more than that."

She jabbed at him again.

"Maybe I'm wrong," he said. "Maybe you're just a pretty face waiting to be rescued."

Heat warmed her neck. Savanna's right arm stretched her flying fist at Max's chin. It connected to his raised palm.

"That's it," he said. "Again."

She increased the intensity of her punches.

Max dodged and matched her swings.

For the first two years of her marriage, she let Richard rescue her. What happened since then?

"Time's up," Max said. "Temperature check."

She followed him to the ropes.

He stuck a thermometer under her tongue, then pulled it out

after it beeped. "Good," he said. "You're within range, practically standing still."

She flicked him a glance.

"You feeling all right?" he asked.

"Physically, yes."

"In that case, let's get those endorphins pumping."

He changed tactics and came after her for the first two minutes.

She started to find her rhythm. The fleeting years flicked through her head, a carousel of choices that had her living alienated from what she felt inside. She'd clung to what she shared with Richard, then he abandoned her because she dared carry his child. She lied to her father. Her further deception almost freed a murdering rapist, placed her job at risk, and ruined her reputation. Then the secret she lived with for ten years returned to haunt her life.

"You gonna let the world crush you?" Max asked.

She punched at his face. Her muscles quivered as she charged after him. Her increased speed backed him against the ropes.

She shifted from his retaliation, but not fast enough. The foam padding slapped her face on the right. The grating sensation lit her skin on fire.

"Come on, princess," Max heckled. "Let's go."

Savanna fumed. Her dancing feet closed in on him. What now?

"You like the safe zone, don't you, princess?" Max broke free and started his taunts again. "Don't stay out there on the edge, come on in here."

Is that what she had been doing? Living on the edge of life? Holding back, refusing to connect, to commit?

She danced toward Max.

He jabbed at her.

She skipped back.

He signalled a come-hither to her again.

She shuffled on the spot, but her feet lost the warmth and agility from moments ago. By Christmas, Nicholas would be gone from her life, again.

"That's right, baby," Max said. "You might as well quit now, there's nothing out here for you."

His insults defeated rather than encouraged her movements.

She dropped her arms and turned away from him. Seconds later, a sharp pain ignited from the back of her head.

Max yanked her ponytail. He held her steadily against his firm stomach. "You need to let go of whatever it is you brought with you this evening. It doesn't belong here. Let it go. Get it out." He held the stifling foam beneath her chin.

Savanna lifted both arms and jabbed her elbows into his gut. Her heel came down on his toe.

He yelped and released her.

She turned and threw alternating punches at his feeble defence, holding him against the ropes in an onslaught of jabs to his foam palms.

His steady gaze penetrated her frustration. He pushed until he found the seed of her anger.

Savanna groaned and skipped back from him.

He walked forward, stretching his arms into her face. Where would she go now? The ropes were her doom. She wanted to look back but feared losing sight of what was in front of her.

The ropes closed in. Her chest heaved with her crumbling nerves. The wretched events of the last few months tumbled down on her. Nothing happened the way she expected and her attempts to right the horrible failures created more despair.

Well, she needed to save herself now. She needed to save her sanity. Everyone threw in their two cents: Rebecca, her father, Nicholas and even Richard with his damning suggestion that she kill the child she carried so he could have the lifestyle he always wanted. She'd had enough.

She blocked Max's punch and stopped him with an uppercut.

He stumbled back and landed on his bum.

"Oh my God," she said and ran to him. "I'm so sorry. Are you okay?"

Laughter sputtered from his handsome face. "That's what I'm

talking about," he said and leapt to his feet. "You know what I like about that? You caught me off guard. I didn't see it coming."

Neither did she. Sweet relief flowed through her.

"I wasn't sure I could get much out of you tonight," Max said. "What did it?"

"Not sure," she lied.

"We should stop for tonight."

Savanna nodded and smiled.

He threw his arm around her shoulder and stuck the thermometer under her tongue again. "Come on," he said. "I'll unlace you."

Chapter 60

For the last ten minutes Savanna paced her living room repeating another of her mother's favourite proverbs.

A day of love is worth more than a lifetime of regret.

She really wanted to believe those words.

An hour ago, she called her father to ask his advice. He listened as she told him the entire story. "Now I'm going to tell Nicholas the truth," she had said.

"Why do you think you're so different from your mother?" he asked after a long silence. "You're exactly like her. Ana sacrificed herself and her family in the foolish belief that it was the only way to protect us. She was wrong. Now you're doing the same." Her father thought that exposing Nicholas to a past neither of them could ever change would only create resentment. But that was a risk Savanna needed to take.

Nicholas would arrive soon. He offered to bring dinner to celebrate the break in the case. She wanted to talk. When he had said he loved her and would care for the baby, her heart warmed, until her guilt chilled the promise in his gaze. How could she allow him to take care of Richard's child when his was gone?

She could never let him stand by her while she kept the truth from him. Yet, telling him about the pregnancy at that moment was a gulf too wide for his love to fill. She would admit her feelings for him, but not before she told him about the abortion. Yes, it was the right thing to do. Regret had burdened her life for too long. Admitting what she had done would wipe the slate clean and give them both a new start.

She padded across the floor. Her bare feet, reaching out from the thick track pants, moved like ice blocks. She hesitated in front of the small accent table against the wall, then pulled the drawer. Weeks ago, as she packed and sorted her documents from among Richard's, she found the brown envelope. The return address stamped in the upper left corner was Women's Health Centre, 800 Commissioners Road. She thought she had thrown out the damn thing.

Holding it now hurled her back to the day she left the clinic numbed and empty. She shook the feeling from her quivering shoulders and lifted the flap, then closed it again. *Maybe her father was right.*

The doorbell rang and startled her. She clapped a palm over her racing heart and stood for a moment staring at the closed door. The bell sounded again. She turned toward it then noticed the envelope in her hand. She dropped it into the drawer and hid it away once more.

Pushing her hair behind her ears, she crossed the floor and opened the door. Nicholas stood on the step with his bike helmet clutched in one hand and a paper bag in the other.

"Hey," he said.

"Hey." She took the bag and rested it on the coffee table. Nicholas entered, dropped the helmet on a chair and freed himself from his jacket. A need to be in his arms drew her to him. He bent his head and dragged his mouth across her lips, then soothed the rising flames with his tongue. She shivered and opened her mouth for him. The tantalizing kiss melted her insides.

"Why didn't you come and see me after the search?" he asked against her mouth. "I waited for you."

She shrugged.

"Detective Thomas said you found the necklace. Why didn't you come back to the lab?"

"I did."

"I thought you would have stuck around for Molly's interrogation."

"I did for some of it. I wanted to submit my report." She sighed. "Then I went to the gym."

"Thomas said Molly gave them everything. She talked about her connection with Moore and Brock. He said Moore was Brock's cutter until he was arrested, then Molly took over. Thomas suspects that's when the formula went bad."

Savanna freed herself from his arms and took the food to the dining table. "Molly was very concerned that Brock would come after her," she said. "Probably why she talked."

Nicholas washed his hands at the kitchen sink. "How much of the drugs did you find?" he asked.

"Hundreds. Opioids. Some in the lightning bolt design. There were at least two other kinds, but it was definitely a shipment."

Nicholas reached in an overhead cupboard for plates. "And the API, did you find that too?" he asked.

Why did he insist on discussing the case? He knew why she avoided him at the lab. "Nicholas." She wanted to stop his stream of questions.

He froze in mid-grasp, his fingers already connecting to the bag of food. Jubilance slipped from his expression. The panic in her voice registered on his face. Within moments, Savanna watched confusion flicker to concern and then to apprehension. He was beginning to understand why now was the only time she would see him.

"Can we put this on hold for a minute?" she asked. "I need to tell you something."

He withdrew his hand from the food and came to her. "Is this about this morning?"

"More than that. It's why I can't say yes to the life you offered me."

"Are you going to end us? Am I not what you want?"

God. She couldn't let him think that, never that. "Oh, Nicholas, you're quite the opposite. That's the one thing I can't hide from you. You're everything I want. I just don't think I deserve you."

"Don't say that. I've enjoyed every moment with you, even the struggles," he said. "But I look forward to the day when we belong to each other. You know I want you in my life."

His frankness disarmed her. She lifted her glance to his face and caught her breath. His love, unguarded and exposed, waited in his dazzling hazel eyes. Why was she so afraid? He loved her.

She raised a trembling hand to touch the growing shadow along his jawline. Her fingertips soothed the scratchy hairs. He would understand why she had done what she had to do. Nicholas would forgive her.

He encircled her fingers in his and lifted them to his lips.

Warming sensations flooded the space between her legs, and she whimpered, then eased her hand from his. Savanna strolled from the kitchen, leaving Nicholas to follow. She tried to say something and eyed the drawer she had slammed shut earlier. She needed to start somewhere, but not there.

"Why are you so afraid?" His voice cautiously probed the growing tension.

"I—"

"Have you heard from Richard?"

"Yes." She pounced on a possible way out. "He called."

"Is this what you want to talk about?"

"No. Richard called because the gossip somehow reached him. He said that I was ruining his tour."

Nicholas stepped in front of her blindingly fast. His lips touched hers softer than she expected. He gathered her into his arms and kissed her without restraint. When he loosened his embrace, she held on.

"Savanna," he said. "I could never get enough of you. Never. If you don't love me, tell me now, and I'll leave you alone."

"It's not that."

"Then what the hell is going on?"

She moved away from him again, placing the couch between them this time. "I never told you that Richard asked me to abort our child," she said.

"He asked you to do that?"

She nodded.

"What reason did he give you?"

She swallowed before answering. "He said because I had done it before."

Nicholas fixed her with a steady gaze. "Had you?"

She nodded again.

"His child?" he asked.

"I did it before I met him," she said. The tears started to roll down her cheeks. They stung her flesh.

"Savanna. What do you mean?"

She lifted her chin and faced him. "Three weeks after I moved to Westbury from Vancouver I discovered I was pregnant." She stopped.

The first part was out. Now she had to keep going. "I didn't know the man's name," she continued, "or how to get in contact with him. I was afraid, and I didn't know what to do. I hid behind the fact that I would never see him again. I aborted the baby."

She waited for Nicholas to say something, but the growing quiet in the room chilled her. No veins fluttered beneath his skin. No straightening of those beautiful broad shoulders. He stood so still, she thought he might have misunderstood what she said. She decided then to tell him everything.

"Six years later, within months of dating Richard, I became pregnant again. We got married and after we returned from the honeymoon I lost the child in a miscarriage. I believed then that I was being punished for what I had done."

Nicholas looked away from her and scrubbed his face with a large hand.

A cry left Savanna's throat. "I'm so sorry," she said.

"This can't be true." He searched her face as if looking for a different answer.

She went to the drawer and removed the envelope. She crossed the room again and handed it to him.

His hand shook when he took it. Or maybe that was her.

His long gaze studied her before he looked away and lifted the flap. His eyes scrolled down the sheet to the end then flicked to the top again. Bewilderment haunted his expression.

She knew then that he focused on the date: August 18, 2002.

Nicholas's fingers pushed through his hair. His eyes never left the paper. He dropped to the chair behind him and a hand swiped his face again, as if he needed to wash away the truth. "How?" he stammered.

Savanna tried to steady herself, but the trembling shook her from inside. She had no words to relieve his suffering.

Nicholas's mouth opened and closed before he stuttered one word. "Why?"

She looked down at her numb toes and then back at him. "I couldn't do it alone," she said. "Not then."

"Alone? I could have found you if only you'd told me your name."

Her body kept quivering. She closed her eyes, unsure now of her memories. "It was never that simple," she said.

"It was a baby! My baby!" His voice, loud and grating, frightened her because she knew how much her confession hurt him. He stared blankly without speaking for a moment, then leapt from the chair.

Savanna couldn't stop shaking.

Nicholas stalked to the door. He stood there, his back to her and his head bent over the paper.

Her heartbeat thundered between her breasts, and she bit down on her bottom lip. She wanted him to stay so they could get through the pain together. She wanted him to forgive her for what she had done to them.

"I'm so sorry, Nicholas," she said through the tight pain in her throat. "I've always regretted my decision." When he didn't respond, she winced and hugged herself. "It was another fork in the road," she said.

He turned to look at her.

"I made the wrong choice," she continued her confession. "Every day since then I wondered what could have been. I thought I was safe from my own guilt and self-loathing, then you turned up. I couldn't simply tell you. When you said you loved me, I couldn't accept everything you offered for Richard's baby."

Nicholas cringed and then measured her with an unblinking stare. His eyes glinted when they slid over her body. By the time he reached her face, she tasted blood.

He clenched his fist around the paper. "It should have been simple," he finally said.

If he believed she copped out, then he needed to know what finally pushed her to the edge. "You once asked me how my mother died," she said. "A soldier shot her, point blank in the face, only three years before you walked into my life. Back then, when I met you, I couldn't..." she paused, the words choking her now. "I could never love a soldier."

His head rocked back. "I wasn't the soldier who took everything from you," he said. "I didn't kill your mother. I didn't take your dreams. I wasn't just any soldier, Savanna. I was Ishmael."

His words broke down the walls she erected to protect herself. She could never imagine hurting this much. But this wasn't all her doing. She blinked to clear her vision.

"Ishmael never called," she said. "I was alone, and I waited as long as I could. You never called."

Nicholas's face turned to stone. He yanked open the apartment door and slammed it shut behind him. He was gone.

His accusation hacked into her with the savagery of a butcher's knife. She doubled over and collapsed on the couch. Maybe burdening him with her secret was a mistake.

Chapter 61

Outside Savanna's apartment, the humid night air suffocated Nicholas. A gust of wind tugged at the abortion requisition as he shoved it into his pocket. He mounted the bike and rolled away from the house. It all happened so fast, he wasn't sure what he said. The entire time after Savanna handed him the envelope, he didn't take a full breath. The requisition. The date. The impossibility of what she was trying to tell him. He had lost a child. His entire body rocked with his attempt to grasp the full reality.

A baby. Their baby. His baby. Much more than a baby ten years later. He would have had a daughter, or a son, if Savanna hadn't aborted his child without a single thought for him. A nine-year-old. His chest tightened and heaved, struggling with the powerlessness that overtook him. He could do nothing to change what she did. Would it have been so bad to keep the child? Even without his knowledge? An abortion took his choice away. The thought of it blinded him.

It had started raining, but he kept riding. Kept going, circling the city. Time disappeared. He and the bike were one. Ten years slipped away to the day she would have done it. August 10, 2002. It was the day before he left Germany for the war zone in Afghanistan.

Her number had been in his wallet since their night together. He'd thought of calling, but convinced himself that Savanna would just add another complication to the mess that was his life.

He gunned the bike forward and took the exit ramp to the highway. Within seconds, he was in the wind speeding so fast on the wet pavement, he was sure he could outrun a police cruiser if one flagged him down. He swerved in and out of traffic. He kept going, hoping to erase those hours they spent together from his memory. The night was still fresh in his head and he'd replayed every moment since his lips touched hers. How was he to know there was more?

The bike skidded. He pulled back in time to avoid a collision with the car in the lane to his left. The cellphone in his breast pocket buzzed and jolt him. He lurched backwards on the bike, accidentally yanking the handle to the right. The back wheel swerved into the left lane. He fought to straighten the machine under him and pull back on the speed. He tugged on the brakes. When the front wheel skidded, and the back lifted in the air, he knew he'd applied too much pressure. He went clear over the handlebar but struggled to hold on. Maybe he could pull the bike under him again.

Without his weight, the machine lost control and wrenched his shoulder sockets. He released the handlebar. The bike flipped over him. Momentum tumbled him along the pavement. Screeching tires from the oncoming car squealed in his ears. The car veered right to avoid him.

Afraid the rear wheels would roll over his head, he attempted to redirect his angle. His back and shoulders skidded along the road. The helmet scraped and hopped against the pavement, sending thundering booms through his skull. He came to a stop sometime after, his head still exploding and his body on fire.

Nicholas leaned to one side and tried to push himself off the ground. The road spun around him. His cellphone kept ringing in his breast pocket. Voices surrounded him.

"Hey buddy," someone said. "Are you okay?"

His stomach churned along with everything else. He inhaled.

Rather than fresh air a stabbing pain pierced his chest. He grunted and rolled onto his back again.

"Can you talk?" someone asked.

He groaned.

"Don't move. You probably broke something in that fall. You landed pretty hard."

Nicholas ignored the warning and bore down, rolling to his side, then pushed onto his knees and elbows. He groaned from the searing pain that coursed through his back.

"You shouldn't move. An ambulance is on the way."

No. He couldn't be carted off in an ambulance. He wasn't going to the hospital. He was going to see Colton Moore. He pushed to one foot. A bad idea, but it was the only way he could climb onto the bike again.

The man next to him kept talking.

Nicholas was in too much pain to figure out what he was saying. His head felt larger than normal. He leaned over and stuck his head between his knees, waiting for his stomach to either calm down or convulse. That's when he remembered he wore a helmet. He unfastened it and pulled it from his head. A rush of air hit his face and his stomach rolled to his throat. He turned away from the man beside him and vomited on the side of the road.

After a couple of minutes, he tried to stand. *Not going to happen.*

Someone said something about an ambulance. He wiped his mouth and twisted to find his bike but swayed instead.

Nicholas tried to stand again. He managed to push to his feet. Another man stood in the middle of the road, directing cars around the bike.

"Are you sure about this?" The man next to him asked. Tanned, balding, grey beard.

Nicholas swayed. He lumbered to the middle of the road and handed the helmet to the man guarding the bike. He then hoisted the machine onto its wheels. He stumbled backwards, but kept upright. He inspected the bike: Front fender bent. Speedometer glass broken. He twisted the handlebar. Not as aligned as he would have liked. He whipped his leg over. His boot bumped the seat and he stumbled again.

"You shouldn't be on the road," the other man shouted.

Nicholas turned on the ignition. It sputtered and died. He tried again. Same response. He paused and took a breath, then pumped the throttle and tried again. The engine coughed and sputtered into a continuous hum.

"You should probably wait for the ambulance," the man holding the helmet said.

Nicholas snatched the helmet from him and snapped it onto his head. "I'm a doctor," he said.

"You're an asshole."

Nicholas felt more like a cripple, and the biggest loser in the world. He gunned the bike. Something was wrong. Where did the road go? He faded, and his body floated. This time when he collided with the hard surface, Savanna was there with him, smiling.

Chapter 62

Wisteria scented the humid Vancouver air. Nicholas lifted his chin and inhaled. A rare cloudless sky looked down on them. "I'm glad you stayed with me tonight," he said.

Backing him, Savanna arched her hips against his crotch. The sweet Brazilian curves fitted flawlessly between his legs as he leaned against his bike. Then she turned to face him. "So am I," she said.

"This, right here, is the image I want in my memory every day for the next few months, especially when the bullets start flying."

She kissed him long and suggestive. It was hard to believe they met only that morning. "I wish I had the power to know when things got ugly for you," she said and splayed her long latte fingers over his chest. "I would show up and save you from a thousand bullets."

Dazed by her words, he choked on his response.

"Tell me what you would never forget about your years as a soldier," she said, all the while tenderly stroking his pecs over his shirt.

A sense of pride cleared the emotion clogging his throat. "Rescuing an entire village from army insurgents," he said. "The work I do with Doctors Without Borders. And seeing a young girl smile because, for the first time ever, she could finally see with the help of glasses someone, maybe even from right here, donated."

"That's beautiful. There's another side, though. I can tell. You carry the images with you. I want to have them too. Tell me. Deputize me to share your burdens."

Where did she come from? Nicholas kissed her.

"I'm ready," she said when he lifted his lips from hers.

"The babies." He cleared his throat and looked away from the distress forming in Savanna's expression. "Limbless and naked and hungry and wailing, some at their dead mothers' breasts. Kosovo, where I would reassemble bones of children to have something for their families to bury."

He shifted his gaze to her face again, prepared for horror and disgust. Her warm chocolate eyes waited for him. They glistened with sadness and compassion. Silence lingered for a moment longer while they stood still holding each other.

"And what about here?" she asked, her voice soft. She placed her palm over his heart. "What promise to yourself do you carry here?"

He despised it all. And he hated that he exposed her to the brutality most civilians in this country would never witness, but her need to know fascinated him. "I carry my own truth," he said. "I would give this world my talents, but I never want my own children to know that such terror exists. I would never want them to realize that nothing I do would ever stop the atrocities." He sucked in a breath and pulled her close to him before he spoke again. "It's for those reasons that I never want to have children."

Savanna's warm lips met his, soft and reassuring. Grateful for the distraction, he let her sweet tongue sooth him. Her long kiss quieted the turmoil that waited for him at the end of the night.

"Let's not talk about ugly now," he said. "You're beautiful, and I want to remember you just like this." He cuddled her closer, and she nestled against him. Together they floated into the night.

Chapter 63

The BlackBerry vibrated on the table and stirred Savanna on the couch. She hadn't moved since Nicholas left. How long ago was that? Daylight had disappeared from her apartment without her noticing. Except for the digital clock on the DVD player that read 9:37 p.m., she sat in darkness.

The phone rattled again. She tried to read the screen, but her vision was too blurry. Maybe it was Nicholas. "Hello," she said.

"Savanna, it's Scott."

She straightened on the couch. Why was he calling her? He probably heard from Molly's neighbours that she'd been arrested. And Savanna was his first call.

"Scott," she said, her tone as nonchalant as she could manage. "I haven't heard from you in a while. What's up?"

"Are you alone? Can you talk?"

"I can. You got something?"

"We've got a problem. Remember those designer drugs I told you about?"

"What about them?"

"That's what I'm trying to tell you. We got a hit on where to find the operation. A couple MPs staked out the place." His voice sounded muffled and there was a strange crackling in the background.

"What place?" she asked.

"A location in Exeter. Lucan Street. Do you know it?"

Savanna pushed from the couch. He was fishing, trying to decipher how much she knew. "Why didn't you tell us about that?" she asked. "I thought we were sharing information?"

"I'm telling you now." He was quiet for a while. Probably gauging how much he could say without giving away his position. "Look," he finally said. "I'm not part of upper brass. I don't make these decisions about who gets to know what. I'm just following orders."

Savanna rolled her eyes. Many a heinous act had been committed just following orders. "What's the problem?" she asked.

"The product was snatched from under our noses."

"What do you mean?"

"Someone else from inside tipped them off."

"Inside? Inside what?"

"Inside our investigation. Someone higher up the ranks who had been in Westbury all along without our knowledge."

"Do you know who it is?"

"We believe it's a doctor?"

"A doctor?" Was he talking about Nicholas? "What do you want us to do?" she asked.

"I was hoping we could meet to discuss next steps. How about in a half hour at the airbase?"

If she went to meet him, she would be safe there. Actually, she could even tip off Nicholas's friend who she met that morning. "The airbase?" she asked.

"Do you know where it is?"

"Yes, I do, but I don't think there's anything I could tell you to help." She didn't want to sound too eager.

"Look," he said. "I know I've gotten more from you than I've offered in the weeks we've been working on this together, and I'm sorry about that. What I can say now is that this might lead to the person who killed the nurse at the end of June."

Savanna slumped against the wall. The son of a bitch was using Janet's death to get information from her. She needed to call Nicholas.

"I can't meet you now," she said. "I'm expecting my father within the hour." Her father wasn't due for another couple of days, but Scott didn't have to know that. "I'll call you later." She hung up.

Sadness sunk deep inside her until she felt the gloomy misery in her bones. She and Janet would have been in Tofino by now, riding bikes on the beach and waiting for the whales to leap from the water. Brock took that away from them.

Savanna dialled Nicholas's number. He probably wouldn't want to talk to her, but this wasn't about them. When he didn't pick up, she spoke into the voicemail. "Nicholas," she paused and took a deep breath. "Brock just called me," she continued. "He's still using his alias. He wants me to meet him at the airbase. Says he has a lead on the person who—" Her voice caught. "The person who killed Janet. Call me, please."

Savanna tried Nicholas a couple more times, circling her living room as she waited for his call. Half an hour later, he still hadn't returned her call. She dialled Quinn's number. No answer. At this hour, he probably thought she wanted to talk. Her partner usually needed more time.

Maybe if she went to Nicholas's house and banged on the door he'd answer her then. She didn't know how much longer Brock would be at the airbase.

Savanna laced on a pair of Nike cross trainers, the only shoes at the front door, then realized she wanted to use the bathroom. The firm soles thumped on the bare floors as she hurried.

A few minutes later, plans to get someone on the line scrolled through her thoughts. She would call the station on her way and have them patch her through to Dave. If that didn't work, she would have to call DS Hannigan.

When she stepped outside, rain was pelting down. She hadn't realized the weather had changed so drastically in the last couple of hours. She grabbed the travel size umbrella hanging just inside the entrance. The shoes weren't rainboots, but at least the double-layered soles gave her a lift and some traction.

She pulled the door closed behind her. With a hand on her stomach, she ducked under the umbrella and headed for the car. George's Mercedes was parked in its usual spot. The windows in his studio were closed, but the light was on.

Keys in hand, she pointed the fob and the car chirped. Oh, wait, her cellphone. Did she pick it up from the coffee table? She patted her pants pocket just as something shoved her from behind. The umbrella went flying and she slammed into the car, stomach first. The collision winded her. She inhaled and groaned when the pain burrowed into her ribs.

Strong ammonia stifled her nostrils. She'd smelled the acrid scent before. She twisted to break free, but her assailant kept grabbing her arm. Since she was wet and slippery from the rain, he struggled for a firm grip on her. She jabbed her elbow backward and connected with a set of ribs.

"Stay still." His voice grunted next to her face.

Brock. Oh, God. It was Brock. He must have been waiting outside her house. No wonder he asked if she was alone. "What do you want?"

The fright seizing her mind kicked into overdrive and she knew escape was possible only if she fought.

She twisted, aiming her elbow and fighting him off. "Help! George!" The words roared from deep within her as she struggled with Brock between the two cars.

"You're a fighter, huh?" He hissed and then laughed into her ear. She lifted a heel, but he shoved his knee between her legs and grabbed a handful of her hair.

"George… George… Help."

He leaned his body into her, pinning her to the Passat. "Shut your mouth or I will cut that baby from your gut."

The menacing growl chilled her. Savanna froze and clamped her mouth shut. Her chest continued to heave and labour for breath.

Brock's fingers closed over her face. An unbearable substance filled her open mouth and nasal passage. Her eyes burned. Her brain worked with lightning speed to assist in the struggle. Then the suffocating substance registered at the same time she realized she would lose consciousness. *Chloroform.*

Chapter 64

$\mathcal{N}$icholas jerked awake. A massive ache pounded just over his left eye. He groaned and lifted a hand to check for a hole, but something tethered him. His eyes flew open and he yanked his arm. A metal pole crashed onto the bed. "What?" He was hooked up to an IV.

"I wouldn't do that if I were you." A familiar voice said from across the room.

His head snapped up. *Bad idea.* Another stabbing pain assaulted his temples. Corbett. "Where am I?" Nicholas asked.

"They tell me this is Westbury General."

Nicholas looked around. *The crash.* He'd passed out when he tried to leave the scene. *Crap.* He needed to get out of here. "Are you here to arrest me?" he asked.

"Are you responsible for this?" Corbett motioned to the IV tube."

"You could say that."

"Was anyone else hurt?"

"I don't know, but I don't think so."

"Then that's a negative, soldier."

"Then why are you here?"

355

"Where is Brock?"

"All indications are that he left Westbury. I thought you would know where he would be by now."

"You think I'm the mastermind in his drug business?"

Nicholas met Corbett's glare and refused to look away despite his thundering headache. If he came here in the interest of saving his own ass, then he could think again. "My investigation is ongoing," he said. "And I'm not stopping until I know who's involved."

Corbett understood his meaning, but the man had been a soldier for forty years. He knew how to play his cards close to his chest.

"I knew I could trust you to leave no stone unturned," Corbett said.

Nicholas looked down at the IV piping liquid into his veins. Whatever ran through that tube was obviously powerful enough to make him hallucinate. "Are you now saying that you are in favour of the investigation?"

"That's right. Finding the ringmaster who ran the drug outfit was the reason I changed your assignment."

"So why not tell me that to begin with? Or is this another tactic of yours to avoid responsibility?" He was past caring about Corbett's threats.

"I know you think that's who I am, and you have your reasons, but your unauthorized interview with Global Research already painted you as a rogue officer. That and the other stunts you pulled earlier."

"You want me to believe that you set this up? A one-man investigation into an illegal venture that threatened the army's reputation? Do you know how many lives were in danger? How many women Brock killed?"

"Wasn't it Colton Moore who killed those women?"

"The police have a witness in custody who said it was Brock."

"I didn't know who was involved in this operation, and you had an axe to grind. An official investigation would have turned unwanted attention to the army. This way, if a rogue officer under sanction ran around asking questions, the people involved would hardly take note, unaware of your natural propensity for digging until you found your man."

"Are you saying you set me up?"

"I'm saying I rubber-stamped your investigation."

"So why recall my appointment before the investigation is complete?"

"You weren't supposed to involve anyone else. I expected a dalliance, but nothing of this magnitude."

Savanna. Nicholas needed to get to her. He'd been a fool. He looked around the room for the rest of his clothes. They hung over a chair next to the window. "And now?" he asked. "Why are you here now?"

"I read your report. I'm here to offer my help."

"Your help? How?"

"The army received credible intel that an API shipment on its way from China to Montreal was intercepted. Our source believes that whoever stole the shipment knew something about the operation."

Nicholas ripped the tape from his arm and pulled the tube from his vein. What Corbett was saying made sense. *Did the police know what they had on their hands?* He pushed from the bed and steadied himself.

"Going somewhere, Lieutenant-Colonel Wade?" Corbett asked.

He looked over at his CO. For many years he'd despised this man. Despised everything he stood for and what the army had become in the hands of generals like Corbett. He was the reason that soldiers like Brock ran illegal enterprises.

Ten years ago, Corbett sent Nicholas to the front with one week's notice because Corbett wanted to teach him a lesson. Before Nicholas shipped out, he flew to Vancouver to see Professor Fraser McDaniel, his mentor at that time, and instead, he met Savanna.

Was he here now to stop Nicholas? Or to really help? Either something had gone really wrong, or Corbett's ghosts were coming back to bite him. Whatever it was, the Major-General meant to take some responsibility.

Nicholas massaged his aching temples. What about himself? Did he ever try to step into the shoes of the people he judged and despised for the choices they made? And who was he to judge anyway? He'd always been good at fixing other people's problems, but when it came to his own, he ran and he stayed gone.

He looked up at Corbett. "If what you say is true," he said, "then Brock has a good reason to run. He's probably long gone."

"You're right about that. He'll tell the Chinese or the Montreal dealer that the police have the merchandise. That wouldn't stop them from going after him, regardless of what Brock believes. They would still hold him responsible for stealing the API in the first place. He'll need cover."

Nicholas looked around for his phone. "I have an idea where he might go," he said. "My business with him isn't over, but first, I've a confession to make.

Chapter 65

The drill chiselling through Savanna's skull raised enough red flags to bring on the panic. A thick and chalky tongue, a head she struggled to lift and burning sinuses?

She twisted her neck and forced her chin upward. Where was she and why was she sitting on the floor? Her eyelids seemed just as heavy as her head. She blinked and flicked her eyes open. She looked around. The semi-dark room looked unfamiliar. *This was all wrong.*

Shallow breathing brought her attention to a shadow standing a few feet away and just to her right. Then it all came tumbling back. *Oh god, Brock.* He'd called and suggested they meet to talk. The call had been no more than a scheme to lure her from the apartment. She fell for it and the madman chloroformed her and snatched her from the driveway. *What did he want with her?*

He stared into a broken mirror, looking past his distorted reflection at something over his shoulder. He wore green camouflage pants shoved into black boots and a snug-fitting green t-shirt. He was broad and lumpy with stiff, hard muscles that looked as though they were better for strength than speed and flexibility. The faint light reflecting from the mirror revealed camouflage paint on his face. He was battle ready. *Who was he going to fight?*

Her shoulders ached, but when she tried to move her arm, she realized they were handcuffed to an old radiator. Her heart sped up. She brought her knees to her chin and tried to stand, but she kept slipping along the dirt-caked wooden floor. She craned her neck and followed Brock's focus. Another mirror. It leaned against a set of broken drawers behind him.

He stared at the infinite reflections that repeated in the two mirrors. "The door is at the top of those stairs." His grating voice startled her. "But you aren't going anywhere. Not yet anyway."

"So you're not only a liar. You're a drug dealer too."

"Don't think you're in a position to judge, sweetheart. He rolled his neck before repositioning to look at her through the mirror. "You've been whoring around on your husband with Wade. Ha. The lovely couple shopping in the baby aisle. I thought your old man should know what you're doing in his absence."

Her scalp crawled. It was Brock who had taken that photo and sent it to the newspaper. Another one of his strategies. Reveal Nicholas's location and publicizing her presumed infidelity with a single picture. "What do you want with me?" she asked.

"Now that you're awake, we can talk about that." An oily smirk curled his thin lips. But first, let me check out what you've been up to since our telephone conversation. From what I see here." He twisted so she could see what he held.

He was scrolling through her BlackBerry.

"Wade hasn't answered your last three calls, but that's Wade for ya. He abandons everyone who depends on him. Did you tell him you're going back to your old man?" Brock grinned into the mirror.

The guy wasn't only a sociopath, he liked the sound of his own voice. "Why were you following me?" Savanna asked.

"I wanted to trust you, but when I saw you with Wade in Exeter the day after your nurse friend met her untimely end, I knew you were bent."

"The only one who's bent is you. I know you killed Janet and I'll make sure you pay for it. She had nothing to do with your sleazy business."

"My business isn't sleazy."

"Why did you kill her?"

"If you and the nurse would have kept your noses out of it, she'd be alive today. And you would be free to tell your musician husband whatever lies you have cooked up for him when he comes home."

"Janet wasn't into drugs. What did she do to you?"

"You're right. She had nothing to do with it, but I spotted her at the Black Pearl pub. She was watching me for the longest time, as though she was trying to figure out where we met. We hadn't of course, but she'd seen me with Suzette one night at the hospital. I had to follow her then to figure out what she was up to. She made a call. I didn't get most of it, but enough to know that she planned to visit the police station to give them a description. I couldn't let that happen."

"So you killed her?"

"Just like I killed the other two."

"Suzette and Theresa. What did they do to you? Why did you cut off their hands?"

"They were just like my mother. She took everything. I worked the streets so she could eat, and she still needed to steal my stash."

"You cut off your mother's hand for that?"

"Both of them. She would never steal what's mine again."

Savanna shivered. Her stomach lurched, but she needed to keep him talking. "Suzette worked for you. Was she also your girlfriend?"

"Because I fucked the bitch that doesn't mean I cared about her."

"She stole your drugs?"

"She was selling my product to a classy nursing home up in Toronto."

"How did she end up with Colton Moore's DNA?"

"How do you think?"

"They were sleeping together?"

"Moore probably raped her. He's an idiot."

"And you're better than he is?"

"Like I said before." Brock started looking around as though he lost something. "You are in no position to judge."

"If Moore was such an idiot why did you work for him?"

"Work for him?" He howled with laughter. "No sweetheart, he worked for me. He might be an ignoramus when it came to getting away with his sexual misdeeds, but he's one brilliant cutter."

"Molly gave you both up when the police arrested her. You can bet Moore will be charged for his drug crimes. Do you think he'll take the blame for all of it and not rat you out?"

"If he knows what's good for him, he'll keep his mouth shut."

Brock seemed to find what he was looking for. It was a notebook. He perched on an old high stool and started flipping through it.

Savanna looked around trying to figure out where they were. "What kind of place is this?" she asked.

"An abandoned campsite. This is where I first met Moore."

Savanna froze. Abandoned. "Beaverton Campground?" she whispered. That was where Moore spent his summers. She'd been so stupid. The information was staring her in the face for months. If she'd only mentioned it to Nicholas, Dave, or even Quinn, they would have some idea of where to find her now. She was shivering, but she didn't want to look scared. The mere scent of fear would probably arouse Brock. He described Moore as a sexual miscreant, but those women were raped by both men. Even if the sex started out consensual, according to Molly it didn't continue that way.

Savanna needed to keep Brock talking. Maybe he would say something that might help her escape. "And after all those years," she said, "you trusted Moore with your business?"

"We were always in contact. There are some people who can't sell their way out of a wet paper bag. Not Moore. He has an organized mind. He knew how to move the products. Get the packages where they needed to be, and on time." Brock's expression tightened.

"You let him run your business while you left the country on tours of duty?" Savanna asked. She wanted every piece of information she was going to use to bury his ass.

"What's it to you?"

"I've been working on Moore's case for a year now. I thought I knew him, but you're telling me he's a mastermind and you were just the owner of the operation."

Brock's steely grey eyes flashed in the shadows. "If you're so smart," he said, "how come you let Wade knock you up and leave?"

She looked away. Whatever Brock thought he knew, it was enough to remind her of how much she hurt Nicholas. "You don't know him," she said. "Just like you may not know Moore. Maybe this is his master plan to take your profitable business away from you. Have it ready for him when he gets out. He knows you killed those women."

Brock laughed again. "Moore may know how to cook and cut the stuff. He may even know how to ship it out, but he doesn't know where to get the raw material. He doesn't have my contacts. He knows what I want him to know."

Brock threw the notebook in the corner and pushed from the stool. He walked toward her.

Savanna swallowed. She'd seen what he did with the other women. She didn't want him near her. "What are you going to do now?" She spoke fast, trying to buy more time. "Molly has already ruined the integrity of your merchandise. How are you going to repair that?"

"What? Are you interested in taking over?" He pulled a set of keys from his pocket and unlocked the handcuffs. "Enough of this chitchat," he said. "I've got a job for you, and if you do it right, you might get out of this with your little bundle of joy still tucked safely in your tummy." He tugged her off the floor.

The semi-dark room spun when she got to her feet. She needed to get out of here and away from this madman.

"Come on," he said, gripping her elbow.

"Where are you taking me?"

He shoved her up the steps. "Don't worry. You'll like it."

---

*N*icholas sat on a chair lacing his boots. His head weighed a ton. He thought it would pull him over. He pushed himself upright when his cellphone rang from the bedside table.

"That thing has been going off for almost the entire hour I was sitting here," Corbett said.

Nicholas shot him a glance as he pushed from the chair and crossed the room. *Nothing creepier than Corbett watching him sleep.* The number on the cellphone's screen read, unknown. Nicholas answered anyway.

"Hello." He waited a couple seconds before the person on the other end replied.

"Hello, Lieutenant-Colonel Asswipe,"

It took Nicholas all of two seconds to recognize Brock's voice. "How did you get my number?"

"You sure that's the question you need answered right now?"

"I know you're Colton Moore's accomplice."

"There you go. No more fucking around. We can finally talk business. But let's get one thing straight. Moore worked for me."

"The OPP are in contact with Ottawa. You will be talking, but not with me."

"Patience. We haven't gotten to that part of the conversation. First, I want you to know that this is your fault. You started this and now you're going to finish it and when it's all over you're the one who will be answering the questions in Ottawa. And if I may say, sir, I hope Corbett burns your ass."

Brock wasn't making sense. Or maybe that was the medicine from his IV drip. "What do you want?" he demanded and instantly regretted raising his voice. The vibration rumbled in his head.

"Glad you asked. The police took my merchandise when they arrested that stupid bitch who knocked around with Moore. I want it back."

"You're referring to the API you stole from the Montreal drug cartel? That's between—"

"Don't interrupt." Brock snapped. "The next time you interrupt I won't be responsible for what happens. Got it?"

"Brock, I don't have time—"

"I said, got it?"

This didn't feel right. How did Brock get his number? He'd have to play along to get the answers. "Got it," he said.

"As I was saying. You will get my merchandise from the police and bring it to me."

"What the—"

"Ah. Ah. Ah. You broke your promise, again."

A slap echoed through the phone and a woman screamed. Nicholas's blood ran cold. "Who is that?" He yelled into the phone. Nicholas's fear for Savanna's life overpowered the pain shooting through his head.

"You will bring my merchandise for me in exchange for your girlfriend. And to be sure this goes according to plan, you will leave the police out of it. Come alone with my product. You got that?"

"You're out of your sociopathic mind. How can I get the stuff from the police and not get them involved?"

"Am I supposed to work out your problems for you?"

Maybe it was some other woman, not Savanna. Lying to get what he wanted wasn't beyond Brock. "You're in deep trouble and the police are the least of your problems," he said.

"That may be true. But here's someone that can tell you more about that."

The throbbing continued. It couldn't be Savanna. He left her at home.

"Say something," Brock said. "Say something, goddammit."

"Nicholas."

"Savanna." Strength drained from his limbs. "Are you okay?"

"My friend Dave can help."

"That's enough." Brock was on the line again.

"I'm coming to get you. And when I'm done with you, you won't remember your own name."

"No, Lieutenant-Colonel Asswipe, you don't get to threaten me. I've got your woman. I'm in charge. Now here is how it will go down."

"You will find us at Beaverton Campground. It's on the border between Exeter and Westbury. Bring my merchandise and you may get to reunite with the lovely Savanna Jones, just like in the movies."

"Savanna," Nicholas yelled into the phone. "Savanna." He swung toward the door and crashed into Corbett.

"Brock, you madman. Lay another hand on her and I will make sure you spend the rest of your life sucking your food through a tube."

Chapter 66

The call disconnected. Nicholas shook with rage. He shouldn't have left Savanna in Brock's path. "He must have waited for her outside the house," he said out loud. "Savanna would never have willingly gone anywhere with him."

He shot from the room. The ache in his head clobbered him. Two nurses, one pushing a cart, stepped aside to let him pass.

Nicholas stopped. "Is this pain medication for room six?"

"Excuse me?" The nurse who scowled at him bore an uncanny resemblance to Janet Whateley. "Who are you?"

"Dr. Wade, the patient from room six. I'll take it now." He snatched the cup with the two pills and downed them. "Thank you," he said and continued down the corridor. The antiseptic scent of the hospital nauseated him.

"Wade."

He'd forgotten Corbett was still behind him.

"Where do you think you're going?" Corbett asked.

"I suspect you caught enough of that conversation to answer that question." He spoke without stopping to look back at Corbett.

"You can't go after Brock."

"Yes, I can."

"Brock is naturally aggressive. He's probably armed and he's past the point of no return. He's trained to take out the enemy. Right now, that's you."

"Then we're both on the same page." Nicholas exited the hospital. Corbett kept up the pace. Without a bike, Nicholas needed a car, preferably a fast one.

"Listen to me," Corbett said. "That woman is pregnant and probably scared for her life and that of her child. If you're right, then Brock has no problem harming her and the child. He has what you want. He would hurt her just to watch you break. What is your plan?"

"How did you get here, sir?"

"I borrowed an SUV from the airbase."

Nicholas looked at him. "Good thing it's a base and not a prison, don't you agree?" he asked sarcastically. "May I have the key?"

"Let the police handle this. She may have a better chance with them."

Nicholas wanted to punch him. "If you believe everything you just told me about Brock," he said, "then I have to take him at his word. He said he would hurt Savanna if the police get involved. I'm going in." He stepped closer to Corbett. "Now may I have the key, please?"

His commanding officer puffed up his chest and squared himself under Nicholas's chin. "Enough lives have been lost in this illegal drug business. You better know what you're doing." He pulled the key from his pocket." Rather than drop it into Nicholas's waiting hand, he tightened his fist. "I'll take the wheel. You're in no condition to drive." Corbett turned and headed toward the air force's G Wagon. It was parked in the handicapped zone.

Nicholas caught up and fell into step with him.

"There must be someone else you can call for back up," Corbett said before he climbed behind the wheel.

Nicholas hopped into the passenger seat and punched the street name into the GPS as Corbett pulled from the parking lot, tires squealing.

Nicholas slid his cellphone from his pocket and started dialling. "Yes, there is," he said. He placed the phone on speaker. "Brent," he said when the line connected. "I need your help. Brock took Savanna."

"Jeezus. Are you serious?"

"I've never been more serious. I know you don't approve of our relationship, but I need your—"

"You don't need my approval. For twenty years I trusted that bloody high horse you mounted. I'm not about to stop now. Just tell me where."

Corbett had already left the downtown area by the time Nicholas finished his call with Brent. The Major-General was quiet for the entire conversation.

"Is there anything I can do?" he finally asked.

Nicholas twisted his head and peered at him. Savanna had said Dave could help him. She too wanted him to call the police. She trusted them. He should too. "I'm calling Detective Dave Thomas," he said. "He works with Savanna. Then, Major-General, I want you to tell me something about Brock I don't already know."

Savanna couldn't stop shivering. Blood from Brock's slap dripped onto her t-shirt. The coppery taste still lingered on her tongue and her swollen lower lip throbbed.

"You did well," Brock said. "Now, before Wade gets here, you and I are going to have some fun. I didn't have the heart to wake you earlier or we would have done it already."

Savanna glared at him. He resembled a mercenary cliché—thick head, buzz haircut, short neck and a large mouth. He was just an inch or so taller than Nicholas, but his height was more in the top half of his body. "You're right," she said. "You don't have a heart."

He grabbed his crotch. "I don't need one. I have this."

Savanna flinched and twisted away from him, taking the opportunity to inspect her surroundings. A rotting L-shaped counter top slumped in the corner. Several boarded windows lined the walls. Nothing but darkness looked back at her through a large hole in the windowpane.

The door had been ripped off its hinges, probably by Brock's brute strength. He'd leaned the door horizontally across the open space. That was her only escape.

"Normally I wouldn't be interested in Wade's game," he sneered. "But I think there's something special about you. Never done it with a pregnant woman. And just before I kill your boyfriend, I'll tell him how easily you gave it up."

"You are a sociopath," she hissed. She pulled away and ran toward the door.

He caught her before she got out of his reach. His cold grey eyes peered at her as if she was a helpless child. He grabbed the back of her head and pulled her to him. His tongue slithered from his open mouth and he dragged it along the side of her face.

She shrunk from the slimy disgust. Her stomach lurched at the smell of his stale breath. "Stay away from me," she said.

"I didn't think you would mind." A lustful snarl contorted his face. He shoved her toward another section of the abandoned building. "In there," he said.

The space they entered was half the size of the first one, with a small broken window. Savanna didn't think her heart could pound any louder, but when she spotted the filthy, stained mattress, she yelped. She would fight him. She had to fight him with every ounce of strength she possessed.

Brock pushed her. She stumbled forward. The fear shaking inside her boiled into rage. She landed on her hands and knees. Without another thought, she lifted one foot and smashed her heel backwards and into his crotch.

He doubled over and grunted.

A second kick slammed into his chin. Brock landed on the floor. She pushed to her feet and swung the tip of her shoe into his jaw. He groaned and lunged for her. She skipped back, but not fast enough. He caught her ankle and pulled.

Her feet slipped from under her and she landed on the mattress. Frantic to escape, she kicked both feet at random. Nothing connected, but she moved too fast for Brock to secure his grip. He kept turning his face and pulling back from her reach.

Frustration drove her persistence. If he caught her, she and her baby would die in the next minute. That couldn't happen. Somehow, she would survive this ordeal. A guttural roar rumbled from deep inside her and she jabbed her heel again. It smacked into Brock's temple.

He stopped moving and fell back.

Savanna heaved from the grimy mattress and ran from the room. She scrambled over the broken door. The rain had stopped, but the overgrown grass was wet and muddy. Her feet sank as she hurried into the dark. The sky was mostly cloudy with a few patches of inky black. She followed the faint light of the misty quarter moon along an overgrown path, hoping it led to the main road.

Beaverton Campground was on the border of Exeter and Westbury, but she wasn't familiar with the area. A wild forest surrounded her. Crickets chirped unseen in the bush and the wind whistled through the treetops. Instinct guided her through the dark.

Savanna couldn't imagine Brock running very fast on those thick legs and that muscle-heavy body, but neither could she with a pregnant belly. Her stomach jostled and swayed as she dodged between the wet shrubs and trees. In the clearing up ahead, she spotted a car in the distance. It was probably Brock's. She cradled her stomach with one hand and headed for it.

A noise distinct from the night creatures crunched on the wet forest bed. Savanna halted her hurried steps and turned in the direction of the noise. Not just crunching. It was an engine. A car or something. She waited for headlights to appear. Maybe it was Nicholas. But what if it wasn't. *Best to keep moving toward Brock's car.* More than likely he had the keys with him. *Damn it!* This couldn't be her only option.

She turned and started running again, but collided with someone. Oh god, no. It was Brock. He had recovered. Panic rose in her chest and she screamed just as his backhand smashed into her face.

The blow thundered into her head and silenced her. Blood squirted from her mouth and she felt dizzy.

He grabbed her by the throat with one hand. His other hand lifted above his head. That's when she noticed the machete glinting in the faint moonlight.

Chapter 67

$\mathscr{N}$icholas whipped off his seat belt. "Stay in the truck and keep the headlights turned on," he commanded Corbett, then he leapt from the passenger seat before his CO brought the vehicle to a full stop.

The strong beams illuminated Brock's fingers tightening around Savanna's neck. Her face was turning purple.

As Nicholas raced toward them, Brock reversed his position and held her in a chokehold.

Nicholas halted. Six feet of wet and trodden underbrush separated him from a sociopath holding the woman he loved in a death grip. Fear crawled down his spine. The terror in Savanna's expression pounded at his heart.

Brock had beaten her. Her left eye was swollen shut. Blood dripped from her mouth. Nicholas hadn't expected to meet them in the forest. She must have escaped somehow. He wanted her to know that he was there to save her from this madman.

Brock stepped back, shielding his body with hers. The machete's rounded tip hovered inches away from her neck.

"Let her go, Brock," Nicholas said.

"Come get her."

"You don't really want to harm them."

"I would do away with your bastard in a heartbeat."

"The baby isn't mine. That happened long before I got here."

"Doesn't matter. You bring my stuff?"

"Let them go. We can work this out between us."

"Nothing to work out. You get her when you give me my property."

"Come on, you don't want to hurt the baby. That child has lots in common with you."

"What the fuck are you talking about?"

"Its father bailed. Walked out the minute he heard she was pregnant. He abandoned them, just like your father abandoned you. Savanna is just trying to give her baby a fighting chance like someone gave you."

"No one ever gave me nothing. I got here on my own. Fought for every fucking thing."

Nicholas swallowed hard when Brock's rage went in the wrong direction. That didn't work. Nicholas raised his hand, hoping to gain control of the situation. "I know what you did for those soldiers," he said trying another tactic. "You took care of them when they couldn't handle the nightmares and the suffering. I get it."

"You don't get nothing. You're a trust fund baby, with the brass's head up your ass."

"You're wrong about that. I battle the generals as much as you do. We think alike, you and me. We stand up for the soldiers when everyone else is using them and discarding them. How about you let Savanna go and I'll take her place."

A sound left Savanna and she jerked forward.

"Easy there, sweetheart," Brock said. He probably promised her he'd kill Nicholas. She was afraid he'd keep his promise the first chance he got.

"Come on, Brock. Take it easy. Savanna can go to the truck and collect your bag. You need that API more than you need her."

Brock's gaze shot to the truck. Nicholas figured he was considering the offer.

Brock lowered the weapon to Savanna's ribs. "Are you armed, Wade?" he asked.

"Just my cellphone."

"Prove it. Strip."

Nicholas grasped the collar of his buttoned front shirt and ripped it open. Buttons flew in all directions. He whipped the shirt off his back and threw it to the ground then quickly unbuckled his belt.

"Slow down, cowboy," Brock shouted and pushed the machete into Savanna's ribs.

She cried out.

"Okay, slowing down," Nicholas said. He needed to distract Brock from hurting Savanna. Get him talking. He'd warned Dave and the other police officers to stay back until he could secure Savanna's safety. When he met up with Brent just before they turned off the main road, Brent had introduced him to a couple of officer cadets, two of his best sharpshooters currently on base. One was Saunders. Along with the police detail, they surrounded the area. Brock wasn't going anywhere. Nicholas just needed to get Savanna away from his machete.

"I know why you started the business," he said. His fingers fumbled with the buttons on his pants. "You did it to take care of the men in your squad. The ones who came back riddled with phobias and other psychological defects. What went wrong? What made you kill McBride and the two privates?"

"I wondered how long it would take you to figure that out. McBride was a pussy. He wanted the drugs, but he was the first one to point out that something had gone wrong with the formula. It messed him up bad."

"Why didn't you help him?"

"I told him to give it time. He went to the other men telling them that I fucked up the formula. By then a couple guys had gone crazy. Acting all manic. One of them beat up his wife. Word started to spread. I went to McBride and told him he had to fix this."

"Then you heard that I spoke to Global Research?" Nicholas asked.

"I knew that he'd blabbed to you and that there would be an investigation. A reporter was already asking questions at the bases. I had to convince McBride before he spoke to the reporter. When I found him, he was in the field with two new recruits. I'd gotten him away from them. I told him if he said another word I would cut his fucking hands off. Tang and Stevenson heard me threaten him. They came to McBride's rescue, holding their machine guns on me. Everybody came to his rescue. What about me? I save their twitchy, stressed-out asses and they were going to let him burn me. I held the gun to McBride's head and the privates backed off. McBride convinced them to lower their weapons, saying I didn't have the balls to pull the trigger. They did what he said.

"So why kill them then?"

"Because they were going to blab. I shot them with McBride's weapon. Then I put the gun in his mouth and pulled the trigger. It was easy enough to make it look like a murder-suicide. Upper brass had already heard about his erratic behaviour."

Nicholas pushed his pants to his ankles. Corbett still watched from the driver's seat and had probably heard enough. "See, no weapons," Nicholas said.

"Turn around," Brock yelled.

Nicholas twisted slowly, thinking of Savanna. *She'll be alright. I'll get her away from that madman. She'll be fine.* "Okay," he shouted to Brock. "I'll come to you and Savanna can collect the bag from the truck. It's on the front seat."

"You got that, bitch?" Brock asked and slapped her leg with the machete.

"Just let her get the stuff," Nicholas growled unable to keep his tone light.

"First, I want you on all fours."

With no objection from Brock, Nicholas pulled up his pants again then grabbed his shirt and started to slip into it.

"Now, Asswipe," Brock yelled.

Nicholas dropped to the wet grass, grasping his shirt. "Your turn," he said.

Brock eased the chokehold on Savanna and shoved her.

Savanna hurried toward Nicholas. Brock was right on her heels. From the bruises on his face, it looked like Savanna's kickboxing saved her life. Brock shoved her again. She stumbled and slowed when she neared Nicholas. Her breathing was rapid and shallow, her body shaking as she focused on him.

He needed her safe from Brock. "No, babe," he said. "Just get to the truck. Grab the bag from the passenger seat." He wasn't sure how much longer her quivering legs would hold her up, but at least she would be safe with Corbett.

Savanna nodded and did as he asked with Brock still watching her.

When she pulled the passenger door, Nicholas whipped one foot around and knocked Brock to the ground. He went down hard but came around fast still clutching the machete. He swung wildly.

Nicholas expected his reaction and had already swivelled out of reach and leapt to his feet.

"I'm going to kill you, Asswipe," Brock growled.

"Well, come on then." Nicholas's heart rate ratcheted up a notch. His stomach churned from the medication he took earlier, but rage surged in his veins.

Brock's sinister grin and his machete glinted in the headlights. Nicholas's only weapon was his shirt.

As expected, Brock lunged toward him, chopping at his neck. With less bulk to constrain him, Nicholas sprung out of reach and flicked the shirt into Brock's face. With the same lightning speed, he blocked Brock's attack and jabbed his foot into his knee.

"Argh." Brock howled and stumbled back from the sting that blinded him for a moment.

Nicholas advanced on him and hammered his fist into his rib cage. Pain ricocheted up Nicholas's arm when his knuckles connected to a solid mass. But the unexpected blow jarred Brock. He grunted, but he still held the blade and swung in rage.

It swooshed through the air and the tip caught Nicholas's stomach, slicing him.

Nicholas released a tight groan and jumped back.

Drawing blood bolstered Brock's conceit. He grinned and rushed forward. Nicholas blocked the machete arm and drove his elbow into Brock's throat.

"Ugh. Ugh." Brock coughed and sputtered reaching for his neck.

Nicholas needed to end this. He grasped Brock's wrist to keep the machete away from him and drove the length of his arm into Brock's elbow. The machete dropped. Nicholas followed up with a knee to his groin.

Brock doubled over. Nicholas pulled back his arm. With the memory of Savanna's terrified gaze filling his thoughts, he swung his fist into Brock's face. The blow connected with a crunch.

"Yeow," Brock yelped and dropped to the ground. He surprised Nicholas when he dove for the machete a few feet away. Nicholas leapt after him and stomped on his shoulder. The bone slipped to one side. Brock groaned, and his eyes rolled back. The sound of rifles uncocking alerted Nicholas that the police was already waiting to handcuff him.

"Thanks, Doc." It was Dave Thomas's voice behind him. "We've got it from here."

Nicholas turned toward the detective, but whirled around again when someone shoved him. It was Quinn. A knife had appeared in Brock's fist.

"What say you keep that hand where it is?" Quinn thrust the rifle against Brock's head.

Nicholas met Quinn's gaze. "Thank you, officer."

"Nothing to it, Doc."

"You broke my jaw, my shoulder and my nose," Brock sounded like a muzzled dog. "You can bet this isn't over, Asswipe."

Nicholas leaned into his face. "That's Lieutenant-Colonel to you, soldier. And you can count yourself lucky that you're still able to swallow without a tube. Come near me or my woman again and I will finish you."

Rather than wait for Brock's reply, Nicholas pushed to his feet and ran toward the truck. He glimpsed Brent waiting, but he couldn't stop.

"Lieutenant-Colonel Wade." His CO leapt from the SUV. "Ms. Jones just went unconscious. You should get her to the hospital, fast."

Chapter 68

S avanna squinted both eyes open and peeked through her lashes. A boxed-in flat screen TV, two high-back purple chairs against the wall. This wasn't her apartment. She wasn't in her bed.

Muffled voices pulled her attention to the entrance. Quinn, dressed in full uniform, stood at the door arguing with a nurse. She was an inch taller than him. Her blonde hair was pulled back, exposing her displeasure. In her baggy green scrubs, she stood firm on her decision. Savanna closed her eyes and opened them again.

"She's my partner," he said.

"What is it with you law types? The other one said she saved his life. Seems to me I have Mother Theresa herself in that bed," her sarcasm egging Quinn on.

"Don't kid yourself. She'd take you out in ten seconds flat if you're the bad guy… girl."

"Good for her. Now, you need to leave and come back during visiting hours."

"Quinn," Savanna tried to smile, but her face felt like it would crack. Maybe it had already. It hurt so much. She tried to sit up, but her arm was tethered to an IV.

Quinn hurried over, his loafers scraping on the bare floor.

"Officer," the nurse charged after him. "You can't stay."

Savanna raised a hand to her. She tried to speak, but her parched throat burned.

Quinn leaned over the bed with a water cup and guided the straw to her mouth.

She drank half the water. "Thank you," she said. "Can he stay for just a few minutes?" she asked the nurse.

"No, he cannot."

The woman was a nurse and that meant she started out with more compassion than most. Savanna only needed to appeal to her softer side. "We're partners," she said. "He can't work today until he knows I'm all right. Just for a minute, please?"

The nurse eyed Quinn, who watched Savanna with a solemn expression.

The nurse looked at her watch. "I'll be back in a minute," she said and stalked from the room.

"Hey," Savanna said.

He avoided eye contact. "So, you still want to be partners after I chewed you out?" he asked.

"You're always chewing me out."

"You should have called me."

"I was about to again when… Did they get him?"

"No, you did. Dr. Freaking Ninja Wade did the rest."

"Look, the other day I—"

"The other day? How long have I been in here?"

"They brought you in two nights ago."

"What?" Savanna struggled to sit up.

"Hey. Stop." Quinn stepped closer to the bed. "If you move around like that, dragon lady would be back here kicking me out and—"

"Am I still pregnant?"

"I think so. Wouldn't you know?"

She touched her belly and felt the familiar bump. She eased back into the pillow. "Sorry. I…" She remembered her dream. Her mother telling her to wake up and handing her the baby.

"You're allowed, I guess," Quinn said.

"What time is it?"

"8:15."

"In the morning?"

He nodded. "That's why she's on the warpath. I snuck in. These places should be more secure."

"Yes, Officer."

"Don't do that again, okay?"

"What?"

"Keep me in the freaking dark." He glowered beneath furrowed brows. His eyes bore into hers.

"I'm sorry," she said.

He swallowed. "Promise."

"I was wrong, Quinn. This would have been much easier if I'd included you from the beginning. I promise, no more secrets. How do you feel about becoming a godfather?" she asked.

"An Irish godfather?" He beamed. "That has a bonny ring to it."

She laughed. "I think so too. But you have to keep your potty mouth to yourself when the baby is pulling out your red hair."

"Hell, I think I can manage that." He stepped closer and kissed her on the forehead so quickly she barely knew what to think.

She tried to smile again.

"Don't do that?"

"What?"

"Smile."

"Why the heck not?"

"When dragon lady comes back, get her to show you a mirror."

Savanna touched her face. Tears stung her eyes. No wonder it hurt so much. Her cheek was swollen and puffy. She could feel the tears working their way around the bruising.

"Shit," Quinn said. "I didn't mean to make you cry. Sorry."

"Out," the nurse said from the door. "That was more than a minute."

Quinn nudged his chin in the nurse's direction. "Gotta go," he said. "We both can't lie around all day. Somebody has got to work."

"Thanks for sneaking in."

"No problem. Just don't tell anyone I kissed that mug of yours." Quinn ambled over to the door as the nurse pushed her cart into the room. She shooed him out and turned the lock.

He left before Savanna could ask the question burning her tongue. *Where was Nicholas?*

Chapter 69

Nicholas climbed from the car and walked up to the early twentieth-century bungalow with a grey sloping roof. Two acres of farmland sprawled around it. Red bricks paved the driveway and a narrow walkway that led to the front door. Blooming summer rose bushes in yellow, white and red skirted the house. A black-and-white collie, probably the inspiration for the exterior paint job, ran toward him.

"Hello, Major." Nicholas bent down and patted the dog's head and offered his chin for a sloppy greeting. He ruffled the floppy ears and pushed to his feet.

He lifted the brass knocker and knocked once. The door opened after a few seconds. A short woman, her black shoulder-length hair now mostly grey since he last saw her in March, greeted him. Her warm brown eyes looked sad for a moment, then brightened. She reached one arm out to him.

"Good morning, Mrs. McBride," he said.

"Oh, you." She swatted his arm. "We're practically family now, when are you going to call me Ma'Bride like the other boys do?"

He smiled and apologized for annoying her again. Her head reached just below his shoulder and he folded her easily into a hug.

It had been at least five months since he visited this farm and even longer since he hugged his own mother. The maternal greeting warmed him.

"Nicholas," she said. "How good it is to see you. Come in."

He stepped inside. The smell of fresh bread baking in the oven warmed him.

"No disrespect intended, ma'am," he said.

"You're impossible." She laughed good-naturedly and with her arm still wrapped around his back she tugged him along with her. "Come on through to the kitchen. I've been using that trick you recommended and now I have the perfect loaves every time."

"I'm glad to hear it," Nicholas said. Not much in the house had changed in all the years he'd visited. The same long white curtains at the double-pane windows let in the warm daylight brightening the taupe walls. Dark and colourful borders framed the McBride family photos and highlighted happier times. Most of the photos featured Kevin from grade school up to his two letters of commendation from the army.

They entered the blue kitchen. The paint job was the last project McBride completed for his mother before his death. The house was lonely now. Frank McBride had died of a heart attack a year before his only son. It pained Nicholas that Verna McBride lived alone with her grief.

"Come and have something to eat," she said.

"Thank you. I will." He forced down his mounting anxiety. Quinn had called. Savanna was awake and conscious. He'd be back in Westbury by the time the doctor discharged her. And unless she rejected him, he wasn't leaving her side again. But for now, he needed to be here.

Verna McBride set a plate in front of him on a round oak table covered in a white lace cloth. "Have you had breakfast?" she asked.

"I had some coffee on the flight."

"You boys need to take better care of yourselves. I'll whip you up some eggs. The bread will be ready soon."

They chitchatted while she puttered around the kitchen. Nicholas wanted to wait for her to sit down before he raised the reason for his visit. She watched him eat while he told her about his appointment in Westbury.

"When do you get back to the army?"

"Next spring," he said. He wasn't sure about that, but it was around the time he would know for sure what came next in his life. He took the dishes to the sink and washed them even though she protested. Then he sat across from her at the table again. He took her hands in his.

"I have some news," he said. Given the gravity of his investigation, he couldn't quite call the outcome good news. "A new development in Kevin's case proves him clear and innocent of the events surrounding his death and the death of the other soldiers."

A cry hurled from her throat. "Oh, thank God," she said. A rush of tears pooled in her eyes and disappeared between the lines on her cheek. He said nothing more, giving her a moment to digest the news.

"Kevin wasn't always a good boy," she said. "Running with the wrong crowd after his father's death. I guess he took it hard. But he didn't deserve what they said about him. He wasn't evil. He never would have killed those men."

"No, he wouldn't have."

"Thank you for making it right."

"You're welcome, but I'm not the one to thank. The army will make the pardon official in a couple weeks or so. I should warn you though, the reporters will probably show up before that."

She nodded still holding onto him. The tears streamed. "You've always believed in him," she said. "You were a good friend to him."

Nicholas dropped his chin. He couldn't agree. If his friendship was as good as she believed, he would have listened earlier.

"I know what you're thinking," Verna said.

He lifted his head to look at her.

"You're wrong." Her voice was firm, and determination eclipsed her sadness. "There's only so much you can do for a friend. You could give them all of your goodness, but that wouldn't make them do the right thing. Kevin wanted to forget, numb the pain of his father's death. You probably reminded him too much of Frank."

"He tried to get clean," Nicholas said. "I know. He came to me."

"I know too, but you were there all the other times he tried and couldn't make it. Don't beat yourself up. You've got nothing to be guilty for. Go live your life and bring some little ones to visit soon. I want to see that you've done well before my time is up too."

Chapter 70

AUGUST 30, 2012 - WESTBURY, ONTARIO

Savanna twisted in the hospital bed trying to ease the sore spot on her lower back. She reached for the remote control and raised the bed into a sitting position. Better. Not great, but better.

The hospital bed was starting to lose its comfort. Either that or her patience for lying around with nothing to do had run its course. She'd been there for three whole days, yet the doctor continued to talk about bed rest for the remainder of her term. He would visit her within the next hour and she intended to show improvement and hope that he would change his diagnosis.

She closed her eyes and leaned her head against the white pillows. The lullaby she hummed in her dream still played in her thoughts and she let it soothe her every time the frustration mounted. Rebecca said she would return after dinner. It was 3:00 p.m. now.

A perfect time to call her father. She reached for the cellphone on the bedside table. Not her old BlackBerry, but a new smart looking iPhone with all her info transferred. She suspected Nicholas, before he left, replaced the BlackBerry Brock took.

Sadness ripped through her like a razor's edge. She inhaled and released the breath. If she kept hurting like this whenever she thought of him, the doctor would never let her leave this hospital. She accepted Nicholas's decision, but losing him would take more time.

She turned on the phone and summoned the nerve to call her father. Making the call meant accepting his worry, and the knowledge that when he arrived in Westbury, he would insist on flying her to New Westminster as soon as she could travel. But she no longer wanted to keep him in the dark about her life.

She started dialling then paused when a knock on the door offered a much-welcomed means to procrastinate.

"Come in," she said.

The door opened, and Nicholas walked in. The man who had saved her life. He looked beautiful in her favourite blue button-front shirt with the sleeves rolled to his elbows and a plain beige pants. Not at all like the last time she saw him. Her breath caught at the memory.

As he walked closer, his soft, tender expression glued her to the bed. When he reached her, his inviting lips eased into a smile.

"I thought you'd left," she said.

His eyes glistened. He shook his head.

"I wouldn't have blamed you. In fact, I'd understand if you did."

He pulled one of the high-back chairs close, sat on it, then leaned forward.

Something seemed different about him.

"You thought that I left you?" he asked.

"You have a good reason."

"What's that?"

"I kept the pregnancy from you. I thought I was saving you from the pain I suffered. Well, there was more to it than that. I didn't want you to despise me either."

He winced and then took her hand in his. His long fingers were still bruised on the knuckles.

"You see," Savanna said, her eyes never leaving his, "I still regretted the abortion after all those years. Sometimes, I even grieved for the loss. So, you showing up like that just kinda made things worse for me."

He lifted her palm to his lips and her entire body quivered, right there in the hospital bed. Yeah, she still loved him.

"Maybe one day the grief will go away," he said. "But you can stop regretting it now." He pressed up from the chair and sat on the side of her bed. "I remembered what I told you that night. I said I didn't want to be a father."

Savanna's throat clogged. Some part of her remembered those words too.

"I told you that I didn't have the heart to bring children into this world to suffer the atrocities I witnessed," Nicholas continued. "I was disillusioned and angry with the army, with the world." His eyes locked with hers. "Savanna, I didn't know what I was saying. I didn't know I was saying it to the woman I would love for the rest of my life."

Her eyes widened, and her heart floated. "Nicholas, I love you too."

His hazel eyes flashed to a warm brown and relief suffused his expression. "Say it again," he said.

"I love you."

He kissed her forehead and let his lips linger. When he drew back, she realized that the torment that burdened him since the night they met in the cheese barn was gone. "I'm going to get the doctor," he said.

"Why?"

"I want to get you out of here. In fact, I'm never letting you out of my sight again."

She laughed, feeling very light and very happy. "The doctor will be here soon and if you tell him that, he might let me go home. But first, I have a question."

"Okay."

"Did you tell Nurse Foster that I saved your life?"

"It was the only way I could get in to see you at 0600 hours."

"How could I have saved your life?"

He sat on the bed again, still holding her hand. "I didn't tell you why I could never forget your face."

"No, you didn't."

"That morning in Kabul, when the second bullet penetrated my thigh, I had already lost feeling in my shoulder. I went down hard. Just before the lights went out, I saw your face like it was a dream."

Savanna shivered. No, he never told her that. The night at her new apartment after they made love she mustered the courage to ask him about the bullet wounds. He'd told her about that day. Though she hated hearing the story that almost took his life, she loved him, and his injuries were now part of her too. She wanted to know it all.

"You seemed so real," he continued. "It was your smile that kept me conscious of more than the dark. You were there. Just like you promised. Do you remember our conversation that night in the park?"

She shook her head. "Not very much of it," she said feeling like she might burst into tears.

"We talked about my work in a war zone. Then you said, if you ever knew that I was in danger, you would show up and save me from a thousand bullets."

Savanna tightened her fingers around his. She must have loved him even then."

"I survived that attack because you showed up in my dreams," he said.

She placed a hand on his chest. He seemed so centred now, serene even. His calm quieted the pounding in her racing pulse. She couldn't stop staring at him. This was the face she would love forever.

"When I walked away from you three days ago, all self-righteous and judgmental," he continued, "I wanted that night, our night, to mean as much to you as it did to me. A child would have done that, but those weren't the sentiments I left with you."

She squeezed his hand again. "I didn't realize how much that night meant to me," she said. "Not until it was too late. After the procedure, I thought our bond would snap, but it merely splintered.

Though I never thought I would see you again, our connection seemed chiselled into time."

"You did what you thought was right for you. Though you regretted it, the decision was yours to make. I wasn't here. You had a right to choose and you did. I don't blame you for it and you shouldn't blame yourself."

Her heart slowed. "Do you mean that?" she asked. "When you walked out, I thought you despised me and every explanation I gave you."

Nicholas kissed her forehead. "I'm pretty sure I'm going to loathe your cooking," he said. "But I could never despise you. I'm sorry I made you believe that I did. I love you."

"Say it again."

He laughed. "I love you. The last thing I ever want to do is hurt you."

"Then don't leave me again, because without you all I do is hurt."

THE END

Epilogue

FEBRUARY 6, 2013 - NEW WESTMINSTER, BC

Savanna was already swaddled in her winter coat when she marched into the kitchen. "I'm going for a walk," she said. Her father frowned.

She pulled a fur-lined aviator hat over her messy hair and tried not to let his alarm get to her. When she reached for her boots, Nicholas got there first. He held one waiting for her foot.

"I'm sure you didn't come all this way to help me into my shoes," she said.

"To tie your laces, walk with you and rub your feet when they're sore." All done with his task, he pushed to his feet. "And you," he said and kissed her nose, "promised to keep me busy, remember?"

"You'll need this," her father said and handed her an umbrella.

She groaned. "No snow in the forecast?" she asked. "A little snow would be nice. Snow in February is lovely. Don't you think? I don't know about you guys, I like snow in February."

She looked up just in time to catch the exchange of glances over her head. Yeah, that was what she did lately, ramble.

These days it seemed that all her requests fell on the universe's deaf ears. The baby was five days past its due date, no matter how much she hoped.

People tried to console her by saying that a few days late was a cake-walk. "Some women went to forty-two weeks before the doctor induced." That was from the gynaecologist Dr. Wagsmith recommended in New Westminster. She'd been seeing him since her false labour started at thirty-six weeks in the second week of January.

Savanna sighed. If she were still in Westbury, she could at least work a crime scene to keep herself busy. Instead, she took daily walks in the rain and fog to keep her sane. At least the time with her father was magical.

"Thank you," she said to them both. "I'll be back soon."

"I'm coming along," Nicholas said.

She tossed him a grateful smile and pulled the kitchen door. The wind tugged at her hat, and raindrops smacked her face. She welcome the fresh air. When she was at her worst, Nicholas and her father's forgiving patience turned her from an ingrate to a love-sick puddle of sappy gratitude.

Back in the summer, after her run-in with Brock, she'd spent another week in the hospital before both Wagsmith and the attending doctor decided it was safe for her to go home. Another month passed before her gynaecologist allowed her back to work. Then she had to argue with Nicholas, who threatened to tie her to the chair if she left the lab for a crime scene.

Four days before Christmas, her last day at the lab and the day before she left town on maternity leave, Nicholas and the gang surprised her with a baby shower. Hannigan awarded her an honorary detective status, and Doreen drunkenly congratulated her on bagging the handsome Dr. Wade.

Nicholas spent Christmas Eve and Christmas Day with his parents then showed up on her father's doorstep on Boxing Day. When he told Kenneth that he wasn't going anywhere and would sleep outside Savanna's bedroom door if he needed to, her father stood with his arms folded across his chest.

"Really?" he'd asked. "And what happens when the child starts to resemble its father, what will you do then?"

"I'll be too busy being a dad to notice."

Savanna broke into tears then, and they both stopped their silly bickering. It was settled. Nicholas slept on a cot in her father's office, Kenneth in Savanna's old room and she on her father's comfortable queen-size bed.

Every Friday after the Christmas holiday Nicholas flew from Westbury to New Westminster to spend the weekend with her. Two days before her due date, he told Coroner Miller that he would manage the team remotely until a few weeks after the baby came, then he'd resume his duties minus the weekends until the end of his appointment, or until she moved back to Westbury.

Yet, not once had Richard contacted her to find out if his child had come into the world. Their divorce became final a few days after Christmas. By then he had disappointed every bit of tenderness she ever felt for him. The day she read the documents, she felt revived. Still, she hoped for a single word of interest from him that would allow her to say something positive when the questions started in a few years.

Nicholas folded her hand in his as they stepped through the gate. They walked in silence. A few yards from the house, she smiled up at him. In the last month and a half, she enjoyed the twinkle in his eyes when he looked at her. Feeling a bit sluggish, she squeezed his hand and bid him to stop walking.

"What's wrong, babe?" he asked. "You okay?"

She wrapped her arms around him as far as she could reach. He held the umbrella over them. He looked adorable with a two-day stubble and sporting the slouchy toque she bought for him on her shopping spree with Rebecca.

She kissed him. His lips, soft and sweet on hers, quieted the angst buzzing under her skin.

He smiled, the one that made his eyes dance.

"I'm truly the luckiest woman in the world," she said, then caught her breath as tightness tugged under her stomach. It wrenched like all the others she suffered in the last two days. She waited for it to pass.

"You better believe it." Nicholas's grin widened.

She'd never get accustomed to seeing him smile at her like she held the Holy Grail he'd been tracking.

"And—" he started to say again. His lips kept moving, but the tightening flared into a sharp slice.

She grasped Nicholas's jacket lapels. The agony weakened her knees. She slid from the comfort of his hand on her back.

He released the umbrella and caught her before she hit the ground.

Savanna bit down on her bottom lip and leaned into him, cradling her belly. For a moment, she was only aware of the cramping. She exhaled, unable to outlast the shooting spasms. Then she heard Nicholas's voice calling to her.

"Sweetheart, speak to me." He lifted her off her feet and headed back to the house. "Tell me what's happening."

She met his eyes hoping the sight of them would stop the pain.

"Honey," Nicholas pleaded, "what's happening?" He was already at the back door, kicking it to get her father's attention.

"The baby… is coming," she panted and heaved into a ball in his arms when another one assaulted her lower belly.

"Kenneth," Nicholas said when her father appeared. "It's time. Call the ambulance." He released her onto a kitchen chair and knelt before her.

The cramps seizing her stomach rippled down her lower body. "Nicholas," she said, "I think I need the bathroom." She released a moan that rumbled in her throat and tried to stand.

"No, wait—" Nicholas said.

Steamy warmth heated her stomach. Liquid gushed between her legs. This was the third time she'd seen Nicholas go pale.

"It's… It's okay, my love," he stammered. "Just breathe. We'll get you to the hospital in no time."

Savanna's head swam. "Nicholas."

"Yes, babe."

"Telephone my dad."

"He's already here."

"Right. Rebecca. Call Rebecca. She's at the hotel."

"I've got her number right here." He wrenched the cellphone from his pocket, still supporting her with one hand.

Rebecca had flown to New Westminster with Peter the day

before her due date, insisting that Savanna wasn't having this baby without her.

Kenneth entered the kitchen dressed to go just as Nicholas finished the call. "The ambulance is on the way," he said. "I also called Dr. Rand. He'll meet us there."

"Thanks, Dad," Savanna said. Another spasm tore through her.

"How far apart are the contractions now?" he asked.

"Five minutes," she said though it felt like they never stopped.

Nicholas's voice whispered in her ear. "I love you," he kept saying. "I love you. I love you."

They arrived at the hospital just in time. With Nicholas on one side, Rebecca on the other and her father just outside the door with Peter, the baby, just as anxious as Savanna, shot from her body after a series of mighty roars.

"Sweetheart," Nicholas said excitedly. "You did it." He kissed her wet face.

"I love you," she said.

Moments later, Dr. Rand placed a wailing baby wrapped in a towel on her stomach. "Meet your son," he said.

Savanna collapsed into the pillow and clutched him. Her heart gushed with warmth. "A baby boy," she said and kissed his head.

"Didn't I promise you a baby," Rebecca said and hugged her. "Congratulations, sweetie."

By the time her father entered the room with Peter, Savanna still smiled down at her swaddled bundle of joy. His skin, paler than her own, wrinkled with baby softness and she kissed the pink fist he reached out to her. She snuggled close and let his fragrant newborn smell fill her senses.

Peter ran over to the bed, his dark brown curls bouncing around his head. "Aunty Savi," his little voice singing for her, "did the baby come for his shower?"

They all laughed.

Nicholas picked Peter up and sat him on the bed beside Savanna.

He reached out and touched the baby's closed fist with his index finger. "You are Aunty Savi's baby."

"He most certainly is, sweetheart," Savanna said.

Kenneth drew close. "Princess. How are you?" He kissed her forehead.

"I'm good, Dad. Do you want to hold your grandson?"

Kenneth Jones's eyes misted. He blinked and reached for the baby. "Have you thought of a name?" His voice choked.

"Yes, I have," Savanna said, watching him cuddle the baby like a pro. "But he's not a girl."

"You must have thought of some boy names." Rebecca touched the baby's forehead.

"Some, but now that I see him, they don't fit. So, I'll have to call him Andrew, in remembrance of his grandmother, and Kenneth, after his grandfather. Andrew Kenneth Jones."

At the sound of his full name, Andrew stretched and yawned.

"It's the perfect name," Rebecca said.

Her father leaned over and kissed her. "Andrew and I agree. We like that name very much."

Savanna looked up at Nicholas.

His Adam's apple bobbed up and then down. "You look tired," he said.

She was about to protest but relaxed into the pillow instead. "I could sleep for a week," she sighed, and gave in to the exhaustion.

"I say you have about a couple of hours." Rebecca took Peter's hand. "We'll go and call home with the news." She kissed Savanna's forehead. "You did good, sweetie. I'll see you later." Rebecca eyed Nicholas, and he nodded.

Savanna's stomach fluttered. They had already cooked up something together. She smiled to herself, happy that Rebecca liked the man she fell madly in love with.

"We'll take Andrew to the nursery," Kenneth said.

"Okay." Savanna watched her father expertly place her son on the small bed. "See you later."

Nicholas held the door open.

Savanna smiled at her three men. They were her family. Her new beginning. She was grateful for all that life had given her. "Hey, Ishmael," she called to Nicholas.

He told Kenneth he would catch up then closed the door and was at her side in a few steps.

"There's something I want you to know," she said. "Something you should never forget."

"What's that?"

"Your face might have blurred in my memory after our first night together, but you touched me inside. You left a sense of security in my heart. Since then I've never really been alone. I only wish that I had always known."

"You know now."

"Can you do me a favour?" she asked.

He kissed her forehead. "Anything."

"Would you be willing to confirm that I am the luckiest woman in the world."

"How do I do that?"

"Marry me?"

His jaw dropped, and then he was kissing her, long and slow and sweet. Then he lifted his head and reached into his pocket. A black velvet box floated between his thumb and index finger. "Yes. Of course. I will" he said. "I thought you would never ask. I'd marry you in a heartbeat."

Savanna's eyes widened. Nicholas opened the box.

She gasped. A blue sapphire solitaire set in yellow gold. She touched it with one finger. Just like the man kneeling next to her bed, it rocked with authenticity. Love warmed and filled her chest. She was indeed a lucky woman.

Nicholas plucked the ring from the box and placed it on her finger, then kissed her again. He lifted his head and met her eyes. "Now," he said, "should I get the old ball and chain to keep this on your hand?"

They both looked at it. The beautiful stone drew light from every source in the room and sparkled a colourful prism against

Savanna's smooth latte skin. She and Nicholas burst into laughter, knowing that she would never be able to wear the ring under latex.

"I love you madly," she said and hugged him.

"Say it again."

"I love you."

"Don't forget the madly bit. I like that."

"Madly," she whispered. "I love you madly, Dr. Wade."

"One more…." His voice choked, but he kept moving his lips toward hers with perceptible slowness. When he finally kissed her, she knew luck had nothing to do with it.

Get Exclusive Access

Hearing from my readers is one of the best parts of writing.

Sign up to my newsletter, *Let There Be Romance* and receive early notification on new books, promo codes and deals in the romantic suspense genre.

Visit my website www.applewhite.ca

Acknowledgments

It's always a pleasure to say thank you to the people who inspired and supported throughout a long and arduous journey.

Thank you to my husband, Mark, truly a partner in love and all things real and worthy. Much love to my wonderful little girl, Emily who has grown taller than me since I started writing this novel.

I'm grateful to my proof reader, Leslie James, and to my beta readers, Amanda Heerschop and Cathy Santaguida. Thanks to Lorin Oberweger for her early input.

Most of all, thank you to my editor, Jessica P. Morrell without whom I couldn't have gone the final distance.

To my readers, thank you for joining my adventure, and as always. . .

Let There Be Romance.

Angela

By Angela Applewhite

Short Stories

Twist of Fate

The Best Publicity

About Angela Applewhite

Angela Applewhite lives in Toronto with her husband and daughter. When she's not writing, she's thinking about writing, or chasing a piece of research. Yes, she admits to being totally consumed by her characters. To relax, you can find her flipping through Britbox, or rewatching Jane Austen movies.

Like Angela's books? Check out her website at

www.applewhite.ca

Click the links below to follow Angela.

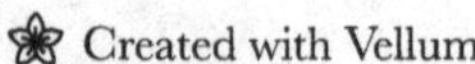 Created with Vellum